BOOKS BY

Lori L. Lake
=====================

The Milk of Human Kindness:
Lesbian Authors Write about Mothers & Daughters

Stepping Out: Short Stories

Different Dress

Gun Shy

Under the Gun

Have Gun We'll Travel

Ricochet in Time

Romance for Life

Snow Moon Rising

Shimmer & Other Stories

Like Lovers Do

Advance Praise for *Buyer's Remorse*

The new mystery series—featuring two of the most fascinating and surprising protagonists yet—is a humdinger. Lake's deft portrayal of her new sleuth rocks. I can't wait for Book 2!
~Jessie Chandler, author of The Shay O'Hanlon Caper Series

Treat yourself to the debut of mystery fiction's newest lesbian detective, Leona (Leo) Reese. Lake takes us on a twisted ride through sinister secrets and lies and gives us a story that promises to keep everyone up way past bedtime.
~Ellen Hart, author of The Jane Lawless Mystery Series

Praise for Lori L. Lake's Work

"It is no wonder that Lori Lake's books are best sellers. Her characters are deep-bodied, multidimensional, and convincing. Her plots unfold like petals on a flower, coming to full bloom at just the right moment." ~Foreword Magazine

"Considered one of the best authors of modern lesbian fiction, her work – part action, part drama, and part romance – gleefully defies categorization." ~Lavender Magazine

"Lori Lake is one of the best novelists working in the field of lesbian fiction today." ~Midwest Book Review

About Lori's Other Books

The Gun Series

Gun Shy is an exciting look at police work through the eyes of police officers who happen to be lesbians. Lori L. Lake has set a fine precedent with her endearing, witty, action-packed story that has plenty of police activity, longing, and romance. It brings to mind one of my favorite TV shows, Cagney and Lacey, a classic 1980's hit about two straight female cops. *Gun Shy* would be a great model for a contemporary version—two female officers, Reilly and Savage, who not only fight crime, but also have the hots for each other.
~The Independent Gay Writer

Snow Moon Rising

It's a smashing book that wears its learning lightly, yet fills the air with a people and an era well-caught, well-delineated, and very moving. ~Caro Clarke, author of *The Wolf Ticket*

Different Dress

"[T]he pleasure, like on some road trips, is in the journey, not the destination, and Lake's tale takes its leisurely good time as this love affair runs into detours and unexpected roadblocks. This lesbian romance is full of entrancing details that make the day-to-day tour come alive as the dazzle of show business and the joy of making music serve as backdrops to the lovers' deepening relationship." ~Booklist

The Milk of Human Kindness: Lesbian Authors Write About Mothers and Daughters

"One of the great things about this collection is that it doesn't only focus on daughters. The stories that take into account the mother's point of view are particularly insightful. Some of these writers are especially adept at showing a mother's confusion about her daughter's lifestyle or fear of the pain this path will bring the child." ~The Lambda Book Report

Shimmer & Other Stories

Lake has created distinctive and memorable characters in settings that will linger with readers long after the stories come to their satisfying and hopeful conclusions. Here are five compelling tales of outsiders: women ex-offenders, lesbians, cancer survivors alone with their altered bodies. All bump up against the harsh real world and find salvation in surprising ways, from the supernatural to a former nemesis turned guardian angel." ~Lee Lynch, award-winning author of *Beggar of Love, Sweet Creek, Rafferty Street*, and many other novels

Stepping Out

"Some writers write stories and have fun. In this collection, Lake fell in love with her characters. She cared for and nurtured them, making this not so much a collection of stories as an anthology of characters." ~The Lambda Book Report

Ricochet In Time

"When Dani and her lover Meg are victims of a hate crime at the beginning of the story, it is anybody's guess how the plot will develop. Will the killer get away with it? Will Dani be able to pull herself together enough to pursue justice for her slain partner? Or will she run away as she has from trouble in the past? The interesting point, here, is that this particular plot element becomes the background for a much more interesting story. Meet Ruth and Estelline, Grace, Bryce, Cleve, and a whole host of distinct characters, all of whom interact in various important ways with Dani as she fights her way back to full health from her physical injuries and emotional pain. You'll have to read the book to see if the perpetrator of the hate crime is brought to justice. The outcome is far more surprising than you can guess. ~Ronald L. Donaghe, author of *The Blind Season* and a professional book reviewer for Foreword Magazine.

Buyer's Remorse

Lori L. Lake

Quest Books

Port Arthur, Texas

ISBN 978-1-61929-001-3

First Printing 2011

9 8 7 6 5 4 3 2 1

Cover design by Donna Pawlowski
Art Direction by Lori L. Lake

Published by:

Regal Crest Enterprises, LLC
4700 Hwy 365, Ste A
PMB 210
Port Arthur, Texas 77642

Find us on the World Wide Web at
http://www.regalcrest.biz

Printed in the United States of America

Acknowledgments

I started this book in March 2007 and completed the first draft by early September 2007. Soon after, all hell broke loose in my life, and four years passed before I was able to get this novel revised and finished. I couldn't have done it without the support of my good friends Ellen Hart and Jessie Chandler who kept me going, even when I wasn't sure if I could. How many mystery writers does it take to screw in a lightbulb? Apparently three: one to scribble, Ellen to hold the light over the book, and Jessie to give it that final surprising twist at the end.

Other people to whom I owe a debt of gratitude: Commander Mary Nash, Saint Paul Police Department, who was a mere sergeant when I first met her and hasn't lost a bit of smarts by being promoted; Det. Lee Lofland, retired, for general law enforcement data, but especially for investigation timelines and forensic information about smothering; Joanne Middaugh, MSW, social worker extraordinaire; Laura Lively, expert on finances, scams, and identity theft; Leslie Budewitz for general legal information; Mary Logue for editorial advice and for planting the seeds that led to a much stronger plot; and Sharon Carlson, RN/PHN, for medical data and wound information.

Readers who slogged through various versions of this book and gave invaluable advice include: Betty J. Crandall, Brenda Adcock, Catherine Friend, Jane Vollbrecht, Jessie Chandler, Laura Lively, Nann Dunne, Pat Cronin, Sandy Wilson, and Verda Foster.

I can't thank my Chief Editor, Nann Dunne, enough for her careful reading of the manuscript (multiple times!) and for being willing to scuffle with me over various aspects of plot and structure. Copyeditor Verda Foster did a bang-up job on short notice. Thanks to both of you for being so "nitpicky." Keep it up.

The Last Minute Lovelies—Mary Beth Panichi, Jessie Chandler, and Judy Kerr—are the best brainstormers on the planet and helped me figure out how to make the final twist work. Let's do that again on the sequel!

As always, I'm grateful to my publisher, Cathy LeNoir at Regal Crest, who was very patient with me during that long drought from 2007 until 2011. Thanks for having faith in me.

And my sisters and their families have stood by me every step of the way. I thank:

Jeannie for buying them all
Angela for reading them all
Debbie for the silent support
Cyndy for the prayers

I know I must have forgotten to thank somebody. Over the last four years I believe many more people have assisted me, and if I haven't listed you here, please yell at me, and I'll be sure to make it up to you.

Lori L. Lake
November, 2011

For Pat and Gary
at Once Upon A Crime Books
It's no mystery why I love you two

Chapter One

THE SUN HID behind a cloud as Sergeant Leona "Leo" Reese walked across the parking lot to the Saint Paul Police Station. She was dismayed to see Bob Hannen near the door, a cigarette burning between his fingers. She hated cigarettes — not quite as much as she despised Hannen, but close. Cops weren't supposed to smoke in the squad cars, but the minute Hannen made sergeant, he'd started doing whatever he wanted.

She hoped he'd go back inside before she arrived, but no such luck. He caught sight of her and broke into a wide smile, his bright-white dentures gleaming in the sunlight. He'd just turned forty, but he had the body of a sixty-year-old and the brains of a teenage boy. A teenage boy with hidden 'Roid Rage. The guy loved to manhandle suspects.

"Well," he said, "if it isn't Little Miss Can't Shoot Straight."

The double meaning was clear, and Leo choked back a reply replete with curse words and references to his parentage. "Get out of my way, Hannen."

"I'm glad to catch up with you, Blondie. I wanted to thank you for your kindness."

She wrenched the door open and hesitated. She hated looking back. The gloating expression sure to be on his face made her feel homicidal.

He dropped his cigarette and ground it into the cement with his heel. "Thanks to your incompetence, I'm the new FTO coordinator."

"Screw you, Hannen."

"You wish," he said, laughing. He followed her inside, the smell of sweat and stale smoke wafting around him.

Leo concentrated on breathing. If she didn't, she was afraid she'd pull out her sidearm, aim at his foot, and show him what a straight shooter she was. Of course the guy's foot was usually in his mouth, so she'd get the delightful experience of also blowing his head off.

"Have fun talking to the commander," he said in a mocking voice. "I'm sure he'll have some sweet nothings to whisper into your queer ear." With a cackle, he peeled off and went toward the Roll Call Room. She headed to the women's lockers.

Leo had always gotten along well with men. Some of the cops may have had reservations about her at first, but she was persistent. Little time passed before she learned the names of wives and kids, the hobbies her coworkers enjoyed, the quirks and prejudices they possessed. Dad Wallace had taught her that one of the biggest compliments you could pay a fellow cop was to listen and be respectful, offering calm support and no judgments.

The tactic worked on the street, too. She kept track of people whose houses had been vandalized, ministers whose churches had been broken into, businesses with robbery and shoplifting calls, and she stopped by periodically to touch base with those victims — even now when her role was supervisory.

But none of this worked with the Bob Hannens of the world. He was all about power: who had it, how they got it, how he could snatch it away. He wasn't particularly smooth, either. In Leo's opinion, Bob's name had one too few O's in it. Her competence was a threat to his ascension, and when she made sergeant two years before he did, Hannen declared war, a silent, festering sort of war characterized by snide comments and constant needling. The man gossiped and passed on lies and inaccurate information more than any neighborhood busybody she'd ever met.

She hated him for it, and today her anger was so close to the surface that she worried she'd say something she'd regret to the commander. *Breathe*, she reminded herself again. *Just keep breathing.*

She changed from the casual apparel she'd worn at the shooting range into her uniform, all the while wondering how Hannen had found out about her situation so quickly. She'd left the range less than an hour earlier. Had the range master called in her scores so quickly?

As she holstered her sidearm, she rethought her shooting performance. Her first few rounds at the target always went fine. After six or eight shots, though, her vision went fuzzy, and despite wearing hearing protection, the gunshots gave her a headache. By the time she was a few minutes into a relay, she felt physically shaky, sometimes even dizzy.

Today she'd clearly seen the irregular pattern of pockmarks in the safety berm behind the target area. Every line, every dent in the dirt, every crease in the wood frame around the box was defined. The color gradations were unmistakable. So her sight — her vision — was fine. Up until she fired her weapon a few times, her vision was always crisp.

After she failed three times to score the required eighty percent, the range master suggested it might be an emotional reaction. Her face flamed now as it had then. Emotional reaction? Who was he to bring that up? She'd been an expert marksman her entire career, and there was no possibility that her failure to pass the shooting qualification was psychological.

"It's probably something easy," he'd said, "a visual problem. Go get squared away, then call me for an appointment. We'll work through a remedial program to get you back on rotation."

Remedial! How embarrassing. In a decade of being a cop, she'd never failed her shooting quals. She couldn't report for roll call and let anyone know she couldn't shoot reliably. Her authority as sergeant in charge of a team depended upon her skills. She currently supervised two rookies, six veteran cops, and two Field Training Officers. How could she show her face to them if she failed routine shooting quals they'd all handily passed?

She closed her locker and concentrated on her breath as she headed up to see the commander.

"Sergeant Reese!"

Startled, she looked up to find Commander Malcolm down the hall in the doorway to his office, the late afternoon shadows pooling around him so that she couldn't make out his face. "In my office," he said. "Now!"

"Yes, sir." She hustled toward him, a sinking feeling in the pit of her stomach.

"Sit down." He slammed the door and stood over her, his normally calm face pink with anger. "When were you going to come see me about your shooting quals?" He paused, but she didn't answer. "Is there any reason why you've withheld this vital information?"

"No, sir."

"How long were you going to go on before informing somebody in command?"

"I thought last time was a fluke. I honestly thought I'd pass today, sir. I'm as surprised and concerned as you are."

He slipped around the other side of his desk and sat heavily in his chair. "You didn't, though, and now I have to make special arrangements for you."

"Commander, I spent all afternoon at the range. I'm doing much better."

"Good for you." His voice dripped with sarcasm. "You should have done much better a helluva lot sooner because now you're reassigned."

She groaned. Hannen hadn't been kidding. She was going to get stuck with the dreaded desk duty. Hours of boredom. "I'll shoot another relay Friday, boss. I'll pass. I promise."

"Should've done that while you had the chance. You'll need to take the remedial course, and in the meantime, you're off rotation." He ran a hand from his forehead across the top of his balding head.

"You're not really going to let Hannen supervise my team, are you?"

"Who else have I got? You've left me no choice."

"Damn," she muttered.

"Damn it all is right."

Hannen wasn't just a power-hungry jerk. He was a hotshot showoff who bragged about every angle of his work and sex life. A few nights with him in charge of her rookies could be detrimental to their training. She needed to get to her FTOs as soon as possible and give them instructions to counteract Hannen's attitudes.

"Isn't there anyone else who can cover for me?"

"No, Reese, there isn't. You know we're short-staffed, and I've got another paternity leave coming up next week. I don't take too kindly to being put in this situation. With some foresight on your part, this could have been avoided. Why the hell didn't you tell me about this sooner?"

A cold chill passed through her, and she could no longer meet his gaze. Leo had always liked Commander Malcolm and enjoyed working for him. He was fair. Very strict, but he usually stuck up for his officers. She'd never been in this sort of situation with him before, and she felt like a traitor, an idiot, and a huge disappointment.

"Do you have an answer? Why did you fail to report this?"

She fumbled for words. "I guess I—I couldn't believe it, sir."

"You didn't pass in July and completely tanked today. I can't believe you didn't think you had a problem."

Her face and neck flared with heat, and for a moment she felt like she might cry. Instead, she said evenly, "That's why I've spent a couple of afternoons at a private range on my own dime. I'm highly motivated. You know that, sir."

"Are you feeling any aftereffects from the Littlefield shooting?"

"No, sir, I'm not. You know the shrink cleared me for work. Littlefield is not an issue."

"You're not having any dreams or flashbacks or anxiety?"

She shook her head.

"You're sleeping well?"

"Yes, sir, I am." She waited while he peered at her, eyes sharp, but she calmly met his gaze.

He sighed and picked up a pencil, tapped its eraser on the desk. "This is alarming judgment on the part of a sergeant, and I'm disappointed. Listen to me, Leo." He met her eyes, and now she knew he spoke not only as her superior, but also as a man concerned for her personally. "I'm forced to take drastic measures. Please understand that this isn't meant as punishment, but it's the only way to adequately police the community."

She stared at him, suddenly fearful that he was going to fire her. But he couldn't. Wouldn't.

Would he?

She had the right to a union representative. And a chance to go before a board of professional responsibility.

"I need bodies," he said. "I need you guys out on the street getting the job done. Since I've got to pull you indefinitely, I'm bringing up two rookies. While you're gone, we can afford to pay them."

Gone? What did he mean "gone"?

"At the rate we're losing officers, by the time you get back, I'll have a place in the rotation for the two new staff."

She forced herself to speak calmly. "Where am I going, sir?"

"Department of Human Services."

"What!"

He continued to tap the desk with the pencil. "They're even more shorthanded than we are. You'll continue to be employed by SPPD, but DHS will reimburse us for your salary."

DHS? She was instantly filled with visions of destitute welfare clients, the Dorothy Day Center, homeless men with mental problems. "I don't understand."

"You'll work in their Investigations Division and report to them."

"You're suspending me?"

"No, no, no. We're lending you, Reese, that's all. You're still an officer in good standing."

"This isn't right, sir."

He narrowed his eyes, but his expression wasn't angry, and he let out a sigh that showed how tired and deflated he felt. "Your only other choice is unpaid leave of absence. I didn't think that would fly with you. Go to DHS, work on the remedial shooting course, and we'll get you back here in about twelve weeks."

She exploded up from her chair. "Twelve weeks!"

"Yup."

Leo leaned over his desk, her palms pressing on the edge. "No way. You can't do that, Commander."

"Oh, yes, I can. Your only choices are to go to DHS on special assignment or take leave without pay. If you do it my way, DHS gets help, I get to train two new staff, and you come back after a little career enrichment." He tossed down the pencil. "In the meantime, you get your shooting skills in order and fulfill the obligation to DHS, and you'll be back on duty before you know it. That's the deal."

She sank back in her chair, hardly able to process this news. She'd be off duty until nearly the end of the year, and she couldn't quite imagine it. Three months working at what? "What in the world would DHS need me for?"

"Their Investigations Division is shorthanded. Couple of medical leaves, somebody had a baby. They're not meeting their mandates. I golf with Ralph Sorenson, the division director. He and I cooked this up over the phone earlier today." Commander Malcolm looked at his watch. "It's 1800 hours, Reese. Don't clock in. You better go home and get some rest. You've got exactly fourteen hours before you report to the DHS building."

LEO CLEARED NEARLY everything out of her locker. She whisked the last items off the top shelf into a duffel bag and sat down for a moment on the bench, head in hands. In a couple brief hours, her life had turned upside down. Why the hell was this happening to her? She didn't deserve it.

She glanced over her shoulder when the locker room door opened. Her fellow FTO, Dez Reilly, strode in. Reilly drew near, and Leo rose so her colleague's six-foot height didn't loom over her quite so much.

"Leo, I just heard the news."

"I hope it was from someone more reliable than that asshole Bob Hannen."

"Unfortunately, the asshole speaks. Way too much."

Leo let out a peeved sigh. "I hope you can keep him in line."

Reilly crossed her arms over her blue uniform shirt. "Not much anybody can do about that guy. He's a lawsuit waiting to happen."

"Yeah, I know. I can't say enough bad things about him. I hope he doesn't make your life too miserable while I'm gone."

"There's something else," Reilly said. "I know what it's like to have a critical incident, and I—"

"Oh, God, not you, too? Dez, there's nothing wrong with me that a little ibuprofen won't cure. Really! This is not about PTSD."

"That's the same thing I told myself when I—"

"No." Leo held up a hand. "Don't go there. I don't mean to be rude, but I'm not having any psychological issues."

"I didn't say that. I just want you to know you're not alone if you do."

Dez Reilly's blue gaze, sincere and honest, drilled into Leo's eyes. She knew Dez was just trying to help, and she let go of the angry tirade at the tip of her tongue. "Okay, thank you."

"Let me just say one more thing before you go. If you change your mind and want to explore anything at all about the Littlefield shooting, give me a call. There's a few of us who get together once a month and talk about this stuff. It's a good thing, Leo. If you need any support, you know I'm there for you."

"Thanks. I mean that. I appreciate your concern." She picked up her duffel. "Now if I can just get out of here without running into Hannen again."

"He's holding court in the front. Take the back stairs and you'll probably miss him."

Leo knew what the cliché writers meant about having a heavy heart. Between that and the piercing headache stabbing between her eyes, she wanted to hit something. She only had to make it to the parking lot. Buck up, she thought. I can do it.

AT HOME LEO found a note on the table: *Still prepping for the Dunleavey case. Hope to be home by six.*

Her partner had been working long hours. The past two nights, by the time Leo had crawled into bed after midnight, Daria had been asleep, and now she'd missed her again. Other than a brief phone conversation the day before, she'd only seen Daria in passing since the previous weekend.

Between loads of laundry and tidying up the house, she braised some strips of chicken, sliced a bunch of green onions, and grated Monterey Jack cheese. Corn was out of season, so she took a frozen package from the freezer.

When she heard a car in the driveway around half past six, she was whipping up eggs, milk, and salt to add to the chicken, corn, and onion already in the skillet.

Daria walked in the door in a rumpled suit, her curly hair in disarray, but her brown eyes brightened. "Smells like something good."

"Chicken Fritatta."

"Yum."

Leo set aside a spatula and hugged her.

"I'm so glad to be home. This case is completely kicking my butt."

"Go change and we can compare notes."

Ten minutes later, they sat at the kitchen table drinking glasses of dark Merlot and eating wedges of hot frittata sprinkled with cheese, drizzled with hot sauce in Leo's case, drenched in hot sauce for Daria.

"What's the scoop with Dunleavey?" Leo asked.

Daria smacked her wineglass on the table. "He says he's not guilty, never been anywhere near the robbery scene, doesn't know what happened to the goods, but the cops have six people swearing it was him. I don't know if I can believe the guy."

"Does he seem to be telling the truth?"

"He's either a very persuasive liar or the biggest dumb-ass on the planet."

"What's your bet?"

With a sigh, she said, "I don't know. I've never had a guy seem so sincere and protest this convincingly. I find it hard not to believe him, and I can't figure out any reason a half-dozen people would lie. I haven't been able to discover how any of them have an interest in this case or that they even knew Dunleavey. I think he's going down in flames."

"Wait a minute. You're the one who always reminds me that eye witnesses are notoriously unreliable."

"Yeah, yeah. I know, but no matter how I spin this, I keep coming up with no other theories that would exonerate him, and he hasn't got an alibi."

"Hence the long hours."

"Right. I keep going over everything, reading the witness statements, checking out details. Shit, I've got two boxes of statements and police reports alone. What a headache. Jury selection is almost done. There's no way to delay the trial. Unless I can find some evidence or a technicality, Dunleavey is going to be convicted."

"Get him to plead to a lesser charge."

"He won't. He maintains his innocence." Daria took the last bite of the frittata and reached across the table to take her hand. "I'm sorry to be so gloomy. I'm tired."

"I bet. You've been burning the midnight oil and the candle at both ends, too."

"I know. What about you?"

Leo looked into her dark eyes, hardly knowing where to begin. "I'm having trouble with my shooting quals."

Daria let go of her hand and poured another glass of wine. "That's not like you, William Tell. You could shoot an apple off my head from twenty paces."

Leo explained about her problems on the range, ending with the news that she was reassigned until the end of the year.

"Hey, that gets you off the evening and midnight rotations."

Daria's tone was so happy and hopeful that the frittata in Leo's stomach turned to a lump. They'd discussed this before—how could Daria forget what a touchy subject it was?

Daria went on. "I think it'll be great if you work days."

"Yeah, great for you. How many times do I have to tell you that I like working nights? If you weren't working so late all the time now, we'd have more time together, especially on Tuesdays and Wednesdays when I'm off. I'm here during your waking hours on the weekends." The argument was ancient, one that emerged from under the ice every so often and made both of them angry.

"Okay, okay." Daria put her hands up, palms facing out. "I

give. I don't want to fight about that again. So, what are you going to do?"

"The range master suggested I get my eyes checked."

"A-ha! Old Eagle Eye is finally succumbing to age."

"You're not listening. My vision is clear and sharp. I'm going tomorrow to shoot a few rounds at the private range over in Maplewood."

"You're fooling yourself. Just go see the eye doctor."

"I hate wasting the money."

"Leo! You've got insurance." She covered Leo's hand and squeezed. "Is it possible that the Littlefield thing is interfering?"

Leo tried to pull away, but Daria held her hand tight in a warm clench. "Admit it. You're still upset. You're still not over that, are you?"

"I wish everyone would just shut up about Littlefield. That has nothing to do with this. The whole damn thing was a shitty situation, but that's got nothing at all to do with my shooting accuracy."

Daria gave her a skeptical grin but didn't pursue the issue. "Then it's something else."

Leo rose to clear the dishes.

Daria grabbed their glasses and went to the sink to rinse them. "I'm not kidding, Leo. What if there's something wrong? Go see Doctor Spence, and if it isn't your eyes, get a physical."

"I just had a physical a few months ago."

"But you never know…"

She went on to cite cases where people turned out to have weird diseases. The longer Daria lectured, the more Leo tuned her out. By the time they'd cleaned up the kitchen, she was so irritated that she stomped into the TV room and flopped down on the couch. Daria followed her in, talking now about a brain aneurysm from which a colleague's relative died.

"I don't want to talk about this anymore," Leo said and clicked the remote.

Daria was clearly taken aback by the venom in her voice. "Geez, I'm just saying—"

The television came on, and loud music drowned her out.

"Thanks for making dinner," she said over the music video. "I think I'll go edit my opening statement again."

After Daria left, Leo felt bad, but not bad enough to seek her out in the den. She'd been on pins and needles all day, and she was sick of it. Tomorrow, after the difficult day she figured she'd have at DHS, she'd spend some time at a shooting range. The damn private range was expensive, and she hated to spend the money, but she had no choice.

Chapter Two

ELEANOR SINCLAIR GRABBED her shoulder bag, stepped out of her apartment, and crossed the hall to the open door to her partner's apartment. Callie's rooms were the exact layout of Eleanor's, but reversed, which always made Eleanor feel like she was stepping into a parallel universe. Other than the mirror vision, the only other difference between the two efficiency suites was that Eleanor's had a sliding glass door leading out to a garden a quarter-acre in size. Instead of a door, a bay window in Callie's living room gave a view to the street.

Callie Trimble sat in a navy-blue easy chair, barefoot, wearing a baggy housedress covered with orange and yellow swirls. Her son Ted was sprawled on the couch across from her. For a forty-year-old tax professional, Ted was surprisingly scruffy-looking in baggy shorts and a rumpled Hawaiian shirt. He hadn't bothered to remove his tennis shoes before putting one up on the couch, the other on the coffee table. Something he was saying was making Callie laugh.

"Hey there, young man," Eleanor said.

Ted sat up, swung his feet to the floor, and grinned, almost daring her to upbraid him for his bad manners. With his dark blue eyes and mischievous face, he resembled Eleanor so much that over the years, he'd often been mistaken as her son instead of Callie's.

"Eleanor, how are you?" He didn't wait for an answer. "I was just telling Mom about all the funny things my computer mouse can do."

Callie said, "He makes the mouse run all on its own with batteries. I want a mouse like that."

"We'll have to go on a shopping trip then," Eleanor said.

Callie brightened. "Can we go now?" She brushed steel-gray hair out of her eyes and smiled with such glee that it made Eleanor's heart hurt. In two minutes or two hours, Callie would have no memory of Ted's little mouse.

"Maybe tomorrow? I'm off to my book group in a minute."

"Tomorrow?" Callie said. "Tomorrow would be fine."

Eleanor winked at Ted. "Take good care of her until I return."

"Always do." He laughingly blew a kiss her way. She had sharp enough peripheral vision to see that no sooner had she turned than he slouched back on the couch with his foot up on it. She decided she didn't care. He made Callie happy.

She strode down the east wing's long hallway. Where the west hall and the administrative wing met her hallway, someone had left a crumpled handkerchief in the middle of the carpet. Eleanor pulled a clean tissue from her shoulder bag and bent to scoop up the hanky.

"Oh, that's Agnes Trumpeter's." Sherry, one of the aides, held out a hand. "She's always losing that dang thing everywhere she goes."

Eleanor handed it over. "It's been well-used. Probably needs a good washing."

"I'll take care of that, Eleanor. You going out?"

"Yes. I'll be back in two or three hours. I let the cook know I won't be in for supper."

"But you'll miss the sing-along."

Sherry's expression was so sincere Eleanor had to smile. "I'll catch the next one." With a nod to Sherry and a wave to Habibah, another aide who stood by the front desk, she made her way out to her car. She let out a huff as she got in. Every day she forced herself not to blow up at any of the workers or the other occupants of the Rivers' Edge Independent Living Apartments, but after ten weeks, her patience was wearing thin.

She drove out of the parking lot onto a street nowhere near any rivers or edges. She wondered why the owners had named the place Rivers' Edge. Unless it was a reference to the River Styx, and they had in mind the mythical ferryman, Charon, waiting to haul all the old people down to Hades as soon as possible. Eleanor already thought she was living in a minor version of Hades, and maybe Rivers' Edge was an allusion to a good place to drown.

She felt such a sense of relief whenever she escaped from the hellhole of her new home. Wishing it weren't so, she resolved to think about it no more and stopped at a diner for a solitary meal with a book for company.

After eating, she left Minneapolis, crossed the river to Saint Paul, and passed through her old neighborhood, wistfully viewing the spacious homes, converted mansions, and Victorian-style brick houses with ivy crawling across them. For old time's sake, she drove along the scenic East River Parkway. The Mississippi River, with 100-foot-tall bluffs on one side, sparkled in the early evening light. The walking and biking paths atop the bluffs were crowded with people eager to enjoy the warm sun.

Eleanor drove to the community library and headed for the entrance. In her canvas shoulder bag, a copy of the evening's book, *Pride and Prejudice*, bumped against her hip. She'd been delighted when an old classic was chosen by one of the twenty-somethings in the group. Eleanor hadn't known that *P&P*, as the younger set called Jane Austen's novel, had been made into a movie starring famous young actors. Apparently the remake had girls hot to read Austen. The young woman who selected this month's book had prattled on about Matthew MacFadyen, Keira Knightly, and several other actors Eleanor had never heard of, but when the girl mentioned Dame Judi Dench as Lady Catherine and Donald Sutherland as Mr. Bennett, Eleanor didn't feel quite so dense.

Nowadays, though, whole days passed when Eleanor never stopped feeling dense. For a moment, she felt a stab of longing to be back in the classroom teaching high school seniors, talking about books and films, and asking them hard questions about ethics. She knew it was easy to create a romanticized memory of the forty-two years she'd spent teaching Language Arts at high schools in Saint Paul, but for the most part, she'd enjoyed the work. Every year she estimated at least twenty percent of her students actually succeeded in reading and thinking and learning. Even after clothing styles became scandalous and rap music took over the airwaves, Eleanor still had serious students who made her school days worthwhile.

She would not have retired so soon if she'd had any other choice, but—

"No, not going to think about that," she mumbled aloud. She stepped through the automatic doors of the library and inhaled the scent of floor polish and books, her favorite combination.

AT HALF PAST seven, Eleanor left the library accompanied by two young women named Valerie and Lindsay.

"Hey, El," Valerie said, "would you like to get a cup of coffee with we two?"

Eleanor ignored the bad grammar and the overfamiliarity and thought, why not? She spent nearly an hour with the girls at Starbucks eating a sweet roll and drinking a surprisingly good cup of chai tea. She'd never cared much for coffee, and she didn't realize so many types of tea could be had nowadays in coffee shops—if you didn't mind spending five bucks, that is. Neither of the girls batted an eye at the expense. She could buy an entire box of teabags for what she'd just paid, but then again, she supposed you were also paying for the ambiance.

"I should be toddling on home," she finally told the girls.

"This is great," Lindsay said. "It's cool that you'll read *Sense and Sensibility* with us. Can we talk about it next month after the group—or maybe we should wait longer to be sure we have time to finish the book?"

Eleanor had read the book so many times she knew parts of it by heart, but she didn't tell them that. "I can be ready by next month if you can."

"Okay," Valerie said. "Let's do it."

Eleanor said her goodbyes and left them sipping coffee. She stepped out into the muggy evening. Temperatures during the day had been scorching, but even though summer was waning, the mid-September evening temperature hadn't dropped much. She hurried to the car, grateful for air conditioning.

On the way back to Rivers' Edge, she thought about how nice it was to chat with such lively young people. Now that things at the new apartment had settled down, perhaps she could volunteer as a tutor or get involved in neighborhood activities. She'd had no chance to check into that, but perhaps it was time now.

She entered the front door and made sure she closed it securely. The pounding beat of piano chords echoed from the dining room — or café, as some of the residents insisted on calling it. The sing-along was in full swing. She stood for a moment trying to place the tune the piano player was banging out. When a wavering voice sang, "Way down upon the Swanee River," she recognized the melody, if you could call it that. She thought a Greek Chorus could have managed a more tuneful monotone.

She crept silently through the lounge area toward the hallway. In the TV room, Walter Green lounged on the couch, his mouth open, white-haired head back against the wall. She tiptoed past and down the east hallway, glad that the singing grew fainter with each step. At her studio apartment, she found the door ajar as she'd left it. Directly across the hall, the door to Callie's apartment was also open, and the overhead light was on. Eleanor poked her head in, but her lover was nowhere to be seen. Eleanor assumed she'd gone to the sing-along.

With a sigh, Eleanor trudged into her own apartment and set her bag on a ladder-back chair just inside the door. She flipped the light switch to turn on a table lamp in the corner. The left half of the apartment was a sitting area with a desk in the far corner by the sliding glass door, two tall bookshelves along the left wall, and a sofa and recliner in the middle of the room. She'd hung up her favorite pictures and framed photos, but so many had gone into storage, especially the largest paintings. She missed them.

The right half of the apartment consisted of a partially screened bedroom area in the far corner, and an enclosed bathroom that took up a quarter of the apartment's footage. For the monthly rental cost of this miniscule 24-by-24-foot studio suite, Eleanor knew she could be paying a mortgage on a home worth a quarter million dollars, which irritated her to no end. But this was the most practical place for the price, so she tried not to think of that.

She shivered. The air conditioning hummed, but then she felt a rush of warm, moist air. Squinting, she saw that the sliding glass door wasn't shut. She crossed the room to close it. The piano and reedy singing voices sounded louder because her apartment opened to the garden, and the dining room's sliding glass door was also open.

Back in the apartment she moved toward the bedroom alcove and saw an orange and yellow splash of color on a white bedspread. Callie lay at an angle, facedown on the double bed. Her bare legs and feet hung off the near side of the mattress.

Through the sliding glass door she caught sight of a swirl of motion in the twilight, a sense of a presence slipping out of her range of vision. Was someone there? She peeked around the corner into the night, but by the time her eyes adjusted, whatever or whoever it was had gone. She shut and locked the slider and went to the foot of the bed. "Rise and shine, old girl. You're napping in the wrong room again."

When Callie didn't move, Eleanor stepped around the side and leaned a hip against the mattress. Callie's steel-gray hair was mussed, and she lay in an awkward position with her right arm beneath her torso.

"Wake up. Your arm's probably fallen asleep." Eleanor leaned over and patted Callie between her shoulder blades, in the middle of the wild orange and yellow housedress. Callie had been a light sleeper all her life. She should have popped awake. Goosebumps rose on Eleanor's arms.

"Callie?" Eleanor reached across the sleeping woman and tugged at her shoulder. "Callie, are you all right?" Once she turned Callie on her side, the body rolled toward her, limp and lifeless.

"Oh, no, no, no..." Under Eleanor's probing hands, Callie's arm and neck were warm, but her body seemed slack, like a rubber doll with loose joints. "Callie! You can't be—you can't!"

She felt a stab of pain behind her breastbone so sharp it took her breath away. The ache flowered, and for a moment she thought she was having a heart attack. As the pain ebbed, she dropped Callie's hand and staggered back. "Oh, God, no." She rushed into the bathroom and pulled the emergency panic cord so hard that she ripped it out of the wall.

PEOPLE CAME. PEOPLE went. A hall full of paramedics and staff and police milled about, but Eleanor paid them no mind. She sat in the easy chair across the way in Callie's room, hunched under a multicolored afghan Callie had crocheted many years before.

She didn't cry. She couldn't even think. She'd rocketed from shock to numbness in so short a time that she found it impossible to focus on anything. When Sherry, the aide, handed her a hot mug of coffee laced with milk and sugar, she accepted it and sipped away, unaware of the actual flavor.

Why now, she kept thinking. Why now? Callie was having good days. She was happy here.

A Minneapolis police officer came and identified himself. His name didn't register. She forced herself to concentrate. His dark, ebony face reminded her of a boy she'd taught many years before.

"Mrs. Sinclair? You probably don't remember me."

"Axley."

"Excuse me?"

Her tongue felt thick, and she struggled to get words out. "You used to say 'axley' instead of actually."

He looked at her blankly for a moment. "Ah, so you do remember me."

"I'm sorry I don't recall your name, young man, but you're definitely familiar."

"Jasper Caldwell."

"Yes. You wrote a paper once about elephants. You made puns about their trunks and big ears and about how they never forget. I didn't know you'd joined the police. Always thought you'd be a veterinarian. Or a zookeeper. Never saw a boy so wild about animals." She realized she was babbling and closed her mouth.

"Yes, ma'am." He shifted uncomfortably and tugged at the sleeve of his blue uniform shirt. "I'd forgotten about that paper. Long time ago. I graduated Class of '88 and never put my elephant knowledge to work. Mind if I sit?"

"Be my guest."

He settled across from her and opened a ring-bound memo book. "The manager here will have more information about Mrs. Trimble's situation, but she's not here right now, so the aides said I should talk to you. You're her next of kin?"

"Yes, I am, legally. Her ex-husband lives nearby. And a son and daughter, too. Well, the daughter's in the Peace Corps. Howard Trimble. That's her husband—her ex. Over in Saint Paul. He's in the phone book." She shut her mouth, aghast at her inability to speak in her normal coherent style.

He made a note. "All right then. The aide said you were off somewhere, out to dinner?"

"Yes." She described her activities up to the point of returning to Rivers' Edge.

"Did you get picked up or drive or take the bus?"

"I drove myself."

"Okay, what happened when you arrived home?"

"I came in here, and — "

"Wait a moment, ma'am. Back up to the parking lot. Close your eyes and imagine yourself parking your car."

She took a deep breath and closed her eyes. "I picked up my shoulder bag and stepped out of the Buick. I locked it from the inside, shut the door, and went to the front door of the apartment."

"Was it locked?"

"Yes. I used my key, and I definitely closed it behind me."

"Go on."

She took him through her next steps, and when she got to the sliding glass door, he asked, "Did you notice anyone outside?"

Eleanor opened her eyes. "Not exactly. I saw...something. Movement. But no one was out in the garden when I looked."

"Then what?"

"I closed and locked the door, and then — then I found Callie. Like that."

"You moved her."

"I'm sorry. I didn't realize she'd passed, Officer. She was facedown on the bed. I thought she was sleeping."

"Did you notice anything strange?"

"Strange? In what way?"

"Anything unusual. An intuition, something that puzzled you? Anything that was off in any way?"

She closed her eyes once more and envisioned the orange and yellow housedress and the way Callie had rested, one arm underneath her midsection. She didn't like that picture in her mind, so she shook herself and met the cop's gaze. "Callie was always a side sleeper. She must have had an attack and fallen onto the bed."

But that didn't seem right either. She'd found Callie with her head near the middle of the bed. She would have been closer to the side if she'd had a stroke or heart attack while standing, and if she'd been lying down, would she have rolled onto her stomach like that? Maybe she crawled that far and then collapsed. "All of this is so unusual. So unexpected."

"I understand," he said. "What time did you last see her alive?"

"I'd say about half past five." When he frowned, she said, "You can verify it with Sherry. Or Habibah. I saw them both on the way out."

"What was Mrs. Trimble doing?"

"Visiting with her son, Ted. Howard's son."

"Trimble his last name?" When she nodded, he asked, "You know where he lives?"

"Off Snelling by Macalester College. I don't know the address off the top of my head. It's in Callie's address book."

"All right then."

He paused for a full minute to make notes. Eleanor thought of the little red address book that Callie had carried for years. In her mind's eye, she visualized how it was filled with Callie's looping handwriting, a script that Eleanor would never see her write again. The realization pressed down on her chest like a heavy weight, and tears welled up.

Officer Caldwell went on. "And you arrived home when?"

"A few minutes after eight o'clock."

"This library book group—do you regularly attend it?"

"Fourth Monday every month. I haven't missed in ages."

"Which branch?"

She gave him the address. He made more notes and went over some of the same questions he'd already asked until she began to feel impatient.

"You saw no one when you entered her apartment?"

"You've asked that already. That's my apartment. This is her apartment." In answer to his quizzical look, she said, "Callie was in the mid-stages of a form of senile dementia. She wandered freely, napping here, there, everywhere. Sometimes I'd find her in the TV room asleep on the couch or in the big recliner. Other times she'd get disoriented and wind up in one of the other residents' rooms. Most people in this complex keep their doors open during the day. I've got everything of value locked away because people are known to wander off with this or that."

"Theft, you mean?"

"Oh, no. Last week Norma Osterweiss came in here, unplugged the lamp by Callie's chair, and took it out to the café where she lined it up with several other lamps she'd liberated from their owners. She didn't remember doing it. Callie went into Mrs. Stepanek's room the other day and lifted an entire vase of pretty flowers and put them over there on her television set. This goes on day in and day out. Nobody gets too upset, and the aides are good about returning things. Those of us who care lock our doors, or we make sure we don't leave anything out that's valuable."

"I see. So you went into the other apartment immediately upon arriving home, shut the slider, and then?"

"I found her right away."

"Thank you, Mrs. Sinclair." He stood and tucked the memo pad into his uniform shirt pocket. "Someone will be in touch."

Eleanor rose. "What's going on, Jasper? Why all the probing questions?"

"This is the normal routine." He gripped her hand in his warm mitt. "I'm so sorry for your loss, Mrs. Sinclair."

His physical warmth made her realize how chilled to the bone she felt, and a bout of dizziness passed over her.

"Whoa, whoa." He maneuvered her into the easy chair and lowered himself to one knee. "I better call someone for you."

"I'll be all right. It's just such a terrible shock."

"Yes, ma'am, it is." He reached behind her, pulled up the afghan, and helped wrap it around her shoulders. He got to his feet and smiled sheepishly, as if embarrassed by his own gentleness. "You weren't too bad as a teacher, Mrs. Sinclair. Never mean like some of the others."

"That's nice of you to say, Jasper."

Chapter Three

THE DEPARTMENT OF Human Services building was nothing special. Leo followed Fred Baldur through the typical maze of cubicles filled with tired-looking bureaucrats. After clearing security, he took her through a side door that bypassed the reception area and brought them to a wide hallway by the elevators, which seemed to take forever to come.

If she remembered correctly from her Old Norse mythology, Baldur was the name of a prince. Or perhaps it translated as "king"? She couldn't remember, but she was certain that Fred Baldur could in no way bill himself as royalty.

He was a pale-skinned man dressed in a wrinkled light-gray suit, no tie, and scuffed black oxfords. Perhaps it was lucky his hair was thinning because his skull hadn't been acquainted with a hairbrush for many moons. He had such a flattened patch of bed-head over his left ear that Leo was sure he must be a side sleeper.

She'd worn a comfortable blue suit that had been around the block a few times, a button-up white blouse, and a pair of plain oxford shoes. As far as she could tell, she was overdressed for the department.

Baldur pressed the elevator button and said, "Stay away from the front desk as much as possible. We've had a long string of temp receptionists, and you'll be pressed into service if you go near them. Let the office manager handle their questions and catastrophes, or you'll never get out of here for a cup of coffee much less be allowed to drink it."

She was surprised they were taking a break so early. She'd arrived at eight a.m. sharp, met with the director, Ralph Sorenson, for approximately ten minutes, and been sent out into the sea of cubicles to find her trainer, Fred Baldur. He'd droned on for all of half an hour, going over general information about the Department of Human Services and the Investigative Division. The important information she'd learned was brief: The State of Minnesota licensed all youth treatment centers, nursing homes, detox services, rehab centers, adult foster care programs, homeless shelters, assisted living complexes, adolescent group homes, child care centers, and day programs for elderly and disabled. Complaints came to DHS regularly and could be lodged by a client, a worker, or a relative of someone involved. DHS was required to respond. All deaths and matters of serious injury were always fully investigated.

If the provider of services was guilty of negligence or dangerous practices, DHS had the authority to cite the provider, suspend staff, recommend fines, or pull licenses and shut down the business.

That was the extent of her training, and now it wasn't even nine o'clock, and they were setting out for a break.

The elevator opened, and Baldur stepped aside to usher her in. She estimated he was near retirement age. He stood with a stoop, as though Atlas had skipped town and left him holding the entire weight of the heavens on the back of his neck. As the doors clunked shut, she asked, "Why is the department so understaffed?"

He shook his head like Eeyore from the Winnie the Pooh cartoons. His voice came out sounding like Eeyore's, too. "One gal's on maternity leave. Another one had twins, so she's on extended maternity leave. And the other member of the team fell off a roof and cracked some vertebrae weekend before last, so he's gone now, too. Brad might not be able to work for months. That leaves me. Wish I could get a leave like the others, but to tell the truth, I don't like the pain involved."

Baldur steered her away from the building's front doors to the entrance for a restaurant called Piccadilly Point. The décor was shabby, traditional English pub with three old-fashioned recessed "snugs" for private meetings tucked along one wall. Dark-stained wood paneling covered the walls, most of which were decorated with old-time sepia photos and dart boards. The room was so dim that Leo squinted, waiting for her eyes to adjust, and she didn't get close enough to determine what the framed pictures depicted before Baldur led her to one of the snugs. She slid into a clunky tavern chair, which was surprisingly comfortable. The tables were made of scarred wood planks with old-fashioned wood pegs as fasteners. The carpet was threadbare, but the overall atmosphere was of cozy gentility.

A waiter appeared. "Hi, Fred. The usual?"

"Please."

"And you, ma'am?"

"Black tea. With milk and sugar, please." If Piccadilly Point served English fare, she hoped they'd have decent tea. "May I see a menu?"

"We're not serving anything except muffins and bagels until eleven."

"That's fine, but I've never been in here before, and I'll likely have lunch here fairly often, so I wanted to get an idea of your entrees."

He whisked a menu over to her, and she took a moment to scan it. They served traditional English favorites such as Shepherd's Pie and Fish and Chips along with other typical selections: steaks, burgers, spit-roasted pork and chicken, and soups.

"Is the food good here, Mr. Baldur?"

"I suppose. I stick with the coffee and gin for the most part. Not together. Oh, and not on work time, either. Please call me Fred." His eyes squinched up with his attempt to grin, but his lips only curled up slightly at the corners. She got the impression that it hurt him to smile.

The waiter delivered a giant mug to Fred that could easily hold two cups of coffee. Her teacup was dainty, and the tea was served loose-leaf in a china pot covered with a fluffy red and gold tea cozy. The waiter set down a sugar bowl, milk, and slices of lemon, and asked if they needed anything else. Fred sent him away.

"I come down here every morning," Fred said. "Used to be able to sit here and have a nice private smoke. Damn do-gooders ruined that. Lawmakers have no backbone these days. They just listen to the rabble. Plenty of restaurants are no-smoking, so why couldn't they leave mine alone? You smoke?"

"No."

"Probably for the better. Guys I know are dropping like flies. Cirrhosis. Lung cancer. Emphysema. I'm fifty-four years old. Sure don't want cancer. Guess I ought to quit drinking, too. But this place does have some nice English Gins. Scotch, too. You drink?"

"Socially. Otherwise, not so much. It's an expensive treat in my book."

"True. Very true." He took a slurp from the big mug and sat with his hands cupped around its heat. The wrinkles in his face slid as though the skin were dripping down into his jowls. Dark bags under his eyes made his brown eyes look even darker. Leo had a hard time believing he was only fifty-four.

"I wanted to get away from the office to make some—ah, arrangements with you, Ms. Reese."

"Leona is fine."

"All right, then, Leona. You see, I'm not cut out for field work. To be honest, I can't stand the histrionics." He paused, shaking his head.

"Histrionics?"

"Everywhere you go, they're all slightly hysterical. Complainants, witnesses, managers, owners, the damn relatives. They've all got an ax to grind. I can't take it. I prefer to coordinate. Brad and I had it going pretty well. He did the field work, and I took the phone calls and completed the paperwork. I figure what with you being a cop and all—I mean, a police officer—you might want to run the show like Brad and I did."

"To be honest, Fred, I don't know that I'll be here too terribly long."

"What? I was told three months guaranteed."

"Yes. Well. We'll see."

She figured the tea had steeped long enough, so she busied herself preparing her cup. When she looked up, he was staring at her with such a sad-sack expression on his face that she had to stifle a giggle. "I'm fine with the street work. Field work is my forte, but I'm pretty good at paperwork, too."

"The red tape is miserable. But less so than interviewing. I'd be indebted to you if you'd agree to split the tasks like Brad and I did."

"Okay."

His face broke out in a smile for the first time, and Leo was taken aback. His teeth were yellowed. She could actually see ingrained tan streaks. Dull stains gave his grinning face a hyena-like appearance.

He jerked as though stung and lost his smile. One knee came up and jounced the table. Her tea slopped over the side of the cup, and she let out a little gasp.

He fumbled in his pants pocket and dragged out one of the smallest cell phones she had ever seen.

"I hate technology. Forgot I had it on vibrate," he said as he flipped it open. "Yeah? No kidding? You can't be serious? I'll take care of it."

He snapped the phone shut. "Drink up, Leona. Here's where you're going to have to keep up your end of the bargain."

What a strange and cryptic man, she thought. What the hell is he talking about?

"There was a suspicious death last night at an elder apartment complex in Minneapolis. It will have to be investigated now."

"What's the protocol? Do we liaise with the police or what?"

"Liaise? Is that a word? They do their job, we do ours and hope they stay the hell out of our way. We try to get information out of them wherever we can. Brad was very good at it. He got excellent cooperation from the various law-enforcement units. You'll want to do the same. Luckily you have the Saint Paul PD in your pocket. Use your badge anytime it greases the skids. If it helps, I mean." He took a giant swig of his coffee, smacked the mug down on the table, and rose. "We better get back to the office so I can load you up with the things you'll need."

Teacup poised near her lips, Leo paused. "You're coming along, right?"

He fumbled in his pocket and threw a couple of folded bills on the table. "Let me get this."

He wouldn't meet her eyes. She'd seen that guilty look on the faces of plenty of suspects—a sort of weasel-like avoidance where they hoped you weren't watching too closely to see their guilt.

Leo's hand shook a little as she set her teacup on the tray. She stood but didn't follow him. He took a few steps, stopped, and wheeled around. "We don't have a lot of time, Leona. Let's get crackin'."

"Wait a minute. You're kidding, right? You're not sending me out in the field with no training, no backup, no oversight—nothing?"

He slouched his way over to stand in front of her. "Oh, come on now. In your regular position, you go out on the street daily, question people, deal with miscreants and lawbreakers. This'll be a piece of cake in comparison. It's a retirement apartment. A walk in the park compared to the creeps you must meet on the street."

She had no response for that. She lifted her napkin to her lips and dabbed, tossed it on the table, and followed him out of Piccadilly Point, certain now that Fred Baldur was no prince.

SHORTLY BEFORE TEN, Leo arrived at the Rivers' Edge Independent Living Apartments. Baldur had loaded her up with forms, a manual of guidelines written in unintelligible legalese, and a battery-operated tape recorder the size of a paperback book. She was glad she'd brought along the leather valise her foster father had given her when she graduated from college. To make room for all the DHS junk, she had to empty the valise of the files and materials she carried with her when she testified at court.

She drove her own car with the mileage counter engaged. Baldur had instructed her to keep careful track of all travel because she'd be reimbursed only with proper documentation. He'd given her more instructions about claiming her mileage than about what to do at the scene of the suspicious death, and she was having a hard time not despising him.

Rivers' Edge, in the southwest Minneapolis Linden Hills neighborhood, was only a couple neighborhoods south of where she and Daria lived in Kenwood. She'd driven completely across Minneapolis from west to east and crossed the river into Saint Paul to get to DHS. When she went back to work later in the day, she'd have to do it again. Then return home. What a waste of mileage.

Linden Hills, bound on the north by Lake Calhoun and to the east by William Berry Park and Lake Harriet, wasn't quite as upscale a neighborhood as Kenwood, but the large bungalows and Tudor homes were nothing to scoff at. Rivers' Edge was in a pleasant residential area, and the one-story building took up an entire city block.

Leo circled slowly enough to examine the complex from all

four sides. On the north side, the building stretched the entire length of the block. When she turned south at the east corner, she saw the end of the facility and a narrow chain-link gate next to a stone wall, perhaps seven feet high, that butted up against the structure and ran west around the corner halfway down the block until it met with another wing of the building. The parking lot took up the southwest corner and could be entered on the south or from the west. She pulled in, wondering what was on the other side of the stone wall in the southeast corner.

The lot was half-full. She parked next to a well-worn four-door sedan that she recognized as a typical unmarked police car. She grabbed her valise, got out, and glanced in the other car's front seat. It contained an oversized computer jutting out of the dash just like Saint Paul's officers used. Good. Police presence. Now she'd get some facts.

Leo approached the front entrance, a covered portico held up by three white pillars on each side. No stairs. Just a straight shot to the front door, which was extra wide and painted stark white. The pale blue siding on the rest of the building was covered in dust. To the right, at thigh level, a brass-colored metal flap was labeled MAIL and could be operated by a narrow handle. Small packages would fit through. She bent and lifted the handle. When the cover was parallel with the ground, it snapped into place so that the postal carrier had two hands free to insert parcels and letters.

She clicked it shut and straightened up. Did she knock or simply walk in? Before she could make up her mind, the door swung open. The profile of a man in a dark-brown suit filled the doorway.

"...and yes, we'll be in touch," he said over his shoulder. The man turned and was startled to see her. His shaggy hair was light brown and shot through with gray, his face craggy, and despite the fact that he was well over six feet tall, his head seemed far too big for his frame. He regarded her as if she were less than human. "Who're you?"

She had no official DHS identification or badge to share yet, so she said, "Leona Reese, DHS Investigations."

He stepped outside, a skeptical look on his face, and pulled the door shut. "I'm aware that you people have to get involved at some point, but we're not done with the official investigation. Let me give you my card and you can call later. Probably be a day or so." He fumbled in the breast pocket of his suit.

Since she hadn't yet read the book of guidelines, she had no way of knowing what level of involvement the State was assured. In Saint Paul, her officers cooperated with investigators whenever there was a death.

But would Baldur have sent her out if the police shrugged off state investigators like the dandruff this officer needed to flick off his suit jacket?

He handed her a business card. *Dennis Flanagan, Homicide Division.* "Give me a ring later this week. I work days, and you can catch my cell after hours."

"Detective Flanagan, I've got to begin my investigation. The State needs to determine if this facility should stay open or be closed down." She hoped that was the right tack to take.

He clapped a dinner-plate-sized hand on her shoulder and tried to gently nudge her toward the parking lot. "Call me in a day or two."

She stood her ground and fumbled in her valise.

"Okay." He let out a sigh. "Call me tomorrow then."

She pulled out her badge. "I'm with SPPD on special assignment to DHS."

He squinted and let his hand drop. "Oh. Why didn't you say so in the first place? Okay, I guess you can go in."

"Is there any background you'd like to share with me first?"

He fished a notebook from his breast pocket and flipped through the pages. "The deceased is a 69-year-old female. Trimble, Callie Louise. Found dead last night at approximately 8:05. Seemed natural, but a resident, name of"—he thumbed through his notebook—"Eleanor Sinclair, she raised a stink. Per regulations, the responding officers called for a medical examiner to come to the scene. The assistant who showed up thought it looked suspicious, too, so the vic's scheduled for autopsy today."

"What was suspicious?"

"Position of the body. Possible broken nose. Might've been hemorrhaging in the eyes."

"You think she was suffocated?"

"Could be."

"What's the scoop on the personnel here?"

He thumbed forward two pages, and Leo hastened to get out her own notebook and pen.

"Owner is Martin Rivers, main office in Plymouth. He's got eight of these homes in operation. Manager of this one is Rowena Hoxley. Two nurses on staff visit all eight homes. They've got six aides here who work varied schedules, a housekeeper, and a couple of cooks. Hoxley'll give you a roster for staff and occupants."

"What's behind the stone wall?"

"Big garden. Same size as this parking lot. Walkways and bushes and such for the residents to enjoy." He pulled at his cuff to check his watch. "Look, I've got ten minutes. Let's go in, and I'll show you around."

He pressed the buzzer. Nobody answered for at least a minute. Finally, Leo heard a scuffling inside. The woman who pulled open the door was a five-foot-tall Latina in black stretch pants, white tennis shoes, and a blue, green, and purple scrubs-type top. "You're back, Detective."

"Yes, could you round up Mrs. Hoxley again?"

"Sure." She let them in and closed the door, pressing against it firmly. "I promise I've always been careful to keep this door shut," she said nervously as she strode away.

Flanagan rolled his eyes. "Talk about locking up the barn after the horses are already out."

She followed Detective Flanagan across the tiled foyer. On the floor next to the door, a sturdy square basket sat under the mail slot. To the right was an office, hardly bigger than an alcove, but it had a door for privacy. To the left was a reception desk counter with no one behind it. The top of the shiny wood surface was clear except for a telephone and an In Box piled with magazines and unopened mail.

Flanagan stopped in a common area furnished with matching couches, easy chairs, and tables with reading lamps. The paintings on the wall were of restful scenes—a forest with a shaft of sunlight piercing through, a blue and gold ocean under a setting sun, a snow-topped mountain illuminated by the moon. The kind of paintings Leo found uninspiring. She'd take paintings of people any day.

The sole occupant of the lounge area, an elderly man, sat on a sofa reading the newspaper. The whole room would look downright cozy except that the floor was covered with the kind of black, brown, and tan no-nap institutional carpet designed to show no stains. Leo figured such a smooth, flat carpet would minimize falls. No throw rugs. No wrinkles. Nothing to trip over. But it sure was ugly.

Flanagan said, "Public cans there." He pointed toward the corner where two doors led to restrooms. "The dining area—cafeteria and kitchen—are off through those double doors to the right." For the first time, she became aware of the smell of cinnamon. Something was cooking that smelled tasty.

"Straight ahead is a staff bunk and bath. The residents live in the two wings over there." He gestured across her to the left with a thumb that was the size of the French baguette she'd eaten for breakfast. "There are six apartments in the west wing, three on each side of the hall. Same for the east wing. You can go over and see how it's laid out. The owner, Rivers, said he designed the interiors of all his complexes exactly the same."

"I see."

"I have to get back to work. Can you find your way around?"

"Which room was the victim's?"

"10-East, but she was killed in 9-East." He saw the look on her face and said, "Things are loose around here. People come and go from one apartment to another. Trimble was found in the room directly across the hall from her own. Good luck. You find out anything important, please call me right away."

She thanked him. After he left, she stood waiting at the edge of the common area. Now that she was inside, Leo got her bearings in the T-shaped building. The residents lived in apartments situated on the top of the T's crossbar. She strolled that direction until she came to the intersection of the two wings. Against the far wall, between apartments 5-West and 7-East, was an open area, a blue-lit TV Room. A silver-haired woman slept in a recliner in front of the TV. The recliner's footrest was up, but she was so tiny her legs didn't reach the footrest's cushion. The TV played silently—some home shopping show flashing a pale blue scene.

Leo saw movement to the left. The woman who'd opened the front door walked toward her.

"I think Mrs. Hoxley—the manager—must be out in the garden. She's nowhere to be found here. Come with me."

Leo retraced her steps to the common area.

"I didn't catch your name," the aide said.

Leo introduced herself and learned the young woman's name was Silvia Garcia. "You work here full-time, Silvia?"

"Yes. The early shift. I start at six a.m." She led Leo through the double doors and into a dining area. The tables were already set up for lunch, and Leo heard clinking and thumping noises coming from a doorway she assumed went to the kitchen. Silvia gestured toward an open sliding glass door, and Leo followed.

Despite autumn coming on, the garden retained some freshness. Along parts of the stone wall a waist-high, dark-green hedge with a flat-trimmed top stood proud and square. Two maple trees sported red and gold leaves. The rhododendron and forsythia were fading, but a line of rosebushes still showed blooming pink roses. The daylilies had died, but the ever-hardy hostas grew in many patches throughout the garden. A smooth flagstone walkway wound under the trees and around the garden beds.

A woman dressed in jeans, white tennis shoes, and a navy blue cardigan sweater over a red t-shirt sat on a wide stone bench angled beneath a maple tree. Her gray hair was cropped short. Very lesbian looking, Leo thought, then wondered if her gaydar was correct. Was this small facility one where lesbians would congregate?

Another woman stood a few feet away, her hands moving so

fast that at first Leo thought she was signing to a deaf person.

"That's Rowena," Silvia said.

The conversation stopped, and Rowena glanced their way, then did a double take. Her hands dropped to her sides, and when she spoke, her voice was angry. "Who's this now?"

Silvia dropped back, leaving Leo to come forward on the smooth flagstones. "Mrs. Hoxley?"

"Is this a necessary visit, because if it's not, I need to ask you to leave. Are you press?"

"Oh, no. I'm here from DHS."

"You've come at a bad time."

Leo was now officially tired of people. Baldur had given her the run-around. Detective Flanagan hadn't been particularly helpful. And now this woman. Leo went straight for the jugular. "I'm afraid this is very important and concerns the Rivers' Edge operating license granted by the State."

Rowena Hoxley's face flooded red. She was forty-ish and dressed in rumpled tan pants and a baby-blue scoop-necked shirt. Her dyed blonde hair was a mess of unkempt curls. She'd be pretty, except for the scowl on her face. She looked extremely unpleasant, especially when she stiffened as though she were going to pitch a fit. Her head jerked toward the seated woman.

The bench's occupant raised a hand. "Don't worry about me, Row. I'll be fine. Go ahead."

"Are you sure, Eleanor?"

The woman gave a curt nod and turned away, but not before Leo noticed her tear-stained face. She was in her early sixties, certainly not much older than Leo's foster mother. She clutched a flowered handkerchief to her chest with both hands. Even in her grief she was sturdy and alive, and Leo wondered what had brought her to live at an apartment facility for the elderly.

Rowena Hoxley said, "Shall we go inside?"

Without waiting for an answer, Hoxley marched off, and Leo followed her to the front office. She invited her to take a seat and went around to the other side of her desk to plop down. When Leo lowered herself to the chair, the space was so tight that her knees touched the desk front.

Hoxley picked up some loose pages, shuffled them together, and stuffed them in a drawer. "All right then, what can I tell you?"

"First, I'm required to tape record this. Also, I have to provide you with some information." Leo dug through her valise, put the recorder on the desk, and flipped it on.

She recalled Fred Baldur's meager instructions. She must insist that witnesses, including staff and owners, speak to her. The people in charge were in a difficult position. If they told her anything incriminating or facts that proved the facility was unsafe, Leo had an obligation to share it with the police and to act in such a way that the residents of the program were protected. She was required by law to inform each interviewee of these facts and already thought of that as a kind of Miranda Warning with no rights. They had no right to remain silent, nor did they have the option of dragging in their attorney, and no attorney would be appointed unless criminal charges were filed. But anything they did say could possibly be used in a court of law. Leo could understand if management balked at talking to DHS investigators.

"I'm required to read a statement about your rights and responsibilities and the ways the State might use your witness statement."

Hoxley let out a snort of impatience. "I've been here since ten p.m. last night. I don't have the time or energy to deal with this." But she listened to Leo's statements with resignation, and when she was done, Hoxley said, "Okay, fine. Can we get on with it then?"

"I understand this must be a very trying time. I'm going to ask you questions that will help me understand how you run your program. I'll interview all staff and residents."

"But the police already did that!"

"And if it happens that Mrs. Trimble didn't die from natural causes, they'll likely be back to do it again. Repeatedly. I can't make any promises, Mrs. Hoxley, but with any luck, I'll only be here off and on for a few days, and then the State's investigation will conclude without any fanfare."

"Oh, this is a nightmare. Nothing like this has ever happened at Rivers' Edge. Never."

"Nobody's died?"

"Not under suspicious circumstances. We had a heart attack in May, but he later passed at the hospital. Three months ago, Mrs. Levinstein fell at the shopping mall and broke her hip. She didn't make it through the surgery to put pins in. Other than that, I don't know that anyone has actually died on the grounds before. In the three years I've worked at Rivers' Edge, we've had no deaths in-house."

Leo made notes on a legal pad. She suspected that the packet of information Baldur had shoved into her hands as she left probably contained a form with an official format for doing this, but she didn't have time to search it out. She could rely on the tape recording if she needed it.

Hoxley brought her hands up to her temples and ran her fingers through her wild fake-blonde curls. When she met Leo's gaze, her blue eyes were bloodshot. She looked like she needed another drink. "Can we just get this over with?"

Leo spoke as kindly as she could. "I'm sorry that you're exhausted. Let me get the basics now, and I can ask you other questions later on. You have twelve occupants?"

"Actually, nine right now. Well, eight now that Callie has—passed. Three vacancies. Guess we'll have four when her lease is legally terminated."

"Is that usual?"

"No, not really. We've had a waiting list at times in the past, but the economy's bad. In the last few months, we've had more turnover than usual. Oh, and I should add that one tenant, Norma Osterweiss, is out of town, visiting a daughter in Red Wing." She took a ring-binder out of her right desk drawer and opened it. "We were last full up in February. A couple of people moved out to be nearer to family. Mrs. Levinstein died. Sol Hausmann had the heart attack. A couple of people ceased to meet qualifications and were sent to new facilities."

"What qualifications are you referring to?"

"We're not a nursing home. We're an apartment house in every sense. The focus is on independent living. We provide quality assisted care to help each elderly or disabled person live as comfortably as possible. We're required to provide help with only three of the basic needs that fall into seven specific categories." She listed them off quickly from memory. "Bathing, dressing, grooming, eating, transferring, toileting, and continence care."

"Transferring?"

"Moving people. You know, lifting them when they're not mobile. When you see how small our aides are, you'll understand why we don't do any transferring."

"So you don't do all seven tasks?"

"No, our home focuses on clients with high-level skills. Residents have to be ambulatory and can only live here if they need ordinary help with bathing, dressing, and grooming. We also do food preparation, but they have to feed themselves. They also have to be able to use the bathroom on their own. We have a service for Registered Nurses on call 24/7. The RNs help us assist the patients with keeping track of their medications. Basically, one or more people are on hand here twenty-four hours a day. My aides get to know the residents and treat them like Mom and Dad—or Grandma and Grandpa. We do their laundry, fix delicious meals, go out walking in the garden with them, and so forth. Anything beyond that requires a facility with a lot more staff and services." Hoxley frowned. "But shouldn't you know all this?"

Leo opted for honesty. "I've been involved in many investigations, but not in homes such as this. Thanks for your patience with me. Now let's talk about who works here."

"I've got six aides who cover every minute of the day, 24/7. This complex is *never* unstaffed. Three aides have overlapping shifts that start at six a.m. and run until ten p.m. From ten at night until morning, I have two aides who take turns working the shift."

"What does the sixth aide do?"

"It's not like that. We have a whole schedule that the six aides cycle through, always with enough coverage to deal with vacations, holidays, and illness. Believe me, I've got them on a nice overlapping schedule because if someone isn't available, I'm the one who gets stuck coming in to cover."

"But someone was here last night?"

"Yes. In fact, I had two aides on duty last night, Sherry Colton and Habibah Okello. That's standard for the dinner hour and for Activity Hour after that. Sherry was to leave at ten, and Habibah was here for the late shift. They're required to stay awake until the last resident shuts out the lights, which is usually by eleven or so. Then they can sleep in the staff bunkroom if they wish. I don't think Habibah slept, though."

"I thought someone had to be awake all night?"

"No, that's the beauty of a smaller facility. The law allows an exemption from the 'awake' requirement when there are twelve or fewer residents. We've got a terrific security-response system for our clients. If they have any problems at all, they ring, and the aide awakens and comes running. We keep a log of every time there's a summons between midnight and six a.m. We have very few incidents."

Rowena Hoxley was in her element now and spoke with pride about her facility, waxing on about the garden, the fine cooking, and the entertainment they often brought in. "A couple of our aides love to sing, and one plays the piano. One or two nights a week we have a sing-along. Sherry led it last night. We have arts and crafts night, too. Anything the residents want to undertake as a hobby, we'll try to help with."

"Besides the six aides, how many others work here?"

Hoxley ticked them off. "Two cooks who generally work half-time each, a housekeeper, and me. We pay a gardening service that also does snow removal in the winter. The eight Rivers' facilities share the services of the nursing consortium, so we have regular visits from the RNs. That's it. Keeps the overhead low and the residents happy."

"Ten staff then." Leo made a note.

"Yes."

"Anyone else on the premises last night?"

"As I was leaving for the day, Callie Trimble's son Ted came in. I didn't see anyone else. It's my understanding that Eleanor

Sinclair was out for the evening. Sherry and Habibah said they had seven at dinner and only five at the sing-along. Callie was sleeping, and Walter Green doesn't sing. Habibah told me Walter watched television in the TV room."

"I'll want to talk to the son and any other family that have visited lately."

"I can't think of anyone else who's been in. I'll hunt up the son's contact info."

During the rest of the interview, Leo got the names of all staff and residents. As far as she could tell, she had twelve primary witnesses to interview: the seven residents plus Eleanor Sinclair, the two evening aides, and the cooks. Of secondary importance were the aides not on duty. She also wanted to speak to the owner.

"Where were you last night after the dinner break and up until the police called?"

"Me? You can't think I had anything to do with this."

"I assume the police asked you the same question."

"They did."

"What did you tell them?"

"I was at home. My husband worked late. He walked in the very moment I took the call from Sherry Colton."

"Can anyone verify your whereabouts before he returned?"

"My neighbors may have seen me drive in after work. I don't know, though. I swear to you, I was at home."

"Mrs. Hoxley, is there anyone else you think I should interview? Anyone else who's been around during the last week or so?"

She shook her head. "Can't think of anyone. Nothing unusual has happened lately."

"All right. I'll be here for some time. When I leave, I'll check out with you or one of the aides. Do you —"

The office phone rang, and Hoxley raised a finger.

Leo whispered, "Go ahead." She busied herself with her notes, but when Rowena Hoxley gasped, Leo looked up.

"Crime — crime scene? No...of course not. Yes...I'll be here." She hung up, her eyes brimming with tears. "Oh, Lord. Detective Flanagan says Callie Trimble was definitely murdered."

Chapter Four

LEO STUFFED THE tape recorder in her valise and followed Rowena Hoxley out the door. The manager came to an abrupt stop, and Leo nearly bumped into her.

Built into the office wall, outside the door, were twelve numbered mailboxes with tiny locks, and the woman from the garden stood there, a key-ring in her hand and a shocked expression on her face.

"Eleanor?" Hoxley said.

"The mail." Her hands shook and the keys jingled. "The door was — I'm sorry. I didn't mean to eavesdrop. I heard — " She broke into tears and bowed her head.

"Oh, my. This is awful." Hoxley took Eleanor's arm and steered her over to a couch in the lounge area. "I'm so sorry. So terribly sorry."

Leo couldn't hear all Hoxley was saying, but she was doing such a nice job comforting Eleanor Sinclair that the manager went up several points in Leo's estimation. Perhaps she wasn't such an unpleasant person after all.

Leo stepped back into the office and examined the open mailbox slots above the chair where she'd been sitting. Someone must distribute the mail each day, but every box was empty, so it obviously hadn't been done yet. What was the point of having locks on the other side of the mail slots if the manager's office was this open and accessible? Across the hall she noted a pile of circulars and envelopes stacked on the counter near the front door. Why bother to lock up the mail if anyone could rummage through it out there before it was distributed to the mailboxes?

"Ms. Reese?"

Leo shot out of the office to see Hoxley get to her feet. "I told Eleanor why you're here, and she'd like to speak to you. But the police want me to stand guard at Callie's and Eleanor's apartments. Could the two of you maybe go into the café?"

"Come along, dear," Eleanor said. "This way."

By the time they were seated across from one another at a square table for four, Eleanor seemed more recovered from her shock, but Leo almost didn't have the heart to begin an official interview. Still, she had to do her job, so she got out the tape recorder and explained the same rigmarole she'd been through with Hoxley.

Eleanor listened placidly through the recitation. "I appear to be the police's number one suspect, so I suppose I ought to be careful about what I say. However, I can assure you I didn't kill Callie. She meant more to me than anyone in the world."

"Had you known each other a long time?"

The woman's eyes filled with tears. "Forty-two years. I came to teach at Como Park Senior High in Saint Paul, and she was a cook there."

"And you've kept in touch all these years."

Eleanor's lips twitched, and it took her a few beats to answer. "Yes. We did."

"Did she have any enemies?"

"Not that I'm aware of. Callie has always been—I mean, she was—" She broke off as tears filled her eyes.

Leo waited. She figured that in this job, as in police work, rarely would the interviewees be happy. She wouldn't go so far as to call Eleanor Sinclair's normal human emotions "histrionics" as Fred Baldur had, and she doubted that these would be the first tears she'd see today. "Go on, Mrs. Sinclair."

"Nobody loved to laugh as much as Callie. She was a happy, loving person. Even after her diagnosis, she never let it get in the way."

"Diagnosis?"

"A little over three years ago, Callie was diagnosed with Multi-Infarct Dementia. It's a kind of vascular disease caused by mini-strokes that damaged her brain. We had no idea how long it had been coming on, but she was having major problems with her memory, so I took her to the doctor. They performed a battery of tests, and when they gave the diagnosis, our lives changed overnight. But, you see, though the doctors said she might have severe depression and mood swings, she never has. She cried a lot at first, but after a while she decided to meet life head-on."

"Which meant?"

"We finished out the school year and took off for a summer tour of Europe. I hadn't been overseas since my college days, and Callie had never been at all. We spent ten weeks traveling and had a wonderful time."

"Weren't you afraid she'd have an attack?"

"We didn't let ourselves think of that. The doctors had her on medication to stabilize her vascular pressure, so we went and had a jolly time."

Eleanor's face took on a faraway expression, as though she were remembering happy times, but then she snapped back to attention. "She made it halfway through the next school year, but her memory was too spotty. She couldn't be trusted to cook anymore, so she took a medical retirement and stayed home."

"So you and she lived together for some time?"

"Yes." Eleanor raised her chin in defiance. "For nearly forty years. Ever since her divorce."

It was clear Eleanor Sinclair was being honest at the expense of her own comfort and privacy. Leo wished she could explain that she understood completely and that not only was she in a relationship with a woman, but her foster sister, Kate, and her partner, Susie, had been together eight years and were raising two children.

But now was not the time to discuss that. Instead she said, "You chose separate apartments here."

Eleanor steepled her fingers and pressed them against her lips. She sat like that for a while, and Leo didn't think she was going to answer. When she finally did, her voice was so quiet that Leo had to strain to hear. "I've been a private person my whole life. It's nobody's business what my relationship was with Callie. She was quite a free spirit, so much more uninhibited than I could ever be. We didn't find many elder care places where we could room together. Most of them were full, and the rest were run by people who weren't very open-minded. I—I couldn't—I was unable to broach the subject with the various administrators. I searched for an appropriate place for a long time to no avail. This one seemed the most ideal. With our apartments right across the hall, she could still come to me in the middle of the night, and no one appeared to notice or care. We were starting to settle in."

"You're very courageous to trust me with this now."

Fire leapt into Eleanor Sinclair's eyes, and Leo got the first glimpse of what a formidable teacher she'd probably been.

"This is the way families should be. One of the big problems in our society these days is how people fail one another. We should be there for one another whether we're blood family or 'found' family." She took a ragged breath. "But what's the point now? Nobody can split us any further apart than we are, forever and always. Someone stole her away from me, so who cares? She'll never again rest easy by my side." Tears ran down her cheeks. She sat impassively, letting the grief roll off her like water from a faucet.

Leo let her have a moment then said, "I hope you realize how sorry I am to be putting you through this."

Eleanor brought her handkerchief to her face. She wiped away the tears and dabbed her eyes. "Go on then. What else do you need to know?"

"When did you move here?"

"Mid-June this year. I finished teaching and had to retire. I'd have liked to continue. I loved teaching. But Callie could no longer cook at home, and I'm certainly not good at it. Besides, she was gradually failing, and I knew I wouldn't be able to take care of her properly when the time came. I believed it was better to scale down right away. So you can see why the police will suspect me." She leaned forward and studied Leo for a moment. "That large, loud detective was clearly suspicious of everything I said, but I was unable to explain to him all the reasons why I'd never hurt Callie. You understand, don't you? Please, tell me you understand this?"

"I think I understand better than any straight man possibly could. Everything you've said makes perfect sense."

Eleanor's eyes widened in comprehension. For a moment her face brightened, then she sagged in the chair as though someone had sucked the life out of her. "Thank you."

"I'll do my best to preserve your privacy, though your life with Mrs. Trimble may come out. But it won't be from me unless there's a specific reason relating to the investigation."

"Oh, my God, I can't believe she's gone. Who would do this to her? Who?"

"We have to get to the bottom of it, Mrs. Sinclair."

Leo waited as Eleanor shook her head slowly. Finally, she said, "You should call me Eleanor. Even though everyone has called me Mrs. Sinclair—especially when I was teaching—I was never married."

"All right, then, Eleanor. Will you tell me what happened last night?"

Eleanor outlined her evening, hour by hour. As Leo scribbled notes, it suddenly occurred to her that she was taking notes like a cop, not like a state investigator. What, exactly, was her goal here? She was supposed to figure out if Rivers' Edge Independent Living Apartments were safe to stay open. And how could she make that determination? Fred Baldur hadn't given her any guidance about that at all. If a killer was on the loose it wasn't safe, but how was she supposed to make that judgment unless she determined who had committed the murder? Only then could she be entirely sure the residents were safe.

She hadn't been listening very closely, so she was thankful the tape was running. Just then, the recorder clicked off. "Uh-oh. Let me flip the tape over."

Eleanor pulled a flowered handkerchief from the sleeve of her cardigan. "I can't believe this is happening. I feel like I've been relegated to a terribly bad dream, Mrs. Reese."

"Now it's my turn to ask you to call me Leona instead of Mrs. Reese. I've never been married either. All right?" Eleanor nodded, and Leo went on. "Let's talk about the other residents. Did any of them have a problem with Callie?"

"Not at all. People here are mostly friendly." She paused.

"Mostly? Has there been a problem?"

"No, that's not it. It's just that it wasn't easy to move into a new place, that's all. Has anyone told you about Callie? I mean, given you details?"

"Not really. Other than what you've told me, the only fact I know is that she was sixty-nine-years old."

"She was also a big, solid farm girl. You're what—five-eight?"

"Exactly."

"Then you're about her height, but Callie had a lot more meat on her bones. She carried heavy trays and shifted huge oven racks and kneaded bread her whole life. She was strong. Whoever did this to her had to be equally strong. Willie Stepanek lives next door to me, and she's Callie's size, but she's all flab, not much muscle. Besides, she's a delightful woman. She was always patient with Callie and would never hurt her. Agnes, Nettie, and Jade are tiny little slips of things. None of them had the strength to subdue Callie. Habibah told me last night that all the women but Callie were in here at the sing-along. So was Franklin. He's strong enough, too, but I can't believe he'd have hurt her."

"Sing-alongs always go on here in the dining hall?"

"Yes." Eleanor pointed past Leo. "The aides roll the piano out, and somebody plays. Sherry is good, but Norma and Jade also play beautifully."

Leo hadn't noticed the piano over in the corner. She took a moment to examine the room, wondering what else she'd missed. There were six tables, each of which would seat four. Near the kitchen door, a long sideboard with glass-fronted cupboards was filled with table ornaments and other dining necessities. That was it.

Leo checked her list of residents. "So, we've got Agnes Trumpeter, Nettie Volk, Jade Perkins, and Franklin Callaghan. Oh, and Willie Stepanek. That's five, plus you. Someone's missing..."

"Walter Green. And Norma Osterweiss. She's on vacation."

"Good memory."

"Forty-two years of high school students make one a quick study."

"What's the scoop on Walter Green?"

"Sherry said he was sleeping in the TV room."

"Could he have attacked Callie?"

"Well, I don't know. Maybe. My students would have called him a Space Cadet. He wanders around, muttering, and asking lewd questions. Never does anything violent, though."

"There's always a first time. Is he capable?"

"Maybe. He's not a big man—certainly not like Franklin who's six feet tall and broad-shouldered. But no one saw Walter leave the TV room. He was asleep when I went by, and I don't think he woke up until after the police arrived."

"Could the aides and residents have been so busy at the sing-along that they missed him leaving the TV room?"

"Possibly." Doubt showed in her eyes. "I told the officer last night that something was wrong when I got home. I was too much in shock, though."

"Oh?"

"Callie would never have opened the sliding glass door in my room. Only Willie Stepanek's room and mine have access to the garden. They charge extra for that." She rolled her eyes. "Originally, I took the room with the garden walk-out because I wanted to be able to go out there whenever I pleased, and I thought it better for Callie. But she preferred watching the traffic go by from the window in her room. Besides, I was afraid she'd wander out there in the dead of winter. I found out quickly, though, that she didn't really like the garden. The one time she went out without me, she got disoriented. I found her sitting on the bench under the tree crying. She couldn't figure out how to get home. She liked to be indoors. I think she felt safer."

"And last night?"

"The sliding glass door was wide open. So was the screen door. When I left, the door was open, but the screen was closed. I don't believe Callie touched it, so who did?"

"Did the police dust there for prints?"

Eleanor shrugged. "I haven't the faintest idea."

Leo made a note to check with Detective Flanagan. "What about Callie's son?"

"Ted? You think Ted had something to do with this?" She laughed. "Besides me, nobody cared as much for Callie as Ted did. I declare he loved her more than his own wife, from whom he has often been estranged. Callie was Ted's port in the storm. Even after her memory became so bad, she never forgot him. She forgot her own brother at times, but not Ted or me."

"The police will examine Ted's motives."

"I suppose they must, but he has no motive."

"The obvious one is always money."

Eleanor laughed again, a deep throaty chuckle. "Callie was a cook in a public high school for almost five decades. She had no money to speak of, and Ted knew it. He does tax accounting for both of us."

"But what about this place? Rivers' Edge can't be cheap."

"It surely isn't, but I'm the one who pays for that. I inherited a lot of money when my parents died, and I parlayed it into a small fortune in the stock market. Callie's husband ate through all the money the two of them ever had. When she sued for divorce, he found some new chippy with money. Callie's never been as financially secure as I have. She got divorced back when women didn't have the protections and fair courts that they do now. The louse even got the house and the kids, though he did a despicable job providing for and attending to them. By the time they were in middle school, they practically lived at our house." She paused and sat breathing fast. "Our house..."

Leo waited respectfully for her to recover her composure. "So you met her at the school where you worked?"

"Yes. She was seven years older and so full of life. She didn't deserve a verbally abusive husband who slapped her around whenever his business prospects faltered. At first I sought to protect her, to urge her to get away from him, and then..." She looked off into the distance. "The kids were in kindergarten and second grade, and I enjoyed them as well. Such serious little people, a girl who looked just like her mother and a boy who resembled me so much that people often thought he was my son. They quickly became attached to me, and for the first time in my life, I understood what it was like to bond with a child. It was wonderful. And then I — well — I suppose I had already fallen for Callie like the proverbial ton of bricks. I loved her desperately." She raised her eyes and met Leo's, a little defiant, but with pride, too.

"And wow, you've been together all this time, all these years."

"That's right. The fact is, Leona, that Callie and I could've been more than comfortable for twenty or thirty more years, and neither of her children would ever have done anything to either of us. If Ted wanted money, he'd have had to kill me, not Callie, then assume the trustee position to which I had him appointed two years ago. But Ted would never hurt Callie. Or me. We both love him. Loved. I mean, Callie did — and I always will."

Eleanor abruptly brought her wrist up to her mouth.

"I know this must all be a terrifying jumble," Leo said, "and I think I should let you be for now. We can talk further tomorrow. I'm going to give you my phone number so you can call if you think of anything else, okay?"

"All right."

The doorbell went off, four descending notes, paused, and repeated. A moment later, a deep rumbling voice asked for Rowena Hoxley.

Leo handed Eleanor a slip of paper. "I'll bet that's the police."

"Come to arrest me?"

"Did you kill Callie Trimble?" Leo asked as she rose.

"No. Of course not."
"Then don't worry."

DETECTIVE FLANAGAN SWEPT into the common area
followed by a shorter, square-jawed man much older than
Flanagan, much more grizzled, with a whiskey nose and rheumy
blue-gray eyes. He wore a light blue suit and a frown. His shirt
collar was open, no tie. With his sunburned face and blond hair cut
in a flat-top, Leo could more easily imagine him on the deck of a
fishing trawler rather than as part of a murder investigation.

She hesitated in the doorway of the dining room. The front door
was propped open, and a man carrying two heavy cases preceded a
woman muscling in a pair of lights on extendable stands.

"Where's the manager?" Flanagan asked. "Oh, hi there."

He met Leo's eyes, and she could tell he didn't remember her
name. "Leona Reese here, Detective."

"Yeah, right. This is my partner, Hal DeWitt."

"Glad to meet you, Detective DeWitt," she said. "I'm sorry to
hear that Mrs. Trimble's death has been ruled a homicide."

"Not half as sorry as I am," Flanagan said.

"I think you'll find the manager down the east hall."

"Thanks."

Eleanor slipped into the doorway next to Leo, and they
watched a parade of people bring equipment through the front
entrance. "Looks like they'll take fingerprints," Leo said.

When it seemed that everyone was in to stay, Eleanor shut the
door.

Flanagan came around the corner. "Hey, there may be more
technicians needing to come in."

Eleanor said, "They can ring the bell."

Flanagan let out a sigh of exasperation. "It's a lot easier if the
door's open so they can come and go."

"Didn't we just have a death here due to poor security?"

Flanagan gaped at her but didn't argue. To Leo he said, "We're
likely to be here a couple of hours. I suggest that you skedaddle for
a while. Maybe go get some lunch."

"Okay."

He looked at his watch. "Mrs. Sinclair, if you'd be so kind, I'd
appreciate it if you'd stay in. Maybe you could wait right here and
keep track of the front door."

"When will I be able to return to my apartment?"

"Not sure. I'll let you know as soon as I can."

"Lunch is going to be served at noon. If you don't find me
here, I'll be in the dining room. Leona, would you like me to see if

the cooks can set a place for you?"

"No, that's all right. I'll come back in a couple of hours. I should check in at the office anyway."

Leo gathered up her things and headed for the parking lot. The air had warmed up, blessing the Twin Cities with an unusually hot fall day, and the humidity wrapped around her like a soggy blanket. She wouldn't be surprised if it hit ninety degrees before the afternoon was over.

She cranked up the A/C, and as she waited for the car to cool down, she turned on her cell phone. No messages. Daria must be busy in court. Leo wondered how her trial prep was going and left a quick message to tell her she was thinking of her and hoping it was all going well.

She hadn't thought to give Fred Baldur her phone number, so she called the department and was transferred twice before his voice came on the line.

"Fred, Leona Reese here. The police arrived at Rivers' Edge and kicked me out for a couple of hours while they work the scene. The woman who died last night was murdered."

"How?"

"They haven't told me officially, but the officer in charge seemed to suspect suffocation."

"I've received four major complaints and sixteen minor."

"You're kidding. About Rivers' Edge?"

"No, of course not. About various licensees. I've systematically dispensed with three of the more worrisome ones and most of the minor issues."

Why was he telling her this? She had a major case to deal with. What did she care about his administrative woes? "And so?"

"I can't help you with the case you're on. You can call for advice anytime, but I've got my hands full here."

"I see. I'm going to take a lunch break, kill some time, then continue recording witness statements at the apartment."

"Excellent! Good plan."

"I won't knock off at five, Fred, to ensure that I've put in a full day. Unless you've got something that would take an hour—"

"No, nothing of that nature at the moment. All the cases I have for you are in-depth and will take concerted effort."

"Then I'll take care of some personal business now and work late to compensate."

"No need to inform me. We're all salaried professionals here. The boss expects us to stay on top of the juggernaut and keep the crazies out of his hair."

"I understand. Still, I thought I should keep someone apprised of my status."

"Yes, fine, fine. Keep me posted if you wish."

"Do you want my cell phone number?"

"Ah, no." He made a humming sound. "Well, perhaps that would be a good idea. I'm not likely to call, though. Things are all-consuming here."

Leo gave him the number, got his, and closed her cell phone. What a weasel. She didn't have enough information about policies and procedures yet, but her intuition shrieked that Fred Baldur was sitting on his ass, drinking coffee, and shuffling paper while she was out doing the real work. She put the car into gear and drove toward Highway 100. As long as she had time on her hands, she might as well make the most of it.

She pulled into the Robbinsdale Rifle & Gun Club lot fifteen minutes later. She opened the trunk, got out her weapon, a box of shells, ear protection, and safety glasses, and made her way down to the gun club's basement. The place smelled of gun oil and cordite. The clerk and another man leaned over the counter to examine a topographical map while they argued about the best place to build a deer stand.

Leo showed the clerk her peace officer's license to expedite matters and paid for an hour's time. She selected a target and took it into the enclosed area. The other lanes were all empty, which was nice. The less noise, the better. But the ceiling was so low that she immediately felt claustrophobic.

As the ventilation fan rattled and whirred, she loaded three magazines for her Glock, then set up the target and sent it out a distance of eighteen feet. For the last decade, she'd practiced at least once per month at distances between five and twenty-five feet. Feet, not yards. Civilians were surprised any time she told them that. On all the cop shows, the shootouts often took place over long distances out in the street, from behind car doors, and on the run down dark, shadowy alleys.

But she still remembered what Dad Wallace, her foster father, had taught her and Kate the first time he'd taken them to a range to learn to handle guns safely: "The majority of police officers are killed at a distance of ten feet or less. Girls, we get up close and personal with people. If they pull a gun, they're more likely to be in your face than far away."

At the time, Leo had been thirteen and Kate twelve, and Dad Wallace's patient tutoring had instilled in them a respect for firearms and a fascination as well. He was never surprised that they'd both gone into law enforcement—only that his sons had not.

Now here it was nearly two decades later, and Leo had recently read that most police gunfights were won—and lost—at distances less than seven yards. The times may change, the weapons may be different, but as Dad Wallace always said, cops working "up close and personal" was still what law enforcement was all about.

She donned her ear protection and safety glasses and assumed her favorite shooting stance, surprised that her heart was beating extra hard. She usually wasn't this nervous. She lowered the weapon and took two deep breaths, willing herself to relax. Her vision was clear, and she could stay as long as she needed to — or for as long as her credit card held out. She told herself to stop fretting and start shooting. She couldn't think of a single reason why she couldn't successfully fire off the entire box of fifty shells.

She decided to warm up by aiming for the target's bull's-eye in bursts of three shots. She sighted down the barrel and squeezed the trigger. "Yowza," she said triumphantly. All three shots nailed near-center.

Lining up again, Leo aimed for the outside ring, to the top and the right. These shots clustered in a triangle with no more than an inch between them. She let out a sigh of relief.

She was halfway through the second magazine when her skull suddenly felt like it would explode. The pounding squeezed at her temples like she'd been hit with a blackjack. She placed the Glock on the ledge in front of her and squeezed her eyes shut. Pain. As bad as the worst sinus headache she'd ever had. With a swipe of her hand, she removed the ear protection muffs.

She took deep breaths, but the pain didn't pass. It reduced to a less intense throb, but the pounding remained. For a while she worried that she'd throw up. When that sensation receded, she removed the glasses and set them on the ledge, too. Why was this happening? How could something she'd done for years give her such an intense headache? She'd shot tens of thousands of rounds, and this had never happened before. Was it the percussion? Maybe she needed a new pair of earmuffs. She'd seen some military grade, high performance ones that cost a hundred bucks and used a gain limiter to suppress sounds exceeding eighty decibels. Maybe that would help.

She had no desire to practice anymore, especially since she knew her accuracy would be shot to hell. She had to acknowledge that something was definitely wrong. She gathered up everything, stepped out of the lane, and exited the range. At the cleaning station, she unloaded and disassembled her weapon, cleaned and oiled it, and put it away in the carry case.

The cymbals crashing in her head synchronized with her footsteps on the way out to the car. After returning her kit to her trunk, she sat in the driver's seat and let the sun's heat warm her. But no amount of heat could bake the pain from her head.

Chapter Five

ELEANOR AND TED sat on a saggy maroon sofa in the middle of the Rivers' Edge lounge area. A couple of technicians wrangled fancy spotlights on adjustable stands through the front door. The two detectives, Flanagan and DeWitt, followed behind.

She could see Ted was in a terrible mood, but he hadn't yet shared what was troubling him. Of course, Callie's death was enough to upset him, but this attitude seemed different. It wasn't like Ted to scowl and stare daggers as he was doing to the police officials entering the complex.

She patted his arm. His suit felt smooth and rich. She wasn't sure what the material was called, but she knew he favored the Baroni brand. Ted always looked good in business clothes, and the gray two-button jacket was especially handsome, especially with the bright blue tie. Eleanor had always been utilitarian. Callie was the one who enjoyed wearing flashy outfits, expensive pantsuits, and splashy colors. But Eleanor could appreciate the style of Ted's outfit.

Ted muttered, "I'd like to have it out with those two."

"Who?"

"Asshole cops."

Eleanor tightened her grip on his forearm and leaned in to examine Ted's wounded expression. "Why?"

"They showed up at my apartment in the dead of night and hauled me down to the station."

"What? But—but why?"

"They asked me some questions about where I was last night, and I guess they didn't like my answers. They hardly let me dress. Just barged in, tried to intimidate me, and dragged me downtown. Thank God April wasn't home. They kept asking questions about Mom, but they wouldn't tell me what was wrong. You'd think that when the police show up to inform a person of a death in the family, they'd be a lot nicer about it."

The two police detectives came striding from the east wing. Without a glance they hurried out the front door and slammed it behind them.

"They're absolute assholes," Ted said. "Rude. Suspicious. Just mean."

"I'm so sorry they got to you before I could tell you. I was in such shock. I should have called you and your sister right away, Ted."

"It's okay, El.

"How long did they keep you?"

"Hours. Made me sit there for hours and didn't even offer me coffee or a Coke or anything. I sweated in some dinky little room with only a chair and table. When they finally did come talk to me, I bet we were done in fifteen minutes. What could I tell them? I don't know a thing. I got home in time to take a shower, dress, and go make arrangements at work. I'd have been here sooner, but my boss was on the rampage. I had to finish off some paperwork for him before I could come see about my own mother's death. I'm sorry it took me so long."

He shuddered. At first Eleanor assumed it was from being upset about work, but when she looked closer, she recognized the anger he was trying to stifle. She remembered him as a small boy when his older sister Olivia took something away and he had to fight to get it back. That same focused, intent fury was evident on his face today.

"You know, El, I've been smacked around before. I had my share of fights in school when I was growing up, but you just don't know how helpless you feel when two Cro-Magnon cops stand over you and shoot questions like crazy. Made me sick that they could possibly think I'd hurt anybody, especially my own mother."

Eleanor started to cry, soundlessly, tears rolling down her cheeks.

Ted put an arm around her and drew her into a hug. She leaned against the side of his chest, her head tucked under his chin, feeling so fragile. She could count on one hand how many times he'd held her in his life. Sure, he'd sat on her lap as a child to read a book, and there were times she'd gotten down on the floor with him to build a Lego project or examine some toy he was assembling, but she hadn't ever been a huggy person. Callie was always the warm, affectionate one. Eleanor had never found a way to escape her own reticence—except with Callie. She knew she would have been terminally stiff and brusque if not for Callie's constant intervention. She'd been Eleanor's lifesaver, the one person who sought the good in Eleanor's heart and brought out all the joy and love hiding there.

Ted let out a strangled sob then cleared his throat to cover it. "I'm so sorry, El. Here I am whining about the dumb-ass cops, and you're dealing with all this—all this—"

"I know," she said. "It's awful. A nightmare." She patted him on the chest and pulled away to dig in her jeans pockets for a hanky to wipe her eyes.

"I don't know what would have happened to me if it weren't for you and Mom. Dad was so awful."

"You would have been okay, Ted. You're a strong person."

"Sure didn't feel that way last night. It was clear they thought I was some kind of animal that needed to be broken. I guess cops think they're successful if they can cow you into feeling small."

"Sounds like we both had a terrible time. I thought my night was awful, too. Today has been just as bad."

"I can't even imagine. The police were walking around the grounds when I drove in. Are they done in your rooms yet?"

"I don't know." Eleanor tugged on his sleeve. "We can go to the dining room."

They went through the open double doors and slumped into chairs at the first table they came to, Eleanor facing the common area and Ted sitting to her right.

He said, "The police told me they'd be checking every detail about my life. They actually seem to think I killed Mom."

"Oh, please! That's beyond ridiculous."

His hands shook, which she could tell embarrassed him. Folding his arms over his chest, he kept his voice level. "They think I was the last to see her alive and that I have a motive."

"Ha. What would that be?"

"Mercy killing."

Eleanor blinked back a wash of tears.

"What are we going to do?" he asked.

She squeezed his arm. "There's nothing we can do but get through this. It's the worst nightmare I could ever imagine."

"Exactly. That's exactly it."

The front doorbell rang. An aide came from the far corridor, went through the common area, and disappeared from Eleanor's sight. A moment later, Callie's ex-husband, Howard Trimble, came chugging toward them like a black locomotive, his face red.

"Uh-oh," Ted said.

Any minute she expected steam to billow out of Ted's father's ears. They both sat waiting for the engine to run them over.

Without a single greeting, Howard said, "I've just come from the bank. They won't let me get at Callie's accounts."

"Why do you need access?" Ted asked.

"We've got to make the funeral arrangements."

Eleanor said, "Howard, I've already got that ball rolling."

Howard glared at Eleanor. "I don't need your interference. I'll take care of my own family arrangements, thank you very much."

Eleanor drew a breath and said sharply, "Callie and I prepaid our funerals long ago. I've already stopped by the Episcopal Church to alert them, and whoever has time tomorrow morning can come with me to meet with Father James. I planned to get the word out this afternoon."

"Why—who are you to..." His face flushed redder. "You're probably the reason the bank denied me access! You have no right."

Ted said, "Dad, have a seat."

"I don't want a seat. I want to know the meaning of this. Have you taken over my wife's money?"

Eleanor said, "Other than an account for her pension and social security deposits, Callie had no money to speak of. And she's your ex-wife, Howard. Remember? You have no control here."

"Preposterous! I'm more than happy to inform the authorities about this." He brought his index finger up in the air and began the kind of diatribe Eleanor recognized from past experience. "Callie always had plenty of money." Ignoring Eleanor, he spoke to Ted. "Your mother probably didn't want you to know. *That woman* she lived with tapped her accounts. I just know it."

"Dad, stop! Nothing illegal or underhanded has gone on."

"And how would you know, Ted?"

"For cripesake, I'm their accountant. I know more about their financial situation than you do. Mom spent her entire savings when Grandma Trimble went into the nursing home."

"That's not possible."

Ted said, "You paid some, Mom paid some. When Mom ran out of savings, Eleanor stepped up and paid the rest."

Howard gaped at Eleanor in disbelief. "I knew nothing about this."

"There was no way Callie and I were going to let your mother be moved from the good treatment she got at the care center to some flea-bag welfare home."

"But it wasn't your place to interfere, Eleanor."

"Of course it was. Until she had to go to the nursing home, your mother lived with Callie and me for three years. Callie nursed her like she was her own parent. She fed her, walked with her, helped her dress. Right up until Mother Trimble had the final heart attack and needed round-the-clock attention, Callie handled the bulk of her care. And when she died and left you the house, which you sold for a boatload of money, you never shared a thing."

Howard sank into a chair and scrubbed at his face with the palms of his hands. "Oh, my God, this is awful. All so awful."

Ted said, "And now Mom's dead and gone, Dad. She's dead."

Ted glanced at Eleanor, wide-eyed. She was sure Ted must feel as surprised as she did. Although Howard had quite a temper, she'd never seen him come so unhinged. She knew well that Ted's experience of Howard Theodore Trimble had run along the lines of loyal subject following the regent's every order. His authority wasn't questioned by his son or Ted's sister, Olivia. Though he never laid a hand on the kids, at times Howard had been downright harsh to the children. Callie and Eleanor served as an oasis in the desert of Howard's unreasonable expectations. But right now, he appeared thoroughly stunned and confused.

He pulled his hands away from his face and stared right through his son. "She's really dead. I can't believe it."

"Jeez, Dad," Ted muttered, "you almost seem human."

Before Howard could respond, the doorbell tones sounded, and they all turned to see who'd be admitted. After a moment, Leona Reese appeared in the doorway.

"Oh, hello," Eleanor said. "You're back."

"Finally." Leona strode toward them, moving with grace. She was dressed in a dark blue pantsuit and a white blouse with a stiff collar and possessed a pair of the most piercing bright blue eyes Eleanor had ever seen. Earlier, when talking to Leona, she had felt like the investigator could see right through to every one of her secrets. No wonder she'd spilled them all. Was the woman trustworthy? She seemed to be. In fact, if Eleanor didn't miss her guess, Leona Reese had her own share of secrets.

She reached the table and extended a hand to Ted. "Leona Reese, Department of Human Services. You must be Callie Trimble's son."

Ted rose. "Yes. Ted Trimble," he said as he shook her hand, "and this is my father, Howard Trimble."

Howard sat with his head in his hands. "You're not with the police?"

Leo hedged her statement. "I don't work with the Minneapolis police." She placed a leather valise on the table, and she and Ted lowered themselves into chairs. "Are there other relatives coming?"

"Just my sister," Ted said. "Our family is small. But she won't arrive for a couple of days. She's — "

Howard interrupted. "Why exactly are you here?"

The animosity in his voice didn't seem to register with the investigator. Calmly she said, "I'm here from the State to make sure the facility is safe."

"How safe could it be," Howard half-shouted, "if my wife was murdered last night!"

"Dad."

"Somebody killed Callie. *Killed her.*" He said it as though he couldn't get his head around it, and Eleanor knew exactly how he felt. "Who would do that?"

Eleanor hesitantly reached out, wanting to touch Howard, but she pulled back. He wouldn't take kindly to her comfort, so she said, "The police will figure this out. Let them do their jobs."

As if on cue, the doorbell went off again, and the echo of deep, bass voices came from the foyer.

"Oh, God, I think I recognize those voices," Ted said. "Please tell me it's not those cops again."

Detective Flanagan in his brown suit filled the doorway like a bull moose come in from the wild. "Ladies and gentleman, good afternoon." His tone was falsely cheery.

Howard stood, a banty rooster eager to claim his territory. "Have you determined what happened to my wife?"

"Not yet. I don't believe I've had the pleasure, sir."

"Callie Trimble is my wife. Was, I mean. My ex-wife. I'm Howard Trimble, and I'd like to know right this moment what happened to her."

Eleanor expected Howard to start stomping his feet, maybe throw a small conniption fit. She caught Leona's eye and shrugged.

Flanagan came into the dining area while DeWitt hung back in the doorway. "I'll inform you about that when I have some answers. We're going to inspect the garden now."

They trooped toward the sliding glass door, Howard trailing. Eleanor looked at Ted, then Leona, and they stood and joined the procession. On the cement patio, Flanagan told them to stay put.

A slim Latino man dressed in cut-off jeans and a baggy white t-shirt stood over a pile of weeds he'd raked out from under the maple tree.

Flanagan flashed his badge. "Who're you?"

The man gripped the rake in both hands and leaned on it. "Garden Service."

"Your name?"

"Carlos Guevarra."

"You here yesterday?"

The man shook his head solemnly. "I come on Tuesdays and Thursdays. Not been here since last Thursday."

"You find anything unusual out here?"

"Nope."

"You hear there's been a killing here?"

"Mrs. Hoxley say."

"Know anything about it?"

"No, sir. Not a thing."

"All right. You can go." The man leaned down to scoop up the weeds, and the detective raised a hand. "Leave that."

The gardener let go of the lawn-and-leaf bag as if it were on fire. He hotfooted it through a narrow gate in the wall, wrapped a chain around the metal supports, and snapped the lock shut.

Eleanor thought if she were the gardener, she wouldn't want to stick around either. The two detectives prowled the garden while she focused her attention on the thick stone wall that surrounded two sides of the yard. She wondered if someone could have scaled it. The wall was at least seven feet tall and punctuated here and there at the base with lengths of hedge. On one end, where the wall met the corners of the building, there were no gaps. On the south side, the wall ended three feet from the apartment. A narrow chain-link fence less than three feet wide was securely screwed into the stone wall. The door in it was wide enough for the gardener to squeeze in a wheelbarrow or mower, but it was chained shut and secured with the lock the gardener had just used.

Eleanor caught Leona's eye. "Isn't there supposed to be an accessible exit from here, you know, in case of fire or emergency?"

"I'm not up to speed on those sorts of codes. I imagine it's safer in some ways if there's no unlocked egress, except through the facility, though I imagine any spry person could get over that wall."

Before Eleanor could answer, Flanagan came toward them.

Dragging along like a limping pup, DeWitt trailed behind, bent at the waist to examine where the edge of the wall met the dirt. "Nope," DeWitt said. "I don't see any signs of disturbance."

Leona muttered, "But the gardener just tidied up all the evidence."

Over his shoulder to his partner, Flanagan said, "I doubt if anyone came over the wall."

Leona Reese surprised Eleanor by stepping off the patio onto the grass and saying, "I disagree."

Flanagan's giant head swung her direction, a smirk on his face. "So you think you know better, huh?"

"Check out the grass. We haven't had rain for days. It's pretty dry and wouldn't show many footprints." She took two fast steps off the patio, hopped in the air, and came down hard with her heels. "Look, not much indentation even when I'm trying."

DeWitt blurted out, "This is a crime scene, lady!"

"Then treat it like one," she snapped. "Besides, you've got bad timing. Looks like the gardener cleared out all the beds. Any evidence you might have had is probably lost."

Eleanor watched the big man's face flush pink, turn red, then glow a sickly shade of dark purple. She was glad Leona had brought up the fact before she had to mention it. Flanagan stood, his hands in tight fists as if he wanted to belt someone.

DeWitt waddled over to the edge of the patio and glared. "We think it's an inside job anyway."

This DeWitt fellow was scarier than Ted's father, and Eleanor was amazed to see how Ted shrank back toward the sliding glass door. He gulped down a breath, obviously trying not to let his alarm show. She moved next to him and tucked her arm through his.

"It may be an inside job," Leona said, "but it could also have been an outsider. Was anything taken?"

Flanagan had recovered his bluster. "We'll have that information soon enough."

Eleanor said, "I can't say if anything's missing. The room's been cordoned off, and I've not been in there since last night."

Leona's bright blue eyes met Eleanor's. "I think someone could definitely have come over the wall."

Flanagan moved fast and came to loom over her, his face mocking. "There's not a bit of evidence that anyone entered or exited. Besides, the sun was down, and if someone came out here, they'd have bumbled around in the dark."

"Not really," Eleanor called. "It was well after dusk, but not full dark." She pointed to where the two stretches of wall met at the corner. "The street lamp overhead sheds a surprising amount of light. I've been out here after dark lots of times. If the mosquitoes aren't on the attack, it's quite pleasant."

"Still," Flanagan said, "it's not likely anyone escaped over the wall. There's no evidence of it. They'd practically need a ladder."

A blur of blue shot past Eleanor. Leona reached the wall, brought her knee up and stuck out her lower leg. With a toe dug into the wall, she changed her forward momentum to launch herself upwards. Her shoulders cleared the wall. Before gravity pulled her back down, she got her hands on top and pulled herself up. She twisted in midair, and with a poof of dust landed in a sitting position on top of the wall.

"Whoa," Ted said. "Pretty neat trick."

"And if I can do it," Leona shot back, "then anyone could have." She pointed down at the grass. "Can you see any marks?"

In a fury, Flanagan marched over. "Enough with the shenanigans. Get down."

Leona peered over her shoulder, leaning precariously to see the other side of the wall. "Before the gardener gets to the outside flower beds, you guys ought to check it out. What if there're footprints or evidence over there?"

"You're interfering with a—with a police investigation," DeWitt sputtered.

Leona hopped off the wall with no difficulty and brushed off the seat of her pants.

For the first time since the previous night, Eleanor smiled.

Chapter Six

LEO CHECKED HER appearance in the mirror of the ladies' room and washed her hands. She wanted to kick herself for being a smart aleck to the two cops, but she hadn't been able to stop herself. They were both so arrogant—no, worse. Condescending. Not so much in what they said as in how they said it. As if she were some sort of dingbat with no brains whatsoever.

She was accustomed to a moderate level of male superiority in her work life, but as a sergeant in charge of patrol cops, most of the ribbing was good-natured. She wasn't used to outright disrespect or being dismissed out of hand. Flanagan and DeWitt were detectives, that was true, but she outranked both of them.

Out here in the civilian world, outside her city of jurisdiction, she possessed no rank. The cops had bona fide badges unlocking every door for them, while she was loaned out to an overworked, understaffed department that was apparently not respected.

She suppressed her fury, picked up her valise, and went to the common area. A man she'd learned was named Franklin Callaghan sat on one end of the center couch under a reading lamp that cast a nice glow. A newspaper sat folded on the coffee table in front of him. He held a book and pencil in his hands.

"Sir? Mr. Callaghan?"

He tore his eyes away from the book, which, as she moved closer, she saw was a thick collection of crossword puzzles. He gazed up at her, his eyes shy.

She introduced herself and asked if he would allow her to interview him.

"You could pay me a double nugget, and I still wouldn't have a thing to tell yer, lass." His voice, a charming Scottish brogue, was deep and resonant and reminded her of the voice of Grandpa Wallace, her foster father's dad.

Franklin Callaghan sounded so earnest that she lowered herself to the cushion next to his, set her valise on the other side, and sat back against the comfortable couch. He shifted slightly and half-turned his broad shoulders toward her.

"You spend a lot of time out here in the common area, Mr. Callaghan?"

"Aye. My flat is small, and I enjoy the people coming and going."

"You seem engrossed in your reading and puzzles."

"True."

"But I'll bet you observe things, and maybe you've seen something you don't realize is important."

"P'raps." He tucked the pencil in between pages and closed the puzzle book. A pained expression flitted across his face. She wondered what it meant.

"How long have you lived here at Rivers' Edge, Mr. Callaghan?"

"Three years and more." He paused. "I came in midsummer after me wife passed, that's over three years back."

"Do you know who's lived here the longest?"

"Aye. Walter has been here since the place opened, nigh on five years ago. Agnes came after him, then me. Others have come and gone, but we three are the mainstays."

"I see. What would you think if we just sit here and talk, and I'll run the tape recorder? No muss, no fuss."

"If that pleases you, lass, I'm sure it'll be fine."

"It's been a tiring day, so let's be low-key."

She got out the recorder and set it between them. In a perfect world, she should take him into the dining room or the admin office and sit at a table where she could take notes. She should also read that long set of rights, but the prospect of getting them out meant she might lose his interest or goodwill. Her intuition said he'd be more forthcoming right here, in his comfortable corner of the sofa, without excessive bureaucracy.

She clicked on the recorder and laced her hands together. "You understand what happened here last night, right, Mr. Callaghan?"

"Mrs. Hoxley told us Callie Trimble died. At the noon meal she updated us to say Callie was murdered. Callie was a wee bit daft, but she was right pleasant to me. I'm sorry she's dead."

"Who do you think killed her?"

His eyes widened. "Why, as I said, I haven't got a thing to tell yer. I hadn't noticed her at all after dinner last night or at the sing-along. We were near the end when the alarm sounded and Miss Sherry and Miss Habibah tore off like startled hares. I spent the rest of the eve reading here and watching people scrabble for hours."

"Who was at the sing-along?"

He sat for a moment, thinking. "Miss Sherry, Miss Habibah, Agnes, Jade Perkins, and Willie Stepanek. Oh, and Nettie Volk. I almost forgot her. She's a sweet old hen, but she can't carry a tune, so she hums along."

"From the moment the sing-along started until you heard the alarm, did anyone leave the dining room?"

He sat still for a moment. "Now that I ponder a little, yes. Habibah left for a while."

"Do you know where she went?"

"I assume to the ladies' room."

"Was she gone long?"

"I don't recall. I believe that was when I talked them into playing an old Scot song, 'The Bonnie Banks O' Loch Lomond,' and I was intent on it."

"You don't recall her coming back while you were singing that?"

"No, she did not."

"Was it a short song, a lengthy one?"

"Why, lass, you don't know that old chestnut?"

"I vaguely recall it."

He cleared his throat and sang in a smooth bass voice:

O ye'll tak' the high road and I'll tak' the low road
And I'll be in Scotland afore ye
But me and my true love will never meet again
On the bonnie, bonnie banks o' Loch Lomond.

He finished and looked her in the eye. "That's the chorus. The song is three verses and as many or more choruses. I always like singing that part as many times as they'll let me. Miss Sherry does a fine job harmonizing. Her voice is lovely, and the song brings back so many memories. Reminds me of my boyhood. I grew up in Argyll, close to the shores of Loch Lomond."

"And you came here to the U.S. when?"

"As a lad of sixteen. My father was an American Army man who fell in love with a wee nursing aide, fresh off the farm in Argyll. After the Battle of Somme when so many tens of thousands died — this is the Great War I'm speaking of here — Mother was sent to nurse in London. There she met my father. Do you know much about the Great War?"

"Some, sir."

"It's nigh on ninety years now since my parents met and married. My sister was born in 1917, and I, ten months later. My father was killed in January 1918. We didnae emigrate to America until the 1930s."

He suddenly shook himself. "I must apologize. I may have took meself a little off the beaten track, lass."

"We were talking about the sing-along."

"Ah, yes. I'm not able to say how long Habibah was gone. Could have been six or eight minutes, p'raps ten. I don't recall her moving about, but I do know she was with all of us when Eleanor pulled the alarm."

"That's helpful, Mr. Callaghan. What can you tell me about

the staff?"

"They're very nice, most all of them."

"Almost all?"

"Hazel can be a wee bit crotchety at times, and Missy McCarver is a genuine terror if anything unusual turns up in her housekeeping rounds. But Miss Sherry and Miss Ernesta are especially kind to me. Oh, and Habibah's sister, Shani, she can't sing, but she surely can cut a rug."

"Dance, you mean?"

"Yes. That gal's got rhythm to burn."

"You've never had any difficulties with any of the staff—not the cooks or the aides or Mrs. Hoxley?"

"Oh, no. All in all, the staff here are delightful. They help make the days pass."

"Do the staff all get along with one another?"

"Well, to be honest, sometimes no. Missy and Hazel have been known to go a few rounds, but short of fisticuffs, mind you."

"What have they fought about?"

"I don't think they care two bits for one another, that's all. Sometimes it happens that way. Hazel is particular about Walter's things—that's Mr. Green, I mean. Missy doesn't always meet Hazel's timelines or instructions, and they've had more than one sprattle. Missy finally gave her a piece of her mind. For a minute I thought there'd be broken glass and flying flinders, but they stomped off in different directions, and that was that."

"When did this happen?"

He stroked his chin. "Oh...I'd say last Thanksgiving. Peaceful ever after. Now they don't speak to one another at all."

"Have you seen anything else recently that appeared odd or suspicious?"

"Can't say that I have, lass. I'm sorry. Nothing seems out of place."

Leo scooted forward and angled to face the old man. He had to be ninety years old, yet his face showed few lines, and his eyes were clear. His white hair was thinning, but for the most part, he looked like a man in his late sixties. She thought he must have gotten some excellent genes from his parents.

"Since you're here quite a bit, Mr. Callaghan, will you keep an eye on things, and if you see or hear anything strange, will you let me know?"

"Aye, that I will. The coppers asked the same."

"Here's my business card—let me write my cell phone number on the back just in case."

He accepted the card and tucked it into his shirt pocket. She thanked him, clicked off the tape recorder, and rose. He leaned forward and dragged himself up off the couch, unfolding himself as though the movement were painful. She was surprised to find that he was much taller than she, but it obviously hurt to stand up straight.

He took a deep breath and rolled his broad shoulders. "Arthritis. Got it in me neck and low back. Well, lass, I'll keep an eye on the place for you." He held out a hand, and she shook, feeling the strength in the clasp.

"Thanks for your help, Mr. Callaghan."

"My pleasure." Reaching behind him, he made a slow, laborious descent to the couch. She felt honored by his old-fashioned grace, but dismayed at his pain. As she walked away, she had to admit that he was the first real gentleman she'd encountered all day.

In the front office, Rowena Hoxley stood at the mailbox slots putting envelopes and magazines into the tenants' boxes.

"Oh, hullo," she said. Her voice was flat, her face puffy. She'd acquired even darker bags under her eyes since Leo had seen her earlier. "Are you shutting us down, or what?"

Leo was taken aback. So far she hadn't seen anything that required any drastic measures, but she couldn't make any promises. At this point, she wasn't sure what the proper procedures were. "So long as you and your staff keep a close eye on everything, I'll continue this investigation, and the facility will keep operating."

Hoxley crammed the last of the mail into a slot and stepped back until she came in contact with the desk. She slumped down against it. "That's good. I don't know where these elderly people would go. It'd be a shame to put them out of their apartments."

"It's important that you step up security here, ma'am, especially after nightfall."

"Don't worry about that. I've already informed Silvia, Sherry, and Habibah that they'll be working overtime, and I've got Hazel on standby. Claire Ryerson from the main office will be coming over as well. We'll be sure that at least one aide is awake throughout the night to make regular rounds. We've got that covered. I'll make double-damn sure nothing happens to anyone else."

"Before I go, could you give me contact information for all staff and for the owner?"

Hoxley hefted herself away from the desk and dragged around to the other side. She opened a drawer and fished around. "I'd appreciate it if this information stayed confidential. I typed this up for the police, and you can have a copy, but my people's privacy should be respected." She handed over a couple sheets of paper.

"Please shred it when you're through."

"Thank you, Mrs. Hoxley."

Leo checked her watch and was surprised to see that it was after four p.m. Rush hour would be revving up, and the longer she waited, the more time-consuming her trip from Minneapolis to Saint Paul would be. She stuffed the papers in her valise and bid farewell to Rowena Hoxley.

Back at the office, Leo found that Fred Baldur was signed out for the day. She assumed he worked until 4:30, so she wouldn't be able to talk to him until the morning. No great loss. She had a hunch he wouldn't be much help anyway.

She slipped into her assigned cubicle—actually, Bradley Rayburn's cubicle. He'd tacked pictures of his family on the cubicle's cloth walls, which she left alone. She picked up a professional portrait of his wife in a stand-up frame on the corner of the desk and put it in the top desk drawer along with a homemade clay paperclip holder, coffee cup, dog-eared paperback mystery, and an opened pack of Wintergreen mints, leaving only a computer and keyboard, phone, inbox, blotter, a jar full of pens and pencils, a stapler, and a tape dispenser. Even starting from scratch in her work area, she didn't figure she'd ever feel comfortable in this sterile environment. She preferred the camaraderie of her cop shop. Who would she talk shop with here? Fred Baldur? The thought gave her the willies. If she wasn't so irritated, she thought she'd shudder.

Leo sat at the desk and relaxed for the first time in hours. All around, people were packing up for the day, saying goodbyes. She got out the agency Standard Ops Procedure manual and skimmed through various sections. After half an hour, with eyes glazed over, she hadn't learned anything helpful. For an SOP manual, it was heavy on instructions for forms completion and remarkably light on actual investigative procedures.

What the hell kind of situation had she gotten herself into? She'd like to take a club to the range master and her commander as well. The whole situation was maddening, and she had half a mind to appeal to the chief. At the very least, she should be riding a desk and doing administrative work at the downtown police department, not sitting here trying to make sense of a bunch of moronic bureaucratic legalese. How could she stand three months of this?

She'd already pissed off the cops on the case; Hoxley at Rivers' Edge was less than helpful; and she felt she'd made little headway in figuring out anything about the murder. How deep was she supposed to delve? Flanagan had made it clear that he and DeWitt completely controlled the murder investigation, but that didn't help her much. How could she tell if Rivers' Edge was safe for anyone without uncovering the murderer? For all she knew, the killer could be wandering the halls at Rivers' Edge this very minute. What if he killed again tonight or tomorrow?

In her experience, most assaults and murders in people's homes were committed by known elements—a family member, friend, or a neighbor. But who would kill an old lady like Callie Trimble? Did one of the staff or tenants have it in for the old woman? If it was an inside job, Leo definitely needed more background on the victim and everyone who'd been at Rivers' Edge the night before. But was it possible that someone came in over the wall? A random killing by a stranger?

Highly unlikely. For her entire career, she couldn't recall a single random in-home homicide that wasn't robbery-related. Someone killed Callie Trimble for a reason.

Callie's family might have positive or negative reasons. On the positive side, there was mercy killing. Was Callie that far gone mentally that someone in the family couldn't bear to see her suffer and decided to put her out of her misery?

On the negative side, the usual motives needed review: uncontrolled anger, revenge, money issues, an accident covered up.

None of that rang true. She had a hard time believing that Eleanor had anything to do with it. What about Ted? Sons had been known to kill their mothers for any number of reasons. That avenue bore examination.

Whoever the killer was, he had to possess a fair amount of strength. Eleanor said Callie was a good-sized gal, so it was unlikely that a dainty, tiny person could have done it. But anyone with enough coordination, power, and persistence could have.

If not a family member, then who and why? Could a fellow resident or aide have gotten so angry that suffocating an elderly woman was the result? Or could there be a cover-up? Did Callie see something she shouldn't have? She remembered a case in Saint Paul a few years earlier where an orderly at a hospital had been sexually molesting unconscious patients. He tried to strangle a nurse who caught him at it. Luckily, she'd been a lot more conscious than his poor victims and had fought him off.

So many loose ends. Leo never liked loose ends. One of the reasons she preferred working patrol was that when she and her officers came upon a scene, they secured it, dealt with the people involved, gathered evidence to assist detectives and prosecutors, and moved on. She enjoyed hearing how the prosecutions turned out, especially if they were successful, but her role didn't require her to dig through seven zillion leads. Others were responsible for making sense of the evidence and fashioning a case, not the patrol officers.

She'd always pictured herself working in that chain of command like her foster father, Dad Wallace, had. As a Saint Paul cop for nearly four decades, he'd been so proud when she made sergeant, and now her goal was to remain a supervising sergeant for a long time. All those young cops coming up through field training deserved to be taught the very best skills. She loved being able to instill good habits and practices. Perhaps she'd get into investigations later and achieve commander status when she was older. Much older. Crap, she thought. How derailed will I be with this shooting quals problem hanging over my head?

She couldn't do anything about that now, much as she wanted to. All she could focus on were the loose ends from the homicide. First thing in the morning, she needed to interview Martin Rivers, the owner of the apartments. Maybe he would give her something useful. She pulled out the information Rowena Hoxley had provided and reached for the telephone.

Chapter Seven

WEDNESDAY MORNING LEO left her house in plenty of time, fought the rush-hour traffic into Saint Paul, and made it to the DHS building a few minutes before eight only to find that Fred Baldur had called in sick. His stock with her plummeted farther. She tried to check in with Ralph Sorenson but was told the director had gone to the state capitol for a meeting. So much for accountability. She was on her own today.

She drove to Rivers' headquarters in Plymouth and hurried into a square, one-story brick building across the street from another independent living apartment called Rivers' Rock, which looked exactly like Rivers' Edge except for the sign on the front.

Inside the headquarters, the waiting area to the left was furnished with dark brown leather couches and chairs and surrounded with honey-colored wood paneling. A pair of framed pictures hung on the wall. In one, a flight of ducks flapped above a rushing river. In the other, a deer loped along the edge of a forest. Definitely a man's office, Leo thought, and a sportsman. The navy-blue carpet showed the undisturbed marks of a recent vacuuming, and she marched across it, leaving footprints in the nap. It was so quiet, she wondered whether anyone was in.

Behind the enclosed reception counter, the office was like a freestanding little building with an open door in the back. Leo thought of it as the business version of a shotgun shack. On either side, hallways led to the back of the building, but she couldn't see very far down either hall.

She moved to the reception counter, set down her valise, and put her elbows on the dark-blue laminated surface. She didn't see a bell to summon anyone, so she called out, "Hello, anybody here?"

A chair scraped back, and a shapely woman appeared in the doorway. Either the administrative office had a rear entrance, or the vacuuming had been done after this lady arrived. Her every step left a footprint behind her.

"May I help you?" The woman smiled, showing even, white teeth and twinkling gray-green eyes. In her mid-thirties, she was fit and attractive, and Leo admired her deep tan. She wore a green-and-white-striped dress with a gold belt accentuating her slim waist. The rings on her fingers flashed gold and diamond.

"I have an appointment to see Mr. Rivers."

"Leona Reese?"

"That's me."

"I'm Claire Ryerson, one of Mr. Rivers' personal assistants."

"He has more than one assistant?"

"Yes. There are two of us, but Iris — Iris Fullerton — has been on vacation the last two weeks. She'll be back next week, and I can take my end-of-summer holiday."

"I'm a bit early. Shall I wait?"

"Mr. Rivers is in, so it's no problem at all that you've arrived now. In fact, it will be easier for him to stay on schedule since he's got a full calendar today. Let me see if he's ready." She disappeared back into her office.

Leo gazed up at a four-by-six-foot display on the wall ahead of her. An onyx frame was speckled with silver flakes, and the raised black lettering on a shiny gold background looked classy.

Rivers' Independent Living Apartments, Inc.

Zestful Living and Independence
With Exceptional Focus on Your Comfort

Plymouth – Rivers' Rock
Coon Rapids – Rivers' Rapids
Minnetonka – Rivers' Hope
Vadnais Heights – Rivers' Heights
Minneapolis – Rivers' Edge
Bloomington – Rivers' Bloom
Burnsville – Rivers' Park
Woodbury – Rivers' Arbor

She recalled that someone — Detective Flanagan, she thought — had mentioned the existence of eight homes, and here were all their names. How could anyone keep them straight, though? She went through them again and noticed some associations. Plymouth Rock. Woodbury Arbor. And parts of city names such as Coon Rapids and Bloomington and Vadnais Heights, but still — how confusing.

Every city with a Rivers facility was substantial in size. The population of Minneapolis was nearing 400,000, and all of the other jurisdictions, though smaller, ranged from 52,000 to well over 80,000. Except Vadnais Heights, but that was a municipality so enmeshed in the Saint Paul area that it might as well be one big Saint Paul neighborhood. Each of the apartment complexes was in a different police jurisdiction, though, so Flanagan and DeWitt would have a difficult time gathering and compiling information from multiple cop shops. Was that planned by Martin Rivers? Or merely a coincidence?

Claire Ryerson came down the hallway on the right. "Mr. Rivers is available now, Ms. Reese. If you'll follow me."

Leo looked down at her long-sleeved silk blouse, tan pants, and flats, then at Claire Ryerson's ensemble. The woman's gold open-toed shoes matched her belt perfectly. Everything about her appearance screamed class with a capital C — and spendy with a capital S.

One benefit of being a police officer was that Leo never had to worry about the juvenile clothes competitions so many professional women engaged in with such vengeance. Police uniforms were one and the same. Not particularly attractive, but Leo never had to worry about matching her duty boots with her belt. Actually, now that she visualized her sexy police outfit, both her belt and shoes were black leather, so maybe she was doing better than she thought.

Claire Ryerson stopped outside a door. "Here you go. Would you like me to bring you a coffee?"

Leo almost said no, but after hesitating, changed her mind. "Sure. That would be nice."

She stepped into an office the size of a family rec room. A dead ringer for Hoss Cartwright in a navy three-piece suit came around the massive desk. His brow was wide, eyes blue, and hairline receding. He enveloped her hand in his giant paw, and she had to crane her head to meet his eyes, so she put him at six-three, maybe six-four. He looked so much like the actor who'd played Hoss on *Bonanza,* that she imagined he probably wore a six-shooter under his suit coat.

"Thanks so much for coming, Ms. Reese. Terrible thing to have happen at Rivers' Edge. Just terrible. Let's sit over here."

He indicated an arrangement of three leather settees in a U-shape. A square oak table squatted in the middle. On a doily, an ugly vase containing a dried grass arrangement graced the center of the table. Leo wondered why anyone would dig up prairie grass and drag it into a professional office. She expected a gopher to pop out any minute.

No sooner was she seated than Claire Ryerson showed up with a full coffee service on a bronze mirrored tray complete with two delicate china cups and saucers, a gold caddy containing sugar and cream dispensers, and two golden spoons. Leo noted that it all matched the assistant's outfit. She wondered if she could get a similar set with black leather trim for her own use. Wouldn't that match her duty belt and holster nicely?

Claire poured. "Please help yourself to cream and sugar, Ms. Reese."

"Thanks. Black will be fine."

"Anything else, Mr. Rivers?" Claire asked.

He sent her away and turned his attention to Leo. "Is there any news about Mrs. Trimble's death?"

"No, I've heard nothing new." Leo scooted forward to the edge of the seat, picked up her coffee cup and saucer, and took her first sip. The coffee was rich and strong, just the way she liked it. "If you don't mind, I need to tape record this interview, Mr. Rivers. I'm required to write a substantial report, and the facts must be correct."

"Oh, I'd rather you not."

She set down the coffee. "I'm sorry, sir, but in this situation, I've got to roll the tape. It's not an option."

He winced, and his face went through strange contortions. For a moment, she wondered if he had control of it. "I was hoping I wouldn't have to call my attorney."

"You're welcome to do so, but it'll only delay this interview." Jesus, she thought, he was acting like she'd arrested him.

He rubbed his hands together in a fussy manner. Big men usually didn't wring their hands like housewives. Grimacing again, he said, "Do you think I need an attorney?"

She slipped into cop mode. "I can't give you legal advice. You need to decide about representation yourself, but you're not under arrest. If you haven't done anything illegal, I'll take your statement as quickly as possible so I can move on to the next interview." She paused, and when he didn't answer, she went on. "I should mention that if you fail to cooperate, DHS rules require that I suspend your license to operate Rivers' Edge. I'll have to launch an investigation into all eight of your homes and —"

"Oh, no! That won't be necessary. Of course I want to cooperate. Of course."

With deft fingers Leo pulled out the tape recorder and turned it on. After the initial comments and warnings, she asked, "How long have you been operating Rivers' Edge?"

"I built it. Built all the facilities from the ground up. I opened Rivers' Rock, across the street, eight years ago, and I've opened a new complex every calendar year since. We broke ground for Rivers' Waterfall down in Lakeville last week. With all this murder mess, it might not open 'til next year. Might be bad press, so I'll probably delay and not keep to my goal of opening one every year." He picked up his coffee in one giant hand. In his grip, the cup looked like it belonged to a doll's tea set.

"And Rivers' Edge opened when?"

"Sorry. Five years ago."

"How do you keep all the names straight?"

"Easy. Each one is like a child to me. I've used the same floor plans for each, but they all have special little details. If you spent as much time in each of them as I have, it'd make perfect sense to you."

"Okay. Tell me about Rivers' Edge."

"Number four. Has the walled garden, which the others don't have. The one across the street here, Rivers' Rock, has a nice-sized fenced yard, but nothing more substantial. Now I'm able to afford bigger lots, so the newest Edge building down in Lakeville will be even more elaborate—a pond, an elaborate walking path, more windows with a view of something besides the street."

He went on for some time about architecture and landscaping before Leo stopped him. "Have you ever had a murder in any of the homes?"

"Of course not. No."

"Have you got any knowledge or information about this murder?"

"How could I? I haven't been over to Minneapolis in weeks. Rowena—you met Rowena Hoxley, right?" Leo nodded. "She's my most competent manager. I never have trouble with the Edge. Never."

"So nobody's died in your apartments?"

"Of course some of the elderly have—have passed. I've got mostly elderly to deal with, and so yes, some have, you know, passed on while living in my apartments."

She was surprised at how difficult it was for him to use the word "died." He took a gulp of coffee and set the cup down on the table, his hand shaking slightly.

"In the eight years your complexes have been open, Mr. Rivers, how many deaths have you recorded?"

"I couldn't possibly know that offhand. I'm the big-picture man. I merely get summary reports. My managers handle the day-to-day events including departure transfers."

"What do those procedures consist of?"

Leo had never heard the term "departure transfer." While Rivers droned on about procedures, she envisioned tiny, emaciated old ladies and dried-up elderly men, all in their best suits and dresses, standing in a row near the doorstep of a Rivers' complex, all holding tickets to the great unknown. What kind of conductor would come by to collect their transfer and help them depart? Apparently not Martin Rivers.

She took a deep breath and forced herself to focus on his blather. He rose and stepped over to a bookcase next to the office door.

"...provide you with every single blueprint—whatever you need."

"Oh, no, that won't be necessary at this time, sir."

He stopped abruptly. "Are you sure? The police reviewed them."

"They have different goals than I do. They're searching for a killer. I'm trying to figure out if Rivers' Edge is safe for your tenants and if anyone is liable for what has happened."

"Of course it's safe. This person's untimely, uh" — he rolled his shoulders and fingered his Pancaldi tie — "passing is a fluke. A terrible event, that's for sure, but it's a stroke of bad luck. No one in my organization is at fault."

Leo bit her lip and reminded herself not to speak. The death of a sixty-nine-year-old woman was simply bad luck for Martin Rivers; for Callie Trimble's family, her murder was a horrific event likely to haunt their memories for years, if not forever. Could this man really be so uncaring?

"What do you plan to do to ensure this never happens again?"

Rivers came around the back of his settee and peered down upon her with a puzzled expression on his face. "I don't follow your meaning."

"Are you concerned about the safety in your apartments?"

"Why, no. I provide a wonderful living situation. This is a total aberration I'm sure will never happen again."

"I'll need information on the background checks for every employee."

He strode to his desk, got a legal pad, and returned to the settee. With a flourish, he whipped a pen from the breast pocket of his suit and said, "Background checks, Rivers' Edge."

"No, sir. I want information for every worker in your employ."

"What? But the police only asked for—"

"The police have an entirely different objective. I need to verify that your staffing has no irregularities. I'll also need records for employees going back two years."

"That's excessive. It'll take my assistants a great deal of time to assemble this material, and all for nothing. Our hiring practices are sterling."

"Surely you've had to provide such data in the past whenever your license was up for review."

His face flushed bright red all the way up to where his hair was receding. "Fred Baldur personally vouched for me."

"You know Mr. Baldur."

"Yes, he was a few years ahead of me in college."

"I see. So you've never provided records to DHS."

"Of course I have. Just not — not to that extent."

"Now you can compile all the data, and you'll be ready for a future audit. Mr. Baldur won't be at DHS forever. Sooner or later you'll have to get the information together, so it may as well be now. I'll also want copies of rental applications and all file data on tenants. That includes complaints from and about all tenants living at Rivers' Edge for the past three years, no matter how short a time they lived there."

"But I don't know those details."

"Your managers will. Please contact them, and assemble the information."

"I'm a busy man, Ms. Reese. This will take considerable time."

"I'm happy to close Rivers' Edge during the interim so you can find the time."

"You don't understand. We broke ground on the new complex." He glanced at his watch. "I need to be in Lakeville in forty minutes to meet with the contractor."

"If you want your license for all eight complexes suspended for failure to provide requested data, that's your choice."

"But it'll take days to pull all that together."

Leo pressed her lips together and ignored the urge to tell him that Hoss Cartwright never whined. "Actually, I wasn't done with my requests. I'll also need records of every single death that's occurred in any of your facilities since Day One. Any death in an apartment, the halls, the grounds, anywhere on your property."

"The police didn't want all that."

"You're not hearing me, Mr. Rivers. You've had a murder in your facility. I don't mean to be unfeeling regarding your business needs, but the State has a keen interest in making sure there are no repeat murders. You're going to have to drop everything and cooperate."

He sat as if she'd poked him with a pin and all the air had gone out of him. With his shoulders slumped and knees splayed out, he reminded her of a muscular version of the Michelin Baby.

With a sigh, he put the legal pad on his knee and scribbled notes. "What's your deadline?"

"By the end of the day tomorrow would work well."

LEO LEFT THE Rivers' administration building with a sinus headache. The air outside carried the faint scent of garlic from an Asian restaurant up the street. Ordinarily the aroma might be pleasant, but today it made her head pound.

She drove off feeling irritated and hating the new assignment. Only a day and a half had passed, and already she missed the comfortable roles she played as a patrol sergeant. Even when she patrolled alone—which was most of the time—with the flick of her shoulder mic, she always knew she had backup. The officials in charge of this new assignment had basically abandoned her. She was stuck out in the field, no peers to rely upon, no supervisor providing support and instruction. What a rinky-dink setup.

She'd intended to return to the murder scene, but instead she did a U-turn and headed back toward Saint Paul.

The DHS office hummed with activity. She went to her assigned cube and left her valise on the desk.

Outside Ralph Sorenson's office, his secretary was talking into a headset. Leo had met Monique Miller the day before and been impressed by her friendliness. She was a big-boned woman in her fifties with bottle-dyed hair of a peculiar maroon color. Given time, the color would fade and appear more natural, but at the moment, it reminded Leo of a puffy burgundy handbag.

Monique raised a manicured finger and pointed to two chairs by a window. Rather than sit, Leo gazed out the window at the city. From the fourth floor, much of her view of the skyscrapers in the center of Saint Paul was blocked by a parking ramp and other office structures, but off to the left, the wide Mississippi River sparkled in the morning sun. She imagined herself and Daria in a speedboat, wind in their faces, spray in their hair...until Monique bid goodbye to her caller and said, "Ms. Reese, may I help you?"

She turned. "You can just call me Leona."

Monique smiled. "First name basis is great with me, too."

"May I make an appointment with Mr. Sorenson for sometime today?"

"No can do. He's out indefinitely. I can't predict when he'll be back. I can get you in tomorrow morning."

"I guess that'll do."

Monique gestured for her to come closer. "Come sit here," she said, pointing to a chair to the right of her wide desk.

When Leo was seated, Monique leaned over and spoke in a stage whisper. "I oughtn't be saying anything, but, well, you probably need to know a few things if you're going to be here awhile."

"Oh?"

"Ralph was so happy to get someone with experience for License Investigations. Even if you're here temporarily, it'll help so much, what with the problems he has with Fred."

Leo liked to think she wasn't much for gossip, but to be honest, every cop she knew survived by finding out the dirt on everyone else, both in the department and out on the street. "What exactly is the problem with Mr. Baldur?"

"Gambling."

"Is he off gambling now? On a Wednesday morning when he's supposed to be at work?"

"Oh, no. He's way too smart to get caught during office hours." Her face took on a delighted expression, and she scooted her chair closer. "He goes off to one of the area casinos and stays out all hours of the night. Imagine his surprise when he can't wake up in the morning. Sometimes he shows up in the afternoon, saying he's over his stomach flu or whatever."

"How often does this happen?"

"At least once a week. He was doing a better job of covering it up when Brad and the gals were here, but with us being short-staffed, he's in for it. I pulled the paperwork today for a PIP—a performance improvement plan for Fred, that is. I hope Ralph will take the hint. He's never been much for PIPs, but nobody needs it more than Fred. Now that you're here until the end of the year, maybe we can get rid of Fred once and for all."

"He's that bad?"

"No, he's just not that good. Not reliable at all."

"What if my term here ends before he's sent packing?"

"An investigator from the Duluth office came down to help out. He just got here this morning."

She wrote something on a pad of paper, ripped off the page, and handed it to Leo. *Thom Thoreson* and a phone number were written there.

"Forget Fred. That's Thom's mobile phone, in case you need it after you go out in the field today. Gracie's leave is over in about six weeks, and Barbara's sometime after. We'll have to make do until then."

Leo relaxed in the chair and resolved to stay in Monique's good graces. She'd learned ages ago that the secretaries and duty sergeants and clerks of the world wielded far more power than most people gave them credit for. "Look, this has turned out to be a murder case I'm working on right now."

"What? I hadn't heard that." Her blue eyes opened wide, and she leaned in even closer. When Leo didn't speak right away, Monique said, "You can tell me everything. I'm Ralph's confidential secretary, and I've got access to documents and information you aren't privy to, so you're not abridging confidentiality or anything like that. Maybe I can help you."

In a few brief sentences, Leo outlined the facts. "My understanding is that DHS has a multitude of cases requiring investigation, but without Mr. Baldur, I don't have a clue where to get that information or how I should prioritize tasks."

"Oh, honey, that's easy enough." She rose. "Come with me. You need to meet Thom Thoreson. I hope he's still in."

Leo followed the heavyset woman through the maze of cubicles. In a loose, yellow linen dress, Monique teetered along in a pair of ropy espadrille platform shoes. Leo had never been fond of any type of tall, block heel. Monique looked like she'd break an ankle with any quick movement. Leo knew her own fashion sense could easily be ridiculed by other women, but if you couldn't run in a shoe — on or off-duty — Leo usually wouldn't wear it. She only made exceptions and wore low heels to weddings and Daria's work parties and even then, the heels were minimal and she could maneuver in them.

Monique led Leo to a cubicle that was papered high and low with posters and magazine pictures from the Harry Potter movies. A man in a wheelchair sat typing at the computer. When he heard them, he spun the chair effortlessly. She guessed his age to be somewhere in the late twenties. His broad shoulders filled out a white polo shirt, and he wore gray linen slacks and shiny black oxfords with red socks. His nearly black hair was trimmed short. Tanned, freshly shaved, and smelling of expensive cologne, he sat grinning, his teeth straight and white. She was struck by how handsome he was and immediately wondered what had happened to put him in the wheelchair. She wasn't about to ask, though.

"Monique, what brings you to Potterville?" He glanced at Leo with interest.

"Did Ralph or Fred mention Leona Reese — "

"No, they didn't. And where is Fred, the shirker, today?" He raised both hands and made quote marks in the air. "Out sick?"

"Um hmmm. Ms. Reese — "

"Please," Leo said, "call me Leona."

"Leona, this is Thom Thoreson. He does investigations and is very good at intake and data analysis. Thom, Leona is our new investigator."

"Temporarily," Leo said.

He held out a hand and shook with her. "So you're the new gal stuck with Old Balderdash."

Monique said, "Thom's the one who runs the Investigation Unit up in Duluth. He does the intake and forwards the cases. He provides all the stats to the team and to management." Monique touched Leo on the shoulder. "I have to return to my post guarding the front office from wanderers and thieves, but I guarantee Thom will take care of you."

Leo thanked her and turned back to Thom.

"Yes," he said, "I guess you could say that I'm Fred's counterpart. Except I go out in the field as much as I can. So tell me, Leona, what did you do to deserve this cherry assignment?"

"Long story," she said. "I could ask you the same thing. I heard you got pulled from Duluth. How long will you be in town?"

"Long as it takes."

"I don't seem to have any cases," Leo said, "except the one Mr. Baldur assigned to me Tuesday. Have you got a few minutes to hear about it?" She sketched out the details of the case, falling into cop-speak at times, but that didn't slow Thom down. He asked a series of questions, and quickly understood the whole scope of the case.

"Everyone's been cooperative?" he asked.

"So far. I've barely started interviewing the residents and staff. Mr. Baldur hasn't given me much information about how to handle the cases."

"Did he acquaint you with that new invention the department acquired well over a decade ago, the computer?"

"There's one in the office, but I don't have any passwords."

"Figures. Okay, let's get you set up." He looked something up on his computer and paused a moment to write on a Post-it note. "Show me the way to your sumptuous digs." She led him to her cubicle where he gave her instructions on how to log in to the computer.

"Here's your password."

Leo tacked the Post-it to the side of the screen. When she opened up the department's internal intake program, she was shocked to see over two hundred blinking entries that Thom informed her needed action.

"Here's how it all works," he said. "I take phone call complaints, receive police reports in the mail, and also get occasional e-mail complaints from the DHS web site. I evaluate each piece of information based upon departmental guidelines and create an intake form for each complaint if it passes muster. We've got northern and southern offices who do the same, but we're often shifting reports and cases back and forth."

"How many come in each day?"

"Oh, maybe sixty."

"Wow, that's quite a lot."

"We classify each one by priority. See there." He pointed at a numerical column next to all the blinking entries. "One's are, of course, Priority One. Two, Three, and Four fall in decreasingly important categories. Click on the box at the top that reads Summary. Okay, see right there? You've got 6 Priority One, 33 Priority Two, 84 Priority Three, and 104 Priority Four for a total of 227."

Leo restrained herself from groaning. Was this the "paperwork" Fred Baldur had referred to yesterday? "How do I know what to do here?"

"Click to the previous page and select any random item." A new screen opened showing boxes neatly filled in with data. "This

Priority Two item, for instance, is based upon a report from an administrator at a halfway house. See the details at the bottom? They've suspended an employee for physical abuse of a client. The admin people are telling us witnesses support the allegations. Since the clients are out of harm's way, it's not a Priority One, but it's still a Priority Two because there's a police report."

"When the cops get called, even if it's minor, it pops it up higher in the queue?"

"It depends. In a case like this, usually when the provider makes the report and the police get involved, you can handle it over the phone. On the other hand, if the report came in from a program participant, and the people at the halfway house weren't being cooperative, then you'd go out and do the whole official investigation."

"How the heck can anyone keep up?"

"We don't. We've got a backlog so deep, we'll never catch up. Even when we're at full staff, we don't have enough manpower to get by. Every two years the legislature further limits or cuts funding while they add more types of transgressions we're supposed to investigate. It's a losing battle. We're constantly out of compliance."

"Sounds like what happens to us cops on the street."

"I can only imagine."

"You'll have to forgive me, Thom, but my head's spinning. I've spent yesterday and today focusing on one single case, and now I find out I have 227."

"If the old Gamble-holic were here, he'd be knocking down some of this. A lot of it requires a simple phone call or two in order to complete the finalized report. Priority One and Two are the real pills. Most of them are big headaches."

Speaking of headaches, Leo's had grown worse. All she wanted to do was get up and walk out. She definitely never signed up for this mess. Writing her police reports was as far as she wanted to go with paperwork. "How do I begin to handle all this?"

"You don't. Let Fred do it. You both have access to this same database, so you can print out the ones that need a personal appearance. He should be here doing that right now. Some of these are a week old, but I don't recall any of them being huge crises, not like the one you got yesterday."

"So I should work through these twenty-six Priority Ones and make decisions?"

"No, I don't think so. You ought to finish with the murder case first. Maybe you can clear that up today?"

Leo let out a guffaw. "I wish. Unless the police get a break in the case, I don't think that one can be cleared up easily."

"At some point, you have to make a decision as to whether someone should be cited. Do you think the facility should be closed?"

"I don't know. I've got no experience with this."

"Does it seem like the staff had anything to do with the death?"

"Can't be sure yet. I've only talked with a few of them."

"First rule, as far as these cases go, is to talk to the provider and their staff as quickly as possible. If you have access to the complainant, try to see him or her first, but you want to get a quick feel for the licensee and everyone officially involved as well."

"Nobody mentioned that, so I've spent time with others, rather than with the staff so far."

Thom tugged at the collar of his polo shirt. "Tough call, then."

"I'll hit the place after lunch and interview all of them. In the meantime, what happens if an emergency is reported? An attack or another murder or something like that?"

"It's often hard to get through on the office line. Tell you what, give me your cell number, and if any critical cases come in the door, I'll call you."

"Great," Leo said. "It's a relief to have you as a contact in the office. Monique already gave me your phone number in case I had questions today. I was trying to meet with Mr. Sorenson to get more direction, but now I'll tell her I don't need to."

"He's not going to be much help. Ralph's role is political— ornamental, really. He's about as useful as a Buddha in front of a Chinese restaurant, except in his case, you can't even rub his stomach for good luck." With a braying laugh, Thom wheeled backwards out the door and was gone.

Leo stared at the blinking cases on the computer screen and wondered once again what the hell she'd done to deserve this situation.

For the next half hour, she reviewed Priority One and Two cases until, bleary-eyed and hungry, she decided it was time for an early lunch. She stuffed the printouts in her valise and left in search of a peaceful restaurant, preferably one without a Buddha.

Chapter Eight

ELEANOR SINCLAIR STUCK her key in the tiny mailbox slot and opened the door. Nothing. She re-locked it and frowned at the vacant reception desk behind her. A foot-tall stack of letters, magazines, circulars, and catalogs had overflowed the wooden inbox and cascaded across part of the counter.

She was sorting the items into neat piles by apartment number when Rowena Hoxley came through the front door.

"Eleanor," she said breathlessly. "Hello. How are you today? Oh, goodness, the mail. I'm sorry I didn't get to it sooner."

"It's been crazy."

"Yes, it sure has." Rowena went into her cubbyhole, dropped her purse on the desk, and returned. She seemed less scattered than she had the day before. Her blonde curls were tamed in place, and her face was no longer gray and haggard. She still had bags under her eyes, but for the time Eleanor had known her, that seemed typical.

"Don't bother with that," Rowena said.

"I've got it all separated out to put in the mailboxes now."

"Thank you. You didn't have to do the sorting, but I certainly appreciate it."

"I wanted to check through it. I need my mail, but I haven't been getting any, not even junk mail."

"I wonder if there's a problem at the post office."

"I'll have to check with them. On a different topic, do I make arrangements with you regarding Callie's situation?"

Rowena looked away, obviously uncomfortable. "You mean moving her things and so forth?"

Eleanor nodded. "And terminating the lease. I'll probably be moving out."

Rowena paused, a handful of mail slipping from her hand. As she squatted and picked up letters from the floor, she said, "Callie's passing terminates her lease on the first of the month unless the family would like to extend the provisions to give time for handling her things. But remember the terms of the contract? For you, the lease you signed stays in full force until it expires, unless you leave for a new facility due to health reasons."

Eleanor vaguely remembered those provisions she and Callie had agreed to, but she'd never imagined that either of them would die so soon before the first lease period ended. The weight of this complication settled on Eleanor's chest, and she felt weak for a moment.

"I'm sorry," Rowena said. "I don't handle the contract end of things. I'd cut you some slack if I could. You'll want to talk to the business office. I can get you their business card."

"No, no, that's all right. I have that information."

Eleanor went to her apartment. The police had taken down the crime-scene tape from her doorway. Even if she wanted to, she couldn't sleep in her own bed again. The police had hacked up the mattress looking for trace evidence. But she wouldn't have the heart anyway. Callie had died there. Without her, Eleanor didn't want to stay at Rivers' Edge any longer than she had to. She stepped into the front walk-in closet, went to a four-drawer filing cabinet, and removed the Rivers' Edge file. She located a sweater, got her bag from Callie's apartment, and left.

On the way out of the parking lot, she thought about how grim the world had become. Despite the pleasant early fall weather, the sun in the western sky seemed too hot, too unrelenting. At a stoplight, she fished around in her bag for sunglasses but couldn't find them. She had no idea where they could be, no sense of where any of the necessities of her life were. Everything was a jumble.

What should she do first? Go to the Plymouth office and straighten out the housing mess? Or stop by the church and check in again with Father Jason? Or should she visit the local post office and ask if they were holding her mail in error? She had no desire to deal with bureaucrats. She'd already spent a contentious morning with Howard and Father Jason at the church, and now she hardly had the energy to deal with anything but the most pressing items.

She decided to go to Plymouth.

Entering the Rivers' administration building gave Eleanor a strange sense of *déjà vu*. The last time she'd been in the building, Callie had sat on the end of the brown leather sofa, her flowered purse in her lap. She'd been happy that day — excited to be touring apartments and meeting new people. Callie had always been so friendly, so outgoing. People naturally flocked to her, to the kindness in her eyes and her open smile.

Eleanor's eyes welled up, and she fought back the tears. No good would come of her breaking down in the foyer. She had tasks to do, matters to take care of. Soon enough she could fall completely apart, but first things first. At the reception desk, she cleared her throat and called out softly.

The woman who came through the doorway was a blonde whom Eleanor had never seen before. "How may I help you?" she asked.

Eleanor outlined the situation while the woman listened, her green eyes serious.

"Are you saying you wish to move at the end of September?"

"Yes," Eleanor said. "After what's happened, I have no desire to stay at Rivers' Edge. So what do I do?"

"Give me a moment." She went through the doorway into the office, leaving Eleanor standing at the counter.

When she returned, she had two file folders in hand. "I'm afraid that you're in a tricky situation, Mrs. Sinclair. Technically, your lease runs through December."

"I'm aware of that. I'd like to break it as soon as I find new accommodations."

"Given the circumstances, I do understand." She opened both folders and arranged them next to one another on the counter. "Do you have authorization to close out Mrs. Trimble's affairs?"

"Would you like to see the power of attorney document?" She reached into her bag, but the woman stopped her.

"That won't be necessary. I see that you're listed here in the paperwork as next of kin." She scribbled some notes on the inside of the manila folder and looked up. "I can't be sure about the cleaning fee or the deposits until I speak to the manager. I'll let you know about that." She slid a business card across the counter.

"You're Ms. Ryerson?"

"Yes. But please call me Claire. You can contact me with any questions that Rowena Hoxley can't answer. I visit each of the apartment buildings during the first week of each month for a general walk-through and submit a monthly report to Martin — Mr. Rivers, I mean. I'll be over to Rivers' Edge on the first or second, so if you're still there, I can touch base with you then about the monetary angle. Otherwise, call me when you're ready to move, and I'll work out the details with you."

"Are you saying I won't be responsible for rent on the two apartments once I move? The lease is waived?"

"Yes. If you stay into October, I'll pro-rate the days. You won't owe after you move."

With relief, Eleanor said, "Thank you. I appreciate your help."

Claire Ryerson smiled, her teeth even and shiny. "Let me know if you have other questions."

Eleanor put the business card in her bag and turned to go.

"Mrs. Sinclair?"

Eleanor paused. "Yes?"

"I'm sorry for your loss."

With a terse nod, Eleanor spun and made for the door, tears brimming over. She couldn't get to the car fast enough. Oh, God, she thought. Please, please, God...

She put her forearms on the steering wheel, leaned forward, and let the sobs come.

Chapter Nine

LEO ARRIVED AT Rivers' Edge shortly after one o'clock, intent on interviewing every aide, every employee, even if it meant driving to the houses of those who weren't on duty.

The first aide who wandered into view was Silvia Garcia, but she had no light to shed upon the situation. Silvia wouldn't say a bad word about anyone. She'd been at a Vikings preseason football game with her husband and two other couples, which she claimed the police had already verified. Leo also learned that Ernesta Campion, who usually worked the late morning/early afternoon shift four days each week, was on vacation.

Silvia strode off toward the laundry room, and Leo returned to the front foyer where Franklin Callaghan sat immersed in his newspaper.

"Anything exciting to report, Mr. Callaghan?"

He peered over the top of the *Star Tribune*. "Not a blessed thing."

"Have you seen Mrs. Hoxley today?"

"Not since early in the morn. Say, lass, you can call me Franklin. No need to be so formal around here."

"Great. And I'm Leona."

With a nod, he went back to his paper.

An aide Leo hadn't seen before rounded the corner from the east wing. She wasn't much over five feet tall and wore horn-rimmed glasses above a sour expression. Her smock, covered in purple and blue flowers, clashed with her rust-colored pants.

She didn't give a glance to either Franklin or Leo, but Leo stepped in her path to flag her down. "Are you Hazel Bellinger?"

"Yeah. Who wants to know?" She squared her shoulders and gazed up at Leo in defiance. Her hair was bleached blonde, but Leo noted dark roots. She had a heart-shaped face, and once upon a time, she was likely to have been quite attractive. Now she was barrel-bodied, wrinkled from too much suntanning, and resembled a cranky troll.

"I'm the DHS investi—"

"Yeah, yeah. Heard all about you. What do you want with me?"

"Could we talk for a few minutes in the dining room?"

"I've got work to do."

"So do I, and it involves getting a statement from everyone

here, so please help me out. This won't take long."

Hazel let out a huff and marched past. Leo glanced at Franklin Callaghan. His eyes were twinkling and in *sotto voce* he said, "Go get her, lass."

Leo set her valise on the table. She went quickly through the formalities. Hazel wasn't keen on being taped, but she reluctantly agreed. "I suppose you'll report everything I say to the others here."

"Actually, what you tell me is kept private, for the most part, except for the summary data that goes into the reports. Any relevant information you give might be made available to a criminal defense attorney if someone is charged with the murder, but none of your peers has access to it."

"They're not my peers."

"Oh?"

"Just a bunch of cheery, young, do-nothin's and people who don't speak English all that good."

"You're referring to?"

"The Kenyans and those Spanish girls. Well," she grumbled, "Silvia speaks okay English, but that Ernesta has such a thick accent that I want to smack her sometimes. I can't tell what language she's talking. And those girls from Kenya laugh and babble to each other like magpies, probably making fun of everyone."

Leo flipped through her notes. "What about the aide named Sherry Colton?"

"She's okay. A little too sickening sweet for my tastes but mostly pulls her weight."

"And the housekeeper?"

Hazel's dark eyes narrowed. "Missy and I don't see eye to eye. She whines too much, so I ignore her."

"The cooks?"

"Lorraine's okay. Dottie can be stingy with the snacks, but neither of them whine like Missy does."

"Let's back up for a moment. How long have you worked at Rivers' Edge?"

"Here? Or for Mr. Rivers?"

"Both."

"I've been here since this complex opened. Before that I worked at one of Mr. Rivers' other places. Me and Walter Green been here since the beginning. We're the foundation of the place. Rest of these people come and go like we ought to install a revolving door."

"Did you know Callie Trimble?"

"Sure. Talked to her all the time. She was pleasant, though her mind was scatty. She didn't deserve to die, and before you go and ask me, I've got no idea who would have done that to her."

"Have you noticed anything unusual around Rivers' Edge lately?"

"You mean other than Habibah Okello's scary boyfriend coming and going like he owns the place?"

"Who's he?"

"A huge guy. Must be seven feet tall. She looks like a little peanut next to him."

"In what way is he involved?"

She scowled. "I didn't say that. You asked if I've seen anything unusual. He definitely qualifies. He drives a Ford F-150 pickup truck with some of those blasting music speakers. The bass thumps so damn loud, everybody knows when he gets here to pick her up. Sometimes she gets off duty after bedtime. Woke me up at midnight a week or so ago."

Leo struggled to hide her irritation. Did this woman know anything at all that might prove useful? Or was she dumb like a fox and successfully managing to divert attention from her own situation?

"Where were you Monday night, Ms. Bellinger?"

"Look here. The police already went over that umpteen million times. I was off work on Friday and didn't come back here until today."

"Tell me about Monday night between about seven and nine. Where were you?"

"That's nobody's business but my own. I told the cops, and that's good enough."

Leo had to assume Flanagan would have done something by now if Hazel didn't have an alibi, so she let that pass. She could check with Flanagan later.

"Have you got any idea at all why someone would want to kill Callie Trimble?"

"No. She was nice. The woman across the hall, that uppity Eleanor, she might've had some reason. She was always bossing Callie around, telling her what to do, not letting her go places."

"What do you mean? Like where?"

"Out. Callie was a grown woman, so she should've been able to take off when she wanted to."

"She had a kind of dementia, didn't she?"

Hazel rolled her eyes. "She was mostly okay. Sure, sometimes she got spacey, but it wasn't anything all that terrible."

"I gather you don't care for Eleanor Sinclair?"

"She's not very friendly. She had some hold over Callie. Kind of unnatural, if you know what I mean." Hazel gave Leo a knowing glance, crossed her arms, and hunched down. "I don't know what to tell you. I come here for every shift, do my job, and hightail it home. I've worked for Martin Rivers since his apartments started opening eight-plus years ago, and I oughta be the manager here now. But oh, no, he brings in that Hoxley woman, and she's in charge. Doesn't know her head from a hole in the ground. She may know how to do the paperwork, but that's about it. She don't know people. Somebody gets a little mixed-up, and poof! She gets them sent away."

"Oh, really?"

"Why d'you think we've got vacancies? She got rid of old Mrs. Brodsky because she had a couple of incontinence accidents. Big deal. Like us aides couldn't help her with a pee pad now and then?"

"When did Mrs. Brodsky leave?"

"Right around Mother's Day. Mrs. B's grandkids were here and everything, and next thing you know, Mrs. B was crying and telling them she was being shipped out." She lowered her voice. "Heartless cruel bitch, that's what Rowena is. Didn't give her a chance."

"How long had Mrs. Brodsky been here?"

"Came shortly after Walter and me. This was her home. Now I don't know where the hell she is. She could've died for all I know."

"Would anyone in the Brodsky family hold a grudge—maybe decide to do something here to get back at Mrs. Hoxley?"

"I doubt that. If you wanted to torture Rowena, the best way would be to take a nice pointy beer-can opener to the side of her car. You see what she drives? The woman's in her forties and still tooling around in a race car. You ask me, she's forty-something going on sixteen. Hasn't she bragged to you about her car?"

Leo shook her head.

In falsetto, Hazel said, "My Corvette this, my Corvette that." She waved a hand as if to dismiss Leo. "Ridiculous. The woman's a menace. Drives like a bat outta hell, too. She probably ran over poor Miss Trimble in the parking lot and dragged her in to cover her tracks."

Leo bit back a smile. Hazel Bellinger wasn't particularly nice, but she certainly had spirit.

Hazel rose. "That's probably more than I oughta say, but it's the truth, and if I have to testify on the witness stand, I'll stick to my guns, so help me God."

She stamped off, her fists tight against her hips, as Leo sat back to consider what a remarkable interviewee Hazel Bellinger had been.

LEO SPOKE TO the cooks, Dottie Winstead and Lorraine Peebles, but neither had anything interesting to add. They maintained they'd observed nothing unusual and that Callie Trimble had a perfectly normal appetite right up to her last meal. "Swedish Meatballs, mashed potatoes, and green beans," Dottie said. "With yellow cake for dessert."

Noting the foyer was empty, Leo went in and sat on the couch nearest the door. She took time to make notes and list who was left to interview. Sherry Colton. The housekeeper, Missy McCarver. And Habibah and Shani Okello, who she'd learned were sisters. The housekeeper had left for the day and didn't answer the phone at home, so Leo decided to talk with her in the morning. Sherry and Habibah would be on duty later in the evening, and she resolved to return after dinner when she could make another round of the residents.

Walter Green, in particular, might have something relevant to say. Besides Habibah Okello, he'd been the only resident who might have had access to Callie Trimble. Nobody had suggested that Walter had anything to do with the murder, but Leo needed to talk to him and decide that on her own.

For the first time all day, she allowed herself to relax. Her shoulders were tight, and the low-grade headache she'd been ignoring was calling for another couple of aspirin.

A whish of air came through the vent carrying the distant tinny sound of a TV. Otherwise, all was quiet at Rivers' Edge. What the hell was she doing here? Not even forty-eight hours had passed since she'd been uprooted from her police work and tossed into this bizarre world of investigations. She didn't belong here. If she'd wanted to be a detective, she could have long ago applied for a Major Case position in Saint Paul. She'd never been fond of puzzles or people who lied or the mountains of paperwork and file-combing tedium she associated with the work done by officers with their gold shields. And the hours! Nobody committed serious crimes on a convenient schedule. At least on patrol she could rely upon regular hours, even if shifts changed periodically.

No, investigative work was not something to which she'd ever felt drawn. So how could she get out of it?

She dug her phone out and dialed Range Master Daniels. He wasn't in, so she left a voicemail to ask when they could get together to work on remedial training.

The phone blinked that she had messages, and she listened to the first one.

"Leona, Thom Thoreson here. Fred called in to say he'd be out sick tomorrow. Something about the flu. Yeah, right. I've reviewed all the complaints that came in today, and there's nothing urgent. If you could finish up the one you're on, I've got some priority items that need review. Let me know if you have questions. Otherwise, talk to you tomorrow."

Leo snapped the phone shut feeling she'd been well and truly abandoned, completely deserted. How did these people expect her to handle this mess without more support? She rose, unable to get over how cavalier Baldur was and how little supervision she'd received. No wonder her colleague didn't get much done. Nobody was watching his back or his work. He'd have never made it as a cop.

On the way out to her car, she couldn't get rid of the feeling of disgust. One thing she liked about police work was that her fellow cops rarely minced words, and if she gave an officer an upbraiding, he knew he deserved it. Her team worked hard for her, and even though they often dealt with the aftermath of people being stupid and violent, she and her officers felt they made a difference every day. How was she going to get any sense of satisfaction with this assignment?

THE ELECTRIC GARAGE door ground slowly to a close as Leo marched toward the house and let herself in the passage to the kitchen alcove. She ignored the doggie bed below the coat pegs on the wall. Her little dog, Beau, had died after the first of the year, and she still missed him. The part Scottie/part Boston Terrier mutt had been a college graduation gift from her foster parents. Beau saw her through police academy, and a series of two's: two relationships; two break-ups; two moves; and two major work assignments, first as patrol officer, then as sergeant.

Unlike her first two girlfriends, Beau had been wild about Daria. Leo met Daria five years earlier at a Continuing Legal Education seminar the police department gave for lawyers, and she was immediately attracted to her dark looks and sense of humor.

When Leo saw how loving Daria was with Beau, she'd known she was someone special. Apparently the third time was a charm, and they quickly moved in together with Beau as a sweet third wheel that never got in the way.

She hadn't expected Beau to die. She'd come home from work, and there he was waiting for her on the deep front window ledge, asleep forever in his favorite spot. After these many months, she had finally stopped automatically looking for him. Everyone kept telling her that getting another dog was the best way to fully assuage the pain, but she wasn't convinced.

When Daria pulled up to the garage at seven, Leo fired up the propane grill for pork chops she'd marinated. Two baked potatoes were roasting in the oven, and she'd tossed a green salad.

"Supper will be on the table in about fifteen minutes."

"Sorry, Leo, I grabbed something already. I'm not hungry at all."

"How come you didn't call?"

Her disappointment must have been obvious because Daria said, "Don't get all upset. It's been one hell of a day."

"I'm not upset, Daria. I just wish you'd let me know."

"Let me change first, and I'll have a drink with you while you eat."

She stood at the sliding glass door, a grilling fork in one hand, watching smoke waft away from the grill. Daria had never handled stress well. She wasn't a Type A personality, but many of her colleagues were. They could take the pace, the constant pressure, but she'd been watching it wear Daria down like ocean water over a sand castle. She'd often encouraged her to quit criminal law and take up some sort of foundation work with a lot less strain and frustration. She wouldn't consider it because the income wasn't as substantial.

She didn't understand Daria's focus on money. Her family had always been wealthy. In contrast, Leo and her mother, Elizabeth Reese, had lived their lives counting pennies and cutting corners. When her mother died, Leo had been placed in a series of four foster care homes, none of them with much income. She eventually ran away from each home, always returning to her old neighborhood with the unrealistic hope that she'd knock on the door of her old house and magically find her mother restored to life and making something—waffles, fried chicken, Irish stew, anything—for dinner.

This went on for over a year. Social Services didn't want to skirt any rules, and somebody always retrieved Leo and took her to the county welfare building where she'd spend hours waiting for them to make decisions. But Leo still remembered the day Dad Wallace and his police captain arrived at the county welfare building in full dress uniforms. She didn't know how he did it, but she went home that day to the Wallaces in the front seat of a brand-new police cruiser. She wasn't quite twelve years old, but she was impressed that cops got things done.

Leo moved in with the Wallace family and was eventually placed there permanently. Money was tight for a police sergeant who supported a stay-at-home wife and five kids on his police salary and the pittance the county provided for foster care reimbursement.

So Leo was used to economy. She didn't desire many material things, yet here she was, ensconced in a giant house in the ritzy

Kenwood neighborhood of Minneapolis. Daria's wealthy parents gave them the gift of a significant down payment for the house at their commitment ceremony four years earlier. The Wallaces' present, a lovely Oriental rug Leo used in her office/sewing room, had cost a few hundred dollars.

She liked the rug better than the house.

The wedding gift from Daria's well-to-do parents still felt excessive, and truth be told, the house the Emersons selected wasn't the choice she'd have made. It was far too big for two. Of course, Daria's mother let it be known that she expected small children to rove the house — and soon.

Daria had recently taken out a fifty-thousand-dollar mortgage to build the garage, finish the basement, and upgrade the bathroom on the main floor. The garage was done, but work inside the house hadn't yet started. Leo dreaded that day. Nothing worse than workmen tramping through the house, dust and tools littering their work areas. The noise alone would drive her crazy, especially when she was on night shift and trying to sleep during the day. Might as well go to a hotel.

But she was on day shift, and she'd probably continue to be stuck on days for the rest of the year. The thought made her want to sit down and cry. She thought Daria was just as worn out as she was. The last two nights, Leo had gone to bed early and Daria didn't join her until sometime in the wee hours of the night. The long hours were killing her partner, and there was nothing Leo could do to encourage her to get more sleep. Oh, well, she thought, Daria's a big girl. She'll have to take care of herself.

She opened the barbecue cover and flipped the chops on the grill.

By the time Daria poured herself a Scotch and joined her in the dining room, she'd already buttered her baked potato and eaten her salad. "So," she asked, "your day was bad?"

"Yes."

"How bad?"

"Hellaciously awful. My dumb-ass client made an offhand comment to a reporter in the elevator, and with my luck, it'll show up in the newspaper."

"What'd he say?"

"Something to the effect that he'd had plenty of experience heisting things when he was younger, and if he'd done the robbery, he never would have been caught."

"Oh, I see. So, people are supposed to believe he's innocent now because he's always been too smart to apprehend?"

"Apparently. But if he was so smart, he wouldn't have admitted there are burglaries and robberies out there that could be pinned on him. The police will probably pull all the open files and compare every damn fingerprint and M.O. to see if they can nail him for other offenses."

"That's what I'd do."

"Yeah, I bet." She took a swig of the Scotch and sat shaking her head, then set the glass on the table.

"You still get paid the same whether you win or lose."

Daria glared. "It's not about the money, Leo. I don't think the guy did it, and if he didn't but still gets convicted, his whole life is ruined."

"You've got investigators working the details, right?"

"Yeah."

"Maybe they'll turn up something."

"I've got a bad feeling about it." With a sigh, she shook herself. "Why don't you tell me about your day. Anything good there?"

"I wish." Leo looked into Daria's dark eyes, hardly knowing where to begin. "I went to the range and tried to work on my shooting again."

"Any success?"

"Not so much. My vision is clear and sharp when I start, but it goes straight to hell when the headache hits."

"Why don't you just go see the eye doctor?"

"Dammit, my vision is fine."

Daria was obviously taken aback by the venom in her voice. "But—but—I'm just saying—"

Leo interrupted. "What are you going to do tonight?"

"Case prep, what else."

"I've got to go back to work, too."

"What? I thought this was a regular eight-to-five job."

"Ran into some difficulties, and I still need to interview some evening employees. I left early so I'll finish out my eight hours tonight."

"Just tell me one thing. When the hell are you going to take care of this headache problem?"

"There's no need to shout."

Daria knocked back another gulp of Scotch and smacked the empty glass on the table. "You seem pretty complacent about your vision considering that you've been kicked off the job because of it."

The glass in Leo's hand slipped and she nearly dropped it. "What's done is done. I can't change what's happened. I've got weeks ahead of me to deal with my quals, and now I'm stuck trying to take care of new duties for an office that hasn't given me a clue about how the hell to get the job done."

"Then complain."

"I've tried. The head honcho is rarely there, and from what I hear, he couldn't help me anyway. There's a backlog sixty miles long, and the dolt I'm working with didn't even come in today. So I'm stuck figuring out how to handle cases by Ouija Board and intuition."

Daria rose. "Lord knows you wouldn't want to use intuition. Not when cold, hard facts in black and white are available." She scooped up her glass and stomped toward the door.

"I can't believe you'd say that."

"Just the facts, ma'am, just the facts."

"Where are you going?"

"To get out the Ouija Board for the Dunleavey case."

ON THE WAY from her house to Rivers' Edge, Leo drove automatically without seeing any of the terrain she covered. Daria's comments at dinner kept whirling around in her head. She hadn't known whether to console her or to flee and deal with her own hurt feelings. She'd chosen the latter but still wasn't sure it was the smartest decision.

What was wrong with Daria lately? She'd been touchy and critical, her lack of patience unusual. It wasn't like her to be so grumpy. She yearned for the old Daria, the woman who liked to laugh and who spread her warmth and humor around like butter and syrup on the blueberry waffles they used to enjoy making on Sunday mornings. The Dunleavey case was killing her personality. How many other cases would work the same evil magic?

By the time Leo drove into the Rivers' Edge parking lot, her headache was pounding again, which made her angry. She hated to admit Daria was right, but tomorrow she resolved to schedule an appointment with Doctor Spence.

The front door was ajar and the foyer deserted. A low murmur of voices came from the dining room. She wondered why nobody was concerned about the open door, shut it firmly behind her, and crossed the common area to the café. She found four elderly women sitting around one of the tables, cards in hand, a cup of coffee at each woman's elbow. She'd spoken to Mrs. Stepanek and two of the others in passing the day before and assumed that the three unknowns were Agnes Trumpeter, Nettie Volk, and Jade Perkins, but she wasn't sure.

"Good evening, ladies," Leo said. "When you finish the hand, may I talk with you for a few minutes?"

"Why, sure, honey. Come on in and pull up a chair." The woman who spoke looked to be the oldest of the group. Her white hair was so thin, Leo could see through it to her pink scalp. She was dressed in dark polyester pants and a neon-green silk blouse.

Giant, gem-encrusted rings sparkled on both hands. Diamonds, sapphires, and emeralds glittered in the corners of a pair of old-fashioned, black cat-eye glasses.

Mrs. Stepanek played a card and looked up at Leo. "Give us three minutes to play out, and we'll give you our full attention. Would you like a cup of coffee?"

"No, thanks." Coffee would keep her up all night. Tossing and turning would only irritate Daria. If Daria bothered to come to bed, that is.

Leo pulled up a chair and sat to watch. All of them were intent, focused on their cards. With a shriek of glee, Mrs. Stepanek said, "Here's a trump, so that trick's mine." Using her trick as a scraper, she swept the three cards toward her, then dropped the ace of hearts and took the next trick, too. She played the ace of spades in trump and captured another round. Flashing a grin toward Leo, she said, "Don't you love it when everything falls in place so nicely?"

"Oh, yes," Leo said, but she couldn't help thinking that nothing had fallen into place for her for quite some time. Perhaps she ought to take up cards. "Is this Pinochle you're playing?"

"Sure is," Mrs. Stepanek said.

They finished the round and tallied the score. Once they'd tossed in their cards, all four examined Leo with curiosity. She introduced herself and said, "Would you mind if I tape an interview with all of you about the death of Callie Trimble?"

"Ask away," said the white-haired lady who sat to Leo's left. "We'll tell you everything."

Leo took a pad of paper and pen from her bag, put the much-used tape recorder on the table and started it. "First, let me get everyone's name straight."

"I'm Agnes Trumpeter." The white-haired lady cocked her head to the side like an inquisitive bird, and the blue and green gems in her cat-eye glasses winked and gleamed.

The next card-player said, "Nettie Volk." She wore a pale blue blouse that gave her silvery hair a bluish cast. Her glasses were gold-rimmed, and they looked exactly like those of the woman next to her who announced that she was Jade Perkins. Jade's hair didn't have the bluish tint, but like Nettie's, it was silver and cut in a bob. Her outfit consisted of a lightweight, red lounging suit with yellow geometric patterns. They looked enough alike to be sisters.

"And I remember you, Mrs. Stepanek," Leo said.

"Please, people call me Willie." She was bigger, wider-shouldered, and more boisterous than the others. Her dark brown hair showed streaks of gray, and she was dressed in a rust-colored blouse, jeans with an elastic waistband, and stark white tennis shoes.

The image that came to Leo was of three blind mice and one

good-sized calico cat.

Agnes pushed up her glittery black glasses and squinted at Leo. "I wish we knew something that could help you, but I can't think what it would be."

"You never know. Maybe some small detail will matter. Let's start with how long you've all lived here."

They went around in order. Agnes said, "Four years."

Nettie said, "I came before Agnes by about six months, and Jade came right on my heels, isn't that right, hon?"

"Yes, I moved in the month after you. Such a good neighbor you were, too. You brought me flowers from the garden that first night." Jade and Nettie beamed at one another.

"I'm the new girl on the block," Willie Stepanek said. "I just moved in two years ago."

"Lucky for us," Agnes said. "We needed a fourth for Hearts and Pinochle, and you filled the bill."

Agnes patted Leo on the forearm. "You can call us four the Merry Widows."

Leo surveyed them, and they did seem merry—in the same way that a barn cat was, before he pounced upon an unsuspecting mouse.

She ran through her litany of questions: What did they see? Who was in the dining room that night? Had there been any strangers around lately? Had anyone acted odd lately?

None of them could add any new information.

"Were you all here the whole evening during the sing-along? Nobody left this area?"

Nettie ran a hand along the poof of blue hair at the top of her head. "Wait, girls. Habibah did get up and leave for a bit."

"How long was she gone?" Leo asked.

The four spoke all at once, spouting various time estimates until Willie said, "I think she went to the bathroom. She was gone for maybe five minutes."

"No," Jade said. "It was longer than that. Franklin did his 'Loch Lomond' number. She was gone the whole time, and—"

Agnes interrupted, "At least two songs."

"No, no, no," Nettie said. "You were all so engrossed in shrieking 'Roll Out The Barrel' that you weren't paying attention."

Jade said, "Just because you don't vocalize, Nettie Volk, it doesn't make you a better observer than the rest of us."

"I'm not saying that. But Habibah didn't come back for quite a while. When she did, remember she went over and took the empty carafe into the kitchen and served us all coffee?"

There was silence for a moment, then the others nodded. Willie said, "Okay, I think you're right, Nettie."

"Could any of you see what direction she went? Did she go to the restroom in the foyer?"

"Sorry," Willie said. "We sit over there, close to the piano. We've got a partial view through the door. I'd have been able to see if someone came in the front door, but not if Habibah went around the corner to the ladies' room or toward the apartments."

Leo asked, "Would you say she was gone ten minutes? Fifteen? Twenty?"

They all babbled on at once.

"Not twenty. Maybe ten."

"Fifteen."

"Much less than fifteen!"

"Not more than ten."

They continued to argue, but Nettie raised a hand and the chatter stopped abruptly. "Perhaps ten minutes, but not as much as fifteen. I think that's as close as we'll agree. Let's say ten to twelve minutes, all right, girls?" She looked around the circle. Her friends seemed satisfied.

"But let's get one thing straight," Willie said. "Habibah is a very nice person. She'd never hurt anybody, much less kill one of us. You ask her—I bet she was in the ladies' room."

"What about the other staff?" Leo asked. "Is there anyone who's problematic?"

They exchanged glances, and Leo saw something was bothering them. She raised her eyebrows and looked from one to another, waiting for someone to break the silence.

After a long pause, Willie said, "Hazel has been downright secretive lately."

"Secretive," Agnes said, "and cranky." The women agreed, echoing the word cranky.

"How does that fit in?" Leo asked.

Jade pushed up the sleeves of her red lounger and folded her arms over her chest. "She's making a play for old Walter."

Leo asked, "Aren't staff required to maintain strictly professional relationships with residents here? Isn't there a fraternization rule?"

Jade shrugged. "Perhaps. But Walter's wealthy."

"Very wealthy," Nettie said. "Also rather—to be honest, rather unpleasant." She leaned forward and said in a quiet rasp, "He didn't like Callie and Eleanor one bit, but I'm not sure they knew that."

"Oh?" Leo prompted.

"On account of their, you know, situation," Nettie said.

Jade picked up her coffee cup. "The special relationship, she means."

Agnes rolled her eyes. "Come on now, we're modern women.

Say the word. He accused them of being lesbians. If it were true, it wouldn't bother any of us at all, but Walter's not so open-minded."

"Oh?" Leo said.

Agnes nodded. "He didn't think they looked enough alike to be related, so he made a number of crude comments, and Hazel was right there, agreeing with him."

"Crude comments?"

"Oh," Agnes said, "general rudeness. He called them the Diddle Biddies. The man has no respect. Says anything that comes to mind. He doesn't talk that much, but when he does, he often brings up topics that aren't his business."

"So," Leo asked, "do you think Walter might have harbored enough resentment that he could kill Callie Trimble?"

Willie Stepanek raised a hand. "I can't see it that way. He avoided them. Besides, Walter's lazy. All he does all day is move from the recliner in his room to the couch in the TV area. He doesn't bother to come to the sing-alongs, and he rarely rides the bus to the casino with us either. He's a great big lazy—"

"Toad," Agnes supplied. The others protested, but she went on. "Don't mince words. He's a toad. Franklin's a gentleman, but Walter is the opposite."

Willie rose and went to the sideboard to pick up the coffeepot. She came over to refill mugs. "Sure you don't want a shot? The coffee here is quite good."

"No, I'm fine. What else can you tell me about Walter?"

Willie topped off Jade's cup. "He won't tell you much. He's never been very forthcoming."

"Frankly," Agnes said, "I don't think he likes women much at all."

"Or people," Willie said. "He hates people in general."

"But women specifically," Agnes added.

Leo made a note to interview Walter carefully to find out what his attitudes were regarding Eleanor and Callie. "Let's talk about Hazel. What's the problem with her?"

Jade said, "She still talks to me, and I think I have fewer hassles with her than the rest of you. She was so good about encouraging me to get back on my feet. You see, I had a minor stroke last year, and she regularly walked with me so I could regain the strength in my leg."

"Lucky you," Agnes said. "She treats the rest of us like dirt."

"Have a stroke, then," Jade said.

Leo choked back a guffaw at the tiny lady's droll comment.

"She's really good when your health is compromised. She was quite kind to me, but now that I'm walking fine, she mostly ignores me."

Leo asked, "Any of the other aides cause problems?"

The four women nattered on about the others, but all their comments were positive.

"What about the manager?"

"Rowena's fine," Nettie said. "I don't think any of us have complaints, right, girls?"

They shook their heads and sat thinking for a moment. Leo waited to see if any other comments emerged. When nobody spoke, she said, "Tell me about Habibah's boyfriend."

Nettie frowned. "Chuck? Are you talking about Chuck?"

"I don't know his name."

Agnes leaned in conspiratorially. "He dresses like a professional basketball player. About eight feet tall and likes to wear those two-piece outfits with lightning bolts and fancy braiding on the legs."

"Track suits," Jade said. "He works over at the U. Some kind of sports coach. Walter calls him Denny the Drug Dealer—as if Walter knew anything! He watches too many crime shows. Chuck is a perfectly nice young man, and he comes to get Habibah whenever she works late. I think that's not only wise, but also sweet of him."

Nettie said, "The world sure has changed. When we were young, no white boy could even think about dating a black girl. And now nobody raises an eyebrow."

"Except Walter," Agnes said. "What a racist he turned out to be."

They spoke for a while about Chuck and Habibah, discussed Sherry Colton's cute children, and from there launched into tales of their own grandkids.

Half-listening, Leo checked over her notes and cut in when an opportunity presented itself. "Can you ladies think of anything else to shed light on this senseless death?"

They sat thinking, shaking heads and muttering.

"Is there anything about the way this apartment house is run that any of you have trouble with?"

"Not at all," Agnes said, "though they do toss you out on your ear when you run out of money."

"No provisions for welfare here," Willie said. "The motto says something about zest and comfort, but really, it ought to be 'No Pay, No Stay.'" She let out a peal of laughter, and the others joined her. "Luckily our husbands provided well for us. I've got enough dough to stay here until I'm ninety."

"Just don't have a stroke," Jade said. "Even with Medicare, I still got stuck with a heap of bills."

FATIGUE WASHED OVER Leo like a wall of tepid water. She left the Pinochle foursome in the dining room, but she resolved to keep on moving. She paused in the empty common area and checked her notes. She needed to talk to Sherry Colton, the Okello sisters, the housekeeper, and the one resident left, Walter Green. Five more interviews, and she hoped to be done with it. She was troubled that nobody seemed to have any clue at all as to who committed the murder. With the exception of Walter, Leo didn't suspect anyone. She wondered if the police had any leads.

When Martin Rivers provided her with the information she'd requested, she might be able to make sense of the situation. What if she couldn't, though? What if Callie Trimble's murder was never solved, the killer never found?

She thought of motive, means, and opportunity: the three golden precepts. Until this job, she'd been able to get away with not worrying much about those terms, even when she and her team canvassed door to door. Her main duties on the street were to identify problems, find ways to nip them in the bud, or apprehend those who committed offenses against people and property. So much simpler, she thought. She could use brute force when it was called for, and she carried a sidearm, taser, baton, and mace for protection, not to mention wearing the uniform, which gave her authority, if not always respect. She liked being a police officer on the street. She felt freer somehow. The streets were open to her, the city vast and seething with activity. Rarely stuck in one place for long, she could satisfy a kind of wanderlust she wouldn't admit to others that she possessed.

She certainly wanted to spend time working in police investigations units before achieving commander status, but she'd never thought seriously about striving for a Gold Shield. Leo knew a dozen detectives with whom she'd worked over the years. Nice guys usually, a few enterprising gals here and there, too. Detectives were an odd lot. Strangely silent. Insular. Somehow apart from the rank and file, despite the fact that all of them had come up through patrol. Once an officer was assigned permanently to investigations, they changed. Leo thought of Pete Ullman, who'd gone through police academy with her, worked in the Eastern District for years, and was now working in the Fraud & Forgery Unit. Like other detectives, he was from the rank and file, but not part of them anymore.

She was happy to canvass neighborhoods for the detectives, to be on the lookout for oddities and to trade theories and share her impressions, but the detectives weren't there day to day when all the street policing was done. At the same time, she wasn't on the hook if and when they were called on the carpet because crimes weren't solved. Her job was to watch, predict, and prevent. Never a need for her to carry a case through to the bitter end, and that's the way she liked it.

At the moment, she was stuck with this job and a vexing case as well. Other than possible homophobia, she could think of no convincing motive for the killing. As far as she could tell, most of the residents didn't have the physical strength to subdue a large woman. Unless someone came over the wall, only Walter and the aide named Habibah had the opportunity to attack Callie Trimble. Walter Green was shaping up to be the sole suspect, and from what the Merry Widows had to say, his alibi didn't sound like a very convincing one.

Should she talk to him now, or wait until tomorrow? She had no clue whether he'd be sleeping after eight p.m., but she knew of one sure way to find out. He wasn't in the TV room, so she bypassed that area and rounded the corner into the east wing. His door, the first one on the left, was open.

Leo heard the TV before she reached the doorway. An old rerun of *Law and Order* played, the volume up so high she wondered why his neighbors didn't complain. The man was sprawled in a dirt-brown-colored recliner that had seen better days. When she rapped on the doorframe, he shifted in the chair, and it made a squeaky shriek.

"Yeah?" he said, his eyes squinting her way.

She spoke loudly over the TV program. "Could I speak to you for a few moments about Callie Trimble's death?"

"At the commercial." He turned to concentrate on the show, while she stood in the doorway feeling awkward. On the TV, Detective Lenny Briscoe made a smart-aleck comment, the music swelled, and the program cut away to a loud commercial for laundry soap.

The old man held out a remote to mute the sound and beckoned her in.

The apartment was laid out like all the others. One half was a sitting area, and the other part consisted of an enclosed bathroom, an open bedroom area, and a huge walk-in closet. His bedroom space was bare of all but a twin-sized bed and a four-drawer dresser.

Spartan described the whole apartment. If Walter Green had lived at Rivers' Edge since it opened, Leo sure couldn't tell. No pictures hung on the walls or graced the top of the one bookcase off to the left of the TV. By the window, a dining-room-sized table with only two chairs was pushed up against the wall and heaped with mail and papers, magazines and newspapers.

The only place to sit other than the recliner was a shabby,

pumpkin-orange, two-person loveseat. Leo lowered herself to the edge of it, set her valise on the floor, and said, "Mr. Green, I'm Leona Reese. I won't take up too much of your time."

"Sure hope not. Damn commercials go on and on, but the show'll start up again in a couple of minutes."

"Maybe I should return after the show is over."

He gave a toss of his full head of white hair. "Good idea." He crossed his arms and turned his attention to the television set.

Leo rose, biting back a chuckle. She supposed when she got to be his age she might not bother to engage in social graces either. "I'll stop by after nine."

She thought she heard a grunt but couldn't be sure.

Out in the hall, all was quiet, so she went to the staff room and knocked on the open door.

A woman's voice called out, "Come in."

A slim black woman in a white smock and light blue cotton pants stood in an alcove in front of a row of industrial washers and dryers. Braided through her hair were dozens of multicolored beads. When she moved her head, the beads clicked faintly. She deftly folded a towel and stacked it upon half-a-dozen others atop a folding table. The rest of the room contained a massive, sturdy bunk bed, and a bank of closed drawers that were built into the right wall. Both mattresses were neatly made up and covered with lightweight blue, purple, and white spreads that complemented the flowery border that ran along the top of all the white walls.

The woman glanced over her shoulder, a smile on her face. "You must be the lady from the State. Ms. Reese, right?"

"That's me. Are you Habibah Okello?"

"I am. People often mix up my sister and me, but she's much older." Her eyes twinkled. "Two years."

Her speech was accented slightly, and Leo remembered that the Okello sisters were originally from Kenya. Habibah closed the dryer door and pivoted, smoothing the front of her smock. "Shall we take a break somewhere?"

They went to the common area and found corner seats on adjacent couches with an end table between them. Leo dumped the recorder out, and for the first time, she wondered about batteries. She saw an outlet behind the table, so she dug out the cord. As she plugged it in she heard a peal of laughter from the dining hall. The Merry Widows must still be playing cards.

She was sick of giving the investigator spiel required by the State, but she did it once more, with apologies.

Habibah listened patiently, a relaxed smile on her broad brown face. "No need to apologize. If anyone understands government bureaucracy, it is me. I still remember being ten years old and standing in line all day for many days in Kenya so that my sister and I could come here."

"Nothing worse than waiting in line."

"It's far worse to sit in a prison, waiting for someone to find the error they've made."

"You were imprisoned in Kenya?"

"Not I. My father."

"How long did it take to correct the error?"

"Too long. He died before he could be released."

"I'm so sorry. I didn't mean to bring up painful memories."

"I like to speak of my father. He was a good man. One day I'll have a son and name him in his honor." Her eyes met Leo's with an openness Leo thought was refreshing. Habibah Okello was a strong woman, and her resolute voice affirmed it.

"Have you been in the U.S. for some time?"

"Almost nineteen years. We love it here."

"How long have you been working at Rivers' Edge?"

"Three years. Mrs. Hoxley hired my sister and me the very week she took the position of manager."

"So you've seen a lot of people come and go?"

"Yes. But some have been here as long as I have. Hazel and Ernesta and Silvia came before I did."

Habibah referred to the workers, but Leo had meant the residents. "A lot of the apartment residents have moved in and out as well."

"Yes, but the crazy ladies," she said and gestured toward the dining hall with a grin, "they have all been here for ages."

"Callie Trimble and Eleanor Sinclair were so new. Had you gotten to know them?"

"Oh, yes. Shani and I—my sister, I mean—we liked them both. Never a problem, even though Callie had the Old Timers' disease."

"Was it Alzheimer's? Or dementia?"

Habibah shrugged. "Either way, her memory was not so good, but she never forgot to laugh. I'm sad she's gone."

"Do you have any idea who would hurt her?"

"No. I don't know anything."

"Tell me about what happened Monday night. What time did you come on duty?"

"Sherry and I were on the afternoon shift. Ten o'clock was end of her shift, and I was on the overnight. We ate dinner with the residents."

"And who were they?"

"Let me see. The four card sharks in there—you know who I mean."

"The Merry Widows."

"Yes, they sat together. Franklin and Callie sat with my colleague, Sherry. I was at Walter's table, but I was up and down. One of the cooks—this is Dottie—wasn't feeling well. She was ill with a cold, so I helped Lorraine fill the plates and serve seconds and coffee and dessert, and Dottie did all the kitchen cleanup."

"Who was missing?"

"Eleanor had a book talk, so she was gone, and Norma is out of town."

"Anyone else?"

"No, unless something has changed in the last few days, we still have three vacancies."

"Then what happened on Monday night?"

"After dinner, everyone went away to their own rooms to rest or be refreshed. We gathered them together for the sing-along at 7:30."

"Who came to that?"

"Small gathering. The four ladies came and Franklin, Sherry, and me."

"Did anyone leave at any time?"

"No."

"You saw no one leave."

"No, nobody moved until we heard the alarm bell."

"What about you?"

"Huh?"

"You left the sing-along for a while, right?"

"Oh, no, I don't think so."

An expression flitted across her face for the briefest moment. Leo waited, watching intently. She often used this tactic on the street: Ask a question, get the first answer, then wait for something further. She was often surprised how much additional information a silent stare could garner.

"I—I'm certain—fairly certain I didn't leave the sing-along."

"Not even for a quick trip to the bathroom?"

Habibah slouched slightly and swallowed, her throat working up and down. "Maybe. I don't think so, though."

"What if I were to tell you that every person at the sing-along agrees that you left the room for ten or as much as fifteen minutes?"

"Oh, no, I could not have possibly been gone that long!"

"I see. So you do recall leaving?"

"I think I did go to the bathroom, but I was in and out of there in minutes."

"You didn't go down the east hall to see Callie Trimble?"

Habibah's eyes widened. Before she could open her mouth to deny it, the front doorbell rang. She popped up from her seat as though ejected from a burning fighter plane.

A gust of warm air made its way to Leo. The sun was down, but night hadn't quite fallen, and the two men standing in the doorway were backlit so that Leo couldn't make out their faces. She recognized the physique of Detective Flanagan.

Flanagan held out his identification. "Ms. Okello, Detective DeWitt and I would like you to come down to the station with us now."

"The station?" she asked in a quavery voice.

"Yes, the police station. Please get your things," Flanagan said as he shouldered his way into the foyer.

"But I can't leave my job."

"If you'd been home earlier in the day, we could have made this easier."

Leo rose. A swarm of gnats swirled around the porch light.

DeWitt shut the door. He glanced Leo's way, his face cast in an unpleasant scowl. "Ms. Okello, you've got two choices. Wouldn't you rather come with us voluntarily? Or do you want an arrest on your record?"

The poor woman looked like her knees would buckle. Leo hastened to her side and got hold of her forearm. "Steady up."

Habibah whipped her head toward Leo, her beads clacking together. "Help me," she pleaded.

LEO HAD NEITHER the status nor the inclination to intercede on Habibah Okello's behalf. The most important thing she could do was extract information from Flanagan. While DeWitt followed Habibah to the staff room to get her purse and sweater, Leo faced off with Flanagan.

"What have you found out? Are you detaining her for murder?"

"We're not arresting her, per se. We need to get a statement and verify some things."

"What things?"

He stepped closer and leaned down so he could speak softly. "Prior to working here, Miss Okello worked at a hospital in Milwaukee where three unexplained mercy killings took place."

"Same MO?"

Flanagan shifted back uncomfortably. "Not exactly. One by a pillow over the face, the other two with overdoses of morphine injected into the IV lines."

"And you think she did it?"

"She worked there at the time. It's possible."

"Please let me know, will you, Detective? I can finish off this investigation as soon as you have verification."

With a sigh, he agreed, and DeWitt escorted a shaking Habibah to the front door.

"Who will do my job?" Habibah asked.

"I'll talk to Sherry right away," Leo said.

"I should do that myself." Holding back tears with an effort, she stared up at the enormous cop next to her. "Please don't do this."

Leo patted her shoulder. "Don't worry. These guys will probably have you back here before you know it." Leo recognized the fear in her eyes. "Habibah, you'll be safe. No one will hurt you."

DeWitt said, "Come along, miss." He tugged on her forearm, as Habibah dissolved into tears. Leo accompanied them to the entrance and closed the door behind them.

The four elderly women clustered silently in the dining room doorway. Leo hadn't seen them congregate there, and she didn't know how much they'd heard.

Agnes Trumpeter fingered her cat-eye glasses, removed them, and ran a cloth over the lenses. "You can't possibly believe Habibah killed Callie Trimble."

Leo shrugged. "I'm just as surprised as everyone else. Where is Sherry Colton?"

The women exchanged glances until Willie Stepanek finally said, "Perhaps she's in with Walter. Or Eleanor."

"Thanks." Leo gathered up her recorder, which she'd left on, and dumped it into her valise. The Merry Widows headed off to their respective rooms, calling good night, and she followed them to the apartment wing. She hesitated. Walter or Eleanor? She checked her watch, but it was twenty minutes to nine, and Walter was still watching his TV program, so she went past his room. The door to Eleanor Sinclair's apartment was open, but unless someone was in the bathroom, no one was there. Across the hall, Callie Trimble's door was closed, but Leo heard a faint murmur, so she knocked.

The voices stopped, and a moment later the door creaked open.

"Hello, Eleanor. Have you seen Sherry?"

Eleanor whipped open the door. Sherry rose from the couch. "Hello, Ms. Reese. What can I help you with?"

From the doorway, Leo quickly explained that Habibah had been taken into custody.

"This is impossible." Sherry scowled and managed to look all of ten years old. "I'm supposed to go home at ten."

"It's possible she might be back by then."

"What if she's not?"

"Good question. You may want to call Rowena Hoxley." She looked from Sherry to Eleanor. The older woman's face was flushed and her eyes red. She held a handkerchief in one hand.

"Forgive me for being slow," Eleanor said, "but I don't understand. The police can't possibly think Habibah killed Callie."

"Apparently they're exploring the notion," Leo said.

Eleanor stumbled over to the couch and sat heavily. "Why? Why would Habibah do that?" She buried her face in the hanky. Though she didn't make a sound, her shoulders shook.

Sherry stepped closer and patted her on the shoulder. "I'm so sorry, Eleanor. So sorry..." She met Leo's eyes. "We've been talking about who could have done this, but Habibah was never anyone we suspected. I'd have expected them to haul off Walter before anyone else."

"Why Walter?" Leo asked.

"He didn't much care for Callie. Or Eleanor. In fact, he's quite the mis... What's that word?"

Muffled by the hanky, Eleanor said, "Misogynist. He's probably more correctly classified as a misanthrope. He doesn't seem to like anyone." She wiped her face and sniffled. "Walter has always been rude, but we avoided him. I agree with Sherry. He's a much more likely culprit than Habibah."

Leo couldn't comment on that, but the brief exchange she'd had with Walter hadn't impressed her. "I'd like to talk to you, Sherry. Could we step into Rowena's office for a bit?"

Sherry leaned down. "Eleanor? I'll be gone a little while. I'll come back and check on you when Ms. Reese is done, all right?"

Eleanor straightened up and shifted to sit closer to the front of the sofa, composing herself with a speed that amazed Leo. "I'll be fine, Sherry. Just fine. You don't need to trouble yourself with me."

"Oh, please. You're never a bit of trouble. I'll be back in a while."

Leo followed Sherry out to the front foyer and into the manager's office. "Thanks for taking the time now."

"Nothing much happens this time of the evening anyway." Sherry slid in behind the neatly organized desk. The paperwork that had littered the surface earlier was gone, leaving only an inbox, a blotter, a photo that Leo couldn't see, and a lamp, which Sherry clicked on.

The interview with the aide took a solid twenty minutes, but Leo found out nothing notable. On the subject of Habibah leaving the sing-along, Sherry said, "I'm clueless. We'd pulled the piano out a bit, so that I was at an angle and able to see the residents, but the piano is tall. I didn't pay a bit of attention to anything but the sing-along."

"Did you have a view of the foyer or common area?"

"Not at all. Even if I had, I might not have seen anything. I'm a pretty good pianist, but I have to work extra hard to read the music if I want to keep up the pace. I was concentrating on playing, not on anything else."

"Who do you think killed Callie Trimble?"

Sherry shook her head slowly. "I don't know. I can't believe it happened. The only thing that makes sense is that someone came over the wall to rob the place, and Callie interrupted them. No way did Habibah do it."

WHEN LEO ARRIVED at Walter Green's doorway, he was watching a new television program — some crime show she didn't recognize.

"Mr. Green?"

He glanced her way, irritation on his face. "Oh. You again."

"Yes, I'd like to have a word with you."

"At the commercial."

Leo strode across the room and clicked off the television set.

The recliner extension thumped down, and the old man sat forward in his seat. "Hey! You can't do that."

She stood in front of the TV and stared him down. When he looked away, she said, "Shall we get this over with?"

"You ain't got any right to come in here and disrupt a person's life."

"That's where you're wrong, sir. If you don't take the time to talk to me right now, I'm going to slap a closure order on this facility and you'll be moving to a motel at your own expense."

"Ridiculous."

Now that he was mad, Leo heard a drawl in his words and wondered where he'd been raised. He certainly didn't have the Minnesota accent.

"You ain't the cops."

"No, I'm much worse. I'm with the State, and if I don't get some answers to this murder pretty soon, the Rivers' Edge license will be suspended, and you'll have to move."

He let out a disgusted huff and crossed his arms over the long-sleeved shirt he wore. Underneath, his t-shirt was yellowed around the collar. His white hair was thinning, and uneven white stubble on his chin and jowls showed he hadn't shaved for a couple of days.

She stepped away from the television, sat on the orange loveseat, and took the tape recorder out of the bag. She didn't bother to hunt for a plug-in. Batteries would have to do. She'd cover the warnings and details afterward, too. She wanted to get as much information as possible before he clammed up.

"What do you know about the death of Callie Trimble?"

"Absolutely nothin' at all."

"You were next door in the TV area at the time of her death. Did you see anyone pass by?"

"I was asleep."

"When did you awaken?"

"I dunno. When the cops came, I guess."

"With your room right here, next to the TV area, why weren't you watching this television?"

He scowled. "A fellow gets shack-wacky after a while. I'm stuck here in this godforsaken damn dinky room." He glanced around. "Why sit in here watching the walls close in on me? Place gives me the flying twitches."

"Why stay at Rivers' Edge at all then?"

"Where the hell else would I go?"

"I see. Where did you grow up, Mr. Green?"

He stared at her, his face hard-edged and gradually turning red. "What the hell does that have to do with anything?"

"Background."

"You don't need no background on me. Get off your dead butt and find the killer, then ask *him* about his background."

"What makes you think it was a man?"

He coughed out a chuckle. "You get a load of the size of that woman?"

"What was your opinion of Callie Trimble?"

"I don't bother with opinions of people like her," he scoffed.

"You didn't like her?"

"Didn't know her. Didn't want to get to know her. Not that other one, either. Both of them unnatural, if you know what I mean. You married?"

"My marital status has nothing to do with this murder case."

"I see you got a wedding ring. S'pose some butchy woman could've given it to you as easy as a man."

Leo refused to rise to the bait, though she was sorely tempted. Instead, she kept her voice calm. "You do know that statements like that do nothing but draw suspicion upon you?"

"Who? Me? I had nothing to do with any killing. I was asleep, and everybody knows that."

"Actually, you could easily have gone down the hall, suffocated Mrs. Trimble, and crept back to your chair. A big man like you could have done the job in a couple of minutes."

"But I didn't. I told you that."

"Why should anyone believe you? As far as I can tell, you're the one wild card, the one person here who held a grudge against Mrs. Trimble and Mrs. Sinclair. You had motive, you had opportunity, and—"

"You—" He lurched up out of the recliner, bowlegged and shaking. "You get the hell out of my room. Get out!" He pointed a gnarled finger, his body quivering with rage.

"I suggest you sit back down, Mr. Green."

"I will not!"

"Threatening me does nothing to help your situation."

"The hell with you!"

Leo let out a sigh. She was weary of this battle of wills but not ready to capitulate. "Please, Mr. Green. Sit down and finish this. For the record, I'm not enjoying it anymore than you are. And whether you liked her or not, a woman is dead. An elderly woman who deserved better than to be killed so callously. So please, let's get this over with."

His arm dropped to his side. He shuffled backwards until his ankles touched the base of the recliner, then he dropped heavily into the chair, his knob-knuckled hand searching for the handle that controlled the footrest. He flipped it up and settled back, crossing his arms over his chest.

"Thank you," she said. "Is there anyone here who you'd suspect of this crime?"

"Not a one. All the ladies who work here are just that—ladies."

"In the last week or two, have you seen anyone or anything unusual? A workman, a strange delivery, unusual visitors?"

"Nope."

"Are you aware that Habibah Okello has been taken into custody by the police?"

"One of those little Negro girls?"

Leo resisted the urge to stand up and smack him on the head with the recorder. "Yes. She's originally from Kenya. Do you have any reason to think she might have committed murder?"

He didn't answer for a moment. Instead, the words that ran through Leo's mind were *Mr. Green in the Library with the Pillow*. She stifled a snort and closed her eyes. Realizing how tired she was, she took a deep breath and steadied herself. Walter Green sat in profile, worrying his lips between his teeth.

"Both them little Negro girls is too dinky. Any chance they could've got up a gang of their people to come in and do it for 'em?"

Leo took a deep breath. There were so many things wrong with that response—and she wasn't thinking about his grammar. "Where did you grow up, Mr. Green?"

"Ironton, Ohio."

"Is that close to Cleveland?"

"Not a bit. It's about the farthest south you can get before shambling over into Kentucky. Near the West Virginia border."

"You lived there your whole life?"

"Until I got laid off from the railroad in my fifties." He sighed. "Then I moved up here where my son and daughter-in-law were living. Got a job in South Saint Paul working in the stockyards. Then the assholes laid most everybody off, so I worked catch as catch can 'til I could retire. Thought I'd live like a pauper on the pittance the Social Security morons were handing out, but my great-uncle died and left me a bundle. So here I am, living in the lap of no luxury at all."

"Your son still lives in the vicinity?"

"He got a job in Chicago two years ago."

"You didn't want to move to be near him?"

"Nah. You got any idea how expensive that town is? 'Sides, I'm settled, got all my stuff here."

Leo took stock of the room. As far as she could see, he could pack up his things in the backseat of any SUV and buy a new recliner and bed elsewhere. But she did know what it was like to find a comfortable place and never want to leave it. If she hadn't been persuaded by Daria, she'd still be living in a cozy two-bedroom house off West Seventh in Saint Paul.

"Can you look me in the eye, Mr. Green, and tell me you didn't kill Callie Trimble?"

"Without a doubt."

His gaze met hers, his expression mocking. Everybody lies, she thought. He could be lying through his teeth.

She rose. "I hope I don't have to bother you again, but if anything else comes to mind, I'd appreciate it if you'd notify the police and also let me know."

"Oh, yeah," he said mockingly, "you'll be the first to know." He leaned forward and fumbled around in the cushion he sat on and came up with a TV remote. As Leo left the room, a commercial for Dodge trucks blared out.

She paused in the entryway and organized things in her valise so she could zipper it shut. Everybody lies, she thought. Some of them to preserve their pride, some to protect others. Who was lying in order to shield himself from a murder charge?

At home, she entered the dark house quietly and locked the door behind her. She set her valise in the entryway, not bothering to empty it. She was bone-tired, it was well past eleven, and she was going straight to bed.

She passed the living room area on the way to the stairs and was surprised to catch sight of a pinprick of red light out of the corner of her eye. At the same time, she smelled cigarette smoke.

She crossed the hall and stopped in the doorway. Now that her eyes were adjusting, she saw the outline of Daria's head over the top of the leather armchair, a cigarette in one hand and a glass held in the other.

"Daria?" She reached for the light switch, but Daria interrupted her.

"Stop," she slurred. "No light."

"I thought you quit smoking."

"Yeah. After tonight."

"What's wrong?"

"Everything and nothing." She leaned forward and put out the cigarette in an ashtray on the coffee table. "I was an asshole earlier tonight."

The admission brought tears to Leo's eyes. A tight band around her chest released, and she realized how nervous she'd been feeling since their fight. "Come to bed, Daria. We've both got a long day ahead of us."

"No shit." She rose, staggered before recovering, and limped toward her. She was in stocking feet, but had stripped down to briefs and a t-shirt. At the doorway, Leo folded her into her arms. She smelled of Scotch and stale smoke.

"I'm sorry, Leo."

"We're both stressed right now."

"Yeah, but that's no reason for me to take it out on you."

Chapter Ten

ELEANOR HADN'T SLEPT well since Callie died, and she knew this night would be no different. She didn't bother to change into her pajamas, only taking off her sandals and lying down fully dressed on the coverlet of the double bed in Callie's apartment. She lay in a languid half-stupor, not fully awake, but not asleep either. An occasional tear trickled down her face, and she roused to brush her cheek dry.

The air conditioning was off, and the window facing the street was open partway. The breeze that gently wafted in was warm, but not yet uncomfortable.

Voices raised in the corridor brought her out of her torpor. She jerked upright. She couldn't hear distinct words, but one voice was deep and rumbled while the other was shrill and female.

Fumbling around on the bedside table, she located the cordless phone and picked it up. Barefoot, she went to the door, unlocked it, and peeped into the hall. In front of the TV Room, Eleanor saw Rowena Hoxley's back. She was dwarfed by the looming figure of a tall man in a powder-blue tracksuit.

He ran a hand through curly blond hair and in a weary voice said, "Tell me where she is."

Rowena held her hands up. "She's not here. I'm sure she'll call you. How did you get in?"

"Please. Nobody answered when I knocked."

"You should have rung the bell. One of the residents would have heard it and come."

"I didn't want to wake up the whole complex. Where were you? Why didn't someone answer?"

"I wasn't here yet, Chuck. If no one answered the bell, how did you get in?"

"Hopped the wall."

Eleanor stepped into the hall. "Excuse me."

He glanced past Rowena and squinted. "Hi, Mrs. Sinclair."

She strode down the hall. "What's the matter?"

"I've been waiting on Habibah for nearly two hours. Granted, she works late quite often, but this is ridiculous." He leaned down slightly and addressed Rowena. "If you're working her a double shift, that's fine. Let me see her for a few moments, and I'll be on my way."

Tight-lipped, Rowena glanced at Eleanor. Ridiculous was

right, Eleanor thought. Why couldn't Rowena tell him where his girlfriend was? From the expression of fear on Rowena's face, Eleanor could tell that she didn't want Chuck informed. Too bad.

"Chuck," she said, "the police came by earlier tonight and took Habibah down to the station to question her."

His handsome face went blank for a moment, then he frowned. "What? Why?"

"They think she might know something about Callie's death."

"What? But—but—"

Eleanor took his arm and steered him down the hallway, toward the foyer. "I wish I'd known you were waiting for her. I could have told you where she is. Go to her. Regardless of what she's done, she needs somebody to help her."

Chuck stopped. "Oh, my God, she'll be so scared. Where do I go? What do I do?"

"I don't know. Let's go find the phone number for the police station. Rowena," she called out.

"Right behind you."

"We need your office."

"Whatever. Go ahead. Phone book's in the upper right-hand drawer."

Eleanor went in first and sat down behind the desk while Chuck hovered like a giant pterodactyl, his eyes glittery with anger.

"Here we go," she said, offering him her cordless phone.

"Got my own, ma'am." He held up a shiny silver cell.

She read out the number for him, and soon he carried on similar conversations with four different people. With each new person, his voice raised a few more decibels. When he finally hung up, he said, "I can't believe this. They won't tell me where she is."

"You need a lawyer, Chuck."

Breathing fast he said, "Yes. Good idea. Great idea." He fumbled with his cell phone before pressing it to his ear. "Come on, Jamal. Pick up... Pick up!"

Someone answered, and Chuck stepped out of the office carrying on an increasingly panicked conversation. Eleanor waited in the office chair and watched him pace. After a moment, he snapped the phone shut and leaned into the office. "A basketball buddy of mine is a lawyer. He's going to call back. Oh, Jesus, why didn't someone tell me? There's no way Habibah had anything to do with your friend's death. No way, ma'am."

Eleanor tried to communicate kindness in her next words. "People surprise us sometimes. Perhaps Habibah was trying to be merciful."

"No, no, no!" He bent forward and put his palms flat on the

desktop. "She no way killed anybody. She was on the phone with me at the time."

Eleanor admired the young man for his loyalty to his girlfriend. Such concern was admirable, perhaps even unusual in this day and age, but she doubted that Chuck could provide an alibi with such a weak story.

"What?" he said. "You don't believe me?"

"I'm not the one you have to convince."

He gripped the phone in his hand so tightly that Eleanor wondered if he could actually crush it. "Every night, whenever they have the sing-along, she always cuts out and calls me. I guarantee she was talking to me. We were having a—a—kind of a personal conversation," he said and his face reddened, "if you know what I mean. They can check my phone records."

Chuck's forehead broke out in perspiration. He unzipped his sweat-suit top to reveal a maroon U of M Golden Gophers t-shirt. Before he could say anything else, his phone rang, and he flipped it open before the ring concluded.

"Yeah? Okay, I'll be there in ten."

He bolted from the office calling out, "Thanks for your help, Mrs. Sinclair." His truck roared to life, and he peeled out of the parking lot. She rose, shut out the office light, and found Rowena Hoxley sitting on the couch in the community area.

"This place is a sieve," Rowena said. "Any damn fool can get in here. The dining room and yours and Willie's apartments are locked up, but someone unlocked and opened Norma's windows."

"You're going to have to install some sort of security system."

"Don't you think I know that?" Rowena slapped her fingers against her mouth and muttered. "I'm sorry. I'm so sorry. I didn't mean that how it came out."

"We're all tired. We're all afraid. Don't worry about it."

Rowena hefted herself from the couch and staggered forward. "Yeah, I'm beyond worn out. And I suppose I'll have to report this to that woman from Human Services. She'll probably close us down, and I'll get fired. All of you will have to move. Oh, God."

"You're exhausted and not thinking straight. Why don't you go sleep for a while in the staff room, and I'll sit out here and keep an eye on things."

"I couldn't let you do that."

"Sure you could. I wasn't sleeping anyway, which was why I heard you in the hall. Seems like I'll never sleep again. You go catch forty winks. I'll wake you if anything important happens."

Rowena dragged herself around the furniture and over to the entrance to the staff quarters. "Thank you, Eleanor. Get me up in an hour or two, and I'll be good as new."

Eleanor doubted that. Neither she nor Rowena would recover that quickly. She sank down into the capacious sofa and thought about her companion, her lover, her world—about their time together, the way they used to laugh at puns and silly jokes, the thousands of cups of tea they'd shared. And now it was over. Never again. She closed her eyes and forced back the tears.

A FAINT HUMMING awakened Eleanor. She straightened up, and pain shot through her neck. She'd fallen asleep, her head tipped against the corner of the couch, and now her neck muscles were screaming.

Sun shone through the slitted windows on either side of the front door, and the light was on in Rowena Hoxley's office. Eleanor rose and shuffled toward the office, rubbing the stiffness out of her neck and right shoulder. She stepped into the doorway, but instead of finding Rowena, Claire Ryerson stood next to the desk with a sheaf of file folders.

In profile, she reminded Eleanor of a student from many years earlier. Cissy had been blonde with beautiful sparkling eyes and a movie star's grin. She was the prom queen, the homecoming queen, royalty in every way, and scores of boys wanted to date her. Cissy had come up to Eleanor in the grocery store just this last Christmas, and Eleanor hadn't recognized the haggard woman with lank hair and a hangdog attitude. Time sometimes played terrible tricks on beautiful girls.

But this woman was fresh and fit. Her navy-blue-striped pants matched her navy jacket, and the gold buttons on the jacket were exactly the same as buttons adorning her open-toe slide sandals. Her white silk blouse fit perfectly, accentuating a shapely figure. She turned to face Eleanor.

"Oh, Claire. I expected Rowena," Eleanor said.

"Good morning. I need to talk to Rowena. Do you know where she is?"

"Let me see if she's in the staff room."

Rowena Hoxley lay face up on the lower bunk, breathing heavily with one arm flung over her brow. Eleanor called out her name softly, and the manager jerked upward. She sat up too fast and nearly bonked her head on the bed frame. By the time she managed to slide out and get to her feet, she was awake but disoriented.

"What time is it?"

"I don't know, but Claire Ryerson is waiting in your office."

"Oh, shit." She leaned against the laundry tub and gazed into the mirror above it. "I look like hell."

Eleanor had to agree. Rowena's shirt and pants were rumpled, and her dyed blonde hair was flattened on one side and sticking straight out on the other. What little makeup she'd been wearing seemed to have rubbed off under one eye giving her the appearance of a prizefighting raccoon.

Eleanor left her and returned to the front foyer. The overhead light in the tiny office was on, but Claire Ryerson was no longer in there. Eleanor peeked through the window of her mailbox. Once again it was empty. The heap of mail on the entryway desk threatened to spill over, so she set to work sorting it all into piles.

When she finished, she and Callie — and every other resident — had received a tire store flyer and a Target circular, and the other occupants had various letters, bills, and targeted mailings. But neither she nor Callie had anything of consequence. This is ridiculous, she thought. I'll be speaking to the mail carrier, that's for sure. And she might as well go off to the bank later, as well. She needed to transfer funds from savings to checking so she could pay for funeral arrangements.

The thought swept all semblance of energy from her, and her legs felt heavy, as though she were wading through mud.

Chapter Eleven

BLEARY-EYED AND bone-weary, Leo rose Thursday morning feeling the pounding beat of a headache. No amount of coffee made her feel fully awake, and after a button popped off her blouse, she pulled a more casual swoop-necked shirt over her head.

Daria had tossed and turned all night, and when she joined Leo at the breakfast table, she said, "We're a real pair, aren't we? Welcome to the International House of Zombies."

By the time Leo entered the DHS building, the headache had abated, but she still felt fatigued. Perhaps working most of the day before from eight in the morning to eleven p.m. with only meal breaks hadn't been such a good idea.

She sat down to use the phone. The secretary at Dr. Spence's office was far more chipper than Leo could stand. She gritted her teeth and listened to the woman's chirpy voice, then scheduled an appointment for the following Friday. The woman took her cell phone number and told her she'd call if there were any cancellations.

That done, Leo rose and made her way to Thom Thoreson's cubicle.

When he caught sight of Leo, Thom bid her good morning, but he didn't seem any more awake than Leo felt. He asked, "How's the investigation going over at the old folks' home? You wrap it up?"

"Sorry to say, but no."

"Bummer."

"Do you know if Fred's going to be in today?"

Thom lowered his voice. "He usually doesn't call in sick two days in a row. I thought I saw his car in the lot, so yes, I think he's here."

"That'd be nice. As far as this situation at Rivers' Edge goes, can you tell me if this kind of crime is a common occurrence?"

"A murder? No. You'll find a number of deaths in places like that, but not a lot of old people get killed unless it's some sort of accident. Or overdose."

Leo debated for a moment about how much uncertainty to admit, but she quickly cut off the struggle. "How am I supposed to know if the place should be closed or not?"

Thom shrugged. "All I can tell you is that we rarely shut anybody down unless there's gross misconduct or ongoing danger."

"The problem is I can't tell if there's ongoing danger. The place isn't necessarily secure, but it's no different from many apartment houses. Once thieves get over the garden wall or through the front door, they'll find many of the residents leave their doors unlocked or even wide open. Management can't control that. But then again, management gives these people the impression that the place is more secure than it really is. So is it their fault? Do I cite them? What usually happens in cases like this?"

"This sort of situation isn't common, I guess. We've got well over two hundred licensed, assisted-living or independent-living places in Hennepin County alone, and I don't recall this kind of thing happening since I've been here."

"I had no clue there were so many."

"Tip of the iceberg. Across the state there are thousands of licensed, registered, or certified health care providers like Rivers' Edge. We've also got housing with services, in-home care, hospice, nursing homes, and so much other service-related stuff going on that you wouldn't believe it. Old people or disabled people—hell, anyone not in the peak of health—can be vulnerable to mismanagement or unscrupulous providers."

"I don't understand why this department is hardly staffed then. With so many licensed providers and such a high volume of problems and complaints, why don't you have dozens of investigators in the division?"

Thom shook his head. "Don't you cops ask the same question about your personnel? Bottom line is it's not a priority with the legislature or the budget bigwigs. Never enough staff to go around. It's not usually quite this big a gigantic nightmare, but with so many staff out on medical leave, the place is going to hell in a hurry."

"No kidding," Leo said.

Someone was huffing toward them, and Leo stepped back from the cubicle doorway to see Fred Baldur proceeding down the aisle like a snoring sleepwalker. She turned back to Thom and mouthed, "Fred." Thom rolled his eyes and spun the wheelchair around to face the computer.

"Leona! Are you done with the Rivers' Edge investigation? I don't see the final report on my desk."

"Well, Fred, nobody has acquainted me with any kind of final report form, so even if I wanted to, I couldn't be finished. And I still have at least one interview left."

"Oh." His face was slightly greasy as though he'd overdone it with some kind of lotion. Once again, he wore a wrinkled light-gray suit. Was it the same one? Or another just like it? Leo couldn't tell. Today he wore a wide, unfashionable black tie with a huge knot. Leo would like to have grabbed it and swung the man around a few times.

"I'll try to get this thing wrapped up today," she said.

"Was it a random break-in? Or an internal job?"

She wanted to say that the murder of an elderly woman was not a "job," but to hasten matters, she simply told him she didn't know and went on to explain that an aide had been arrested.

Baldur beamed at her, his yellow teeth gleaming under the fluorescent lights. "Well, now, that's such good news. Wrap it up, why don't you. Can you finish that last interview by noon?"

"I'll try."

"Excellent." He rubbed his hands together like a pasty, oversized praying mantis. "Tell you what. Let's meet at Mickey's Diner after the lunch rush, and we can plan your next investigation. How about one o'clock?"

"Okay." She wondered how much planning the next case would take—and why—but she was too weary to ask. Before she could say anything more, he whirled and marched off with more energy than Leo had seen him display to date. She peeked back into Thom's cubicle to find him beckoning. Leo stepped closer.

Thom whispered, "Wow, he smiled. He must've scored last night."

"What?" She squelched a giggle.

"Let me correct my terminology, because I can see you don't believe he got laid. Look at the guy." He snickered, then recovered, but his face still wore a merry expression. "He's always all cheery whenever he has good luck at the casino. Bet he scored a jackpot."

"I see." So the efficiency of her colleague's workdays would be wrapped up in his gambling losses and wins? She didn't find that a pleasant prospect and turned to go.

"Wait a sec, Leona." Thom wheeled the chair over to the desk surface, scooped something up, and spun around. "I ordered you DHS business cards. Here are some temporary ones. Write your name and your temp number. Monique will let you know when the regular ones come in. Usually takes a week or so."

"Thank you. Guess I'd better get going. Maybe this'll be my last visit to Rivers' Edge."

"Good luck with that. You'll probably need it."

ON THE WAY to Rivers' Edge, Leo's cell phone rang. One-handed, she dug it out and fumbled to turn it on.

"Hello, this is Fran at Dr. Spence's office. I know it's short notice, but we just got a cancellation for a nine o'clock. Are you interested?"

Leo debated for a moment and checked her watch. "I might not be there right at nine. I'm on the road toward Minneapolis and have to turn around. I can be there shortly after nine, though."

"That'll be fine. See you soon."

Traffic back into Saint Paul wasn't as bad as Leo expected. She rolled into the parking lot before nine and crossed the threshold to check in at precisely nine a.m. She sat alone in the waiting room for several minutes. With increasing irritation she watched the clock.

At twenty after nine, the nurse finally called her in and began the process of checking her vision and filling in her chart. By the time the eye doctor arrived, it was half past nine, and Leo had to stifle her crankiness.

"Hello, Leona," Dr. Spence said heartily. "You're having some headaches, ay?" He picked up her chart. "How long since your last eye exam? Ah, it's been a couple of years." He prattled on awhile, then proceeded to have her do some of the very same vision tests the nurse had completed. She wondered why. Had the nurse forgotten to write down the results?

Spence was a big man, not fat, but muscular with beefy arms, broad shoulders, and shaggy brown hair that he often brushed out of his eyes. He lowered himself to a padded rolling chair. "Your vision is 20/20. Are you having any trouble with your reading?"

"No, not really."

"Hold this card here. Okay, what's the lowest line you can read?"

She could see all of them clearly, including the bottom one.

"Excellent. Let's get you dilated, and I'll take a peek."

"Can't you examine my eyes without doing that?"

"Sorry. I have to dilate the pupils or I can't see in."

"I won't be able to drive."

"Sure you will. I'll give you some of those handy-dandy plastic dark glasses. I've got some terrific high quality ones that let in very little light. Lean back."

She let out a sigh of exasperation but allowed him to apply the drops.

"Relax and I'll have you out of here lickety-split." He tucked a tissue in her hand. "I'll give you ten minutes to dilate."

Leo dabbed at her stinging eyes. The dim room blurred in and out. She closed her eyes, remembering why she hated eye exams. It could be hours before her vision returned to normal. Daria was right about zombies. For the rest of the day, that's exactly how she'd look—like she was on drugs.

But if Dr. Spence could figure out what was wrong with her vision and quickly correct it, perhaps she could get Daniels to run her through relays at the firing range again, pass her quals, and resume her regular job before the end of the year. Maybe by Halloween. She couldn't imagine staying with DHS one minute more than she had to. She belonged on the street, directing her unit. While some people might think that police work was dangerous and unpredictable, Leo didn't feel that way. She usually felt gloriously in control. Every situation—whether it was a domestic dispute, a robbery in progress, or a drive-by shooting—was an opportunity to come on the scene and impose order. She got a sizable shot of adrenaline every time she and her officers mastered a difficult or dangerous situation. She knew they were often lucky, but they were also well trained and effective.

Every day on the street was a mini-battle, and every night that she came home safe was a triumph. All through her teen years, she remembered Dad Wallace arriving after his shift and announcing, "Another successful day of upholding the law."

She and Kate would run to him and ask what exciting things had happened. Most days he said, "Routine. Nothing of note."

But sometimes he'd sit down to the dinner Mom Wallace made and regale them with tales of capturing crooks. She and Kate were fascinated by it all and asked pointed questions about shootings and assaults that usually had Mom Wallace interrupting to say, "Not at dinner, girls. We're trying to eat."

Kate wanted nothing more than to follow in her father's footsteps, and Leo hadn't lived with the Wallaces for long before she felt exactly the same. She and Kate both served honorably in patrol, took the sergeant's exam at the first possible opportunity, and passed with flying colors. Since she'd joined the police force a year earlier than Kate, Leo had more seniority and made sergeant on her first application. Twenty-two months later, Kate achieved that goal as well.

The door to the exam room flapped open, and Dr. Spence came in. "Let's take a gander, shall we."

He swung the slit-lamp toward her, and she settled herself into the chin rest. The light he shone into her right eye was bright, and her eyes watered slightly. Abruptly, he shifted his lamp over to the left eye. After a moment, he flipped it back and shifted again.

"Hmmm…" he said.

"You seeing anything unusual?" she asked.

"Give me a few seconds here."

Much more than seconds passed. He put a pad of paper on his knee and scribbled notes. Though he thoroughly examined her left eye, he spent the most time on the right one.

After what seemed like ten minutes, he said, "You can relax now." He pulled the slit-lamp away and slumped down on the rolling chair.

When he didn't turn on the light or speak, Leo felt a stab of fear in her chest. "Is there a problem, Doc?"

"You've had severe eye pain?"

"I guess. It's been some regular headaches. Behind my eye."

"More on the right side than the left?"

"Yes, I suppose."

"Are you seeing flashing lights?"

"No."

"Floaters?"

"No, not really. When I get the headache, my vision sometimes gets blurry, especially if I'm trying to concentrate."

"So, you're focusing, concentrating hard —"

"Yeah — like when I'm shooting at the range. Even through ear protection, I always get an immediate headache. In fact, lately the smell of the cordite is enough to set off the throbbing. Is it from something with my eyes? Is there something seriously wrong?"

"Yes, Leona. You have a mass in your right eye."

"A mass?"

"A tumor."

"You must be mistaken."

"I wish I was. The tumor is sizable, so much so that I think it's periodically pressing against your lens and causing irregular astigmatism."

"I don't understand."

He set the pad of paper on the counter. "I've never seen such a large tumor. No wonder you're in pain." He slid his chair around to her side and covered her forearm with a meaty hand. "I have to tell you, in my eighteen years as an ophthalmologist, I've seen at least a half-dozen cases like this, and in every instance, it's been choroidal melanoma."

"Melanoma — isn't that something like skin cancer?"

"Not exactly. Our eyes have a spongy membrane called the choroid that lies between the white of the eye and the retina. The choroid passes nutrients to the retina. Most people never have a problem with the choroid, but something has happened that's caused a tumor to grow in yours."

"Can you take it out?"

"No. Not without destroying the eye."

All the air went out of Leo's diaphragm, and she suddenly had trouble breathing.

"That's not the worst of it. If it isn't treated, choroidal melanoma can spread to other parts of the body. Your mother had cancer, right?"

Leo nodded, unable to speak.

"We don't want to take any chances." He squeezed her arm

and let go. "I'm going to send you to the best ocular oncologist in the Cities. My receptionist will get you an appointment right away. They can do echography and fluorescein angiography..."

He went on, talking about dyes, and patterns, and sound waves, but Leo could no longer take it in. Her mother died of ovarian cancer when Leo was one week short of her eleventh birthday. Elizabeth Reese's death was terrible, a slow, anguished, painful process. Was this to be Leo's fate as well?

Dr. Spence continued speaking, but it was like hearing distorted babble in an LSD dream. Not until he helped her to her feet did the distortion cease.

"Come out to the appointment desk, and Fran'll get you set up with Dr. Marvin Winslow. He's the region's most experienced specialist and surgeon. Don't worry, Leona." He patted her arm and led her through the exam room door. "I'm sure he'll be able to devise a treatment."

On her feet, she snapped into high alert. If she had cancer, there wasn't anything that could be done, was there? Someone may as well shoot out her right eye. She took a deep breath and tried to banish the vision of a black-clad gunman taking aim at her.

By the time she lurched out of the office and toward her car, her valise contained an appointment sheet and referral documents for Dr. Winslow, and she wore a pair of heavy-duty plastic wraparound glasses to thwart bright light. Despite the glasses, the light still made her eyes water—or were those tears? She wasn't thinking clearly, and the hair on the back of her neck stood on end. She felt so edgy she wanted to scream.

In her car she sat in the heat until she was sweating. Like a robot, she started the car and put the AC on high.

The time was ten o'clock, and in one hour, she'd been sucked into a vortex over which she had absolutely no control.

Chapter Twelve

LEO DIALED, AND the phone rang five times with no answer. Near tears, she pulled the cell phone away from her ear, but before she pressed the END button, she heard a tinny "Hello."

"Kate?"

"Hey, sis. I'm on patrol. Just got back in the car. What's up?"

"I'm sitting here in a state of complete shock."

"About what?"

"I may have—I have cancer."

"What? Where are you?"

"In the eye doctor's parking lot."

"At Central Medical?"

"Yeah."

"I'm coming over. ETA ten minutes."

The phone went dead. Leo sat holding it in a shaking hand and feeling such intense gratitude toward Kate that new tears sprang into her eyes.

The childhood friendship between Leo and Kate had been forged during a summer of grief and anguish. Fourth grade had ended for Leo, third for Kate, and the two of them were in awe of Kate's sixteen-year-old brother, Paul. They hung around the Wallace garage watching Paul work on a dinged-up Honda motorcycle. Leo wanted nothing more than to learn to ride, but Kate was downright obsessive about it. All she talked about was the motorcycle and how she wanted one of her own. She peppered Paul with questions night and day until he instituted rules whenever Leo and Kate stepped foot in the garage. "You can each ask one question, then it's quiet time. You can watch, but no talking."

Paul's fingers were nimble, whether he was cleaning a spark plug or disassembling the gearbox. Fascinated, Leo and Kate handed tools to Paul, held parts, swept the garage, ran errands — anything in order to encourage him to let them be a part of the process.

The day he finally kick-started the bike's engine, Leo stood coughing in the exhaust and feeling a thrum of excitement course through her veins.

"Take us for a ride," Kate shouted over the revving engine.

"Nuh-uh." Over the loud motor, he said, "No can do. Mom

would kill me."

"Please," Kate begged.

"Hand me my helmet."

He grinned as he strapped on the helmet with one hand and put the Honda in gear. With a jerk, he shot out of the garage and braked at the end of the driveway. Kate ran behind him shouting his name.

Paul glanced over his shoulder, waved, and pulled out.

Kate stopped in the street, looking forlornly at his retreating back. She stamped her foot. "I wanted to go with him."

"He deserved the first ride to himself. That's okay, isn't it?"

"I guess."

Kate's mother called out to her from the front porch. "Lunchtime, kiddo."

"I gotta go," Kate said, "but I'll be watching for him. He better teach us how to drive it later today."

Leo doubted that Kate would be allowed to ride the motorcycle by herself, but she wasn't going to be the one to shatter Kate's dream. In a hopeful tone, she said, "He won't be gone long. We'll get a ride later." Kate ran in her house, and Leo went across the street to hers.

But Paul didn't come back.

The Wallaces weren't home all afternoon, so it wasn't until after her dinner that Leo realized something was wrong. Through her front window, she watched the Wallaces' paneled Ford station wagon wheel into their driveway. Two of Kate's four brothers got out of the car, heads down, and went to the front porch. She squinted. Was Robbie crying? Mr. and Mrs. Wallace moved slowly, lumbering toward the house. Kate emerged last, her face red and her hands balled up into fists. Like a sleepwalker, she crossed the lawn and went into their side yard to shinny up the linden tree.

Leo went to her mother's room. Elizabeth Reese lay on her side, her legs tangled in a mauve-colored sheet. Her eyes were closed, and her eyelids looked bruised, as though they'd been smudged with blue ink. They fluttered open, and her mother reached for her.

"What is it, honey?"

Leo stepped closer and took her mother's hand. "Something's wrong at Kate's house."

Her mother winced. "Like what? Not something dangerous, like a fire—"

"Not like that, Mom. I don't know."

"Go check it out, then." She released Leo's hand and gave her a light tap on the hip. "Come back and report in."

"Do you need something first? Water? Something to eat?"

"No, baby, I'm fine." She shifted and settled on her side with a wince of pain. "I'll just...sleep...a little more."

Leo grasped her elbows in her hands and pulled her arms tight against her middle. She watched as her mother's breathing evened out and the pained expression on her face faded. Only then did Leo tiptoe from the room.

Outside, the sun was low in the sky. A mosquito whined past Leo's ear, and she twitched. The air was warm and heavy, like a blanket pressing down during a bad dream. She approached the linden tree in the Wallaces' yard, searching the branches for her friend. She caught sight of a tennis shoe in the farthest reaches, much higher than the two of them usually climbed.

"Kate?" No answer. "Kate, what's wrong?"

Nothing.

Leo's stomach turned over. Never before had Kate snubbed her or failed at least to recognize that she was there. Leo wondered what she'd done. Had she upset Kate somehow? She couldn't think of how, though.

A window on the main floor in the Wallaces' house shrieked open. "Hello, Leo," Mrs. Wallace said. "Is Kate in the tree?"

"Yes." Leo could see Mrs. Wallace's outline through the screen. She wanted to ask what was going on, but something held her back.

After a moment, Mrs. Wallace called, "Kate, come in now. It'll be dark soon." Leo waited, feeling awkward.

"Katherine Michelle Wallace. Please come down from that tree right now. I said right now."

Not a sound came from high in the tree. Leo said, "I don't think she's coming."

The window whooshed shut.

After a deep breath, Leo grabbed a tree limb and pulled herself up. Branch by branch, she climbed high into the tree until she came to where the trunk narrowed. She paused when her head was even with Kate's sneakers.

"Kate?" She tapped on a scraped-up shoe. "Hey, Kate. Talk to me." She wormed her way around the trunk of the tree, found another toehold to push up from, and squirmed onto a sturdy limb until she was sitting even with her friend. Kate's face was pressed against a forearm resting on a branch at shoulder level.

"What's wrong?"

Kate lifted her head. Her face was red and tear-streaked. Her nose was running, and her blonde hair was mussed. A thin twig the size of a toothpick stuck out of the mop, over her ear.

"Please tell me. What happened?"

"Paul wrecked the motorcycle."

"What?"

"He crashed." She coughed out a sob. "A truck hit him by the 7-11. He crashed, and he died."

"Died?" Leo whispered. "Paul's dead?"

"What am I going to do without him?" The words came out strangled, as though Kate were choking. More tears rolled down her pale cheeks. She tried to wipe her face on the sleeve of her t-shirt succeeding only in smearing tears everywhere. "I wanna die, too. I could just let go."

She brought both hands up and pulled on her hair, letting out little gasps as she cried. Leo shot out her hand and steadied her. She gripped the lightweight, braided belt Kate wore. "If you let go, then I do, too."

Kate met Leo's gaze for the first time, her blue eyes bloodshot and miserable. "Don't be stupid. You have to take care of your mom."

"What about your mom?"

As if summoned, Mrs. Wallace's voice wafted up from the base of the tree. "Kate, please come down now. I know you're terribly upset. We all are. Please come down."

"I won't," Kate said. "You can't make me."

Mrs. Wallace shaded her eyes and craned her neck. "All right, take some time up there. But come down soon—before it gets full dark." In the moonlight, Leo squinted at Mrs. Wallace and noted the runnels of water dripping down her face. She lifted a handkerchief and stumbled away, her shoulders shaking.

Leo had never seen Mrs. Wallace cry, and it shocked her. Her whole body went cold. How could Paul's mom stand it if Paul was dead? Handsome, laughing Paul? She couldn't get her mind around that fact. She and Kate had spent the whole morning helping him. How could he be dead and gone now?

The tree was warm, and its branches and leaves surrounded Leo protectively. She settled her shoulder against the narrow trunk and tightened her grip on Kate's belt.

Through the branches and shifting leaves, Leo watched the sun at the horizon as it blazed purple and orange and molten gold, the last tendrils of light fading gradually.

She didn't move when Mr. Wallace came out to order Kate from the tree.

She didn't answer when Mrs. Wallace informed them it was after ten p.m. and they needed to come down.

And she didn't argue when midnight rolled around, and Kate finally let out a sigh and said, "I'm done." They climbed down, and without a word, Kate went into her house and Leo went to hers.

They'd been ten that summer with Kate five months younger and a year behind in school. Leo didn't turn eleven until July, and a week before her birthday, she had her own tragedy to contend with.

But that evening in the tree had cemented a bond between Leo and Kate, something unbreakable and akin to a sister relationship. Leo grew up relying upon the connection, even during times when she and Kate went different directions in high school. And she knew now, as she sat weeping in her car at the medical plaza, that Kate would always be there for her and she for Kate. No tree would ever be tall enough to stand in the way.

A police cruiser pulled into the parking lot and made its way toward her. Seeing Kate arriving calmed Leo. She watched her park, get out, and stride over, her blue police uniform looking a bit rumpled on her trim, lean body. Except for blue eyes and similar height, Leo and Kate shared no other features. Kate's dark brown hair, willowy build, and Black Irish beauty marked them as opposites.

She slid into the passenger seat, reached out and patted Leo's shoulder, and left her arm lying across the top of the seat. "Love the shades, sis."

"I know. I can't help it. The minute I take 'em off, I go half-blind."

"What did the doctor say, exactly?"

Leo repeated what Dr. Spence told her. "I was so shocked, though, I might have missed some of it."

"Bottom line is you have some sort of growth inside the eye that the ophthalmologist can see."

"Yes. He took an interior photo with this new machine and showed it to me. With all those veins and globs of this and that, it was pretty gross. But I could sure see that the right eye is completely different from the left."

"You're going to get a second opinion, right?"

"Oh, yeah."

Kate shook her head slowly. "This sucks for you, Leo."

"I know."

"What did Daria say?"

"Haven't told her yet. She's in court."

"You gotta be kidding — get her out."

"I can't do that to her. She's up to her neck in hot water with this Dunleavey case."

Kate pulled her arm off the back of the seat and steepled her fingers in front of her. "What are you going to do now?"

"Pray that my dilated eyes return to normal fast so I can at least bury myself in paperwork."

"I'm sorry you can't do your regular patrol job. That'd be

easier, wouldn't it?"

"Hell, I don't know. Maybe it's just as well that I'm doing this other thing. If I have to go through treatments of some sort, I'll feel a lot better if I'm not causing problems for the patrol team."

"What can I do? You need me to take you to any appointments or anything?"

"Maybe. I don't know yet. That's the hard part. I don't have a clue."

"Yeah, yeah, I know. Man, this is frickin' unfair."

Leo smiled at Kate's attitude and posture. When she was upset, she reminded Leo most of the child she'd been when they first became friends. A noticeable piece of the cranky, petulant Kate still existed in the adult.

"Unfair, awful, shocking. It's all of that and more."

"I wish I could stay and talk now."

"Yup," Leo said, "but duty calls. For me, too. Thanks for coming to calm me down."

"Well, I didn't do a damn thing."

Leo socked her lightly on the shoulder. "Just knowing you're here is all I needed. It's okay telling people on the phone, but to talk about it in person makes me feel a lot better. I don't know what'll happen, but I know you're there for me."

"When are you going to tell Mom and Dad?"

"I'll get that second opinion first."

Kate opened the car door and let in a wave of heat. "Call me tonight, okay?"

"You bet."

She hustled over to the squad car and was gone with a squeal of tires.

Unspoken between them were all the times Kate had shown up to sit and wait with Leo as Elizabeth Reese slowly but surely lost her battle with cancer. Kate never lasted more than an hour, but in Leo's mind, it was the effort that counted. Kate liked to be active, on the move, getting things done — waiting was torture for her.

BY ELEVEN A.M. Leo knew she could do nothing further until she got in to see the eye specialist. Her head pounded in a steady, painful beat, so she took two aspirin from the omnipresent bottle, washed them down with a slug of warm water, and put the car in gear to return to Minneapolis.

As she drove, she wondered if she'd be able to catch Daria when lunch break rolled around. The Dunleavey trial was unpredictable, but surely the court would recess around noon. In the meantime, she'd keep busy with her work.

At Rivers' Edge, the lighting was muted enough that she was able to take off the giant bug glasses. She tracked down the housekeeper, Missy McCarver, who was vacuuming the staff room. Missy's youth and her rangy physique surprised Leo. She didn't know what she'd expected, but it hadn't been a six-foot-tall dead ringer for Olive Oyl. She supposed those long arms would be handy when it came to dusting high corners. The young woman's broad shoulders and muscular arms would be a real asset for any kind of heavy labor.

She was shy, too. As soon as Leo called out Missy's name, the girl flipped off the vacuum and blushed and stuttered. The staff room was quiet and out of the way, so Leo set up her tape recorder on top of one of the washers in the laundry alcove and gave Missy the boring statement of rights and requirements. She could almost see Missy's dark eyes glaze over, so she rushed through to the end and said, "How long have you worked here?"

"Since the Christmas before last."

"Okay. So what can you tell me about the death of Callie Trimble?"

"Uh, well, I guess nothing."

"You worked that day, right?"

"Yeah, ten to six-thirty."

"You didn't eat with the group that day?"

"I usually never do." She blushed. "I don't really like old-people food."

Leo chuckled. "And that would be...?"

"You know, stewed veggies and steamed meats. Mashed potatoes and slimy gravy. I'd rather have Taco Bell or Culver's."

"I see. How about the cooks—you like them?"

"They're kind of old-fashioned. Dottie is always real nice, and I guess Lorraine is, too. They don't come out of the dining café much."

"Okay, back to Callie Trimble then. Did you see her Monday?"

"Sure. She followed me around and talked while I cleaned her room."

"What did she talk about?"

"Nothing important."

"Let me be the judge of that. What topics did she bring up?"

A flash of irritation crossed Missy's face. "Really, nothing at all. Just some talk about the weather and some questions that didn't make sense."

"What kind of questions?"

"I guess I don't remember. She always asked weird stuff, like, did I borrow her reading glasses when she was standing there wearing them. Or, like, did I know this person or that person. I think she asked me Monday if I knew when her mother was coming to visit. Whenever Eleanor was nearby, she'd tell Callie that I hadn't met any of her family. Besides, Callie's mother had, you know, died ages ago."

"I see. Did you see anything at all unusual on Monday?"

Missy said, "Nuh-uh."

"How about lately? Anything at all?"

Missy gawked up at the ceiling for a moment. "Nuh-uh. Can't think of anything. You know, she was a nice old lady, and it's icky that someone killed her. I'm sure glad there wasn't any blood to clean up." Missy's eyes widened and her hand went up to her mouth. "Oh, I'm sorry. I didn't mean it the way that came out."

The girl was so alarmed that Leo wanted to reach out to assure her, but she didn't know her well enough, so she restrained herself. "Don't worry. I understand exactly what you mean. I've worked for a long time as a police officer, and nobody ever likes to see blood. Let's talk about the other residents." She went through the various names, but Missy had nothing new to add. Like so many others, she didn't like Walter Green. In fact, she sounded a little frightened when she brought him up. The rest of the residents were no problem, though she thought Agnes Trumpeter was pushy and demanding, especially about the bathroom's cleanliness, but that was it.

"How about the employees here?" Leo asked. "Hazel, Sherry, and Habibah worked that day. And Rowena of course."

"I don't know. I don't pay attention to them most of the time. 'Cept Rowena is my boss so I'm always, like, extra careful with her. They're all regular people, but they're so much older than me."

"What about Hazel Bellinger?"

Missy's eyes narrowed as she looked away.

"Is there something strange about Hazel?"

"Not really. She's just mean."

"Mean to the residents?"

"No, she sucks up to them. She's mean to me. And she's way mean to anybody who has an accent."

"Do you think she could have something to do with Callie Trimble's death?"

"I wish. But she was standing around in the dining room yesterday bragging about how she had an unbreakable alibi."

"Did she say what that alibi was?"

"No, not that I heard."

"Did you hear that Habibah was arrested?"

"Yeah." She rolled her eyes. "Like Habibah could've tackled Callie? I don't think so. I mean, Hazel and I are practically the only people here strong enough. Of the women, anyway. Walter's pretty tough, and Franklin's strong, but he's also a little wobbly."

"Where were you Monday night?"

Missy blanched. "I—I didn't mean that I was—or that I would—" She gulped. "I wasn't here. I went out to Taco Bell first and to the movies with my sister. The police already know that."

"Don't worry, Missy. For the record, I always have to ask that question. Thanks for talking to me. If you think of anything else, will you call me?" Leo handed her the generic DHS card with her phone number penciled in.

Missy accepted it, her face still pale.

Leo clicked off the tape recorder and put it away. In an offhand tone, she asked, "How do you like working for Rowena Hoxley?"

Now that the tape recorder was off, Missy let out a breath and relaxed. "She's okay. Kinda spacey. Forgets to hand out paychecks on time. She doesn't remember to lock her office half the time. I swear, I spend more time locking up around here than anybody, and I probably get paid the least."

"Ah, so if you go to an unoccupied apartment and the person isn't home, you let yourself in?"

"Yeah, but nobody locks up. I always lock up when I'm done, even if they left the door wide open."

"What happens if residents come home and don't have their keys?"

"Doesn't matter. Someone's always here to let 'em in. Hey, I know this is kind of strange to say, but did you know your eyes are, like, real big?"

Leo laughed. "They're still dilated. I had an eye exam." She bid farewell to Missy McCarver and strolled out to the front foyer. Franklin Callaghan sat in his favorite spot with the newspaper folded down into eighths so he could work the crossword puzzle.

"Say, lass," he called out, "what's a nine letter word for uncertain?"

Leo thought a moment. "Have you got any letter clues?"

"Fifth letter is a G, and the last is an S."

"How about ambiguous. Will that fit?"

"Aye. Good thought. That's the one, lass. Thank you."

She sat down near him and in a low voice asked, "Have you seen anything unusual lately?"

"No, but I'm on the case." He smiled, his eyes dancing, and Leo thought he had probably been extremely handsome in his younger days, a real lady-killer. The Freudian slip amused her, and she smiled back at him.

"Thank you, Franklin. Here's my card if you need to call me with any news."

He slipped it into his shirt pocket. "Seven letter word for

ungainly. No clues."

Leo rose. "Maybe awkward?"

"I'll pencil that in."

She headed for the parking lot, passing Rowena Hoxley's open office. Nobody was inside, though the desk lamp and overhead lights were on, so she doubled back. Leo wondered if resident and employee records were locked in the desk, so she flicked off the glaring lights and slipped into Rowena's chair. Both file-size drawers opened easily, and the files within were labeled clearly and placed in alphabetical order. In the police admin offices, everything was kept under lock and key. She didn't think she'd want to work in a place where any sneaky passerby could pull her personnel jacket and review it.

She glanced out into the corridor and didn't hear anything, so she eased out Hazel Bellinger's inch-thick file. None of the other employees had such a fat file.

Various personnel forms were tacked on the left side. The right held a thick stack of performance reviews going back ten years with the newest ones on top. In between some of the older evaluations were memos with the subject of "Warning" and "Performance Improvement Plan." Ever since Rowena Hoxley had been at Rivers' Edge, however, Hazel had received stellar marks. Did Hazel like management better and therefore she behaved herself? Or did she have something on Rowena? Once again Leo made a mental note to ask Flanagan about Hazel's alibi.

She exchanged the file for Habibah's much slimmer jacket. All the evaluations indicated that the young woman met or exceeded standards. The file contained two letters, one from a former resident, the other from the daughter of someone who'd died the previous year. Both letters praised Habibah for her kindness and good cheer.

Leo stuffed the file into the drawer and pulled out Walter Green's file folder. Besides a receipt for deposit, all she found was his original application filled out in large block letters, the pen strokes so forceful that she could feel the indentation through the page. She scanned the form, but nothing interesting stood out.

Suddenly she realized that being able to read the file was a gift, a blessing she'd always taken for granted. What if Dr. Spence was right and she really did have a tumor? What if she lost her vision? She was relieved to be sitting down, because for a brief instant, she felt ever-so-slightly dizzy.

From the foyer, Franklin's voice called out, "Say, you don't happen to be good at crosswords?"

Leo shoved the folder into place, shut the drawer, and rose. Who was out there? Someone had answered Franklin, someone with a quiet female voice.

At the doorway she peered out. Two women faced Franklin, their backs to Leo. She recognized Rowena Hoxley's unkempt blonde mop and scruffy blouse and pants, but she wasn't sure who the other blonde woman was. She stepped soundlessly across to the welcome desk and set her valise on it.

Rowena said, "Never been good at word puzzles."

"Thanks for weighing in, anyhow," Franklin said.

As the two women turned, Franklin grinned at Leo, and she gave him a grateful nod. Rowena let out a startled, "Oh!" and stopped abruptly. "I didn't hear you come in."

"Good morning," Leo said in an all-business voice.

"Not for long," Claire Ryerson said. She glanced at her wristwatch. "It's nearly afternoon." The statuesque woman held a thick manila envelope. "I brought over the records you requested from Mr. Rivers."

"That's great. It saves me a trip over to Plymouth."

"I had to drop some other things by, and I thought you might be here."

Leo felt envious of Claire Ryerson. She was the kind of woman high-level executives wanted on staff as their right-hand assistants. She was also the kind of woman who turned heads, not only for her Grace Kelly beauty, but also because she had exquisite taste in clothes. Her slim pencil skirt was navy blue, and she wore a white silk blouse with a button-front and puffed cap sleeves. Around her neck hung a cowl scarf of splashy blues and white. Her pumps accentuated lean, muscled legs. The whole effect was so classy, so elegant, that Leo felt that her plain black slacks and scoop-necked shirt looked like they'd been purchased at Dumpy & Dowdy.

Where did that leave Rowena Hoxley? Shopping at Sluggy & Sloppy?

Leo bit back a smile, covering it by saying, "I've interviewed everyone, and I'll be writing my report."

Rowena said, "I haven't heard a thing from the police. Are they closing the case now that Habibah's in custody?"

"I don't know."

Claire stepped forward and handed over the envelope. "I do hope you won't find it necessary to cite this facility."

"I'll let you know as soon as I've talked it over with my supervisor."

"Thank you," Claire said, her voice smooth as velvet. "I just know you'll do the right thing."

"I'll be on my way, then," Leo said.

From the couch, Franklin called out, "See you around, lass."

She waved to him, nodded to the two women, and left,

fumbling to don the clunky sunglasses.

Though she'd left the driver's window open a crack, so much heat rolled out that she thought she could fire pottery inside. She leaned in to start the car and stood next to the open door and broke the seal on the two-inch-thick envelope. A cover page listed the contents:

> All-facility employee background checks – 2 year retrospective
> Rivers' Edge tenant data – 3 year retrospective
> All-facility deaths – entire historical record

She leafed through the packet. She didn't imagine that Martin Rivers had compiled the data. Claire Ryerson must be every bit as efficient as she was elegant. Leo couldn't wait to dig into the records.

She dialed Daria's cell phone, but she didn't answer. Just as well. She wasn't sure that cancer was something you shared with your partner over the phone. She snapped the phone shut, no message. Daria rarely checked missed calls. If you wanted her, you had to leave a message.

THE NEON ART deco sign above Mickey's Diner in Saint Paul read *Free Parking* with a flashing arrow pointing to the right, but there were never any open slots in the tiny lot. The closest parking ramps were hidden a couple of blocks away, and street parking was at a premium. Once upon a time, before the city center had spread and commercial corporations gradually took over, many mom-and-pop joints and small businesses dotted Seventh Street. Now the dining car squatted at the base of an enormous two-tone stone building. With the Children's Museum to the east, Assumption Catholic Church across the way, and the county juvenile justice center kitty-corner from the diner, the area was active day and night. While on patrol in that area, Leo and her officers constantly ticketed illegal parkers.

Searching on the street, Leo had no luck finding an open meter, so she parked in a multistory monstrosity that charged more per hour than her lunch would probably cost. A quick survey of her pupils assured her the dilation wasn't so bad now, so she put on her regular sunglasses.

By the time she strolled up to Mickey's, the insistent sun was making her sweat. The sight of the old-fashioned railway car made her smile. When she and Kate were in their teens, sometimes they'd ride the bus down Seventh Street and meet Dad Wallace there for his dinner break. She'd consumed more pancake dinners and grilled cheese sandwiches than she could count while interrogating her foster father about the police calls of the day.

She'd thought the 1930s diner was ancient back then, but someone had maintained it, and the diminutive restaurant had aged gracefully. The façade sported yellow and red porcelain steel panels, red letters on yellow that spelled out *Mickey's Dining Car*, and a horizontal band of windows exactly like railway cars had, even though it had never been used as such.

Once she was through the miniature glass vestibule, she smelled the heavy odors of grease and syrup. Inside, the fixtures were mahogany and stainless steel. Mirrors made the interior seem less claustrophobic, but the place was packed and the booths tight. Luckily, two patrons rose, and she threaded her way toward their table.

She was relieved to have arrived so early. She didn't relish the thought of sitting knee to knee with Fred Baldur, but before he arrived, at least she'd have some time to herself for a quick review of the documents Claire Ryerson had collected.

Instead, she heard her name called. Ahead, in the far corner, Fred waved, a cup of coffee in front of him.

Just her luck that he'd come early, too. She wended her way through backpacks and shopping bags on the narrow floor and squeezed into the seat across from him. His cheap polyester tie glistened with a spot of spilled coffee.

"You're early," he said.

"I could say the same for you."

"I was glad to get away from that endless ringing phone. Are you done with Rivers' Edge yet?"

"I need to check in with the police detectives, but yes, I guess I've found out all I can without staking out the place."

"And?"

"And what?"

"What's your assessment?"

"Is there some kind of template I can use to figure that out?"

"Surely you're kidding? Don't you do reports and handle cases all the time for the cops?"

He said it with such irritation that she wanted to yell, "Hey, will you lay off? We've only known each other a couple of days, and certainly not long enough for you to harangue me." But she took a deep breath and instead said, "Fred, this is completely different from my regular job out on the streets where I have a team of officers keeping the peace. Sure I write reports, but this is a completely different animal."

"Oh."

A waitress swooped by, leaving two menus on the table in her wake. Leo said, "You must have some general form I can follow, right? An old murder file, a previous report—something that will help me adhere to the proper format?"

With a sigh he said, "Sure, I'll get you one. Can you move on to a new case now?"

"I guess."

"But you'd recommend leaving the facility open?"

"I don't think it does anyone any good to close it. You'd probably get a lawsuit served from Martin Rivers, and nobody would be one step closer to finding out who killed Callie Trimble."

"It happens like that sometimes. You have to let it go. In the meantime, we've had a rash of complaints, and it's probably best to move on. Why don't you work on the report, submit it to me in the morning, and start fresh tomorrow."

The waitress skidded to a stop at their table, pad in hand. She pulled a pencil from over her ear and took their orders. Fred got bacon, eggs, sausage, and more coffee. Leo ordered a club sandwich and lemonade.

After the waitress left, Leo looked out the window at the people passing by. A woman with a stroller the size of a baby elephant attempted to corral three small children. Luckily the sidewalk was wide or Leo would worry about one of the kids stumbling into traffic.

A pulse beating behind her right eye gradually intensified. She recalled her morning appointment once more and felt sick to her stomach. With a start, she realized Fred had asked her a question.

"Excuse me? What was that?"

"I asked how long you've been in police work?"

"Since I was 22."

"Weren't you involved in a shooting recently?"

Leave it to this guy to brazenly bring up topics that a police officer doesn't discuss with civilians. She was surprised he didn't know how inappropriate his question was. "Yes, we did have an officer-involved shooting on my shift. I don't much like to talk about it."

"I imagine. I know a copper up in Forest Lake who shot a ten-year-old. Seems like he took forever to get over it…"

Fred droned on and on, pausing twice to hold out his coffee cup for the waitress to pour a shot from a foot away. When Leo was younger, the waitresses filled Dad Wallace's cup the same way. Had this waitress been here since Leo was a teenager? How did she manage not to slop all over everything?

Leo watched Fred's mouth move, with those yellow teeth periodically smiling as though he were talking about something anyone would care about. Their meals arrived and she bit into her club sandwich. How the hell was she going to get through this lunch? She'd never been a fast eater, but today, she chewed quickly and guzzled most of the lemonade in record time. She pushed her plate away.

"...and I served on the governor's task force for nursing home reform. Governor Perpich's blue ribbon task force, that is. We haven't had a guy in office like him since."

Leo choked back a laugh. Rudy Perpich, affectionately called "Governor Goofy" because of the slightly hare-brained ideas he sometimes proposed, had died over a decade earlier. He hadn't been in office at any level since his gubernatorial term ended in 1991. That gave her an idea of how long Fred had been around, and if Perpich's task force was his last major claim to fame, no wonder Thom had no respect for him.

She looked at her watch. "I can't believe how fast time's flying. I need to run."

"But you get an hour for lunch."

"I know, but I had a doctor's appointment this morning, so I better get going. I'll stay a bit later tonight to make up for the extra time."

"This isn't the police department, Leona. There's no roll call and no lieutenant watches your every move."

"Actually, the department no longer has lieutenants."

He stared blankly.

"After sergeant, there are commanders and senior commanders. We did away with the lieutenant category when we ushered in the new millennium." She rose and tossed more than enough money on the table. "See you back at the office, Fred."

She stamped out of the diner, angry that he'd tried to bring up the Littlefield matter, which was none of his damn business.

Early in the summer, Zach Littlefield had been in a stolen SUV with three others who'd decided to take a joyride. Two officers in one-man cars were pursuing them when Littlefield lost control, sideswiped three parked cars, skidded through an intersection, and crashed into a Vietnamese bakery front. Leo arrived at the scene as three guys bailed and ran. Her officers bailed from their cars and ran after them shouting, "Stop! Police!"

She was out of her cruiser when one of the car thieves wheeled around and fired. The shot sounded distant, but it registered in her mind as gunfire. One of her officers went down. Leo pulled her service weapon and shot the man.

Not until she approached the suspect on the ground did she discover he had the pink-cheeked, acne-ravaged face of a teenage boy. He lay in the street, mewling and crying like a grade-schooler. Zach Littlefield, the driver and ringleader, was fourteen.

Afterwards, when she thought about the event, she couldn't remember unholstering her Glock, aiming, or firing. She recalled the sound of the two loud reports and could recollect the figure falling. But not even moving or breathing registered until after she cuffed the shooter and handed off his .45 to one of her rookies. Everything came into clear focus when her fellow officers called out that everyone was secure. She was relieved to find that none of her officers were injured after all.

One of the joy-riders had wisely hit the ground and didn't resist arrest; the other was captured two blocks away. The fourth kid, injured in the crash, was unconscious in the SUV.

Hands cuffed behind his back, Zach Littlefield lay on his side in a fetal position. Blood flowed from a wound below the kid's collarbone. Leo keyed her shoulder mic and requested backup and paramedics. She got her uniform shirt off and knelt next to the boy, rolled him so his back was against her knees, and leaned over him to press her shirt against his chest to stanch the blood flow. She heard sirens and shouting. Red and blue lights flashed all around her. She felt like she was in a strange dream, as if the world was slightly out of focus. Someone appeared at her side with a first-aid kit.

"Sarge?"

She looked up to see a patrol cop from another sector and assumed they'd called in the cavalry.

"What can I do to help?" he asked.

"Can you get pressure on the other wound?"

"Where?"

"The kid's arm is bleeding."

They attended to Littlefield until the medics finally arrived and she could step away. Only then did she see the amateur photographer with a video-cam. Just what she needed — some jerk ready to sell rights to film at eleven.

The intersection was a mass of flashing lights, squad cars up on the curbs, officers all over the place. Scores of people from the neighborhood stood watching as well. Two people held up their cell phones to film what was happening. She trudged over to the commander's cruiser in her t-shirt and vest, noticing blood, which felt wet against her thighs, staining her uniform pants.

Later, she was grateful for the home movie, which showed her attending to the boy, calling out orders, and following procedure. Zach Littlefield wasn't a particularly nice kid. He'd been arrested previously for assault and expelled from one junior high for bringing an unloaded gun to school. The expected media salvo didn't materialize, and the department cleared her in record time of any wrongdoing.

She spent time with the department shrink and met all the psychological requirements before returning to regular duty a week after the shooting. Leo knew officers who had developed post-traumatic stress syndrome, but she had not. Despite the severity of the events of that night, she didn't believe she carried any lasting horrors. Only anger and frustration that she and her fellow officers had been put through the wringer. On the side, her commander told her he thought she should have gotten a commendation for firing twice and hitting her target both times. It was remarkable shooting considering the circumstances and the fifteen yards distance.

Of course, nobody could celebrate her accuracy or anything else about that day. Zach Littlefield was only fourteen, and the public didn't take kindly to police shooting kids, even if they were armed and dangerous.

Thank God he hadn't died. Leo thought about him often, but she didn't care to talk about the incident, especially with a lunkhead like Fred Baldur.

She wasn't sure how the heat had increased so much in a mere twenty minutes, but on the way back to the car, she felt as though she were roasting. Her face was damp. She reached up to wipe away the moisture and instead of perspiration found tears.

Chapter Thirteen

ELEANOR LEFT THE First National Trust building, still feeling as though she were wading through a mudslide of monumental proportions. She got into her car and sat shaking uncontrollably, shocked that her emotional state could be so overpowering. She let the afternoon heat soothe her, and gradually she calmed down.

She held a sheaf of papers she'd been gripping so tightly that she'd creased them down the middle. A kind banking representative had printed out information from her general accounts as well as her charge account. He'd also given her copies of various authorizations she'd supposedly signed to increase her credit. How had this happened? She'd signed nothing. Who did this to her?

She leafed through the pages until she came to the charge card statements for the last two months.

Over nine thousand dollars to Jetter's Gems and Jewels.

Eleanor had never heard of the place, but the address was in Saint Paul, so she put the papers in her bag, started up the car, and got on the freeway.

Jetter's shop was located in a strip mall on Larpenteur Avenue between Mister Chang's Wok and Marta's European Bakery & Cookie Emporium. Eleanor found a parking place next to Famous Footwear and slammed her door with real vigor. As she stepped up on the curb outside the jewelry store, she realized she'd stomped across the lot. She stopped to take two solid breaths and told herself to calm down.

The windows on either side of the door contained jewelry boxes and cases of various shapes and sizes, all resting on folds of black velvet. The rings and necklaces and brooches twinkled in the sunlight.

She entered the store and her eyes took several moments to adjust to the dim light.

The small showroom was quiet with not a clerk in sight. She moved forward and stopped in the U created by three glass display cases packed full of gems, jewels, watches, necklaces, and earrings. A glittery sign on the rear wall read *JETTER'S GEMS & JEWELRY*, then underneath, *Philippe Jetter, Proprietor.*

The left wall was covered with cuckoo clocks, and the right sported coats of arms decorated with shining gems. In the left corner, beyond the display cases, sat a cluttered worktable littered with tweezers, magnifiers, a loupe on a movable stand, and various watches, rings, and other bits of shiny metal.

A tan curtain to the right whisked open, and a barrel-chested man in his fifties stepped through. He was dressed in a gray herringbone suit and a bloodred tie.

"Good day, madam, good day." He had a slight accent, but Eleanor wondered if he was putting it on.

He strutted over to stand below the store's sign behind the showcase filled with wedding rings. With a grand gesture, he half-turned to point at the sign behind him. "As you may suspect, I am Philippe Jetter, proprietor of the most extraordinary gems and jewels in the Midwest." He smiled, and she wondered how much time and attention he paid to the natty little bandit mustache he sported above his dainty red mouth. He had a full head of dark hair, but his face was round, and the mustache was so small that it looked fake.

He threaded his fingers together in front of his belly. "We import jewels of the finest quality so that you receive only the highest value. The selection of diamonds, pearls, sapphires, rubies, and emeralds is unrivaled by other stores. Our cultured pearls are—"

Eleanor cut him off before he systematically described every single gem in the store. "Excuse me. I have a quick question about a purchase."

"Certainly. How may I help?"

She slapped her charge statement on the glass case. "Last month you sold something on this account, and I want to know more about it."

"Oh, madam, I cannot share customer information. I'm so sorry."

"This purchase was made on my own account."

"And you've had a case of buyer's remorse?"

"No. I'm having a case of fraud and theft. You sold something illegally on my account."

His face twisted into an expression of disbelief. "I have never seen you in my life, madam, and no one else works in this fine establishment. I remember every single customer, and you have not been one of them."

"Yes. Exactly. Please get out your records for this purchase." She stabbed her index finger at the statement.

"Come with me, madam." He picked up the sheet of paper and carried it toward the front of the store.

When she'd stepped in the shop, she hadn't noticed a table and chairs in an alcove behind her, below the front window. "Please have a seat there," he said. "I'll check on this purchase."

A few feet from where she sat, a recessed area below a row of cuckoo clocks contained a computer screen, a keyboard, and a credit card device. With his back to her, Jetter clacked away at the computer then spun around and sat in the chair across from her. "Madam, if you would be so kind as to show me some identification?"

She fished in her bag for her wallet and showed him her driver's license.

He squinted at it for a moment and gave her the charge bill. "That is satisfactory." He cleared his throat. "My records show that for $8,429, you purchased a lovely three-stone wedding ring with one center oval diamond of approximately one carat. The diamond was flanked by two exquisite, hand-matched half-carat emeralds, and you selected a classic polished 14-karat gold setting to complete the design."

"A wedding ring! Do I look like I'd be getting married?"

"Oh, madam! Women marry all the time."

"You said eight thousand and some dollars. The bill is over nine thousand."

"We cannot ignore the state sales tax."

She glanced around the shop. "You've got a video camera in here somewhere, right?"

"But of course."

"Where is it?"

"That is a trade secret, but I assure you even now our exchange is being recorded."

"Wonderful! Will you pull out the tapes for the day you sold the ring?"

He sputtered. "But the sale took place last month."

"Are you saying you don't keep the tapes?"

"No, madam, not for that long."

"But you admit you've never seen me in your life."

"True. The woman who came in to purchase this ring was not you. I can see that."

"You remember her? What did she look like?"

"Light hair, I think, though it was up in a scarf. Pretty smile. Very nice teeth."

"Did she have dentures or what?"

"I cannot say. She wore a lovely lavender-colored suit. Beyond that, I can't help you."

"Would you recognize her if you saw her again?"

"Possibly."

"She couldn't have given you a credit card. She gave you a number, right?"

"No, madam, I am a reputable business owner. I would never charge an account without the card."

Eleanor dug through her wallet and came up with a credit card. "But I have it right here. How could she have used my card when it's never been out of my possession?"

He shrugged and gave her a tepid grin that only angered her more.

"Did you even look at her ID to make sure she was me?"

He let out a huff and his nose came up in the air. "I ran her credit card, and it was accepted. I had no reason to believe there was a problem. She was most genteel, a well-bred woman of impeccable taste."

"But Mr. Jetter, this was a robbery."

He stood up abruptly and stuffed the calculator in his pocket. "I can help you no further, madam."

Eleanor felt like her legs weighed a hundred pounds apiece. She rose, shaking her head. "This is a crime. I don't know what's going to happen, but you might want to check ID from now on. I'll be reporting this to my credit card company, and I have a hunch that it won't go well for you."

His face flushed red, and his eyes narrowed. "I have done nothing wrong. Nothing."

"And neither have I. We're both victims here, Mr. Jetter."

THE WEDDING RING on Eleanor's charge bill was the most egregious fraud, but none of the other charges were hers either. The account balance exceeded nineteen thousand dollars, just short of her twenty thousand limit. Nineteen grand, Eleanor thought. How could this have happened? Suddenly she felt so tired that, for a moment, she almost decided to leave the investigating to the police. But then she looked at the bill again.

In monetary order, the next highest amount, $4,278.93, was charged to an electronics store. She'd love to know what the thieves had bought. A stereo system? One of those big-screen TVs? A computer? She knew next to nothing about electronics, and the store was way out in Crystal, so she decided to visit the store that had sold the next most expensive item.

Norton Fine Furniture sold somebody $2,027.65 worth of goods. She drove to their showroom and found expensive end tables, leather sofas, and entertainment centers of every size, shape, and material, all of which were tastefully displayed on Persian rugs and decorated with afghans, potpourri bowls, and various table lamps that sometimes cost more than a sofa. The salesman was obsequious, eager to show her anything she wished. When he found out the purpose of her visit, he became petulant, but eventually he tracked down the records and told her that her charge account had purchased a massive wooden armoire, a piece of furniture that was designed to hold a TV (or two or three), and all the extra TiVo, VCR, DVD, or receiver components anyone would ever buy.

The salesman admitted they had video surveillance running in the store, but nothing more. She got the owner's name. She didn't hold out much hope. The furniture was charged the day after the items at the electronics store, so after this much time, she suspected video records might not have been kept.

Her next stop was Chez René Fine French Food in Saint Paul. If she read the word "fine" one more time, she thought she'd scream.

The lunch rush was through, and only two diners, businessmen by the looks of them, were seated in the far corner. The *maître d'* was nowhere to be seen, so Eleanor stood in the foyer and waited, the aroma of spices and sauces tickling her nose. Her eyes adjusted to the dim light, and she saw a stack of faux-leather menus atop the *maître d'* station. She picked up the heavy book and opened it.

The left side of the menu listed *Escargots Curnosky* for $17 and *Huitres Auu Beurre Blanc*, $19. The least expensive item, *Soupe A L'Oignon Gratinee Au Champagne*, cost $14. She didn't speak French at all, but thought it was French Onion Soup. The least expensive item on the right side of the menu was *Crevettes a La Mode De Provence* for $29. The entrees ranged all the way up to $48. No wonder the charge on the credit card statement was over eight hundred dollars.

A man in a black suit carrying a couple of menus came around the corner and started when he saw her. "I'm so sorry, ma'am. I didn't hear you come in."

His hair was sandy blond and his eyes a piercing blue. He spoke like a native Minnesotan—that is, with no French accent.

"Hello, I need some assistance, sir."

"I'm the *maître d'*. How may I help you?" He set the menus he carried atop the stack and stepped behind an elaborate counter with a gold filigreed screen that hid a cash register.

Eleanor set down the menu and once more hauled the charge bill out of her bag. She'd handled it so much that the paper was now wrinkled and creased. As she introduced herself, she smoothed it out on the counter. "I'm afraid I've been the victim of credit card fraud. Someone stole my card number and has somehow been using it."

"That's terrible. A friend of mine had his identity stolen last year, and he's still trying to sort it out."

"Last year? He's been dealing with it that long?"

"Over a year now. It's a real mess."

Eleanor knew about identity theft, but until this very moment, it hadn't occurred to her that the situation could be any worse than the credit card theft alone. "I can only hope and pray that I'm not that unlucky."

"I take it you want me to check records for you."

"If you'd be so kind. The charge is from three weeks ago. A Friday night, I believe."

He jotted a note on a pad of paper and ripped it off. "I have to go back to the manager's office to resurrect this data. Might I interest you in a glass of iced tea? Or a good stiff drink?" He smiled sympathetically.

"That would be nice." In several hours, she hadn't eaten anything or had so much as a sip of water. All of a sudden her stomach was growling.

"Tell you what," he said, "come with me, Mrs. Sinclair." He led her into the restaurant and seated her in a cozy semicircular booth designed for two. "My name's Brian. Please give me a few minutes. In the meantime, George will be right with you."

Before Brian had crossed the restaurant, a waiter appeared at her side with a menu and a glass of ice water with lemon.

She said, "I'd like a Scotch Sour, please, and a bowl of that fourteen dollar soup."

The waiter nodded and reached for the menu.

"I'd like to hang on to this, if you don't mind."

"Yes, ma'am."

She gulped down a slug of water, set the glass on the table, and tried to make herself breathe normally. A creepy sensation hovered in the pit of her stomach. With the events of the last few days, she felt like she was in the middle of a strange dream, one of those she occasionally had where she woke up disoriented and frightened. She wished she were in a dream, one that would end unexpectedly and leave her waking up in her apartment, ready to start the day with a cup of tea and some toast with Callie.

Not three minutes passed before the waiter returned with her drink. He waited for a moment, an expectant expression on his face. She sipped the Scotch Sour and pronounced it delightful.

"Thank you." He bowed slightly and went off again.

She plucked an orange slice off the side of the glass and bit into it. The fruit was fresh and crisp, flooding her mouth with the sweet taste of orange citrus. She thought they must have soaked it in sugar water because she didn't recall having such a sweet orange in ages.

George magically appeared with a tray and unloaded a wide

bowl filled to the brim with French onion soup garnished with bits of cheese. He also set down a basket of French breads and pastries and a tray as long as her arm containing crackers, cheeses, plums, cherries, and orange slices.

"This is the most amazing array of food I've ever seen, George, but I only ordered a bowl of soup."

George smiled. "One should get her money's worth with a fourteen dollar bowl of soup. Now, is there anything else you might need? I can grind pepper for your soup?"

"No, this is fine. Perfectly wonderful. Thank you."

The Scotch had gone to her head, flooding her with a lighthearted glee. If she wanted to drive home, she thought she'd better get something in her stomach, so she dug in.

By the time the *maître d'* returned, she was able to say, "I'm in heaven, Brian. This soup is worth every dollar, and the fruits and breads and everything else are outstanding."

"I'm so pleased you're enjoying it," he said. "Our *Entremetier* responsible for the soup is truly a master, and the *Pâtissier* makes the best pastries I've ever eaten. I'd weigh five hundred pounds if I didn't exercise some discretion around all this good food."

"I can imagine."

He held several sheets of paper. "Would you mind if I took a seat?"

"Not at all. I have a hunch you've got bad news for me."

Nodding, he slid into the booth and arranged three pages in front of him.

She flipped open the menu. "What is this right here?" she asked, pointing to the *Medailon D'Agneau Balsamico*, $48.

"Those are Lamb Tenderloins."

"And this item for forty-two dollars?"

"*Magret de Canard Aux Airelles*. That's Duck Breast with Berry Sauce. I always get the sauces mixed up for that and the *Medaillon Beurre de Cassis*, which is Beef Tenderloin in Red Currant Sauce."

"I've never had an affinity for any language but English, so I'd never be able to keep it all straight."

"To be honest, I need to work at it myself."

"What did you find out about the eight-hundred-dollar tab?"

He consulted the papers in front of him. "I'm afraid I might not have enough information for you to press charges. What I can tell you is that there were six diners who each had an entrée. We served six appetizers—four bowls of that French onion soup, the oysters in shallot sauce, and the crab, shrimp, and scallops au gratin. They drank three bottles of wine, one of which was a 1988 Chateau Mouton-Rothschild Bordeaux that cost $295."

Eleanor choked on a piece of pastry. Coughing, she grabbed for the water glass and washed down the lump in her throat while he watched, alarm in his eyes.

"Are you all right?"

"Yes." She set down her fork and sat back, her hands in her lap. "That's quite a meal these people had at my expense."

"It is. The good news is that Stephan waited on them, and he's got a terrific memory. Not only will he probably be able to recognize this party of six, but he'll likely remember many details about them, especially if any of them have been here before."

"Is he here now — or will he be tonight?"

"No, not now, but he'll be in tomorrow. If you end up getting the police involved, I can give them his home address. I wish I could share that information with you —"

"It's all right, young man. I understand issues of privacy completely."

"Thank you."

"What amazes me is how easy it was for this person — these people — to use my credit card. I don't even know how they got hold of it. And apparently nobody blinked when they rang up over eight hundred dollars in charges."

Brian winced, but he met her gaze. "This restaurant's been in business since 1994. We cater to a wealthy clientele and rarely have problems with fraud."

"I have to say, it's a brazen thief who shows up at a restaurant like this and actually dines using a stolen card. If your Stephan is as clever as you say, you'd think the thieves would figure out they could be identified."

"True. That makes me think perhaps it was a one-time visit on their part."

"Or that they live out of the area."

"Yes. That could be."

"Brian, this is the third business I've been to today, and I'm shocked that nobody checks identification."

"We do a cursory check of the signature on the card, but if the charges are accepted by the credit card company, we don't ask for ID. Our clientele wouldn't take kindly to it, you see."

"Yes, I do. You've been most kind, Brian. Thank you for helping a naïve old lady."

"I hardly think you're naïve, Mrs. Sinclair."

"The technology of this world has outstripped my ability to keep up."

"It seems to me that it's the avarice that's done that, ma'am." He rose. "I'm very sorry for your troubles, and if I can be of further assistance, please call on me. Here's the manager's business card."

"Thank you," she said as she tucked it into her wallet.

"May I have George bring you some dessert?"

"Goodness, no. I ate enough pastry already. If he could bring the check, I—"

Brian brought up a hand to halt her. "Please accept this meal on the house. It's the least we can do considering the situation."

"I couldn't."

"Yes, you could, and I hope that one day you'll visit Chez René again under happier circumstances." The *maître d'* winked as he spun on his heel and strolled to the front of the restaurant.

She didn't leave right away. Another sip of Scotch called to her, and she sat thinking about the fact that the world was full of many decent people. She didn't understand why there had to be so many rotten ones, too.

When she finally gathered up her bag and slid out, she left George a nice tip—a ten and four ones.

Chapter Fourteen

LEO'S AFTERNOON PASSED in a haze of periodic focus on the Rivers' Edge report, punctuated by long spacey periods of nervousness. Each time she felt weepy, she forced back the feelings, upbraided herself for weakness, and redoubled her efforts to study documents and write the report on her investigation. She didn't want the whole office to know what was happening to her. With any luck at all, nobody would ever know.

But that was assuming she didn't lose her eye. Each time the thought flitted through her mind, she wanted to throw up. And what if cancer had spread through her body? At one point, she was sure she'd sat frozen to the chair for at least ten minutes, trying to force the fear of death out of her mind. She shook herself, rose to take some deep breaths, and seated herself again just as Thom Thoreson appeared.

"Oh, good, you're here," Thom said. He rolled up next to her and in a whisper said, "Fred came in from lunch and asked me if I thought you got high."

"W — what?" Leo sputtered, her face heating up uncomfortably. "What's he talking about?"

"He said your eyes were all weird at lunch."

Leo couldn't help the bitter laugh that escaped. "You mean the weird dilation a person gets from going to the eye doctor?" She pointed at the clunky plastic sunglasses on top of her valise.

Thom straightened up, threw his head back, and let out a honking bray. Leo thought the decibel level was astounding, but he recovered and said, "The man is an ass — a complete and total mental midget. Didn't I tell you he was worthless? For an investigator, he can't even figure out the most rudimentary things."

"I mentioned I'd been to the doctor, but to be truthful, I don't think I said what kind. So I'll cut him a tiny bit of slack."

Thom crossed his arms, all the while shaking his head. "God, I wish he'd retire."

"Any chance of that?"

"I'll have to sneak a peek at his record. I think he's only in his fifties, though he seems to be about eighty sometimes."

"He told me he's fifty-four."

"Oh, my God, really? That's what fifty-four looks like?" Thom rolled his eyes comically. "I better go. Had to check in since my take on you didn't include druggie in the description."

"Hey, before you leave, one question. Is it possible for me to get access to credit bureau information?"

"Sure, so long as it's for a case. We get the 3-in-1 credit report summary from all the major credit bureaus." He glanced at his watch. "If you want to come to my cube at about three, I can show you what you have to do to pull up the database."

"I'll be there."

"See you then."

Thom was still giggling when he left. Leo decided that Thom might be a good friend and ally. Fred Baldur, on the other hand, was now on her shit list. She'd have to watch out for him.

She concentrated on the notes she'd scribbled on her legal pad, lifted her pen, then stopped. With a sudden sense of disbelief, she scanned the drab gray cubicle. She'd been working at DHS for three days now, and what for? Why bother? Why didn't she get up and walk out right now? She could cite medical leave as an excuse.

The thought brought to mind the gut-slamming news from the eye doctor. She dropped her pen, brought her hands up to her head, and leaned forward with her elbows on the desk. Everything was a mess. Her job. This assignment. Daria's Dunleavey case. But most of all, the cancer.

Cancer. The word gave her chills. Bad enough that cancer had killed her mother, but was she going to die of the Big C as well?

She wanted to get up and scream. Throw things. Destroy every gray cubicle in the sterile gray office. Above all, she wanted Dr. Spence to be wrong. Couldn't he be mistaken?

Her instincts said no. He'd shown her the internal photographs of each of her eyes. Something gray and spotted with fuzzy black patches interrupted the normal-looking orange circle and pattern of red veins that made up the inside of her right eye. In the photo of the left eye, no such blur appeared anywhere.

Something was very wrong, and nothing she said or did would change that.

Leo sagged in the chair and let her hands drop into her lap. Since Monday, her life had turned upside down. She was off her regular job, she had cancer, and she was such a poor investigator, she couldn't even figure out who killed a little old lady in a semi-secure apartment complex.

Tears pricked at the back of her eyelids. She took a deep breath and composed herself. Throwing herself into her work was the one thing guaranteed to block out all the sorrow and confusion.

She picked up the phone, dialed the Minneapolis Police Department, and asked for Detective Flanagan. He wasn't in. She asked for DeWitt. He was out, too. Of course the two partners would be off investigating together. She found the card Dennis

Flanagan had given her Tuesday, dialed his cell phone, and listened to it ring.

When she thought it would roll over to voicemail, he answered. She identified herself, but before she could form a question, he said, "We're in the middle of something here. You in your office?"

"Yes."

"Why don't we come by later, say around four? We can compare notes then."

"All right." She told him how to find her and hung up, all the while wondering why Flanagan would go out of his way to come over to Saint Paul.

She ripped off the top page of notes and drew a giant box on a clean page. Slicing it into four quadrants, she labeled them Suspects, Alibi, Unlikely, and Out of Left Field.

In the Suspects box, she inserted Habibah Okello and Walter Green. After a moment's thought, she added Ted Trimble. He seemed like a good guy, and Eleanor Sinclair loved him, but who could tell. A lot of people liked Charles Manson, too. She'd heard that Jeffrey Dahmer had a charming side. Ha.

Under Alibi, she wrote aides Silvia Garcia, Hazel Bellinger, and Sherry Colton. Ernesta Campion and Shani Okello were out of town, so they went in that box, too, along with the two cooks and the housekeeper, Missy McCarver. None of the Merry Widows could have done it. She didn't bother to write their individual names, just jotted "MW." All of them gave Franklin Callaghan an alibi. Eleanor Sinclair wasn't home when Callie Trimble died, and the final resident, Norma Osterweiss, was out of town.

Into the third box, labeled Unlikely, she put Rowena Hoxley. She almost wrote Habibah's name there, too. She had a hard time believing that the young woman would do harm to anyone.

She wasn't sure what to put in the last box, which she'd called Out Of Left Field. What about Habibah's boyfriend, Chuck? She didn't know his last name, but she scribbled him in. Martin Rivers would also be an entirely unexpected possibility. Claire Ryerson and her colleague, Iris Something-or-Other. Where were all the managers Monday night? Had anyone asked Rivers if he had an alibi? She made a note to check with the detectives. Perhaps she ought to listen to the tapes again.

Granted, neither Chuck nor the Rivers administrators seemed to have a motive.

She went back to Suspects and in block letters wrote: Unknown Outsider—Thrill Kill Motive. She'd hate to think that was what happened. In her years on the police force, she knew of a couple of gang initiation murders and a pair of thrill killings committed by two teens. So that category of homicide had been known to happen, but all of them occurred on the streets.

Who was left? The gardener? Any repairmen? Who else had access? Who else had any kind of motive at all?

Her phone rang. Thom's cheery voice informed her that he was ready early if she wanted to come over and learn all about the credit report process.

Leo parked herself in the visitor's chair in Thom's cubicle and tried to take in the intricacies of the complex computer program. Thom's nimble fingers flew over the keyboard, and Leo wished she typed with that speed and ease.

After she learned how to access the database, she asked, "What do I do with all the cassette tapes I have with witness interviews?"

"You file them with your report and hope and pray nobody ever asks you for them."

"They sometimes get asked for? That's no big deal. Doesn't the State have a department—or contract with somebody—to transcribe them?"

"It's not that easy. They have to be typed word for word."

"And is there a department they go to?"

"Yes. It's called the Transcription Department of Leona Reese."

Leo laughed. "We don't have any clerks or typists?"

"Almost never. Budget cuts. If there was an emergency, we might prevail upon the typing pool, but that's rarely happened."

"So I'll get paid big bucks to type up interviews?"

"Uh-huh. Waste of resources, isn't it?"

"How often do they get requested?"

"Often enough. That's one thing Fred's good at. The guy makes more than any other investigator on the floor, and he spends most of his time transcribing tapes so he doesn't have to go out in the field."

"I see. Well, in that respect, it's not all that different from the police department. We don't have enough clerical support either."

Back in her own cubicle, Leo pulled up the credit bureau database and scanned records for workers at Rivers' Edge. Hazel Bellinger was in hock up to her eyeballs. House, car, credit cards from JC Penney, Best Buy, Kohl's, Sears, Target, and two Visa cards.

Habibah and Shani Okello had no debt, and Missy McCarver only had one charge card, which Leo found interesting since it seemed the vast majority of Americans charged up a storm on a regular basis. For all of them to be so young and not owe significant amounts was either seriously suspicious or a testament to their thrift.

Rowena Hoxley had recently purchased a car for $32,879 from

Buerkle Honda, but she must have had a trade-in or made a significant down payment because the monthly amount owed was only slightly over three hundred dollars. Sherry Colton and her husband had bought a house in south Minneapolis six months earlier.

The staff's bank accounts ranged from a few hundred to a couple thousand dollars — nothing terribly notable. Hazel Bellinger's checking account was overdrawn, and she was behind on her payments to several creditors, but not criminally so. Everyone's purchases looked "normal," though Leo did wonder why one of the cooks spent a minimum of one hundred dollars per month at Victoria's Secret.

She moved on to view accounts for the residents. The Merry Widows had pots of money. So did Norma Osterweiss and Walter Green. How had his great-uncle amassed nearly a million dollars? No wonder Walter had been so smug. And now she knew why Hazel Bellinger was sucking up to the old guy.

The credit reports for Eleanor Sinclair and Callie Trimble were eye-opening. Callie had one savings account into which her monthly social security check was deposited. The balance of the account was only eleven thousand dollars. In contrast, Eleanor had a portfolio of investments and a couple of bank accounts stuffed to the gills with money. Eleanor had recently withdrawn large sums from one of the bank accounts, reduced the funds in a money market account, and spent heavily on a credit card. How odd. From Eleanor's interview and the comments of others, it seemed that she lived a simple life. Her apartment was spare and elegant. What would she have charged to the tune of twenty thousand dollars in the last month?

Without warning, pain sliced from Leo's temple, through her eye, and deep into her head. Again, and again, like an ice pick jabbing her in the eye.

She closed her eyes and bent forward in her chair, tasting the club sandwich bacon from lunch. For a moment she thought she was going to vomit, but the intense pain gradually abated.

When she sat up, feeling cold all over but also perspiring, she was startled to see a giant form step into her cubicle's doorway.

Detective Flanagan hesitated, his suit jacket over one arm and one hand using a handkerchief to mop his brow. His eyes narrowed. "You okay?"

"Yeah, yeah." She couldn't prevent her face from flooding with heat. "I'll be all right. Bad food at lunch, I think."

He stepped into the small cubicle, followed by DeWitt. They lowered themselves into the two visitor's chairs. The tight space made them seem even more broad-shouldered than they actually were. Leo felt claustrophobic.

Flanagan pulled a notepad out of the pocket of his rumpled dress shirt and thumbed through the pages. "This case is the damndest thing."

"Have you nailed the killer?"

"No. That's the thing—we're not making any headway. Can we compare notes?"

"Sure. I don't know that I can help you, but I'll try."

"We were sure it was a mercy killing. Then Habibah Okello's boyfriend came up with a half-ass alibi for her."

"He was with her at the time?" Leo asked.

DeWitt crossed his arms. "On the phone."

"And that checked out?"

"Yeah." He looked so fatigued Leo wondered if he might be hung over. His eyes were bloodshot, and the intricate webbing of veins in his nose and craggy face stood out more than before.

"Her phone was connected to his during the time they say it was," Flanagan said.

"Phone sex," DeWitt said, his voice so raspy he almost sounded like he was growling.

Flanagan shook his head. "She could have put down the cell and gone off to do the job. But Kippler says she was on the phone whispering sweet nothings in his ear the whole time."

"Kippler?" she asked.

"Charles Lavondre Kippler. Her boyfriend's full name."

Leo picked up a pen and crossed Habibah Okello off her quadrant of suspects. "I never thought Habibah killed Callie Trimble anyway."

"They could have been in cahoots."

"I seriously doubt that. So who's left?"

"Our best leads are the two men, Trimble and Green. That Walter Green is a real piece of work, and of course, there's always the son. What'd you get on him?"

"I spoke to him briefly, but I didn't interview him at length. I couldn't compel him to talk to me since he doesn't live in the facility, and he was apparently gone by the time Mrs. Trimble died."

"That's where you may be wrong. As you so handily illustrated when you hopped up on the garden wall," Flanagan said, and his face took on an expression of distaste, "anybody could have come into the garden and entered the premises. Kippler has admitted to occasionally getting in that way, and the flower beds on the outside showed plenty of scuffs and indentations. He has an alibi, though. So I like Trimble for the murder."

"But why would Ted kill his mother?"

"Mercy killing."

"I don't think so. From what Eleanor told me—and the aides and housekeeper said as much, too—Callie still had a lot of brain cells left. Ted Trimble seemed to genuinely care for Eleanor and Callie. Killing his mom makes no sense."

"Then we're stuck with Walter Green," Flanagan said. "Or it's some unknown. Do us a favor. Let's go through the facts for every interview you did."

"Okay." One by one, in chronological order, she detailed her interviews and impressions. The detectives asked few questions and occasionally scribbled in their notebooks.

When Leo finished, Flanagan put a big meaty paw over his mouth and sat, eyes downcast, for a good ten seconds. When he looked up, he let out an exasperated sigh. "That all pretty much jives with what we've got."

Leo met DeWitt's gaze. "Do you have any theories?"

"Money." DeWitt said.

Flanagan chuckled. "That's Hal's answer to everything. He's always following the money train."

DeWitt said, "The money train is almost always the answer in cases like this. I'm pretty rarely wrong about it, Denny, you know that."

Leo was surprised at the sound of DeWitt's voice. He'd said so little until now that hearing him speaking in a melodic deep bass seemed strange. She wondered if the guy sang. She thought his singing voice would come out sounding like the crooning soul-singer Barry White's: low-toned, sexy, resonant. The contrast between that and his rode-hard appearance was remarkable.

Leo gestured toward her computer. "I've been going through credit reports for these people."

DeWitt asked, "Did you happen to peruse Ted Trimble's credit records?"

"No, I haven't done that."

"Go ahead, pull him up," DeWitt said. "Here's his social."

Leo went through the complicated steps of tracking down the correct Theodore Trimble and waited for his file to download. She paged through the report, surprised by how many accounts were delinquent. "He's not doing so well, especially considering he's an accountant."

Flanagan said, "He ought to know better if he's supposed to be a financial wiz. He trades in his car every two years and gets a spendier model. His condo payment is twenty-four-hundred bucks a month. He likes fine food, nice things, and exotic vacations."

"Money," DeWitt repeated. "I tell you, it's the root of all evil."

"Actually," Leo said, "it's the love of money that's the root of all evil. At least according to the catechism classes I took when I was younger."

DeWitt shrugged. "Whatever."

Flanagan flipped a few pages forward in his notebook. "For the record, this guy does love money. Or else he loves what he can buy with it. We found a stack of vacation receipts on his desk at home. Get a load of this. The charges from June—you see the ones from Pueblo Bonito Rosé?"

Leo squinted at the fine print. "Whoa, they add up to what—something like eight thousand?"

"Yeah," Flanagan said, "something like that. Remind me to schedule my next vacation down in Cabo San Lucas. Nothing I'd like more than a relaxing three-hundred-dollar massage."

"Do you think Ted Trimble has a motive?"

"More than anyone else."

"But why would he kill his mother? The logical victim would be Eleanor. She's the one in control of all the money, and if she died, Ted would be responsible financially to take care of things. He could dump Callie in a cruddy nursing home and milk her accounts for all they were worth. Killing his mom doesn't get him anywhere near the money."

DeWitt said, "Maybe there's a larger plan we're not yet seeing."

The men lapsed into silence. Leo was surprised that they were letting her know how puzzled they were. After her initial contacts with them, she'd assumed they'd act all macho and that getting information from them would be like prying embedded nails out of concrete.

She said, "I have questions for you guys. What's Hazel Bellinger's alibi?"

Flanagan whipped through his notepad. "From seven to nine, she was at the movies with a group of women. Bachelorette party for her sister's kid. Afterwards, until sometime after midnight, she was over in Saint Paul at a house on Ford Parkway for the actual party—some kind of naughty lady thing. Her sister alibis her."

"I've got a bad feeling about that Hazel," Leo said. "She's got a money problem herself."

"Yeah," Flanagan said, "we saw that. But what would she gain by killing the Trimble woman?"

Some details fell in place for Leo. "What if she's got her sights set on Walter Green?"

"Does she?" Flanagan asked.

"According to the housekeeper."

Flanagan smirked. "Can we trust anything Missy McCarver says? We got from a number of people that there was bad blood between the two of them."

"I got that, too," Leo said. "But Missy's affairs are in order and Hazel's aren't."

"McCarver lives with her mother and stepdad," Flanagan said. "She hasn't had time to run up the debts Hazel has."

"And at Hazel's age, she won't be reducing those debts any time soon. How old is she—pushing sixty? She needs a sugar daddy."

For the first time ever, DeWitt broke out in a smile. His teeth were uneven, but the smile didn't falter. "Now that's a theory I can get behind. Black widow cases are my specialty."

Flanagan said, "Walter Green isn't going to be easy pickings. He's not the kind of man who'd let some gold digger come along and bilk him out of his money."

Leo said, "If you ask me, I believe Hazel thinks she has a chance. She's turned him into her pet project. She dotes on him, and she's doing all she can to get in his good graces."

"So what," DeWitt said. "Makes no sense why the Trimble woman would be a target."

"What if Hazel did see her as a problem, like, say, Walter decided he didn't want to live at Rivers' Edge anymore because the women drove him crazy? He's told some of his neighbors that Callie and Eleanor were more than friends, and he showed me he's a racist jerk. What if Walter threatened to move out?"

"That's pretty unlikely," DeWitt said. "And I still don't see why she'd kill the old woman."

Leo said, "Hazel might not have had the guts to go after Eleanor Sinclair, but maybe she decided to kill Callie because she'd be easier to trick or to subdue. Maybe she thought that with Callie dead, Eleanor would be likely to move on, and presto! Bye-bye to the problems, and hello to Walter's money. Hazel's certainly spry enough to come over the wall, do the deed, and get the hell out. What theater does she claim to have been at?"

"The Franklin 16."

"That's close to Rivers' Edge," Leo said. "She could have made like she was going off to the restroom, skipped out of the theater, and been gone only fifteen minutes. Nobody would have paid any attention if it was a big group."

Flanagan rose. "It's an idea and a lead worth following up. We'll get the names of the people at the bachelorette party and talk to them. Maybe the theater staff noticed something."

"If I find out anything particularly interesting, especially about Ted Trimble, I'll let you know."

"Sounds good. Thanks for your help. C'mon, Hal."

They rose, bid her goodbye, and swept down the hallway, leaving behind excess warmth and the faint odor of sweat.

Chapter Fifteen

"HAVE YOU LOST your mind?" Daria shouted.

Leo sat in an overstuffed chair, her feet tucked to the side. She swirled the contents of a sweating glass of Mike's Hard Lemonade on ice.

Daria repeated the question then said, "What the hell are you thinking? You've got a mass or—or—whatever it is, and you're going to sit and wait for the specialist's appointment in a week? That's bullshit!"

"That's when they could get me in."

Daria paced back and forth in front of her, her blouse unbuttoned and her dark hair standing on end from constantly running a hand through it. "We're going to the doctor tomorrow. Not a moment later."

Leo felt curiously disconnected, likely due to the fact that she was drinking her second glass of the malt-based lemonade. On an empty stomach, the alcohol had gone straight to her head, exactly as she'd intended.

Daria said, "I can't believe you're just sitting there. What's wrong with you?"

"Nothing that a little eye removal can't cure."

In a flash, Daria moved to squat in front of her, hands on Leo's knees. "Get your head on straight, Leo. You need to see a specialist immediately. Tomorrow at the latest. We'll go down to the Mayo Clinic."

Leo giggled and covered Daria's hand with hers. "Don't be silly. You're in the middle of the Dunleavey trial."

Daria's expression went from worry and concern to horror. "Who gives a rat's ass about the trial? This is your health, your life. We need to go to the doctor tomorrow. Otherwise, we'll have to wait over the weekend." She rose. "I'm calling the prosecutor. I'll get a continuance."

"Daria, that's not—"

But she was gone. Feet pounded up the stairs to the office.

The inquisition had gone on for ten solid minutes, and Leo was relieved to be left in solitude now. The dull throb behind her eyes slacked off as she held the cold glass up to her forehead. She hadn't expected Daria to get so bent out of shape, but part of her was pleased. Lately they'd been going separate directions, and at some dimly conscious level, she'd registered concern. After over four years of living together, their ardor had cooled, and she was worried about it. Better than any empty promise or apology, Daria's over-the-top response to this health crisis showed Leo that she was still invested.

Daria came thumping down the stairs and stomped into the living room, cell phone to her ear. "I know for a fact that your hospital is open all hours. I want to talk to an eye cancer specialist. I'm aware that it's after business hours... This is an emergency! We don't need an ambulance, we need—"

Daria pulled the phone away, looked at the display, and angrily pushed the OFF button. "Damn fools hung up on me."

"Listen, babe, just stop. Sit down and let's talk about this."

Daria paced like a wild animal in a cage. "We'll drive down to the Mayo Clinic first thing in the morning. Better yet, let's go now, get a hotel, and show up when the doors open."

"No. Listen to me." Leo set the glass on the end table and rose. Feeling lightheaded, she lurched over, wrapped her arms around Daria's middle, and buried her face in her neck. Daria's body was tense, but she held her tightly. "Dr. Winslow is the region's best with this kind of eye condition."

"Why can't he take you tomorrow?"

"He's in surgery. They'll get me in as soon as there's a cancellation. They'll call as soon as they can squeeze me in. They know it's high priority."

"That's not good enough."

She loosened her hold and peered into Daria's face. With wild hair and her face so red, she resembled a crazy woman on a bender. Leo cupped her cheek. "Dr. Spence said everything's steady for the moment. Another few days is not going to make a difference. I'm okay, really."

Daria crushed Leo to her. Despite Leo's own fear, she felt a kind of elation. She wasn't alone in this.

AFTER A TROUBLED night of sleep, Leo rose before Daria and ate a solitary breakfast. She had a hard time stomaching much. All night she'd debated whether she should call in sick, but since she was up and around, she decided to go in. She hadn't finished the report Fred Baldur thought he'd be getting bright and early, and she needed to tell him she had a few more things to check out. If she could track Ted Trimble down at his job, she hoped to schedule some time with him.

She went to wake Daria, a mug of coffee in hand. Her partner rolled over, one arm over her eyes. "What a horrible night of sleep. What time is it?"

"Twenty to seven."

Daria groaned.

"I brought you some coffee." Leo placed it on the bedside table and sat on the edge of the bed.

"Why are you dressed for work?" Daria asked. "Why don't you stay home?"

"I'd rather be busy."

Through slitted eyes, Daria gazed up at Leo then slid a hand from her waist and down to her hip. "You call me today the minute you get a cancellation. If they don't call this morning, you call them."

"I know you're in court—"

"It doesn't matter," Daria said sharply. She sat up and put an arm across Leo's shoulders. "I decided how to handle this. I'll inform the judge and prosecutor right away. You call me on the cell immediately—as soon as you know the time. If court's in session, my paralegal will have my phone on vibrate. He'll pick up, exit the courtroom, and get the info from you. Don't hang up if no one says anything for a minute."

"Okay, I'll let you know right away."

"Good plan." Daria kissed her goodbye and threw off the covers. "Guess I better get ready myself."

Carrying a go-cup filled to the brim with coffee, Leo left the house. Her headache was milder than usual, and the coffee helped to sharpen her thoughts. At DHS, she settled into her cubicle at half past seven, long before most of the other staff. Feeling drained but calm, she decided not to worry about anything but finishing off the case. Once she made it through the workday, she could fall apart over the weekend.

The two-inch-tall stack of Rivers' Edge reports sat on her desk. She pulled the data toward her and leafed through the pages.

Martin Rivers employed 106 full- and part-time staff in his eight facilities and administrative office. Seven new staff had been hired in the last two years, a surprisingly low turnover rate. From the starting salary information, it was clear that Rivers paid his staff well, slightly above the Twin Cities average. She paged through the background checks. Each employee appeared to have been fully vetted, with proper nursing credentials listed for all the mobile nurses.

Nobody had mentioned mobile nurses. Did that refer to the RNs Rowena Hoxley had told her about? Leo didn't know what their role was, so she made a note to check into that.

Appended to that section was a typed list of contractors who periodically took care of gardening, painting, maintenance, electrical problems, and exterior window washing. According to

Flanagan, they'd all checked out. Other than the gardener, none of the contractors had been on the Rivers' Edge premises for weeks.

She was concentrating so hard that she didn't see Thom until he rolled his wheelchair in, next to one of the visitor's chairs.

"How are the interviews coming along?" he asked.

"Pretty good. Some of the residents were less than forthcoming, but most people tried their best to remember all they could."

"How about the owner and managerial staff?"

"Compared to what happens when I work patrol, I'd have to say it's par for the course. I've been reviewing the paperwork supplied by the main office, trying to parse out what I can. I count 106 staff in all the facilities, and they all seem to check out as decent, law-abiding citizens. The Rivers' Edge tenant data for the last three years is interesting. Until June, all twelve units were occupied, but four tenants moved at the end of June and one in mid-July: Georgia Grabenstein, Patty-May Decker, Corrinda Clark, Tillie Anderson, and Sallie J. Herman."

"Anybody say why the big exodus?"

"Rowena Hoxley is the site manager. She was fairly vague."

"These kind of places do have turnover. I've seen that in similar complexes I've investigated. We should find out where all of them went—make sure nothing odd was going on."

"One of the residents, Willie Stepanek, moved in two years ago. Every other resident, except Eleanor Sinclair and the victim, Callie Trimble, has been at Rivers' Edge over three years. I talked to them all. None of the tenants reported anything unusual about their financial or legal circumstances. As far as I can tell, they're all a bunch of regular retirees, some of whom have substantial financial resources."

"So this is no low-rent, urine-soaked, flea-bag kind of a place, huh?"

"Definitely not. Their quarters cost more per month than my partner and I pay for our first and second mortgages."

Thom gave her an acknowledging nod. She wasn't sure whether that was about the finances or the admission that she had a partner.

He asked, "What else did management give you?"

"Historical record of all deaths since the owner opened the business. There've been six on-site, not counting Callie Trimble. Look." She handed him the single sheet of paper listing the names, dates, and locations. "No one has died in four of the complexes. The ones in Bloomington, Burnsville, Woodbury, and Rivers' Edge in Minneapolis have had no deaths. Those are the newest apartments, by the way."

"So, we've got deaths of one resident at Minnetonka, one at Vadnais Heights, and two each in the Plymouth and the Coon Rapids homes."

"Those last two are the oldest facilities."

"From what I've seen, that's a pretty good track record, considering the ages of some of these residents." He scanned the document. "The guy who died at the Minnetonka site was 92. Either the owner is amazingly lucky or else he's trained his staff well to get anyone who collapses to the hospital immediately. As long as he can be sure a heart attack or stroke victim makes it out of the apartment before dying, Rivers' record will stay low like this."

"If you were investigating this case, what would you think?"

"It's screwy. Who got in there and why? Why kill this old woman?"

"Exactly my question all along. Even the cops are stumped."

"The whole thing sounds damn fishy, if you ask me. You sure all those employees check out?"

"Seem to." She handed him the section of the report that contained that information.

He thumbed through it. "Where's Rivers' information?"

"You mean for Rivers' Edge?"

"No, the high mucky-muck. Martin Rivers. Where's his data? And who works with him? Doesn't he have an army of accountants and administrative personnel and so on?"

"He's got two exec assistants. No one mentioned an accountant or anybody else fulfilling other functions."

"From what I can see here, they've given you staff and resident info, but nothing on anyone else. What about the administrators? That's a little hinky. I learned my lesson because one of the first cases I worked on when I joined investigations was at a nursing home where the head honcho was forthcoming about everything except his own data. Turns out the complainant, who said he wasn't getting services, was right. The nursing home was charging off services to Medicaid, but not actually providing them. The administrator pocketed the money instead. One of the first things I always do now is check out the people in power."

Leo felt her face grow warm. "I'm embarrassed I didn't think of that."

Thom let out a hearty laugh. "Please don't think I did either. I was working with an old coot who'd been round the block a couple thousand times. Learned a lot from him before he retired."

"The cops working on the case may have something on the owner. I never asked them about that, but lately they've been good about sharing information."

"How would you like to proceed, Leo? Do you mind me calling

you by that nickname? It seems to fit you."

"Yup, that's okay."

"Excellent. And you'll call me Thom with an H." He grinned.

"What?"

"Thom with an H when you write it. In first grade, there were two other boys named Thomas in my class, so I've always put the H in. Makes things less confusing."

"Well, Thom with an H, I think I need to do some more interviews at Rivers' Edge."

He nodded. "Sounds good. If you don't mind, I'll tag along, and I'd be happy to drive."

"I need to check in with Fred and let him know I can't get the report done as quickly as he expects it."

"Fred? Old Baldurdash?" He let out a derisive snort. "Is he even in today?"

"Heck if I know."

"Forget him. Grab your stuff, and we'll go. I can give you some background on the way for how to deal with him."

A NERVOUS ROWENA Hoxley ushered Leo and Thom into the foyer at Rivers' Edge. After introducing Thom to Rowena, the first question Leo asked was about the mobile nurses.

Rowena said, "I thought I told you about that. We contract with a highly recommended professional nursing company called RN/LPN Solutions. We have specific nurses assigned to our complexes. They make periodic health visits to offer wellness advice and touch base with the residents."

Leo asked, "How periodic?"

"At least quarterly. They show up every day for the better part of a week. In addition to basic health checks, they do ongoing physical and cognitive assessments of each tenant. Any time someone is ill, but not so sick that they need an ambulance, a nurse can be here inside twenty minutes."

Thom nodded to Leo and said, "The State regulations require a nurse on call for a facility such as this." Turning to Rowena Hoxley he asked, "Who handles medications for the occupants?"

"Most of our aides are certified, but the majority of these residents handle their own meds. These elderly are very high-functioning."

Leo thanked Rowena and watched her clomp off to her office. The woman looked as tired as Leo felt. "Shall we stop in the dining room and give you the lay of the land?"

"Sure," Thom said.

Leo hadn't arrived at Rivers' Edge this early before, and for the first time, she saw the dining café in full swing. Three of the Merry Widows, Nettie Volk, Jade Perkins, and Willie Stepanek, were at one table swilling coffee and laughing.

At a table in the corner, Walter Green hunched over the food on his plate like some kind of twisted gargoyle. Hazel Bellinger sat next to him, speaking earnestly. He didn't appear to be listening.

At another table, Agnes Trumpeter, in her cat-eye glasses, faced the door, one hand patting Eleanor Sinclair's arm. Across the table from Eleanor, Franklin Callaghan buttered a muffin, nodded, and added some comment of his own.

Silvia Garcia and the cook named Dottie Winstead circulated the room, Silvia with a carafe of coffee and Dottie carrying a plate of cinnamon rolls.

The room smelled of maple syrup, and a hunger pang tickled Leo's stomach.

Dottie came toward Thom and Leo. "Good morning," she said. "We've got these rolls going to waste. Would you care for one with coffee?"

Leo was going to politely refuse, but Thom spoke up before she could. "Sure. They smell great. You make 'em yourself?"

"I sure did." The woman smiled with pleasure and hastened over to the sideboard to collect plates and cups.

Nettie Volk picked at her blue-gray hair with fingertips as she waved with her other hand. She called out, "Come on over here and sit at the table near us."

Before Leo knew it, the Merry Widows had pulled a table up next to theirs, and Jade Perkins swept a chair away from the end so Thom could roll up under it. Leo seated herself to Thom's right, next to Nettie, and Dottie Winstead delivered cups of coffee and plates with the best-looking cinnamon rolls Leo had seen in a long time.

The women made small talk for a few minutes, asking Thom about his job and why Leo had brought him. Jade said, "What on earth happened to put such a handsome fellow as you in that chair?"

Leo was taken aback by the woman's bluntness, but Jade's expression was benign, merely curious.

"A fall," he said. "A freak accident at college. I lost my footing and went down a flight of cement stairs. Broke my back, injured my spinal cord."

The ladies all gasped. "That's terrible," Willie said. "Just terrible."

"Tell me about it," he said, an easy smile on his face.

Leo thought he must get that question fairly often because he seemed to have no trouble describing what had happened. She thought of her eye problem. If she lost her eye, she wondered whether she'd ever be able to talk about it so matter-of-factly. She was certain she wouldn't.

"When did this happen?" Jade asked.

"I was twenty. Middle of my junior year at Arizona State. Worst thing was that I ended up losing my football scholarship. Took over a year just to get into the swing of things again at school."

Willie said, "It must have been terrible to be an athlete and now you can't play sports anymore."

Thom laughed. "Who says I can't play sports? I'm in a wheelchair basketball league. We have games all over the state. Also play some flag football. It's great."

Jade looked horrified. "What if you collide with someone? What if you fall out of the chair?"

"Believe me, I've dumped my sports chair plenty of times. I can manage a pretty effective fall. On the basketball court, sometimes I need help, but I can right the chair. If I have something to grab on to and pull myself up, I can get back in." He made a fist and punched his bicep. "I lift weights."

Leo was amused by the way all three of the women oohed and ahhed, batting eyelashes, and flirting with him. She sipped her coffee and ate the cinnamon roll as Nettie launched into a tale of her grandson's sports exploits.

Agnes Trumpeter left the other table, sauntered over, and slid into the chair across from Leo, all eyes for the handsome man. "I saw a PBS show on spinal cord injuries. It was very interesting. They're doing amazing things with technology."

Thom said, "If you want to see a movie that shows what it's like for athletes in wheelchairs, check out *Murderball*. It's on DVD."

Leo had never heard of the film and made a mental note. She watched Nettie shape and style her hair one-handed, her eyes glittering with excitement. Had the room filled up with testosterone or what? Funny thing: No matter how old a woman got, a handsome man was still an enticement to talk. And preen.

After a while, Thom said, "I'm sorry to change the subject to serious matters, but we're here about the death that took place earlier this week. I know you've all talked to Ms. Reese, but since then, have you thought of anything new?"

Leo half-listened as the Merry Widows eagerly retold their stories and gave their impressions. Eleanor Sinclair rose from the other table and marched toward the door. Leo winced. "Excuse me for a moment," she said to Thom. He gave a nod, and she picked up her valise and strode out into the foyer.

She didn't catch up with Eleanor until right outside the

Trimble apartment.

"Mrs. Sinclair," she called out. "Eleanor."

The eyes that swung around to meet hers were defeated. Blank. Weary.

"I'm so sorry you had to hear that conversation."

"It's all right. I realize the other residents didn't know Callie like I did, so this is all an exciting novelty to them. Like an episode of *Law and Order*. But it's my life."

"Yes, it is. I do understand."

"I don't suppose the police have found out anything further."

"Not that I've heard."

Eleanor reached for the doorknob and closed her eyes. Leo stepped closer, worried she was going to faint. "Are you all right?"

"I've had another shock, and I'm trying to deal with it."

"What kind of shock?"

Eleanor turned the knob and pushed the door open. "Why don't you come in. I don't seem to have the energy to stand out here."

The blinds weren't open inside. Only one lamp near the couch shed a puddle of light that didn't illuminate much of anything. Eleanor made her way through the dim light and sank into an easy chair. Leo took the couch and asked, "What happened?"

"I appear to be the victim of identity theft."

"Really? How did this come to light?"

"I haven't been getting my bills. Credit card and bank statements, I mean. I finally went to the bank yesterday and found out alarming news. They explained that someone who seemed credible had put in a change of address. My bills have been going somewhere else, and the information was used to rob me. The thieves ordered checks for one of my brokerage accounts and cleaned it out. They also got a credit card in my name and charged expensive things. I found out yesterday. I've been running down some of the credit card purchases, trying to find out who did this. I don't know what to do about the brokerage account."

"Was it a substantial sum?"

"Over two hundred thousand dollars plus close to twenty thousand on the credit card."

"Oh, no. What about the address they forwarded your mail to?"

Eleanor shook her head. "Some sort of mail drop. I suspect they used false ID there, so that's no help."

"Have you gotten any mail at all since you moved in?"

"I did. Got a postcard from a former student now living in Montreal. I know I got my June business statements. They always show up six or eight days into the next month. July seemed normal, but I've received nothing in August. I have to go back to the bank and see what other paperwork they want completed. They said something about affidavits."

"You've found out a lot already. Have you reported this to the police?"

"I figured when the detectives came by again about Callie, I could tell them then."

"I wonder..."

Eleanor looked at her sharply, more alert now than she had been a few minutes earlier. "What?"

"I wonder if this has any bearing on Callie's death."

Eleanor's eyes filled with tears, but she controlled herself. "I've got all my files. Would you like to see?"

"That's okay. The police will want to, though. The bank will also contact the authorities, if they haven't already, but perhaps we ought to put in a call." She dug out her cell phone, dialed Flanagan's number, and left a message. Snapping shut the phone, she asked, "Have you called your credit card companies and cancelled your accounts?"

"I did that yesterday. Just one account, though. I suppose that's lucky."

"I occasionally got reports of this while I was working patrol. ID theft is a federal as well as a local crime. There's a federal number, a department at the Federal Trade Commission you ought to call. I'll get that for you. Has anyone called you about this matter?"

"Only the bank and credit card company are aware, and I haven't done all the paperwork yet."

"The thieves and their cronies know. You could get a call from some criminal posing as your bank representative or as a law enforcement official. Don't trust anything by phone. They may request your personal information under some pretext, but you have no way of verifying who's actually on the other end of the line."

"All right. I've frozen what little is left in my accounts, and the bank is doing some checking. The credit card company is sending me something by registered mail."

"What about Callie?"

"What do you mean?"

"What about her accounts? Has she been cleaned out, too?"

"No. She had one account for her pension and social security checks to be deposited. Those accounts are frozen due to her death. The fellow who helped me at the bank said the last activities were the July and August deposits. With all that's happened since we moved here in June, I haven't touched the funds. Ted and I will have to handle that eventually."

Leo's mind raced ahead, thinking through the possibilities, and whole new vistas opened up in her mind. She rose quickly. "Will you be all right here if I go?"

"I'm fine. Why?"

"I think we finally have a motive."

Chapter Sixteen

LEO WATCHED THOM navigate his van through traffic, one hand deftly managing the wheel, the other the brakes. He cut around a turning vehicle and whipped into the other lane to hit the on-ramp for I-94. Once he settled into the flow of freeway traffic, he glanced over. "Too bad we didn't bring all the company's reports with us this morning."

"Wouldn't have mattered. We need the computer for some of this."

"You're pretty sure it's an inside job now?"

"Oh, yeah," she said. "Has to be. Only somebody who has access to the Rivers' Edge mail could do this. They had to swipe the statements."

"Damn thieves work fast, too."

"No kidding. I can't believe everyone in the U. S. isn't quaking in their boots. This happens all the time, and nothing much is being done to curtail it."

"The thieves probably killed Callie Trimble, but why?"

"She must have seen or heard something, and the killer was afraid she'd pass it on."

"Even though she had Alzheimer's or dementia or whatever?"

"I guess. From what everyone says, she had moments of lucidity. Maybe she confronted the person or said something that spooked him."

Leo's phone rang, muffled by her valise. She rooted through her leather bag, her fingers finally closing on the cell. The scheduling receptionist's voice was matter of fact. If Leo could get to Dr. Winslow's office at three p.m., he'd be able to squeeze her in. She thanked the woman and clicked her phone shut. All of the fear and worry she'd effectively banished during the last couple of hours came rolling back at her like a tsunami.

"You all right?" Thom asked. "You look like you just got bad news."

She kept her voice light. "No big deal. I need to leave early today for a doctor's appointment this afternoon."

"Let's nail the murderer of Callie Trimble by lunchtime, and we can both quit early today and celebrate."

She forced a laugh. "I hope it's that easy."

At the office, Thom detoured to check in with Ralph Sorenson, and Leo took that opportunity to call Daria's cell phone. After some cloak-and-dagger whispering by her assistant, Leo left a message and was off the phone by the time Thom returned.

"What have we got?" he asked. He parked his wheelchair to the side of her desk and leaned an elbow on the corner.

"I don't think any of the residents could pull this off, even though they all had access to the mail. From what I saw, the postman delivered the regular mail for the whole facility via the front slot, and whoever took it out of the basket dumped it on the counter across from the manager's office. More than once I noticed residents picking through the pile, Eleanor Sinclair included. When Rowena Hoxley had time or got around to it, she distributed it to the tenants' locked mailboxes."

"So Hoxley might be our doer?"

"I don't know, Thom. To be honest, she doesn't seem that bright."

"People do hide their intelligence at times."

"She's perfectly competent at her job, but she doesn't strike me as being the slightest bit clever. I think this crime would require a high degree of cunning."

"She delivered the mail, but that's it?"

"Yes, but for some of the day, all of it sat out there where anyone could get to it. That would include visitors, vendors, the nurses, repairmen, anyone."

"I thought you said no vendors or repair contractors had been in."

"True. It had to be someone who had access around the end of June or the first week of July. They got hold of Eleanor's mail, copied the important pieces, and returned it so that by the time the August statements were mailed, she'd no longer get anything from the broker, bank, and credit card company."

"Wouldn't they have to open her mail, then? Wouldn't she have noticed?"

"I don't know. Let me call her."

Eleanor Sinclair picked up the phone before it rang a second time. She sounded like she'd been startled awake, and Leo apologized. She asked about the bills and listened to Eleanor's explanation. When she hung up, Leo said, "She did notice. The last time she received her bills, they'd been sliced open, but someone put a Post-it on that said 'This was in my mail by mistake. Sorry I opened it along with all my stuff,' and she didn't think anything of it."

"Any signature on the Post-it?"

"I don't think so. She says she remembers it wasn't signed, and she thought that was odd, but didn't follow up or think anything more about it."

"We're still nowhere on figuring out who did this," Thom said, "but at least I think we're on the right track. Who do you think the thief is?"

"The gardener is out. He comes and goes by the back gate, and someone surely would have noticed if he came tramping through. Franklin Callaghan is out there on the couch a lot. He would have mentioned seeing that."

"What if this Callaghan is the thief?"

"I don't think so. He's not that physically mobile now, so I'm not sure he could have killed her. Besides, he's a charming man. I can't believe he'd hurt anyone."

"A lot of sociopaths are charming," Thom said.

"I definitely know that. I've dealt with hordes of them on patrol. But Franklin doesn't strike me as being anything other than exactly what he appears, a nice man who's living out his last years quietly doing crosswords and chatting with passersby."

"We could have two unrelated crimes — a theft and a murder — that are separate."

"But why, Thom? Why kill a harmless old lady if it wasn't for the purpose of covering up this theft? They got over two hundred grand out of Eleanor Sinclair's brokerage account and twenty-K from her credit card."

He let out a whistle. "She's got some money."

"She had some money. The credit card company is going to eat the losses from the charges, but I'm not sure about the investment money."

"Who would have the access and ability to swipe all that money and then need to come here and kill Callie Trimble?"

"I don't think it was a resident. I think Walter Green is the only one who could physically have killed her, but he doesn't have any motive. He's richer than a pharaoh."

"What about the gold digger?"

Leo laughed. "You catch on fast."

"One of those little old ladies filled me in on Hazel The Black Widow and how she's chasing Wally Green's ass all over the complex."

Leo choked back another laugh. "I hope she's more subtle than that."

"Not according to the teensy-weensy lady with the blue cotton-candy hair."

"Yes, that's quite the hair color, isn't it."

"Reminds me of the treats at the State Fair, which, by the way, we ought to sneak off to enjoy next week when we've got this case in the bag."

"You're joking, right?"

"Of course." He beamed at her, his eyes sparkling and his smile bright. He looked like he must have been a very mischievous kid.

She said, "If it's not Hazel, my money's on Rowena Hoxley or the son."

"What's the son like?"

"Overworked, overextended, and underpaid for the lifestyle he's keeping."

"Deadly combination."

"I rather liked him, though. He seems to love Eleanor, and they have a great rapport."

"I hear Ted Bundy had a great rapport with people, too, especially women."

"I hope it's not Ted Trimble. And I never believed that the aide, Habibah Okello, could have done it, either. She's a tiny little slip of a thing with a good heart. But I haven't checked out her boyfriend, Chuck. He drives one of those humongus Ford pickups and wears a lot of fancy bling and designer sweat suits."

Thom let out a hoot. "Designer sweat suits? What self-respecting guy would dress up in those?"

"He's quite handsome, to be honest."

"Who else is a possible suspect?" he asked.

"A visiting nurse, possibly."

"Despite the news reports about nurses doing mercy killings, that's so incredibly rare. For every medical person who secretly kills a patient, I bet there's fifty-thousand family members who pull the plug, purposely or secretly."

"And you base that knowledge on what exactly?"

"Knowledge of human nature and experience dealing with the families and residents in nursing homes. I'm a student of psychology and human nature. You've heard of Armchair Psychologists? Well, consider me a Wheelchair Psychologist."

"You're good, Thom. Very funny. Disarming, too. I bet you manage to get people to confess to all sorts of things."

"Sometimes. Guys don't find me threatening, and the women seem to like my hair or something."

"Or something." She bit back a smile. "How should we approach the reports then?"

"I'm thinking we should trust your instincts and rule out the residents at Rivers' Edge. So let's cut right to the chase and examine the death records and see if any connections lead to employees."

Leo leafed through the pages arrayed on her desk until she found the packet titled All-Facility Deaths—Entire Historical Record. "We've got six deaths to check. Do we have to go to the jurisdiction where the deaths occurred to get this info?"

"Why don't you give me those documents, and I'll call the Department of Health. I've got a contact there who can access the information. Meanwhile, write down the six names and do some credit bureau searches to see if you can dig up any irregularities."

She quickly complied, put a Post-it on top, and handed him the stack of papers. He set them in his lap and started to roll back, then stopped. "I told Ralph I was going to help you, and he said to move closer to your spot and set up in Barbara's cube. Do you know where Barbara's desk is?"

"I've got no clue."

Thom rolled backwards, out into the hall, and disappeared to the right. Leo flipped on the computer, but before it could boot up, Thom was in her doorway again.

"Obviously Ralph hasn't paid any attention to the various cubicles."

"Oh?" Leo said.

"I found Barbara's area, but every square inch, and that includes the floor, is covered with files and stacks of paper. Looks like the most bizarre filing project in the universe is going on. No way am I disrupting her system. I'll zip over here, into this office. This is more convenient, and no one seems to be using it."

He rolled into the cubicle across the aisle from Leo. If she leaned to her left, she could see part of the doorway. Despite the visitor's chairs in the way, he managed to navigate around the desk.

"You want me to haul those seats out of there?" she asked.

"Nah, I'll push them in the corner and use it to stack stuff on. Gotta do my best to catch up with Barbara."

LEO TOOK DARIA'S hand. They sat in front of Dr. Winslow's desk as the thin, elderly doctor peered at them through the thickest glasses Leo had ever seen. How strange that an eye doctor would have such bad vision. Why didn't he have laser surgery? His irises were magnified to what seemed like twice the normal size, and with his sparse hair and parchment paper complexion, she thought of the Gollum character in the *Lord of the Rings* movies.

He picked up a photograph of the interior of her eye and pointed with a pencil. "Here, you see? This is the mass." He waited, but when neither she nor Daria responded, he set the photo and pencil on the desk. "The tumor is a choroidal melanoma. Dr. Spence's diagnosis is accurate. There isn't any doubt of it." With regular bobs of his head, he punctuated his words with a gentle karate chop into the palm of his left hand.

Daria sputtered, saying, "How—how can you be sure?"

"Miss, in my long career, I've diagnosed hundreds" — chop — "perhaps slightly over one thousand" — chop — "such tumors." He held his right hand ready for the next chop.

Leo hadn't expected to feel the shock she did. Somewhere in the back of her mind, she'd hoped Dr. Spence had erred. Hearing the diagnosis confirmed was every bit as upsetting now as when she'd first heard it.

"What do I do?" she asked.

"You've got three courses of treatment, Leona. Enucleation is the standard therapy for most large choroidal melanomas, especially those that are invading the optic nerve."

"E-what?" Daria asked.

"Enucleation. The complete removal of the eye."

Daria slumped in the chair as though she'd been shot.

Leo said, "Is there anything more, let's say, more hopeful?"

"The other two treatments are moderately new procedures that have proven some success. Episcleral radionuclide plaque brachytherapy is the first. It's useful on medium-sized tumors. I'm not optimistic about its use based upon the location of your tumor, so close to the optic nerve. The second is an external-beam, charged-particle radiation therapy performed with a proton beam or helium ions. That second method could have some success. We may want to try it. Both of these treatments tend to reduce the size of the tumor and often save the eye, though your actual vision is likely to worsen substantially in that eye. For both options, the more substantial the tumor, the less effective the course of treatment. In your case, the tumor is large, impinging upon the optic nerve, and likely to continue to grow."

Leo said, "And I could go blind in that eye."

"Yes." Chop.

"And it's cancer for sure."

"Yes." Chop. As if he suddenly realized that his karate chop motions were irritating her, the doctor clasped his hands together. "The major concern is that the tumor is malignant and could eventually spread to other parts of the body, thus compromising other organs and systems."

"My God." For a moment, Leo couldn't speak. He referred to her body as if it were a machine, with systems and functions, instead of the soft, frightened thing it felt like to her. She didn't want to ask the next question, but she had to know. "What if it's already spread?"

He pushed his glasses up on his nose. "Very good question. My nurse will take a blood sample for the lab to analyze. We'll see what it indicates. In my experience, tumors that present as yours does are sealed off. The malignancy is likely contained to the interior of the eye at this point."

Daria said, "You've got to be wrong. This can't be happening."

Dr. Winslow's chin went up slightly. "I assure you, young woman, my diagnosis is accurate."

"What if we went to the Mayo Clinic?"

The doctor gave her a cold stare then met Leo's gaze. His expression changed from haughty to compassionate as he said, "Leona, you're free to go to any eye specialist in the region, the state, in all the world, but you should know that I'm the consulting expert for the Mayo Clinic. In fact, I regularly consult about cases such as yours with over seventy specialists throughout the country. I know this is difficult news to hear, but I'm certain of the diagnosis."

Daria exploded up out of the chair and paced behind Leo. In her peripheral vision, Leo saw hands flailing, and the air currents in the room suddenly seemed to be swirling. Daria paused for a moment. "Why can't you remove the cancer with surgery and save the eye?" she demanded.

Dr. Winslow was back to the karate chop. "The eye is compromised by the cancer. Cutting through the sclera, into the vitreous humor, and excising the tumor would likely result in the release of cancerous cells."

"Likely?" Daria asked. "You keep saying likely. What do you actually know?"

"I know that between thirty-six to sixty months after doing the kind of surgery you're suggesting, several of my patients died. For the last three years, I have chosen not to attempt such risky surgery on cases like Leona's."

Sixty months or less? That timeline hit Leo like a punch to the gut. "So then, Doctor, what should I do?"

"That decision doesn't have to be made today," he said kindly. "Let's do the blood work, and I'm going to provide you with some material to read at home so you can learn terminology and understand the different courses of treatment. I know that terms like episcleral radionuclide plaque brachytherapy don't roll off the layman's tongue. I've got diagrams of the eye that are labeled with the parts so you can make sense of it all. I'm also going to write you a prescription for a mild painkiller to minimize the headaches. We'll meet again next week to discuss this further." He rose and held out his karate-chopping hand.

ON THE WAY to the parking lot, Daria gripped Leo's hand tightly, which was uncharacteristic for both of them in public. But the connection to Daria was the only thing that helped Leo stay on her feet. Leo's other hand clutched her valise, which now contained an additional three pounds of pamphlets, diagrams, and books about the human eye.

Before they left the air-conditioned entryway, she pulled Daria to a stop. "Do you want to go get a cup of coffee, or an early dinner?"

"Can't. Have to go back to the office."

"Dunleavey?"

"Yeah."

"Are you making any headway?"

"The prosecution rested early this morning. I didn't manage to shake any of their witnesses much, and it doesn't look good. The judge was fine about recessing early, but I've got to go to the office to update Myron and Dan as soon as possible." She checked her watch. "I'm sorry, Leo. I feel like I'm being pulled five directions at once."

"I know."

"You go home and rest. You should take it easy."

The prospect of rattling around the giant house with this on her mind was too frightening to consider. "I'd rather go back to work."

"No, don't do that. You deserve a break. Take some time to yourself."

"I don't want time to myself." Her words came out sharper than she intended. Exasperated, she went on. "I prefer being busy. It's easier if my mind is on something else."

She let go of Daria's hand and folded her into a hug. A part of her wanted to let down her guard and cry all over her, but what was the use?

"What are we going to do?" Daria whispered.

Leo stepped out of the embrace. "I guess we'll read all these materials and make a decision." She hated to see the expression on her face—a mixture of anguish, pity, fear. She wondered if she appeared the same to Daria. Other than the fear, she didn't feel much else, only fear, apprehension, and more fear, along with a sense of finality that pressed against her chest as though she were trapped in a vise.

At some deep level, she believed she already had an idea what she'd do. She wasn't ready to let it come to the surface, though. Acknowledging it at this point seemed too soon.

At the car, Daria kissed her goodbye, and after a final squeeze to her shoulder parted to seek her car at the opposite side of the parking lot.

The late afternoon sun felt merely warm, but the interior of Leo's car was unbearable. She sank into the seat, the door open and the AC running. It was hard to think, partly due to the heat, but also because she felt so overwhelmed by the confirmation of the diagnosis. Oddly enough, though, her head didn't hurt, which was a welcome change.

While she waited for the air conditioner to cut through the heat, she called Kate and told her the bad news. Kate was on patrol, so she couldn't stay on the line long enough to get the details, but she assured Leo she'd call later.

The drive to DHS barely registered. She felt like she dreamed her passage through the building entry and up to the Investigations Unit. As she entered her cubicle, she was surprised to hear a voice call her name. Turning, she saw Monique Miller standing next to Thom at his desk in the cube across the aisle.

"Hey," Thom said, "you came back."

"And it's nearing five and you're still here."

"Yessirree," Thom said. "Monique pulled some records for me on other investigations at the Rivers' homes, and I called around and got some info from the cops. You're not going to believe who deposited a big chunk of change in the bank yesterday."

She set the valise on her desk and crossed the aisle to lean in the doorway. "Who?"

"It just cleared today," he said with a satisfied smile.

"Let me guess." She ran through the various suspects and came up with Ted Trimble, Hazel Bellinger, Rowena Hoxley, and Chuck Kippler. "The son."

"Nope. The gold digger."

"Really. I hadn't expected that of her. How much?"

Thom said, "Ten thousand smackaroos."

"Only a drop in the bucket of what's missing from Eleanor's accounts, though."

Monique said, "She may have a confederate. I did some cross-checking to find out more about your gold digger."

Thom held up a sheaf of papers. "I ran her name through a bunch of databases we keep. Before Rivers' Edge, about ten years ago, she worked for a large nursing home that had multiple patient and relative complaints and then a couple of suspicious deaths. The place was cited several times. They never cleaned up their act, and we eventually shut them down. Hazel Bellinger was investigated because an old man died a few months after giving her several thousand dollars."

"Doesn't that sound familiar?" Leo said. "I'm not sure what any elderly male would see in her, though."

"That's the same thing Thom mentioned," Monique said. "She's not too easy on the eyes, huh? Well, one of the investigators who's retired now looked into it, but nobody could prove that

Hazel did anything illegal."

Thom said, "So she pocketed the money and moved on."

"How did the old man die?" Leo asked.

Thom thumbed through the report. "His family suspected foul play and had an autopsy done, but the M.E. said he died of natural causes. The guy was 88, so that's as far as it went."

Leo said, "I didn't spend a lot of time with her, but she didn't seem the type to stoop to murder. Character assassination was more up her alley."

"Either way," Thom said, "the cops have gone to pick her up. Sorry I didn't wait for you. Wasn't sure if you were coming back today. I called them as soon as Monique brought me the report."

"No problem at all." Leo wondered what they should do next. Wait for Flanagan to report in? They'd already been through this with Habibah, thinking that the murderer had been found, and they were wrong.

"I'm going home," Monique said. "See you two on Monday."

Leo bid her goodbye. She stepped into Thom's newly acquired cubicle and sat in a visitor's chair inside the doorway. Everything was neat and tidy, nothing stacked on seats or floor. "You still haven't given this place the Barbara treatment."

Thom glanced up from the report. "Decided it was too much work."

She shifted and winced. The hard plastic she sat on was clearly not designed to accommodate the human body. The back waffled, giving no support, and the seat pan was tilted forward slightly so she felt like she was going to slide out of it at any moment. Perching on the edge, she asked, "Why would Hazel kill Callie Trimble? That doesn't make sense."

"Yeah," Thom said. "Good question. Had to be something Callie saw. Maybe she caught Hazel pawing through the mail."

"Maybe." Something seemed out of whack to Leo, but she wasn't sure what. "Did you find out anything by checking on the deaths at the other facilities? Hazel worked somewhere else for Martin Rivers before Rivers' Edge opened. Was she employed at any of the four apartments where the people died?"

"You've got those records. Let's check them out."

She crossed the aisle, grabbed the background checks from her desk, and leafed through the pages. Before she could find the information, someone cleared his throat. Fred Baldur lurked in her doorway. He still looked tired, and his cheap blue suit was shiny, particularly at the knees, but he appeared to have washed his hair recently. Instead of the flattened patch of bed-head over his left ear, his thin, dust-colored hair stuck out in tufts along both sides.

"Listen here," he said, his voice stern, "I was expecting you to finish off the murder case."

"Some other details came up," Leo said. "I wasn't able to complete the report without more documentation."

"If you're dragging your feet, I'll have no choice but to report it."

"I'm not dragging anything. There were some new developments, and —"

"I'm not interested in excuses. I want to see results. We've got scores of cases coming in the door, not just this one."

A deep voice from behind Fred said, "Nothing's stopping you from jumping on the bandwagon, Baldur."

With Fred blocking her doorway, Leo hadn't noticed Thom wheeling out from behind the desk across the way.

Fred jerked around and found Thom planted in the doorway of the cubicle across the aisle. "What are you doing here?"

"Ralph sent for me."

"He never told me you were coming," Fred said, his chin held high in the air.

"That's because he doesn't answer to you."

In a haughty voice, Fred said, "I'm doing everything I can to keep this department going, and —"

"You mean you're doing everything you can to avoid going out in the field. Don't dump it all on Leona because the office is short-staffed."

"Don't be ridiculous. I've been an investigator more than twenty years longer than you, Mr. Know-It-All."

"Baldur, investigators investigate. You sit in the office answering phones, typing, and avoiding the great outdoors. I don't care if you've been classified as an investigator since birth. If you aren't out doing the job, you're nothing more than a chair jockey."

Leo looked back and forth between the two men, suppressing a grin. She'd seen this before on patrol when a competent younger cop challenged a burned-out officer. She'd also seen it come to fisticuffs, but she didn't expect that from Fred Baldur. Thom had a huge advantage. Nobody in their right mind would hit a man in a wheelchair. Thom glanced her way, and she saw the challenge in his eyes, along with a twinkle.

Fred's head whipped toward her, glaring at Leo, and she barely had time to compose her face. Just as quickly, he turned back to Thom. "If I'd known it was you coming down here—"

"Maybe," Thom interrupted, "if you showed up on time for work once in a while, you wouldn't miss out on valuable information."

Fred's eyes went wide, and he all but snarled. "I've had enough of your bullshit." He stepped past the wheelchair and stabbed an index finger toward Thom. "You watch yourself here. This is my office, not yours."

He spun and stomped off, his hands in fists and shoulders stiff and drawn up so high Leo could hardly see his neck.

"What was that all about?" she asked.

Thom sighed. "I can't help poking my finger in the tiger's cage. The guy infuriates me."

"It's more like you infuriated him."

"I did my initial training down here, and he did the same thing to me that I suspect he's doing to you."

"You mean sending people out to crime scenes completely unprepared and then not being available for questions?"

"Exactly. It's possible he doesn't understand how unsupportive he is, but over time, he's been personally responsible for at least half the staff in this office transferring elsewhere or even quitting before they pass probation."

"Why isn't he let go?"

"That's the thing—he used to be a good worker. He's still riding on past successes. Sooner or later, somebody needs to either read him the riot act or fire him."

"You needled him pretty badly."

"Yeah, I did. I had good reason for it, though. You can unite with him in mutual disgust at my tactics."

"That's not a real likely scenario."

"Sure it is. You're set up beautifully now. Next time he comes to talk to you, he'll be all embarrassed and falling all over himself to be helpful. Suck up a bit and tell him you thought I went totally overboard, and he'll go out of his way to be more supportive. He may be a crappy worker at this point in his career, but if he takes the time, he does know the procedures."

"What about you?"

"Sometimes the best defense is being offensive. And you've got to admit, I was plenty offensive." He rolled the chair back and forth as though he were doing a dance.

"He probably hates you."

Thom shrugged. "So? I don't care. Unlike so many other investigators, I'll call every one of his bluffs, bring up every transgression. Most people would rather die than make a scene. I've actually made more friends by announcing the obvious than by grinning and bearing abuse or stupidity."

"I'm not sure that bodes well for your opportunities for advancement."

Thom laughed so hard he leaned forward, one arm across his midsection. "I've got no desire to be in management here. I'm learning all kinds of investigative techniques and enjoying the variety of cases. Eventually, I think I may open my own shop."

"Private investigations?"

"Yeah. I'm thinking of putting up a graphic of three spying eyes and calling it Ironside International Investigations." He grinned up at her, but his smile faltered. "What? You never watched *Ironside* reruns? Raymond Burr as a San Francisco detective in a wheelchair?"

"I've seen him in old *Perry Mason* shows, but not anything else."

"It's way before our time. Late 1960s, I think. Probably you can catch it on DVD. Okay, then, where were we?"

Leo contemplated the report in her hand. "Deaths in the various homes and whether Hazel was present at the time." She flipped through the background checks while Thom waited in the hallway. "Here she is. She worked at Rivers' Rapids in Coon Rapids."

"Who died there?"

Leo fished around the array of pages on the desk until she found the list. "Bettie Beckman and Francine Stahl."

"Women. Not necessarily our gold-digging black widow's typical marks."

"No, not exactly. What did the six victims die from?"

Thom wheeled into the other cubicle and grabbed a legal pad. "Beckman, natural causes, died in her sleep. Stahl, heart attack. Both of them from the Coon Rapids site. James Milstein at the Minnetonka site, stroke. Conrad Johnson, Vadnais Heights, heart attack. From Plymouth, Benjamin Johanssen, heart attack, and Marjorie May Warner, natural causes, died in her sleep."

Leo picked through her own notes. "That's certainly interesting."

"Why?"

"Because the financials for two of those people suggest a death pattern similar to our Rivers' Edge death. Guess which two."

Thom pondered for a moment. "Three women, three men. The men all died of heart attacks and strokes. One heart attack for the ladies, and the other two natural causes. Are you saying the two who died of natural causes maybe were suffocated like Callie Trimble?"

"Makes you wonder, doesn't it? And looking at their credit histories shows some strange irregularities."

"In what way?"

"Bettie Beckman purchased expensive items on credit at two jeweler's shops the month before she died. The accounts weren't paid and went into collection. She's got flags all over the account. I bet her heirs, whoever they are, challenged the bills, and the credit card company is still duking it out. I see other purchases here, too, for substantial amounts, but I'm not sure what kind of stores these are. Sixteen days before she died, Marjorie May Warner spent thousands of dollars at various places on her Visa card. Bettie was 59, and Marjorie 67. Kind of young to be dying in their sleep, don't you think?"

"When were the charges made?" Thom asked.

"Two summers ago for Marjorie. Last summer for Bettie."

"Is it a coincidence that Callie, Marjorie, and Bettie all died in the summer?"

"I don't know," Leo said. "But it looks fishy to me."

"It's been a rough market, you know. Lots of flight to cash."

"Flight to cash?"

"When the market's tanking, you get a lot of widespread selling of investments. The market feels unsafe, so people convert stocks, bonds, mutual funds and all that, to go from illiquid to liquid. Sometimes they'll convert from money to luxuries like diamonds and gold. Bad news for long-term investors. It's not so much a panicked sell-off as it is a calculated attempt to preserve funds in an unstable market."

"I'm impressed, Thom. You're not just a Wheelchair Psychologist but also a Wheelchair Economics Expert."

He blushed. "I try to be a Renaissance Man. Interested in tons, master of none."

"I doubt that's true." Before he had a chance to argue, Leo said, "I think we have a lot to do on Monday."

"Uh huh. But if you get any hot leads over the weekend, give me a ring."

"How about revving up that wheelchair and closing up shop for the weekend? It's twenty to six."

"I could roll with that."

Chapter Seventeen

ELEANOR SAT THROUGH the meal in the dining room, picking at her food and consuming little of the noodle casserole while downing far too much decaf coffee. Dottie presented her with a piece of peach pie, but Eleanor took only a single bite, which she nearly choked on. Peach pie had been one of Callie's favorites, and the surge of grief Eleanor felt was so strong that, for a moment, she didn't think she'd be able to swallow the bite.

She rose, slid open the glass door, and went out into the garden. The sun was still warm and hovering low in the western sky. She walked along the flagstone path in the shade of a majestic maple tree. The light breeze felt good on her skin, warm but insistent. She'd been sitting too much, and her legs needed this stretching.

As she strolled under the trees and near the flower beds, a line of Mary Oliver's poetry came to her. *Tell me, what is it you plan to do with your one wild and precious life?*

Callie had asked her a similar question after they'd heard the dementia diagnosis. "One day I'll have lost my mind, El," she said. "You'll still have a lot of life left to live, and I hope you'll live it. You will, won't you? Promise me you'll continue on."

Tears sprang into Eleanor's eyes. She stopped for a moment, one hand on the rough trunk of the largest maple tree, and let herself sob into her hanky. The tears passed after a few moments, and she felt lighter. She wasn't sure if she was ready to contemplate what the rest of her life was going to be like without Callie. She'd been losing her by bits and pieces for months now. Still, to lose her all at once, so violently...the horror of it wouldn't leave her.

She closed her eyes, helplessly imagining what Callie's last moments would have been like. The panic, the fear, not being able to breathe. She hoped Callie's confusion was so great that she hadn't been entirely aware of what was happening. But Eleanor could never know, would never be sure, and that hurt her heart.

She'd never been a violent person, but for a moment she allowed herself to imagine wrapping her hands around the throat of the killer, pressing with her thumbs, choking the ever-living life right out of him. He was faceless. Formless. What did he look like? Who was he? Not knowing was a nightmare. She rubbed her bare arms and shivered, suddenly feeling chilled through and through.

Eleanor was impatient for the funeral to be over, if only

because afterwards, she hoped Howard would leave her alone. Ted had been a great deal of help and support, but Howard questioned everything — the time of the service, the music selected, the cost of the catering, and more. Howard insisted on conjuring up old impressions of Callie, details about her that hadn't fit her personality or temperament since she was in high school. He truly didn't know his ex-wife or what she'd been all about. To make matters worse, he insisted on speaking on behalf of the family, though she felt Ted would be the better choice. She shuddered to think of what Howard would say.

She couldn't let any of that matter. In a carefully protected part of her heart, she would keep her love tucked silently away. She could take it out and examine it any time she wished.

For now she had no relief from grief, no place to be, and nothing to do. The funeral preparations had all been made, and now it was a matter of waiting. And waiting some more. Ted's sister, Olivia, would arrive in a few days, and various other distant cousins, nieces, and nephews would probably show up as well. But nothing was happening right now, and she hated waiting.

She left the garden and found her way to Callie's room. Standing in the doorway, she looked back at her own apartment, realizing that at some point she'd need to make arrangements to clear out their rooms. Ted would help. She'd hire movers, and they could do the packing and heavy lifting. She moved across the hall to the doorway of the room Callie had died in. She still hadn't been able to enter.

It was all too much. She had to get away.

She retrieved her car keys and shoulder bag, tucked an extra handkerchief in her pocket, and locked her door. In the common area, Franklin Callaghan sat on the couch, hunched over a crossword puzzle book. He gave her a solemn nod, and she waved in return but didn't stop to chat.

The car started right up. The air-conditioning fan pumped out hot moist air. Eleanor broke out in a sweat and some of her chill faded. After a moment, she backed out the Buick and drove aimlessly. Quite a bit of time passed before she realized she had no recollection of where she'd driven. Strange how the mind could work on automatic like that. She crossed the river into Saint Paul, wishing with all her heart that she and Callie had never left there. Why did they have to move to Rivers' Edge? If they had stayed in Eleanor's bungalow in Saint Paul, Callie would still be alive. Eleanor would still have her excellent credit rating. She had enough money to last for decades. Bitterly, she thought, *that's what I get for being proactive and trying to plan ahead.*

She drove through the early evening, the traffic dispersing

more the longer she traveled. What night was it? Friday? She recalled that Brian at the Chez René restaurant had said the waiter would be working — what was his name?

Stephan.

She pulled into a left-turn lane and made a U-turn. The parking lot at Chez René was jammed, and she had to circle three times before she saw a couple leaving. She took their slot and hurried into the restaurant.

The foyer was crowded with people dressed in business attire, men in professional suits, women gussied up in nice outfits, heels, and lipstick. Eleanor examined her shabby tennis shoes, jeans, and short-sleeved blouse. Not quite bag-lady, but close. She didn't care. She marched up to the the *maître d'* station. A young blonde-haired woman wearing a slinky black dress and far too much black eyeliner stood behind the podium listening to a man try to convince her to give him a table.

"I'm sorry, sir, but the *maître d'* has overbooked reservations for the evening. I can reserve a table for four two weeks from now."

"That doesn't help me much tonight," he groused.

He spun around and bumped into Eleanor. As he shouldered past, the young woman rolled her eyes and whispered, "Some people are so rude."

"Yes," Eleanor said. "Very true."

The hostess gave Eleanor a surreptitious once-over. "May I help you, ma'am?"

"I'm here to speak to a waiter named Stephan."

"I'm so sorry, but that's out of the question. He's serving."

"Is Brian working tonight?"

The woman pressed her lips together in a grimace. "What is it you need?"

"Is he here or not?"

"Yes, he is. He should be back any moment."

"I'll wait for him."

"Any moment" turned into ten minutes. Eleanor leaned against the wall, clutched her shoulder bag to her chest, and tried not to meet the eyes of well-dressed diners who milled around and regarded her with curiosity.

Finally Brian strode in, and the blonde woman pointed her out. With a wave, Brian summoned Eleanor.

"So we meet again. Mrs. Sinclair, isn't it?"

"Good memory. Yes, I'm hoping to speak to your waiter."

"Tell you what. Come with me."

He stepped out from behind the *maître d'* station and led her into the restaurant, through a maze of tables and into an alcove next to the kitchen's swinging doors. They traveled down a narrow, dark hallway and came to a room furnished with a sofa and a battered-looking pair of wing chairs on one side. Two break tables with six chairs each were crammed into the other side of the room.

"Staff break room," he said. "Have a seat, and as soon as Stephan has five minutes, he'll come talk to you. You may have to chat with him in installments, so this may take awhile. Shall I bring you some coffee?"

"Oh, no." She lowered herself into one of the wing chairs, facing the door. "I'm fine."

ELEANOR WOKE WITH a start. She didn't know how much time had passed and didn't remember leaning her head against the wing chair, but her already-sore neck was stiff again.

A man stood in the doorway, his waiter's outfit neat and unwrinkled. He was compact, not much taller than Eleanor, and probably not much over twenty-one. His hair was unnaturally dark, cut short, and styled in that purposefully disarranged mess that seemed all the rage lately. She wondered why it was so important for young people to effect a windblown look. He'd obviously sprayed something on his hair to maintain the mess, because outside a wind machine, he could never have kept the thatch in place.

"Hey," he said as he plopped into the other wing chair. "I'm Stephan. I hear you need to know about some customers."

"Yes, yes, thank you." Bleary-eyed, Eleanor fumbled in her purse, hunting for the credit card bill on which she'd made notes about the food and wine served. She found it crumpled up at the bottom. "You waited on some people several weeks ago. I'm hoping you remember something about them." She handed him the statement. "I've listed the appetizers and meals Brian told me they had, and—"

"Oh, yeah, these people. I remember decanting the spendy Mouton." He closed his eyes for a moment. "Table number eight in the corner. They passed on ordering cocktails but eventually ordered the wine." He opened his eyes. "They were very polite people. If I'm remembering correctly, I served two couples, the pastor, and one other woman who I'm pretty sure wasn't the pastor's wife."

"A pastor?"

"Yes. The minister and some others from the church were having a celebratory dinner. After the main course, they asked for the wine menu. I was surprised that they requested the Mouton since it's so expensive. I poured them each a glass, and they toasted their success. The pastor said that last month, when we got that storm with the straight-line, million-mile-an-hour winds, their roof was damaged. They'd been having fund-raisers ever since, and I guess they finally met their goal. They were nice enough customers even if they did leave a mediocre tip."

"Customers to you, thieves in my book. I'm afraid they're planning on repairing their roof with my money. Not only did they steal my credit card, but they cleaned out most of my brokerage account."

"I'm real sorry to hear that, ma'am."

"Can you describe them?"

"The pastor was a heavyset guy with lots of gray in his black beard. He had a priest collar on and wore a gray suit, otherwise I might not have pegged him for a priest. He looked more like an ex-biker, if you ask me. The two couples were average, middle-aged people. The guys were like successful businessmen, very professional, you know? I remember one of them wore a huge black onyx ring on his right hand. He was bald."

"Who paid?"

"Blonde lady in an old-fashioned hat. She wasn't young. She was like somebody out of one of those old 'Thin Man' movies—you know what I mean? Very proper. She didn't say much, but if I remember correctly, while I was making my table rounds, they toasted her. I couldn't hear what was said, but she was blushing and seemed seriously pleased."

"Is there anything else you can tell me to help me identify these people?"

"Sure. I asked the pastor the name of his church. It's Saint Vladimir's. I remember because of Vlad the Impaler. I was a real Dracula and horror fan in my teens."

Chapter Eighteen

LEO PUZZLED OVER the details of the Rivers' Edge case as she lounged on a bamboo chair on her deck. Was it possible that three older ladies had died to cover up thefts from their accounts? The idea struck her as preposterous, but upon reflection, she thought that lately everything in her life, both personal and professional, was slightly bizarre. Her situation at work, her eye, this crazy case she was working on. She thought she'd entered the arena of the absurd. What would happen next? The house burn down? Aliens landing in her backyard?

A quart pitcher filled with Bacardi Mojitos sweated under the umbrella on the glass table next to her. She'd eaten a tuna sandwich when she arrived home, but the rum in the Mojito had still gone straight to her head. Her headache easing up had been a nice side effect. Maybe if she kept up a steady diet of Mojitos, the eye pain would go away permanently. Maybe cirrhosis of the liver would kill her before the cancer. Or was cirrhosis cancer, too? She didn't know.

She snagged the pitcher and topped off her tumbler. The lime wedge slipped off the side of the glass and fell into the cocktail. "Oops." She laughed and took another swig of the minty, lime-flavored drink.

Daria appeared at the sliding glass door, and Leo flinched. "Oh! I didn't hear you come in."

Daria stepped onto the deck, rolling up her shirtsleeves. She'd removed her jacket and shoes. In stocking feet, she strode over and kissed Leo's forehead.

"How are you?"

She hoisted her drink. "There's nothing a good Mojito can't cure."

"Enough for me?"

"Sure. I've made a dent, but you may manage an ounce or two."

Daria disappeared into the house and returned a moment later with a glass that she filled from the pitcher. She sank down onto a lounging chair and crossed her legs at the ankle. With a sigh, she sucked down a third of the drink.

"How was the meeting about the case?"

"Not good. The partners are getting pressure from Dunleavey's father-in-law."

"Daddy Warbucks?"

"Just about. He's a big man in some sort of investment banking. Lots of money. A guy like Dunleavey would never get this kind of representation without a wife who came from money."

"Did you put anybody on the stand yet?"

"Yes, five witnesses before I had to leave. That's the only good thing about me having to ask for a recess. I've got the weekend now to see if I can pull out one last Hail Mary. Did you see the newspaper?"

"No."

"I think I told you Dunleavey made a wise-ass crack in the elevator the other day. I was hoping it wouldn't be a big deal, but the Trib reporter definitely heard and ran with it. He wrote a whole article about my client's sordid past, and Dunleavey came off looking like crap."

"The jury won't see it, right?"

"Maybe. They're not sequestered. Not yet anyway, and what's the use at this point? The prosecution could find someone else who overheard Dunleavey bragging and put them on the stand to testify, and then we're screwed. Dan and Myron practically nailed me to the cross. Said I should have controlled my client. Told me I ought to have asked the judge to sequester. Trouble is, I didn't see the article until this afternoon. Myron laid a pound of guilt on me, said he didn't want to see me blow this one because it would have repercussions later. I'll put on the last of my case Monday. After that, I can kiss being a partner goodbye, I guess." She drank deeply and closed her eyes.

Not for the first time, Leo wondered whether Daria was cut out for courtroom cases. As second chair, working tirelessly behind the scenes, she'd received many accolades. Somebody else's head was on the chopping block then. While the lead attorney took the heat, Daria had the time and energy to explore strategy and options, which she was extraordinarily good at. She'd drawn the short straw for the Dunleavey trial, though. Her second chair was a greenhorn who wasn't much help.

"What about your eye, Leo?" Daria hadn't opened her eyes. She lay on the lounge looking half-asleep.

"I don't know." The buzz she'd been enjoying had gradually abated, and the ache in her forehead reasserted itself.

"You have to make a decision. I vote for that plaque treatment."

"How can you say that when neither of us has even read the materials from the doctor?"

"The doctor made it sound the most effective."

"And you want me to call up Winslow and tell him we'll take

Door Number Two because the scanty details we heard sound effective?"

Daria leaned forward and swung her legs off the side of the lounge chair. "No, that's not what I meant."

"I need to read all that literature he gave us." Leo set her glass on the table and pressed cool fingertips to her brow. "It's just that reading gives me a headache."

"Did you get the painkiller scrip filled?" When she didn't answer, Daria said, "Why the hell not? The doctor said it would help."

"I hate taking drugs like that. I feel too fuzzy-headed and can't think clearly."

"And having a constant headache doesn't affect your thinking skills?"

"I may be cranky, but at least I'm wide awake."

Daria lurched up, took a final swig of the Mojito, and smacked the glass down on the table.

"Jeez, you trying to break the glass?"

Daria stomped into the house. Leo watched her retreating back with sorrow. Daria had never been good at handling emotionally difficult matters. Leo chalked it up to her having lived a fairytale childhood with a successful businessman for a father, a society dame for a mother, and older siblings who doted on her. Her family had a live-in maid when she was growing up, and the most arduous manual labor she'd done was vacuuming when the maid was on vacation. She hadn't lost a grandparent until she was thirty, and the family dog she'd loved since the age of fifteen was still alive. She didn't think Daria had ever learned how to lose anything, not a case, not a family member or pet, and certainly not her partner's eye.

LATER, AS THE sun gradually dipped toward the horizon, Leo scooped up the empty pitcher and took the glasses to the kitchen to wash. She wiped the bread crumbs off the counter and tidied up.

On the second floor, Daria's office door was closed, so Leo didn't bother her. She went downstairs to the TV room and curled up to watch a *Lifetime* movie, but she couldn't get interested in some perfect blonde's rocky love life when all she could think about was having cancer in her eye.

Luckily, Kate called. Before she could broach the subject of Leo's health situation, Leo asked, "How are the kids?"

"Jenny is in time-out, and Paul fell asleep in the high chair. They went to the zoo today with daycare and didn't get their afternoon naps, so they've been little terrors."

"Poor things."

"Poor nothing. They told Susie today that Paul was the original wild child at the zoo. He tried to climb into the monkey cage. Lucky it's fully enclosed. I can tell already that he's going to be a handful when he gets older. He gets time-out now—he'll probably get grounded regularly by the time he's in grade school."

"He's quite the little climber."

"No kidding. Enough about the kids. What about you? What did the specialist say about the cancer?"

"Might lose the eye."

"Oh, shit." Kate's exhale sounded as though someone had slashed a tire. "There's got to be something they can do."

She gave Kate the rundown on all she'd learned from the doctor, and Kate listened and asked all the right questions. She loved that about Kate. Though Kate always fought shedding tears, she was warm and occasionally weepy when bad news came her way. At heart, though, she was immensely practical.

"It seems to me," Kate said, "that the most important thing is that the cancer be contained."

She didn't have to say another word for Leo to understand. Kate and Mom Wallace had been with her at the hospice when her mother died. Kate had been strong—as strong as a ten-year-old child can be—but Leo knew there was no way her foster sister would want to see Leo go through the same slow, sapping death. The thought frightened both of them, though neither would ever admit it out loud to the other. Voicing it would make it too real.

Leo said, "I'll see the doctor and decide on a course of treatment."

"I'm there if you need me."

"I know."

"How's Daria taking this?"

"Almost as well as could be expected."

Kate let out a sigh. "Crap."

"It's not so bad. She'll come around. She's just in shock right now."

"And you're not?"

"I can't afford to be."

Chapter Nineteen

LEO AWOKE SATURDAY in the late morning bleary-eyed and exhausted. She'd gone to bed after midnight but had awakened when Daria came in at two a.m. She whispered in the dark, asking how the case prep was coming, but Daria didn't want to talk about it. She settled in and told Leo to go back to sleep.

She hated it when Daria was out of sorts. She was usually such a cheerful person, but when she was in a mood, she was impossible. Days might pass before she got out of a blue funk.

Leo left her tossing fitfully and took a relaxing bath, hoping to soak away her hangover and remembering why she didn't like to take in more than one drink or a couple of beers in one sitting. Six or eight ounces of rum in the Mojitos had left her muzzy-headed.

By the time she got down to the kitchen, it was noon. She found the remains of Daria's late-night snack—crackers, cheese, and seven empty Michelob bottles. Leo's valise, which she'd tossed on the counter when she came home, emitted a beeping noise. She'd forgotten to take her cell phone out and put it in the charger. When she got it out of her bag, she discovered it was beeping because she had a message, not due to a low battery.

She flipped it open and checked voicemail. The sole message, left the night before, was from Eleanor Sinclair. "I'm sorry to bother you after work hours, but I've discovered some further information that I believe is relevant. When you get to work on Monday, could you call me at your earliest convenience?"

Leo didn't want to wait for work hours. She was relieved to have something to do, even if it was Saturday. When Eleanor answered, her voice was strong, perhaps slightly outraged. "I tried to reach the detectives last night, but they were out on another case, and I still haven't heard from them."

"Are you in danger?" Leo asked.

"Heavens, no. I don't believe so. I've just learned some additional details about who might have stolen my mail. I went to a restaurant last night called Chez René over in Saint Paul, and the waiter described the user of my credit card as a blonde woman, middle-aged, dressed nicely. Two couples and a minister from Saint Vladimir's Lutheran Church were with her."

"I know where that church is. Might be a lead we can follow up on. I'll see if I can locate the minister. What about the blonde woman?"

"Stephan, the waiter, said she was attractive, but much older than he is. Stephan was all of twenty, so I'm not sure what middle-aged constitutes in his estimation. Whether she was thirty or fifty, he couldn't say. However, the jeweler I visited also described a similar woman."

"Your credit card could have been sold to someone, but it's also possible that the woman is the one who stole it. Is Hazel on duty?"

"No."

"How about Rowena Hoxley?"

"Rowena? No. She's usually off from Friday night until Monday morning. Habibah and Sherry have the afternoon shift. I think it's Silvia on night duty."

"I want you to lock your doors and don't let anyone in. Don't go out until dinner, and make sure you lock up while you're gone. Stay in the company of the other ladies, and don't open the door later tonight for anyone but Habibah and Sherry. All right?"

"I hadn't intended going anywhere."

"Good. Take no chances, Eleanor. I'll drop by tomorrow and check on you."

"Thank you, Leona. I apologize that I called after hours."

"Please don't worry. You were right to make sure I got the information. Let me know if you hear from Flanagan or DeWitt."

"You can count on it."

Leo hung up and connected the phone to her charger. She wandered into the living room, sat at the writing desk in the corner, and took a legal pad from a drawer.

She wrote Hazel Bellinger's name. She was belligerent, sometimes rude, and she had received funds recently. Could she be the one? She wasn't a big woman, so could she have subdued Callie Trimble?

Or was it more likely that Rowena Hoxley was involved in the theft and murders? Where had she been when Callie was murdered? Leo remembered ruling her out, and she hadn't given her another thought since. She'd felt the same way about Hoxley as she had about Habibah Okello. Neither of them seemed likely to have killed anybody. But now that she thought about it, Rowena Hoxley was certainly a sturdy, well-muscled woman, plenty coordinated enough to have gotten over the garden wall. Of all the employees, she was the most likely to have a key to the gate. She could have even come in through the front door, and it was possible nobody noticed her. Not likely, but possible.

Based on her behavior since Leo had met her, Rowena must be a great actress if she was guilty. She seemed genuinely shocked about Callie's death and concerned for Eleanor. Not once had Leo sensed anything out of line with her. But what if she was a particularly glib sociopath?

Leo remembered a recent police training where the presenter went through the characteristics of the sociopathic personality: charm, manipulation, convincing lies, and a childish selfishness that would be funny if it didn't so often lead to heinous and violent crimes. Leo had dealt with many such people on the street. They were remorseless, impulsive, lacking shame, and often displayed little emotion or empathy about the problems of others.

Rowena Hoxley didn't appear to fall into those categorical descriptions, nor did she work in a field where a sociopath would thrive. Still, the elderly and disabled people in the Rivers' facilities would be easy marks, and sociopathic criminals were adept at changing their image, their stories, and their personalities to avoid being caught.

Where had Hoxley worked before coming to Rivers' Edge? Leo wanted to kick herself for leaving the reports on the desk at DHS. She should have brought them home with her for the weekend, but when she'd left, she hadn't intended to think about work until Monday.

She hadn't made a single useful note on the legal pad or paid attention to what she was doodling. Instead, she'd covered a fourth of the page, starting in one corner, with spindly webs that extended into the middle of the sheet. Obviously she'd begun to see the murderer's web, but she still lacked a good picture of the grotesque spider who preyed on old women.

She tossed the legal pad back into the drawer and rose. In the kitchen she flipped open the cell phone, found Thom's number, and hit SEND.

He picked up on the second ring. "Thom Thoreson here."

"It's Leona Reese—from work." A chorus of cheers blared through the phone.

"Hey!" he shouted, sounding slightly distant. "Keep it down for a sec, guys." He returned to the phone, and his voice sounded stronger. "Sorry about that. Denver sacked our quarterback. I'm watching a pre-season football game with some buddies."

"I apologize for interrupting you."

"Not a problem. What's up?"

She updated him regarding Eleanor Sinclair's call and ended by saying, "I think we have a lead. If we go by the church Sunday, maybe we can track down the minister's name."

"Hang on a second…"

Another cheer went up, and she assumed the football game must be pretty exciting. After a moment, she heard men's voices arguing, which she couldn't quite make out. The commentary gradually became fainter.

"Okay," Thom said, "I'm on Pete's computer, and I pulled up the church on the Internet. St. Vladimir's has a whole website. The senior pastor is George Trent. He's got two associate pastors. One does faith formation, and the other handles visitations and outreach stuff, and they've got a woman who is listed as a lay administrator. Got pictures of all of them. One's a little weasely guy with blond hair, another is about forty years old and bald. Trent is a burly-looking guy with a dark beard. Reminds me of Teddy Roosevelt. He's got to be our man."

"Is the woman blonde?"

"Yeah." He hesitated. "But how do I say this without sounding like a sexist pig?"

Shouts and loud groans came from the background.

"Your buddies think you're a sexist pig?"

"No. I think the Broncos just fumbled. Sorry about the noise. Anyway, the lay administrator is not pretty at all. If the waiter and the jeweler described the woman as attractive, this gal won't fit the picture."

"You sure? A bit of makeup can go a long way for a lot of women."

"No, not with this one. If I have to be blunt, she's built like a Mack truck. She has a nice smile, but no twenty-year-old waiter is going to say she's pretty."

Leo paused to consider. If they had two pastors and an administrator, the church had to employ other people, too.

"Have I offended you?" Thom asked.

"Oh, no," she said. "Not at all. I'm wondering about other church staff."

"They've got a secretary and a bookkeeper. They've also got the typical nonemployee types like an organist, youth minister, and building coordinator. I'm looking at all their pictures. None of the guys match the description, and the youth minister is a dark-haired woman. I think we need to go over to the church in the morning and see if we can roust anyone."

"What time are the services?"

"Eight and ten a.m."

"Let's go to the ten o'clock and time it so we arrive after the service has begun."

Chapter Twenty

ELEANOR FELT LIKE she existed on a different plane, in a different aura than the people around her. Everywhere she looked, people carried on, their hands busy, voices loud, as they flitted about the apartment complex. She wandered among them, feeling as disconnected as a wraith in a churchyard.

To force herself to come down to earth, she'd taken a turn around the garden after supper, but the setting sun beat upon her at too sharp an angle, and she retreated through the dining hall and back to Callie's apartment. She could be coming and going through the sliding glass door in her own apartment, but even after all this time, she still couldn't bring herself to spend any time in the room where Callie died. She knew it was irrational and she'd have to eventually clean everything out of there to move, but for now, she couldn't make herself cross the threshold. If she needed something, she asked Sherry or Habibah or Silvia, and they were more than happy to assist.

Habibah appeared in her doorway. "Eleanor, I hesitate to bother you, but Callie's son is on the office phone."

Eleanor rose and followed her through what felt like waves of extra-heavy air. She imagined this was what sleepwalkers felt like.

Rather than go into Rowena's tiny office, she picked up the phone at the entryway counter.

"Line two," Habibah said.

"El?"

"Ted? Why didn't you call me direct?"

"This is my one call. I couldn't afford not reaching you."

"What do you mean—your one call?"

"The police picked me up for questioning again, and now they're going to charge me."

"Charge you? Whatever for?"

"They found a wallet they say is mine at another murder. But I've got my wallet. I don't know what they're talking about." He made a choking sound, and when he went on, his voice sounded thick and garbled. "Please believe me, I didn't kill Mom. I would never do such a thing. You've got to believe me."

The anguish in his voice cut through her stupor, and suddenly Eleanor felt more clear-headed than she had for days. "Who's your attorney?"

"Attorney? I don't have an attorney. I've never needed one."

"Surely you know somebody, someone who can come get you out of there?"

"I know a lot of corporate guys, but no criminal lawyers."

"All right. I'll be there in a few minutes, Ted."

She got her bag and a sweater and stepped into the muggy evening air. What a terrible time for Ted to be arrested. How could she bail him out after-hours on the weekend? To make matters worse, her credit card was cancelled, and she hadn't yet received a new one. If she could track down her PIN number, she could get two hundred dollars from a cash machine, and she had at least a hundred dollars in her purse. But surely that wouldn't be enough? If Ted was charged with a felony crime, it was more likely that several thousand dollars would be needed.

What else could she do but show up and try to help? Perhaps she'd have to see a bail bondsman.

Just after ten p.m., she arrived at the station, but it was nearly eleven before an officer came out to the lobby to talk to her.

She rose. "I'd like to see my nephew immediately. What do you require—identification?" She opened her wallet and tried to give the sergeant her driver's license.

He stepped back, palms up and facing her. "Oh, no, ma'am. That's not necessary. You see, I can't let you in with or without ID. Visiting hours are long past, and Mr. Trimble is being processed now anyway."

She stood speechless, her mind blank, with no idea what to do next. The officer took pity and patted her on the shoulder. "I'm so sorry, ma'am. You probably can't get access until tomorrow or Monday."

"What about Detectives Flanagan and DeWitt—where are they? I've been trying to reach them all day."

"They're out on a case. I can leave a message for them, but I have no clue when they'll be back."

Behind the officer, she saw two men come into the lobby, one in street clothes, the other in a uniform. They shook hands, and the civilian waved and marched off toward the front door. The cop turned, and Eleanor recognized him. She surprised the officer in front of her by stepping around him and calling out, "Officer Caldwell. Jasper Caldwell."

He stopped and squinted, then strode toward her. "Mrs. Sinclair. How you doing?"

"Not so good. My nephew has been arrested."

"Oh, I didn't know. I'm sorry."

"Can you help me? Please?" She tried to force down the panicked edge on her voice, but she saw the alarm in his eyes.

He glanced at the other cop, and something passed between

them. "Let me handle this, O'Donnell, why don't you?"

"No problem, Jazz. She's all yours."

He faded back, and Eleanor focused on Jasper Caldwell. "Is there anything you can do to help me get my nephew out on bail?"

"Let's go find a cubbyhole where we can sit and talk."

He led her through a maze of passages, stopping along the way to duck into a break room and pick up two cups of coffee in Styrofoam cups. The cubicle they ended up in contained a scarred table with four chairs crammed around it.

He set the coffee down and invited her to sit. "I know what happened the evening of Callie Trimble's death, Mrs. Sinclair, but tell me what's happened since then."

She quickly outlined the facts and wound it up by saying, "The funeral is Thursday, and Ted's a pallbearer. I have to get him out before then. In fact, he needs to be released now."

"Let me go check something, will you? I'll be back as quick as possible."

When he left the cubicle, it seemed he'd taken all the air with him. Eleanor closed her eyes. Elbows on the table, she put her head in her hands. Maybe she should have called Howard. He probably would know a lawyer. Maybe she ought to search the yellow pages and find an attorney now, any attorney. Surely there must be all-night services available for these kind of cases. She opened her eyes and took a sip of the bitter black coffee. Though she didn't much care for it, the liquid was hot and somehow soothing. She'd drunk half the cup before Jasper stepped in and sat, his big frame filling up the space.

He patted her hand awkwardly. "A buddy of mine is checking on him."

"Thank you, Jasper. You don't know how much I appreciate this. Am I keeping you from your work?"

"No. I've been off-duty for half an hour. Just haven't been able to get out of here."

"I'm so sorry. I didn't mean to keep you from your family. Do you have a wife at home worrying?"

"Nah, she doesn't worry until after midnight. I'm never home right away. If I'm not finishing up paperwork, I'm working out in the gym or having a beer with the guys. She's used to it."

"I don't know what I'd have done if you hadn't happened by. This is all a nightmare. Unbelievably so."

"I'm sure it is."

An officer stopped in the doorway to the cubicle. "Jazz, boss says she can see him before we take him to lockdown, but only for a couple minutes. I'll give you a holler."

"Thanks," Jasper said. " 'Preciate it."

Tears filled Eleanor's eyes, and she fought to keep them from brimming over. "Ted is from a good family. I've known him his whole life. In fact, I held him the day he was born. He grew up to be a good man and never committed a crime in his life." Jasper's expression shifted. "Oh, Jasper, I know what you're thinking—that he probably never got caught—but I'd stake my entire fortune on his innocence."

"You may have to, Mrs. Sinclair. He's being charged with two counts of murder."

Chapter Twenty-one

SUNDAY MORNING DAWNED muggy and hot. Leo sat slumped at the breakfast table in the solarium off the kitchen. Through the sliding glass door, she had a good view of the sun coming up over the top of the hedge that bordered their backyard, but she was avoiding the bright light.

She'd slept poorly and been up for a couple of hours reading the pamphlets and books Dr. Winslow had provided. After the first read-through, she'd gone back over a lot of the material again, most of which was difficult to digest. With every section she read and understood, her spirits sank lower.

I can't believe I have cancer, she kept thinking. Cancer. The word gave her the shivers and made her want to spit up the cinnamon tea she was drinking. Cancer. The horrible disease that had ripped her mother from her life, leaving her forever wondering what her world would be like if she had parents. Her father, dead before her birth, had missed her entire life, and her mom had missed so much: Leo blossoming from a child to a young woman, her track-and-field awards, graduation from high school, completing the police academy with high honors, promotion to sergeant, and her commitment ceremony with Daria four years earlier.

How strange it was to realize her mother hadn't lived long enough to ever know Leo was a lesbian.

But it wasn't just the rites of passage where Leo missed her mother. She missed the steady, approving presence, the unconditional love she'd always felt in her childhood. Until she was well into her teen years, Leo had fallen asleep at the Wallaces' home imagining her mother coming to her in the night, sitting by the bed, stroking her hair, and saying that it had all been a mistake. When she awakened, the world would be a different place. She and her mother would still live in the house across the street, and the Wallaces would be their friends, not Leo's foster parents.

Each morning her hopes were dashed. She must have been a sophomore in high school before she let go of the fantasy.

What would Elizabeth Reese think of Leo today? Would she be happy with the path Leo had chosen? With the life she'd built with Daria? And what would her advice be about this diagnosis? Would she say to take the chance that it was benign and would grow slowly? Tell her to undergo the frightening treatments? Or might she advise Leo to get it cut out as quickly as she could?

Leo didn't know. So much time had passed since her mother's death that sometimes she couldn't quite conjure up how she looked. Over the last several years, when Leo found herself unable to remember the shape and color and life in her mother's face, she hastened to the bookcase, pulled out the photo album, and studied as many pictures as she could until once more she could imagine her mother in three-dimensional, fully rounded, living, breathing detail.

Her tea had cooled, but she drank a sip anyway. She wished she'd told Thom to pick her up in time for the early service at St. Vladimir's. Chances of her going back to sleep now were slim, and she had a lot of time to kill before he arrived.

She thought about Daria, who was still moping around the house as though she'd already lost the Dunleavey case. Leo had tried to encourage her the day before, suggesting she complete one last comprehensive review of the facts, then do something pleasant, something restful for the remainder of the weekend, so that Monday morning she'd feel sharp and energetic, able to jump all over the witnesses. Daria had nodded and stalked off to her office, emerging every couple of hours for snacks and beer and never saying another word.

Leo felt helpless to do anything to lighten Daria's load. She'd tried to interest her in lunch and had suggested going out to dinner, to no avail. Daria stayed holed up in her office and didn't come to bed until after three a.m. Once awakened, Leo never slipped off again, so here she was, under-rested and over-worried.

At least she didn't have a hangover today.

By the time she showered and dressed for the church service, the temperature outdoors had risen to an unseasonable eighty degrees. She wore a pair of light cotton slacks, a short-sleeved blouse, and white sandals. After transferring her badge and wallet from her valise to a white leather bag, she unplugged her phone from the charger and squeezed it in, too. No room for a gun, but churches tended to frown on visitors showing up armed.

When Thom's van skidded to a stop in front of her house, she stepped out from the air conditioning into thick, humid air so soaked with water that the small leather bag felt sticky. By the time she got into the van, she was sweating, and her legs felt unpleasantly clammy.

"It's a muggy one," Thom said, by way of a greeting.

"I can only hope St. Vladimir's has AC."

"No kidding." Thom wore loafers, tan pants, and a royal blue polo shirt. His black hair, combed back off his face, still looked damp from the shower. "Shall we play good cop/bad cop?"

"With a minister?"

"Come on, plenty of men of the cloth are well-known to be troublemakers and criminals. Consider the pedophile fiasco in the Catholic church or the Ted Haggard scandal. Some of those guys on TV are raking in the dough to finance their own lifestyles, not provide for real ministries."

"I remember Jim and Tammy Faye Baker vividly. They practically ruined TV during my childhood years. I take it you're not a huge fan of churches?"

"I wouldn't say that. I was an altar boy at St. Aggie's until I was seventeen. I'm pleased to say nobody ever touched me inappropriately. I'm still on Father Michael's Christmas card list, and my parents haven't missed many Sundays in about forty years. But in this line of work, you tend to get a little suspicious about people's intentions, don't you? You're a cop. Don't you see the worst from a lot of the people you encounter?"

She admitted that was true and drooped in the seat, feeling fatigued. Out the window, the city streets flashed by, and it was all she could do to keep from dissolving into tears.

"Hey," Thom said, "what's the matter?"

She hesitated. She hardly knew the guy, so why pour out her tale of woe? "I didn't sleep well at all. I'm not feeling as sharp as I'd like to."

"I can sympathize. I had a few beers last night so I didn't want to drive. I camped out on my buddy's couch and woke up with a kink in the side of my neck."

She glanced at him. If she wasn't watching him manipulate the brake and accelerator by hand, she wouldn't be able to tell he was crippled and couldn't jump out of the vehicle and walk. "I hate it when my neck does that. Of course, lucky me, I didn't sleep long enough to manage to get kinked up."

"You *are* lucky, then." He gave her a big grin. "So we'll go into this thing as The Crip and the Wasted Woman, and we can both be the bad cop."

Leo felt her face flush with heat. She'd just referred to Thom in her own thoughts as a cripple, but for him to say it out loud embarrassed her.

"What?" he said. "You're offended by the characterization? Okay, then let's make it The Crip and the Lethargic Lady."

"No. Not about me, the way you're speaking of yourself."

"Me? But I am a crip, aren't I? I've even got the crip sticker to prove it." He said it with a hint of glee in his voice and pointed at the blue and white disability tag hanging from the rearview mirror.

She wasn't sure what to say. "But—but it's not very respectful."

He turned off Lexington Avenue onto a side street and gave a jerk of his thumb toward the backseat. "The chair is not me, but it defines me in a lot of people's eyes. It's the first thing people see when they look at me."

She met his gaze, still embarrassed and at a loss for words. She wanted to tell him that the first thing other people saw when they met him might be the chair, but his dark eyes and pleasant demeanor were what they'd remember. She felt that was too personal, too forthright, so she kept silent.

What was the first thing people noticed when they looked at her? And if she lost her right eye, would that define her in the same way Thom's chair seemed to define him?

"Aha, here's the church." He pulled into the parking lot.

She was relieved about not having to respond to Thom's comments or further contemplate her own questions. All the handicap slots were full, so he found a spot in the farthest corner. Last time she'd ridden with him to Rivers' Edge, she hadn't paid attention to how he got from the driver's seat to the wheelchair. This time she stayed put and watched. His wheelchair was folded up and tucked into a slot directly behind his seat. He pressed a button overhead and the passenger's side door next to the chair slid open. He popped open the driver's door and swung his legs out. With one hand outside and one inside the vehicle, he neatly slid the chair out and leaned down to set it on the ground where it opened up with a clank. Grabbing the overhead handle and the doorframe, he lowered himself. For a moment he seemed to be standing, and then he twisted and landed gracefully in the chair.

She got out and went around the van to find him attaching a pack to the handles of the wheelchair. "I'm pretty sure I'd never be able to do what you just did."

"What? Flop out of the van? It's easy."

"You've got to have incredible strength to do that."

"I lift weights, and I stay active. I don't want to be like some of the guys I know who can hardly get around because they don't stay in shape. But I have to admit it helps that I lost so much muscle mass in my legs. In my football days, I weighed as much as two hundred pounds. I'm maybe one-sixty now." He pressed a button inside the rear door, and the slider shut.

She slammed the driver's door. "What's the plan, man?"

"I think we should play it by ear. Why don't you take the lead, and I'll jump in whenever it feels appropriate."

With a nod, she headed across the parking lot. High above her, the church's pitched roof was under repair. Tar paper was tacked down, and the roofers had installed a gangway and a cat ladder on the steep surface. Bundles of shingles lay spaced out below the peak, in another row near the middle of the roof, and here and there along the gutters.

Thom said, "That's some roof project. It's amazing how expensive a roof is for such a good-sized church."

They entered the church through the center door of three entrances. From the foyer, a huge, arched door in the middle and two sets of open double doors on either side led into a giant sanctuary. Voices sang a hymn—something about hailing the power of Jesus' name—but the sound was muffled in the enormity of the sanctuary.

Thom rolled to the right, and they went in and saw clusters of people throughout the church. Leo estimated they could cram over 400 people in, but only about a hundred were present today.

He gestured for Leo to slide into the last row, and he maneuvered his wheelchair next to her in the aisle. A man seated several feet away handed her a program, and she whispered her thanks.

The church was a strange mix of new and old. The building was obviously modern, and its lines were crisp, accented with lightly stained wood. Three windows on the side walls contained stained glass panels, and they were dark enough not to let in much light. Most of the illumination in the church came from overhead hanging lamps or through banks of lancet windows high up, near the ceiling. Light from those windows reflected inside from a parchment-colored ceiling.

The pew Leo sat on was smooth wood with no cushioning. The seat back was more upright than she found comfortable, and she could already tell that it wouldn't take long before she'd feel stiff.

The floor was covered in a short-napped carpet speckled with brown, red, and tan. A thicker carpet in a rich red ran up the middle aisle all the way to the steps that led up to the altar. The chancel area was surrounded by an elaborate railing made of heavy dark wood that matched the wood of the altar. Behind the altar, Reverend Trent stood with his hands raised. Once the hymn ended, he intoned a prayer. His dark beard was bushy, peppered with gray. Over his white robes he wore a beautiful green brocade vestment with a golden cross.

Above the minister's head, Jesus hung from a rough wood cross in a particularly grisly-looking, life-size crucifixion pose. The thorns in his crown seemed so sharp that it was no wonder drops of blood dripped down His agonized face. Blood oozed from the sword wound in His side, and His hands and feet glistened with blood. The artist who had painted the figure had outdone him or herself for gore. Leo shuddered. This Jesus was so real she didn't think there was enough money in the world to get her to stand below that cross. Any minute now she expected drops of blood to cascade down and spatter the Bible on its stand.

Leo glanced through the list of readings and took note of the order of the service. St. Vladimir's was a member of the Wisconsin Synod, which she recalled was the most conservative of all Lutheran churches. She passed the program over to Thom.

As an adult, Leo hadn't been a churchgoer. As a child, she'd only attended on big holidays with her mom until she'd gone to live with the Wallaces, staunch Catholics who rarely missed mass. Often they attended the Saturday evening service, though, because Dad Wallace's work schedule required him to work most Sundays.

Up until five months before her death, Leo's mother had worked as a police and fire dispatcher. Leo loved sitting at the dinner table and listening to her mother's stories of helping people give first aid, of children rescued from burning houses, and of crimes averted with the help of the dispatchers. From as early as she could remember, she'd planned to be a dispatcher like her mom.

After her mother died, the TV program *Rescue 911* premiered, and Leo and Kate spent many a Tuesday night curled up in front of the TV rooting for the paramedics, cops, and firefighters. For several years, they both agreed that being firefighters would give them the best chance of saving cats and dogs and kids from fires, but as Leo grew older, she came to understand that the dirty, dangerous job of fighting fires wasn't for her. Dad Wallace had such an influence that she set her sights on a police job. Kate held on to the firefighter dream quite a bit longer, but when she saw how few openings there were, she eventually decided to follow her father and Leo onto the force.

The people around Leo suddenly rose, and she realized she'd completely lost track of the church service. It was time for the Gospel to be read. Thom leaned toward her, and as she stood she bent to hear what he had to say.

"Aren't I a lazy ass?" he whispered. He glanced down at his chair, then shrugged.

Smiling, she straightened up and faced front, wondering how Thom had liked being raised Catholic. His body language and that comment pegged him as irreverent, but she thought there would be more to the story.

When the Gospel reading ended, Reverend Trent mounted the stairs to a carved wood pulpit. After asking them to be seated, he adjusted his stole, cleared his throat, and roared, "The fires of hell await those of us who are not vigilant!"

Somebody gasped, and people shifted in their seats. The congregation seemed as taken aback as Leo was.

"My words are harsh," he said, "but these are trying times. We must be ever vigilant as the forces of darkness, perversion, greed, and sin close in around us every day."

Oh, she thought, so he's *that* kind of preacher. Doom and gloom. Sin and Satan. She tuned him out and concentrated on her hands, which she laced together in her lap. She should have suggested they show up closer to eleven, after the service was nearly over.

Leo didn't much care for church. She'd been baptized as a baby, was confirmed at the same time as Kate, and had attended Catholic Youth Organization events with Kate through her teens. But every time she entered a church, she half-expected to see that baby-blue casket at the front, the one with the silver trim that had contained the body of her mother. She knew it was irrational, but her memories of the day Elizabeth Reese was buried came back each time she walked through a holy door. She saw the shiny blue casket in her mind's eye and re-experienced the horror she'd felt that her mother's remains were in there, all alone, and spending eternity buried at the cemetery so far from the house where Leo lived with her as a child.

She didn't know how she'd gotten through the wake and the funeral. She'd been a week shy of eleven, and somehow she had the feeling that she ought to stand tall on her own. She hadn't cried at the church, but halfway through the funeral, she finally burst into tears, and if she could have crawled up onto Mom Wallace's lap and stayed there permanently, she would have. After the pallbearers carried the blue casket away, everything was a blur. She didn't know how she got to the cemetery; she remembered nothing about the graveside service; she couldn't recall returning to the Wallaces' house afterward.

Another thing she didn't have any knowledge or recollection of was the funeral arrangements. Years later when Mom Wallace mentioned that Leo had chosen the hymns for the funeral, she couldn't dredge that up from her memory. She was out of college before she understood that the Wallaces had footed the bill for the funeral. Leo had no other family willing or able to do so. She still had a sense of awe over the idea that a policeman and stay-at-home mom with five kids managed to pay the entire bill for her mother's final send-off.

What she did remember was going to the ball field with Kate and hitting softballs for what seemed like hours. Kate pitched ball after ball, and when the bucket was empty, Kate was the one who chased down all the balls, leaving Leo to stand in the early evening sun feeling empty and alone. She knew how much Kate liked to bat. Usually Leo was stuck pitching to Kate the majority of the time, but on this one day, Kate never once touched the bat except to transport it back and forth to the field.

Leo remembered Kate's fierce resolve, her refusal to let Leo pitch that day, and it made her heart feel overlarge in her chest— then, and now. Kate had never been overly emotional, and even as adults they weren't all that outwardly affectionate toward one another, but one thing Leo knew deep in her heart was that Kate would be there for her, no matter what. Too bad Daria didn't seem as reliable. Leo felt she ought to smack herself for that thought. How could that be fair to Daria? But it was true, she thought wistfully.

The strains of the organ wailing full force from the pipes startled Leo. The preacher had finished his sermon, and the congregation rose to sing a hymn. Good God, would this service never end? She couldn't believe how long it had dragged on.

Thom saw her checking her watch and rolled his eyes. The expression on his face was so comical that she had to force back a laugh. It was after eleven, and the Prayers for the People droned on and on. She paid no attention at all until suddenly, Thom poked her shoulder.

"What?"

He mouthed, "Listen."

"...and we thank every member who contributed to the roof fund, in particular, we thank Victoria Bishop, our own special guardian angel." The lector paused to look around the church, but didn't seem to find whoever he was searching for.

"Victoria Bishop?" Leo whispered to Thom.

He nodded.

Communion and more prayers seemed to take forever. The final benediction didn't come until half past eleven. Leo watched as the minister and altar boys marched down the center aisle. The church gradually emptied while she and Thom waited patiently.

"Leo," Thom said when there were only two rows left to leave. "Why don't you go out and greet him last so you can ask him to speak to us. I'll roll around and meet you by the front entrance."

Reverend Trent had loomed as such a giant, burly man up on the altar, but once she reached him at the church's front doors, she saw that he was only about an inch or two taller than her five-eight. He was broad, though, with shoulders made to seem even wider by the robe and vestments.

He shook her hand, and as he leaned forward, she focused on his miniature red lips, lost in the forest of his bushy beard.

"Good morning, ma'am. So nice to see you on this lovely day. Your first time visiting Saint Vladimir's?"

"Yes, Reverend, and if you have a few moments, I'd like to

speak with you." Thom came to a rest on her left, and she said, "We'd both like a word."

Trent's eyes lit up. "Let me touch base with one of the council members about the roof project. He's waiting out front. I'll be right in." He called out to someone named John, and asked the man to escort them to the council room.

They were led down the side aisle through the church sanctuary to an elevator behind the altar and descended to yet another hallway ablaze with light. Every overhead lamp in the place was on, probably because without artificial light, the basement would be pitch dark. As they made their way along a passage painted the ugliest shade of pea green, Leo saw the whole level was like a rabbit warren. There were small cell-like rooms along the way, most of which were so jammed full of stuff that the doors wouldn't even shut. She saw shelves of paper and janitorial supplies in one, boxes stacked to the ceiling in another, and old desks and broken chairs in yet one more. As she passed a closet-sized alcove that lacked a door, she realized it was crammed full of decrepit-looking vacuum cleaners. Ten? Twelve? They passed too quickly for her to count. Who kept all this junk—and why? Saint Vladimir's ought to have a garage sale and clear out all the crap. Or maybe someone needed to back up a pickup and cart it all to the dump.

She didn't know what to expect from the council room. Maybe they'd have old statues and carpeting and wallpaper rolls lying around. But the room they entered contained only a huge square table with chairs for sixteen, four each on a side. If they were all extremely skinny—or good friends who didn't mind sitting close—sixteen could squeeze in there. The table was really meant for twelve.

John stepped in, dragged a couple of chairs out of the way and invited Thom to roll up and make himself comfortable. Leo went around to the other side, leaving the head available for Trent. She set down her little bag and plopped into the chair. After John departed, they inspected the room for a few minutes. The paneled wood walls were decorated with 9x12-inch pictures of the Stations of the Cross. At the end of the room farthest from the door, built-in bookcases were jammed full of old books. The room smelled musty, like some of those books had long ago been water-damaged.

"What a snore," Thom whispered.

"My sentiments exactly."

"I've never heard of a Saint Vladimir. What kind of saint is he, anyway?"

"Not a clue."

George Trent came bustling in and stopped at the head of the table. He'd changed into a blue serge suit with a red tie. "Welcome, welcome, Mr. and Mrs. — ?"

"No, sir," Thom said. "We're — "

"Let me guess," Trent said. "You're planning to marry, and you'd like to hold the wedding ceremony here?"

"No, sir, we — "

"You're not living together and coming for some kind of absolution?" Trent sat heavily, looking from Thom to Leo and back.

She decided to let Thom off the hook. "No, Reverend, we're here about the roof."

His brow furrowed. "The roof? What about the roof? It should be completed by early next week. Are you needing a referral? I can give the company the highest recommendation for their — "

She held up a hand. "Please, let me explain. We understand the roof was damaged recently in the storms, and your parish didn't have the funds to replace it."

"That's right. High winds blew off whole sections of shingles. We had leaks in the sacristy and right in the middle of the sanctuary. Terrible, just terrible."

Leo folded her hands and set them on the table. "Someone came forward and donated the funds to repair the roof, correct?"

"Yes, thanks be to God. We'd only managed to raise about twenty-five thousand dollars, but then one of our most treasured parishioners received an unexpected inheritance, and we commenced work right away. We're infinitely grateful that our prayers were so immediately answered."

Leo asked, "What's it cost to put a roof on a church like this?"

"Well in excess of sixty thousand dollars. I don't have the final totals yet. We're hoping it doesn't hit seventy thousand."

"Wow, that's a lot of money," Thom said. "When you got the sizable donation, you must have had quite the celebration."

"Indeed. Not only did we have cake and punch here in the Fellowship Hall, but our benefactor insisted on treating my fellow pastors and myself at a fine restaurant."

"A fine restaurant?" Leo asked.

"Yes, a French place nearby called Chez René. I'd never been there before, but it was outstanding. Have you dined there?"

"No, not yet." Leo's heart raced as though she'd run six blocks, but she forced herself to stay calm. "Who is the benefactor?"

"Her name is Victoria Bishop."

"Is she a long-time member?" Thom asked.

"No, I've been here three years, and she came some time after I did. I'd say perhaps two years ago."

"That's an enormous commitment Ms. Bishop made," Leo said. "A lot of money for such a new member to donate."

"But she's a wonderful woman," Trent said. "Very giving. Very loving. She's here almost every Sunday. She works with the Altar Guild, and she rarely misses the Welcome Dinners we give for new members. She's one of the most active people I know. She helps our secretary create and assemble the church bulletins, and she often does all the shopping for the final farewell events — that's the group of ladies who prepare the lunch after funerals. Most of them are quite elderly, and to have Victoria Bishop helping has been a godsend. Not a bulletin goes by that we don't thank her for some major initiative. She makes an immeasurable contribution to our faith community."

"Was she here today?" Thom asked.

"No, I didn't see her. Could you tell me what this is all about?"

Thom hesitated so Leo jumped in. "Let me introduce myself. My name is Leona Reese, and I work for the State of Minnesota. My department investigates unusual monetary transfers, and we're checking up on Ms. Bishop's generous offering."

A frown of concern passed over Trent's face. "Is there a problem with Victoria's contribution?"

"Perhaps. But probably not."

"Listen here, we're a bona fide church, and we have the properly executed paperwork verifying that we're a tax-exempt religious organization. We're meticulous with our recordkeeping."

"Yes, yes, Reverend Trent," Leo said, "we understand that completely, and we're not casting aspersions upon your ministry or your membership. But we should speak to Ms. Bishop personally and were hoping we'd catch up with her at this morning's service. Now we'll have to track her down at her home."

"She travels a lot for her work. I believe she flies out of state several times a month. Victoria is probably gone because of her job, otherwise, she'd be here. She rarely misses a Sunday."

"Do you have a current address for her?"

"I'm sure we do." Trent rose. "I feel uncomfortable about releasing it, though."

Thom fumbled behind him to pull his backpack onto his lap. From a front zipper pocket he removed a leather folder and flipped it open to display his badge. "This may allay your concerns, Reverend. My name is Thomas Thoreson, and here's my State ID."

Trent let out a breath of relief. "All right. Let's go upstairs to my office, and I'll find her address."

As they entered the elevator, Thom said, "Reverend, what can you tell me about Saint Vladimir?"

"Do you know anything about him?"

"No, sir, I don't."

"He was a tenth century prince in Kiev who brought

Christianity to Russia and the Ukraine. He arranged for baptism of his subjects in the Dnieper River after receiving the tenets of the faith from Constantinople." The elevator doors opened, and Trent stepped out and held the doors open for them. "Vladimir spread the Holy Word throughout his realm and is the founder of the Orthodox Church."

He led them down the hall as he rambled on, but Leo tuned him out, instead thinking about the twisted path the case was taking. Who was this Victoria Bishop person, and how could such a kind-hearted, pious, upstanding woman have anything to do with a murder and grand theft? Was she a pawn of another person's greed and thievery? Or would this financial crime be considered grand larceny? The theft was substantial enough and was certainly accomplished under false pretenses. Leo had a hunch that whoever the con artist turned out to be, he must be clever and cunning.

They were out of the church and in the van five minutes later. Leo looked at the slip of paper Trent had given her. "Uh-oh. I've got a bad feeling about this."

"Why?" Thom asked as he started the van.

"The address is clear across the city, and it's a box number. Why would she live such a distance from the church? There are plenty of Lutheran churches closer to the PO box. With the traffic, it'd take her forty-five minutes to travel to St. Vladimir's."

"Let's go check it out."

The address was in a strip mall between a Game Stop video store and a dry cleaner. Leo hopped out and entered the foyer. Both of the side walls and half of the wall straight ahead were jammed with mailboxes of various sizes. The other half of the wall before her was taken up by a counter, but because the store was closed, a metal grate was pulled down to block it off. A five-foot-tall sign proclaimed "The Lobby Is Open 24/7!" A smaller sign indicated that mail service personnel were only there 6 a.m. to midnight Monday through Saturday.

She found box number 133 and peeked into the sliver-sized window. She could make out a couple of envelopes, but couldn't see anything else.

Back in the van, she said, "One of us will have to call or come over here Monday. The office is closed. But it's a mail drop all right."

Thom backed out of the slot. "This is how crooks and thieves are operating these days. They get a temporary mail drop under a false name, have materials sent to themselves there, and when the box comes under scrutiny, they abandon it."

"How is it so easy to do that? I've seen plenty of fake IDs on the street, but shouldn't these places have rules?"

"Yes, but clerks in these kind of places aren't trained to spot fake ID, and it's pretty easy to mock up driver's licenses."

"But Minnesota instituted new safeguards on licenses."

"The crooks are probably using out-of-state identification. It's easy to come in with some cock-and-bull story about being new to the area or only working here for six months or something like that. The clerks definitely don't have a clue about what a Georgia or Utah or Connecticut license looks like. There's steady trade for stolen identification, too. I've seen a fair number of bogus IDs turn up when we go in and investigate staff at nursing homes, and I'm not just talking about undocumented workers. Seems like there's always some orderly or janitor or dishwasher with a criminal record who gets his papers on the black market to avoid questions. It's a thriving business behind the scenes."

Leo shook her head. "You won't believe how often we picked up people on patrol and their ID didn't come close to matching their pictures. We recently had an older man sit for days in a holding cell because he wouldn't tell us his real name. We had to identify him by his fingerprints, and everything's so backed up that it took practically a week. We found out the old guy had warrants that went back twenty years in three different states."

"Violent offenses?"

"Nope. All con games and theft. The guy was a real slick player."

Thom came to a stop at a red light. "Where to next?"

Before Leo could answer, her purse let out a trill. She flipped open the clasp. The phone was wedged in tightly, but she managed to pull it free and answer it.

"Detective Flanagan here."

"Hey, I've been trying to call you all day. Iris Fullerton and Claire Ryerson—did their alibis stand up?"

"Well, yeah. Fullerton is on vacation. We verified it. Ryerson was meeting with a guy who verified her whereabouts."

"What about Martin Rivers?"

"He's in the clear, too. Look, I've got more important fish to fry. Thought you'd want to know there was another Rivers murder last night."

"What? Not Eleanor Sinclair?"

"No, not at Rivers' Edge. We're in Bloomington."

"Thank God. But who died?"

"An older woman named Celia Deveaux. We've been at the Rivers' Bloom facility in Bloomington all night. At this point, I think you might want to meet with us."

He gave her the address, and she said, "Thom Thoreson and I will be over shortly."

Chapter Twenty-two

RIVERS' BLOOM WASN'T far from the Minneapolis/Saint Paul airport, and the flight path was overhead. Before they'd exited the van and made it to the front door, two planes had already gone zooming by, the noise drowning out all but shouts. Thom waited for the jet to pass, then said, "I'd hate to live here. The noise would drive me insane."

Leo rang the doorbell. "I think they shift the flights around so it's not always so loud."

"Still not my idea of a good time."

The door creaked open, and a petite woman in a hot-pink nurse's outfit stood in front of them looking dazed. Thom held up his badge, and she stepped back to let them in. Leo introduced herself and Thom.

"The police are this way," the young woman said. "Please follow me."

Rivers' Bloom was laid out exactly like Rivers' Edge, but the accent colors were gold and maroon. The Berber carpet was thick, the lighting dim, and the walls in the common area were cluttered with gilt-frame paintings of hunting dogs, ancient castles, and men in jodhpurs. Overstuffed couches and chairs with mahogany wood trim were arranged around a massive square table upon which two sets of magazines were artfully fanned out.

"It's like walking into a strange dream," Thom said. "The place is so much like the other, except weirdly different."

"Yeah, the difference between the twenty-first century and the Renaissance."

The aide led them down the west hall—or, as Leo suddenly realized, it would be the north hall here. Though the facility was obviously built with the same exact floor plan, the building faced north, rather than west as Rivers' Edge did.

Outside a room at the far end, a yellow duffel bag, a jumbled pile of brown paper bags, and spotlight racks on a tripod blocked the doorway. As they drew nearer, she saw the bags were labeled as evidence.

Flanagan poked his head out. "Oh. You're here." He said something to someone behind him then stepped over the paper bags and into the hall. "What a dirty shame. These poor Bloomington cops are about as busy as us."

"What happened?" Leo asked.

"Another old woman, but now we're on to him. He blew it this time."

"Who?" Thom asked.

"I don't believe we've met," Flanagan said.

"Thom Thoreson, State Investigative Unit." The men shook hands.

"I should have kept that maniac in custody when Mrs. Trimble died," Flanagan said, "but we didn't have enough to hold him. Now we do." He seemed to have developed new lines around his eyes, and frustration showed clearly on his careworn face. His brown hair was lank and dull as if he'd failed to wash it for a couple of days, and bits of dandruff contrasted well with his dark green shirt. He'd rolled up his shirtsleeves, and powerful forearms belied his stooped, tired posture as he leaned against the wall.

"Who is the suspect?" Thom repeated.

"Sorry," Flanagan said, as he rubbed his eyes. "Ted Trimble. The son from the other murder."

Leo's mouth dropped open. She didn't know what to say, but Thom jumped in.

"Did you catch him red-handed?"

"No, but he left a little something behind. He lost his wallet during the commission of the crime."

Leo found her voice. "How did the victim die?"

"Looks the same as Callie Trimble. Suffocation. The Hennepin County medical examiner will verify it for us as soon as he can."

"Detective," Thom said, "we've been following a lead that's gone a completely different direction. We need to sit down and discuss this."

"We can talk all you want, but we've nailed the guy." He leaned around the corner into the apartment. "Hal, you got a minute?"

DeWitt shuffled toward the door. If Leo thought Flanagan looked the worse for wear, DeWitt was even more disheveled. In addition to a similar appearance of exhaustion, the legs of his tan slacks were smudged with dark marks, and his shirt was wrinkled nearly everywhere, as though he'd pulled it from the laundry basket and put it on without ironing it. If she didn't know better, she'd wonder if he'd been on a three-day drunk. He said something to another man about being right back and stepped into the hallway to be introduced to Thom.

"Let's go to the staff room," Flanagan said.

One of the dryers was running, and the staff room was unpleasantly warm. The bunks were both made up, and one chair sat next to the foot of the bed.

"Let me grab a couple more chairs," DeWitt said.

"I'll pass," Thom said with a smirk.

DeWitt didn't seem to get the joke. He exited, and Flanagan lowered himself to the edge of the bottom bunk, his elbows on his knees. He sat silently with head in hands until DeWitt came back with another chair and everybody was seated.

"You guys must be whipped," Thom said.

"We had a drive-by shooting Friday night," Flanagan said as he straightened up. "Then we got this call around eight last night. Before we could even get here to assist and see the Bloomington guys process the scene, some lunatic shot his wife and her boyfriend down at the bar on Lexington, so we got called out on that. Half the squad is on summer vacation, and bodies are dropping right and left."

"Oh, man," Thom said, "sounds like a recipe for exhaustion."

DeWitt said, "Bottom line is that Trimble screwed up. Not only did he lose his wallet, but the victim's bank account was cleaned out, and the exact amounts were deposited to Trimble's own account."

"How do you know that on a Sunday?"

DeWitt's face blanched white. "Actually, we noted the deposit late on Friday. We've been monitoring various suspects' accounts. We'll get the new bank surveillance footage tomorrow. We couldn't tell where the deposit had come from so there was no way for us to prevent this." He stared down at the floor, as pallid as a corpse.

"That's terrible," Leo said. "How much was deposited?"

Flanagan shifted, and the coverlet on the bunk bed came untucked. "The idiot had the deposit slip in his wallet. I can't remember the exact amount, but it was something like forty-four hundred and some change."

"Literally pennies?" Leo asked. When the cops nodded, she said, "Doesn't that strike you as odd? I'll bet the funds went to the bank through the night depository so you won't have any video. That's the only way it makes sense. I mean, we have a thief who's killed at least five people, three of them undetected, and suddenly he gets all careless?"

"What?" Flanagan and DeWitt said simultaneously. Both men seemed to zing with electricity.

"What three undetected deaths?" Flanagan asked.

Leo exchanged a glance with Thom. "Let's start at the beginning." They ran through all the details of their investigation, taking turns laying out the facts about the other three elderly women's deaths and their discovery of the mystery woman, Victoria Bishop. Leo ended by saying, "I can't help but think Ted Trimble was set up. I don't see the guy killing anybody. Why kill a family member if there's a whole raft of strangers to bilk and murder? Has he rolled under interrogation?"

Flanagan shifted uncomfortably. "No. He swears he knows nothing about any of this, but we've got too much evidence for it to be coincidental. For chrissake, the guy's an accountant. He knows how to steal, that's for sure."

"The blonde is the key," Thom said. "I predict that this Bishop woman is the mastermind."

Flanagan stood and paced to the closed door. "Could be she's in league with Trimble. This is the kind of con that would benefit from a couple working it."

"Or a team," DeWitt said.

"If there are bank surveillance tapes," Leo said, "they'll show who deposited that money. If it was Ted Trimble I'll be shocked. What else was in his wallet?"

Flanagan said, "Twenty-one bucks, Visa plastic, and some business cards, including one of his own."

"Driver's license?" she asked.

The cops shook their heads.

"Bet he had his license on him when you picked him up, didn't he?" The detectives didn't answer her. "He's been set up, guys. You know it, don't you? The situation is too suspicious. Feels wrong."

Flanagan let out a sigh. "Jesus, I don't know."

Thom said, "Eleanor Sinclair is also part of the solution here."

"Yes," Leo said. "Eleanor is our sole living witness, and why is that? Her accounts were plundered like Celia Deveaux's and the other three ladies' were. Why wasn't she suffocated? Instead, Callie Trimble was murdered. I've been thinking about this. My theory is that the killer doesn't actually know the victims. That's part of the safety valve. If the mark doesn't know the thief, and the thief doesn't know him — or her — or them — it's a lot harder to link them, right? But that also means mistakes could be made. In this case, Callie Trimble was sleeping in Eleanor's apartment, and since the killer didn't know one from the other, he — or she — killed the wrong woman."

"That's pretty farfetched," DeWitt said.

"But possible," Thom said. "You have to admit it's possible."

The cop's skepticism made Leo mad, and she had to temper her words before they flew out in an attack. "These are money crimes, eventually covered up by what appear on the surface to be natural deaths. What about Celia Deveaux? I'll bet you never would have known this was a murder without the wallet."

"That's not true," Flanagan said. "Any death at a Rivers' facility will be on our radar now for a long time."

"You've had three deaths already that weren't on your radar." As Flanagan's eyes narrowed, Leo regretted the sharpness of her words as soon as they came out. Quickly, she added, "Celia Deveaux — was it readily apparent that she was murdered? Would you have thought anything out of the ordinary if it weren't for the wallet?"

"Maybe not," Flanagan admitted.

"I rest my case, Detective. You're being manipulated, and not by Trimble. We've got to find this Victoria Bishop."

DeWitt rose. "There's no 'we' in the equation. Dennis and I will find her. We appreciate how forthcoming you've both been and all the work you've done, but at this point, let us handle the situation. It'd be best if you'd skedaddle now and come investigate tomorrow when the Bloomington techs have got the crime scene wrapped up."

Thom rolled his chair backwards toward the door. "Right. We're going to have to open up a whole new investigation on this death. More interviews, more poking around here at Rivers' Bloom. Of course we can wait until morning. We don't even have the official report yet. We'd appreciate it if you'd keep us in the loop, though."

Leo was silent as she followed Thom to the front door. The thought of a whole new investigation for a similar murder made her angry. She felt she'd somehow failed.

She reached for the front door as someone turned a key in the lock. She pulled back just in time. The door swung open with real velocity.

Martin Rivers stepped into the foyer, his eyes blazing. "What the hell is going on here?" He slammed the door, glared at Leo, and frowned at Thom. "Who are you?"

As Thom introduced himself, Leo watched Rivers closely. Mr. Hoss Cartwright was genuinely distressed. His shaggy hair was windblown, and he was dressed casually in a red polo shirt, tan shorts, and leather sandals that showed a pronounced golfer's tan around his ankles.

Rivers slammed his car keys on the counter to his left and ran a hand over his face. "How can this be happening to me?" he muttered.

"Are you just finding out about this, sir?" Leo asked.

He focused on Leo, his eyes hard and angry. "No, I found out last night and have just spent fifteen hours driving like a bat out of hell from Canada. No sooner did we arrive at the fishing shack than I got this call." His tone was scathing. "I think you can assume my alibi is good. Where's my manager, Ms. Reese?"

"I don't know. We've only conferred with the police since we got here."

"Oh, God. Let me through." He pushed past Leo and Thom

and stomped toward the dining hall.

"Such a nice man," Thom said.

"Yeah, but I suppose you'd feel the same way if your business was taking the same kinds of hits his is." She opened the door. "Let's go regroup."

LEO AND THOM went over the facts in the van all the way back to Leo's house, but neither one of them could come up with any brilliant solutions.

"Victoria Bishop," Leo said. "You're right. She's the key."

"Blondes have more fun. Who are the blondes you've interviewed?"

"Sherry Colton. Rowena Hoxley. Oh, and Hazel Bellinger, but she's a bottle blonde."

"If I remember correctly, Hazel also has a shaky alibi. What about Nettie Volk?"

"Nettie?"

"Yeah, that cotton candy blue could easily be dyed yellow anytime."

Leo laughed. "She's built like a tiny bird. There'd be a better chance of Ted Trimble getting away dressing in drag with a blonde wig."

"Now that's a good theory. What was Hoxley's alibi? Hoxley's the manager, right?"

"Yes. She claimed she was home alone until about ten when her husband came home from work."

"She's my number one suspect then," Thom said.

"Wish I hadn't left the paperwork on the desk. I have her address, and we could have tracked her down and talked to her."

"I hate that today is Sunday. What an obstacle. Any other day, and we might be able to make some progress, but nothing's open. Do you have a key to the office?"

"No. Sorry. I'm so temporary they haven't given me any keys, not even to the executive washroom."

Thom laughed. "If there was one, you'd never get it away from that buffoon Fred."

"What's wrong with that guy? This is an interesting job. What's his problem?"

"I'm not sure if he's lazy or burned out or what. All I know is that when I first came for training, he was no help at all. I've got no use for anybody who can't function as part of the team. Sure, we're all individual investigators with our own cases, but there's no reason to dump the majority of the work on others. Besides, the guy's a glory hound. Have you figured out yet that he wants you to submit the report so he can personally bring the facts to Ralph, perhaps also to the assistant commissioner, and take credit?"

"No. All he said was that we needed to move on to the next case."

"As my grandpa used to say, that's horse-pucky. Old Baldurdash gets everyone else to do all the labor, and he tries to take all the credit. I worked with him during my first eight months before they sent me to the Duluth office. He burned me a couple of times taking credit for my work. I don't trust him, and you shouldn't either."

"How far are we supposed to delve into these murders, Thom?"

"Heck if I know. Haven't had too many cases like this. Usually when there's a homicide, it's an accident or some kind of altercation that went on between clients or a client and staff."

"I guess I'm not sure how I'm supposed to finish off the report and make recommendations. Seems like the best recommendation would be for Martin Rivers to close his facilities as long as his residents are getting murdered."

Thom pulled off the main thoroughfare and slowed at a stop sign. "Rivers certainly could beef up security for a while."

"After the Callie Trimble death, I'm surprised he didn't hire a temporary security service to watch over things, maybe have someone do a complete safety assessment."

"But how was he to know that someone at a different complex would be targeted?"

"True," she said.

Thom stopped in front of her house. "I guess I'll be late, but I'm off to the Twins game now. If anything comes up, call my cell phone. The Target Field isn't conducive to hearing a cell phone call, but I'll have it on in case."

"I didn't know you were due at a game. I'm sorry you're missing it." She opened the door and slipped out.

"Don't worry about it, Leo. See you tomorrow."

She shut the door, and with a wave he drove off. Thom had used her nickname. Usually only family and friends called her Leo, or sometimes Lee. Though she didn't know him well, it sounded natural coming from him.

She trudged up the walk to the house and let herself in. "Daria?" She'd left her valise on the bench in the entryway and tossed her bag next to it. The stuffy air felt warm and heavy. Daria had left the thermostat set too high. Leo turned it down, and the air conditioner cycled on.

In the kitchen she found a note. "Working – won't be back for dinner – D."

It figured that she'd spend the day at the office. Leo should have assumed she would. No rest for the weary and all that.

The remainder of the day, and the evening, too, was hers to do as she wished. The thought made her feel tired. But her head wasn't pounding, and she decided to take advantage.

She went upstairs and changed into shorts, a t-shirt, and workout shoes. When she returned to the kitchen, she buttered two pieces of toast and ate them with a carton of blueberry yogurt. With a water bottle from the fridge and a change of clothes in her workout bag, she took off for the police station.

AFTER HALF AN hour of lifting weights and forty minutes on the elliptical trainer, Leo felt she'd had a good enough workout. She headed to the locker room showers feeling her muscles pleasantly relaxed. The throbbing in her head was back, faint, but bearable. She hadn't kept up her workout regimen in the last couple of weeks since the pain had intensified, and she didn't feel anywhere near as strong as she had before the problem had gradually worsened. She needed to increase her workouts, even if she did get headaches from them. Once she returned to patrol, feeling fit and flexible was critical.

When Leo exited the police station, the heat felt suffocating. She squinted into the mid-afternoon sun, wishing she were already home. Before her eyes could fully adjust, a man's voice said, "Didn't expect to see you hanging around, Reese."

She raised a hand to her brow to block the bright sun. "Oh, hello, Hannen."

"You here begging for your patrol assignment?"

His tone was so condescending that Leo had to bite back a smart remark. Instead she said, "Just working out. I hope you're treating my team well."

"Heh. Well, they're my team now."

"Don't get too comfy. I've got seniority over you, not to mention experience."

"Tick-tock, tick-tock. Every day you're away, my seniority increases. Too bad you came on the force six months before me. Big deal. While you're off contemplating your navel, won't be long before my active duty time will match or exceed yours."

She smiled sweetly. "Obviously, Bobby, you've misunderstood the circumstances." He hated being called Bobby, so she rubbed it in. "Didn't anyone tell you I'm working investigations full-time, Bobby? Every hour, every day counts toward my career longevity. You're never going to catch up."

"Oh, yeah, I will. I heard your squeeze over at the courthouse one day talking about having kids. You'll eventually get knocked up, and your maternity leave will do it."

She'd like to knock him upside the head, but she merely tightened her fist around her workout bag and continued to smile. "We'll see about that. You have a nice day, Bobby." She sauntered off, clenching her teeth with every step. The thought of that pigheaded, sexist jerk supervising her squad infuriated her. But what could she do? He was the kind of cop who knew how to suck up to the brass, but out in the field he was a petty tyrant. He'd covered for her a few times when she'd been off-duty, and she knew her team, particularly the women, were uncomfortable with him.

She'd avoided thinking about her eye treatment options all day, but as she drove out of the lot in the oven of her car, she felt panicky. What if she had to have surgery and was off work for months? Could Hannen actually catch up with service dates? He was one mean and miserable man, and though it was a minor point, she didn't want him to exceed her seniority.

Back to her eye. She agonized over what she should do, especially since she couldn't avoid making a decision for much longer. More than anything, she wanted to go home and find Daria there. They could dial down the lights and cuddle on the couch with good strong drinks. She'd be able to pour out her fears and with any luck come to a decision.

But when she arrived home, the garage was empty. She'd expected that but had hoped she might be wrong. She parked and stopped in the backyard to note that the flowers lining the walk were droopy. She got the hose out and spent time watering the beds around the house, all the while fretting about the pain behind her eyes. The thought of losing an eye was enough to make her want to throw up. Would she be disabled? If she was having trouble shooting now, what would it be like without her dominant eye? She'd always squinted her left eye nearly shut, sighted down the barrel, and been an accurate shot, an expert marksman in fact. Could she retrain herself to sight with the left eye?

She shut off the hose, went inside, and transferred her workout clothes from her bag to the laundry basket. The house was cool and quiet, but she felt restless. In the kitchen, she picked up the half-filled watering can and wandered through the main floor to douse the various plants. She hadn't paid any attention to them for days, and the fern was particularly bedraggled. She upended the can and let the last drips trickle on the fern, picked a few leaves off the table, closed the blinds on the west side of the living room, and returned to the kitchen.

Why did it have to be Sunday? Nothing on TV; nothing

interesting going on. She considered calling Kate, but thought if she did, she'd only whine about how much she missed Daria, and she didn't want to do that.

In a perfect world, she'd have brought home all the notes and reports for the Rivers' Edge case, but she'd expected to spend time with Daria, so she'd left it all behind. Stupid of her. Again. That'd be the last time she'd do that. From now on, she was carrying her deskwork with her. She refilled the watering can, set it on the counter, and stood staring out the window.

Who would murder little old ladies for their money? What kind of people committed such heartless crimes? She hadn't known Callie Trimble nor had she met any of the family of Celia Deveaux, but being acquainted now with Eleanor — not to mention Nettie, Jade, Willie, and Agnes — she couldn't see how anyone would want to harm them. Those women were the quintessential cliché, the salt of the earth.

In a decade on the police force, she'd seen the aftermath of a lot of despicable crimes: a pregnant lady stabbed, drive-by shootings that killed innocent children, robberies gone bad where thieves clubbed homeowners to death. She was often asked why she stayed, given all the ugliness, but amidst the violence and occasional horrors, an undercurrent existed that sometimes approached a kind of beauty. Or maybe she would call it the sublime. At no time was this more apparent than a couple of months earlier, before the Zack Littlefield shooting, when she and a rookie trainee had been called to the scene of a house fire in a shabby part of the east side of Saint Paul.

She and Mike Minton had beat the fire department there, but the neighbors had arrived before the police. In the light of the raging fire, three men in pajamas, two in their underwear, and the rest in jeans or khaki pants all stood below a window trying to coax a young girl to jump.

"Jump," they hollered over and over. "We'll catch you!"

The girl screamed. Flames burned above and behind her. Leo counted eight men under the window and several women standing back comforting a sobbing figure who was on her knees, arms around two small children.

Leo ran to the trunk of her cruiser and pulled out a blanket. "Minton! Let's use this."

They ran toward the group below the window. Before Leo had a chance to say anything, a stocky man wearing nothing more than his BVDs grabbed the blanket.

"Guys, grab hold," he said. "Like this. Get your elbows under for extra strength." He gripped the edge and pulled his fists up to his face, his elbows out under the blanket.

Minton joined the others and grabbed on. They stood below the window, the blue cloth a taut square of safety.

Leo waved to get the girl's attention. "Hey! Look here."

The woman on her knees cried out, "Her name's Allie."

"Allie," Leo yelled. The girl met her eyes for a brief moment. "It's safe, Allie. Jump into the trampoline now. Now!"

With a shriek, the girl launched out the window, her nightgown on fire. She fell and fell, plummeting as though in slow motion. Leo watched her squirm in the air, the fire arcing behind her, and then she was lost inside the circle of men.

For a moment, all was silent. To Leo, it seemed that even the fire ceased to crackle for an instant. And then a great roar of excitement went up.

Moving as one, the men set their bundle on the ground oh-so-gently. A deep voice shouted for help. Where were the paramedics? She heard sirens whining — why weren't they here yet?

Leo dashed over. The girl, long-legged and terrified, kept screaming, "Mama, Mama," over and over. Up in the window, she'd seemed older, but now Leo didn't think she was more than seven or eight. A substantial section of her pink and white nightgown was burned, but the plunge into the blanket must have put it out.

The woman with the two children scurried over, and suddenly it was pig-pile on the blue blanket. The three kids sobbed all over one another, and the mother was a wreck.

Leo leaned down. "Ma'am, is everybody out?"

"Yes, yes. Thank you."

"Are you sure?"

"Oh, my God, yes, thank you."

The fire department arrived. Firefighters jumped off the truck before it came to a stop, and suddenly the yard and street were crawling with cops, medics, and half a dozen of the fire crew dragging hoses.

Leo stepped back and scanned the crowd. All the guys in the impromptu blanket brigade were pumping fists in the air and stomping around as though they'd just scored the winning touchdown at the Super Bowl. Their excitement, their glee was contagious. She grinned and looked for her rookie. Minton stood, arms folded over his chest, and watched silently. His eyes glistened. She took up a post at his elbow so he could have some privacy in the midst of strong emotion.

"Sweet Jesus," Minton whispered, "this is why I became a cop."

In that one simple sentence, Minton had said it all. Neighbors soothing frightened youngsters. Men in their underwear dancing around a yard, celebrating the saving of a child's life. A community of public servants racing to help. Above all, the overwhelming tide of emotion, of people connected by invisible links. People caring about others who were strangers.

No newspaper article, no TV news spot could capture the euphoria. A person had to be there to fully understand, and few police officers could do justice to explain it either. But this was why Leo liked the street, why she didn't want to ride a desk. Investigators cleaned up after the mess was unavoidably permanent; patrol cops sometimes prevented those disasters. Sometimes they had the opportunity to save a life.

So she loved the job. She loved preparing other young officers for it. Law enforcement felt like a calling to her.

What would she do, and who would she be, if she no longer qualified for patrol? She was still young and fit and strong. She didn't feel ready to give it up, so what would become of her if they bounced her right off the job?

She couldn't bear to think of it.

With tears smarting, she turned away from the kitchen window and went upstairs to the fourth bedroom, which she'd set up for her storage, office work, ironing, and sewing. Her off-season clothes and uniforms went into the walk-in closet, along with a couple of boxes of memorabilia and old tax records.

Skirting the ironing board, she went to a table in the corner and flipped on the desktop computer. While it hummed into action, she sat slumped in the chair, wondering if she should call Daria and see how she was doing. Before she could decide, the computer powered up, and she opened a browser and typed in "Rivers' Independent Living Minnesota."

When she found the proper page, Martin Rivers grinned from a full-color photo. She read that Rivers had kicked off construction and planned to open a new facility in Lakeville shortly and another in Crystal in the spring. In the photo, he wore a hard hat and held a shovel as he broke ground for a new site. Next to him stood a swarthy, bow-legged construction worker. Next to Rivers, the guy looked like Gimli the Dwarf from the *Lord of the Rings* movies.

Farther down the page was a close-up of a smiling elderly man holding a newspaper and peering up over half-moon glasses. His teeth were so straight and so blindingly white that they had to be dentures. Next to his picture, printed in bold royal blue, was the business's logo: "Zestful Living and Independence with Exceptional Focus on Your Comfort."

If murder could be considered "Zestful Living" to the survivors, she supposed the logo would do.

She did a search for Saint Vladimir's Church. Reverend Trent's photo on the main page showed him as a younger-looking man with no gray in his beard. She clicked over to the staff page and found names listed alongside thumbnail photos. A middle-aged bald fellow was James R. Lucas, and a young blond pastor was named Matthew Frawley. The lay minister, Jo Ellen Wiesniak, had a hearty, windswept appearance. Her face was broad, her blue eyes small. Thom was right. She wasn't someone you'd call pretty, but she had a solid, friendly look about her.

On a hunch, Leo got out the phone directory and found a listing for Wiesniak, J. E., at an address six blocks from the church. She also found Frawley's name, but there were over a dozen Lucas, J's.

She signed off the computer and headed for the car.

JO ELLEN WIESNIAK lived in a bright-yellow Craftsman-style house with overhanging eaves, a low-slung gabled roof, and a tiny front porch. The house nestled into a narrow lot bursting with plants and flowers. Some of the houses on the street looked a little worse for wear, and every third or fourth house needed the grass cut, but the Wiesniak yard was immaculately groomed.

Leo admired the pinkish-red bloom on the sedum. Purple, pink, and white asters contrasted with big bunches of mums in white, yellow, gold, lavender, and burgundy. The heliopsis stood tall in between bushy, purple Russian sage plants.

And her roses made Leo smile with pleasure. Bloodred, buttercup yellow, and a lovely deep shade of pink, they were open and still blooming.

In the front yard, in the midst of all the color, a woman kneeling on a thick blue pad was weeding a flower bed next to the porch. When Leo called out her name, she dropped a miniature garden hoe, shaded her eyes from the sun, and rose.

She was heavyset, but she'd sprung to her feet quickly and looked strong and fit. Her tan arms stuck out of a sleeveless blouse. She wore loose Capri-style pants that hit her mid-calf and a pair of white canvas shoes that Leo's mom used to call tenny-runners. Leo guessed her age to be around forty. After introducing herself officially as from the State, Leo asked if she could take ten minutes of her time.

"Let's go sit in the backyard shade," Ms. Wiesniak said. "I've got some drinks in an ice chest." She slipped off her garden gloves, wiped her face on her forearm, and went around to the side of the house. Leo followed her through a gate on a cement path that was edged perfectly. Climbing ivy grew abundantly along the fence that separated her house from the neighbor's.

Every step took them closer to an Eden-like garden. The backyard was a riot of colors, and Leo commented on how beautiful the plants and flowers were.

"This is my one major hobby. I love gardening." She led Leo to a patio table and gestured to a chair. Adjusting the umbrella overhead to block the sun, she said, "Reverend Trent told me about your visit to church this morning. I sort of wondered how long it would take you to track me down." She opened an ice chest under the table and rummaged around. "I've got Sprite, A&W Root Beer, and Diet Coke."

Leo accepted a can of Sprite, popped the top, and took a sip.

The other woman flopped into a chair and sucked down several gulps of Diet Coke. She let out a sigh. "Gosh, it's hot."

"Especially since you've been weeding in the sun."

"I meant to do it in the morning before worship service, but things have been too crazy at the church lately."

"In what way?" Leo didn't know why, but a strange kind of electricity in the air gave her a feeling of tense expectation. She felt wired, but in a good way, as if she was about to discover useful information.

"It's been very bad lately."

"Tell me about it, Ms. Wiesniak."

"Please, call me Jo Ellen." She took another sip.

Leo noted that Jo Ellen's double chin contributed to a merry face, used to laughing. But she wasn't laughing now.

"Things have been wrong for quite some time," Jo Ellen said. "Then the roof was damaged, and suddenly it all got even worse. It's close to seventy thousand dollars to replace such a large and complex roof, and we didn't have anywhere near that in the treasury. I kicked off a fund-raising campaign the likes of which the church has never seen. We've got some older parishioners who've been extra careful with their money, and I worked hard to get some of them to part with a smidgeon of their fortunes—whatever they thought they could afford. I was doing well, and then along came Victoria Bishop, spinning her nasty little web."

"Victoria Bishop?"

"Yes. Her." Jo Ellen said it with disdain. "She's such a lovely woman, everyone says so. She's comes off so intelligent and caring, and she has many experiences that she is more than willing to share, ad nauseam, with anyone willing to listen. She's been everywhere, done everything, seen it all."

"But she's a fake?"

"Well, I don't know. I tried to like her, but from the beginning, from the moment when she joined the church, I couldn't trust her. There was something off, something strange in the way she scrutinized me, as though I were a bug under a microscope, and she was ready to pull off my wings. She tries to be all warm and friendly, and she's sure made friends with a lot of people. Most of the members think she's God's gift to the parish."

"But she's been less than pleasant to you?"

"I don't know if it's that I'm overweight or because I haven't done a good enough job in the lay ministry. I really can't say. All I know is that she undermines and sabotages me at every turn. The roof is a good example of it."

"I understand it was her donation that helped meet the target goal."

"Yeah, but I wouldn't be surprised at all if she mugged old ladies and stole from babies."

Leo jerked up straighter in her seat. "What do you mean by that?"

Jo Ellen put the soda can against her forehead and closed her eyes. "I'm sorry. That wasn't very Christian-like of me. But she's a nasty, cruel, heartless woman, and I must be going nuts because I'm just about the only one who can see it. It's been absolutely crazy-making."

"I don't think you're crazy. Make me understand why you believe this."

"Okay." She opened her eyes and set the soda can down with a thwack. "I kicked off the fund-raising with a big bang. Called for donations for a raffle. Made plans for a White Elephant rummage sale. Got the teens involved with sales of Christmas cards and wrapping paper. We sent out a letter to all four-hundred-plus members. The secretary and I spent hours cutting out the letter in the shape of a church just to catch people's eyes. We were getting checks and lots of moral support, and then out of the blue, old man Mueller demanded an audit of the funds that had come in the door. He's on the church council now, along with Victoria Bishop and seven others. We started with about ten thousand in the bank, and we'd already raised over nine thousand more, and suddenly there's a rumor going around that I've got a gambling problem and have embezzled funds. I tell you I was shocked."

"I can only imagine. An accusation like that could kill a career such as yours."

"Damn straight, pardon my French. I immediately handed over the whole kit-and-caboodle to Reverend Trent, and who did he appoint to continue my campaign?"

"Let me guess—Victoria Bishop."

"Exactly. Meanwhile, I tried to track down where this rumor started. I went to Councilman Mueller, but he refused to discuss it other than to intimate shameful things about my moral state. I talked to a couple of others who'd been at the meeting where Mueller originally raised the topic. Neither of them would go on record. Both told me they didn't want to cross Mueller. Said they'd deny it if I repeated their comments, but they each told me that Mueller and Victoria Bishop were cozy and thick as thieves. One of them said she wondered if Victoria had her eye on Mueller. He's a widower and one of the wealthy ones I specifically focused on for a sizable donation.

"It ended up taking me a couple of weeks to extricate myself from that mess, and the entire time, every time I saw Victoria, she'd smile this wicked, mean smile, kind of like she was saying, 'Hey, hon, didn't I get the best of you?' And then she up and announced she'd inherited some money and would be gifting the church with fifty thousand for the Victoria Bishop Roof."

"They're not really going to call it that, are they?"

"Mueller proposed it right in church. And she preened and blushed and got all weepy about it, so yeah, I guess so."

"Amazing."

"No kidding. Now she's donated money before, but in much smaller amounts. Fifty bucks here, a hundred there, but never this kind of dough."

"Have you actually seen the money?"

"Who, me? Are you kidding? I'm now persona non grata. I'm getting the suspicious eye from many people in the congregation. I'll probably spend the rest of my time on staff being accused and suspected of this, that, and everything. To make matters worse, Victoria took the ministry team out for dinner to some fancy restaurant to celebrate reaching the goal, and I wasn't invited. I'm the fourth member of the team! Sure, I'm a lay minister, not ordained, but Reverend Trent has never left me out of a single ministry event."

"This sounds very painful."

Jo Ellen's eyes flooded with tears. She looked away and picked up her can of soda. "I'm trying to decide whether I need to start a search for a new job."

"So you have no way of knowing if this alleged fifty thousand has been received by the church?"

"I do know that the roofing company requested substantial money up front for materials, and the secretary told me Victoria instructed her to write out a check from the church's bank account on Friday."

"Does Victoria Bishop have access?"

"I don't think so. But I don't know. I've been cut right out of the loop. If you don't mind me asking, why are you investigating this?"

Leo debated what to tell her. Jo Ellen Wiesniak seemed like an honest, trustworthy person, but she was in a lot of pain. Leo didn't want her to confide in anyone, even a trusted confidante. She couldn't afford for any details to take some strange path back to Bishop.

"I can't go into it right now. I wish I could. The one thing I can promise you is that whatever I find out I'll share with you." She pulled a small notebook from the breast pocket of her blouse. She asked for and wrote down Jo Ellen's home and work phone numbers. "Do you know where Victoria Bishop lives?"

"I've never been to her house. She's always used a post office box, so I don't know if that's actually the address where she lives. That's what's so weird. Why would she come all the way to this side of the Twin Cities to go to Saint V's when there's a perfectly good Missouri Synod Lutheran church less than a mile from her address?"

"A good question. Do you happen to have a picture of her?"

"No," Jo Ellen said. "If I did, it'd probably be unrecognizable on my dart board. Oops!" She put her fingers to her lips to cover a slight smile. "Did I say another uncharitable, un-Christian thing? How terrible of me."

The humor was infectious, and Leo grinned with her. "Don't worry. I won't tell."

Jo Ellen glanced at her watch. "Oh, no," she grumbled. "I've only got half an hour to get cleaned up and over to my sister's for a baby shower."

Leo stood. "I'm sorry I took up so much of your time. Thanks for the Sprite."

"No, no, please. Don't worry. I'll get there in time, and believe me, it was good that I got all that off my chest." She rose, started to reach out to shake, then let her hand drop. "Hey, it just occurred to me that you should talk to Jim. Jim Lucas, I mean. He's one of the two associate pastors. Victoria did something to him, too."

"Oh? Do you know what?"

"No. But something. He's scared to death of her. I remember a time when he was all high on her, lighting up whenever she came around and sharing lots of admiring looks. He couldn't stop talking about what a wonder she was. But in the last year—no, probably more than that—he changed completely. I don't know what happened between them, but I know it's not good. He practically runs whenever he sees her coming."

"You make it almost sound like an affair."

Jo Ellen's expression was troubled. "Hmmm, that's exactly the tone. I guess I put it out of my mind and tried not to think of it that way, especially since his wife is the sweetest woman. They seem so devoted to one another, but you know what? That's exactly the kind of thing Victoria would do. She's sneaky."

"Have you got an address for Jim Lucas?"

"Sure do. Oh, and if you like, I'll hunt around at church tomorrow and see if I can find a photo that has Victoria in it. She doesn't like to have her picture taken, but we've had a ton of barbecues and welcome dinners. She's got to be in one of them. Write down your e-mail address, while I go get Jim's address."

ARMED WITH THE address for Jim and Sarah Lucas, Leo drove off to locate Laurel Street in Saint Paul. Victoria Bishop, mystery woman. Who was she? The difference between Reverend Trent's glowing evaluation of her and Jo Ellen Wiesniak's experience was so extreme that Leo didn't know what to make of it. Was Victoria Bishop one of the most adept con artists on the planet? Or had some terrible misunderstanding occurred?

One thing was clear, Reverend Trent confirmed that he and the ministry team had eaten at Chez René, and the meal was definitely paid for by Bishop, using Eleanor's Visa. At the very least, Bishop was guilty of theft. Perhaps she bought the credit card on the black market. Leo had to admit it was also possible that Ted Trimble gave it to her.

Could they be in league with one another? Men did a lot of stupid things for women, and if Bishop was half as manipulative as Jo Ellen had described, Ted could have fallen for her and done things he wouldn't ordinarily do.

A hazy outline was starting to assert itself, and what Leo was seeing was a Black Widow kind of woman, someone who beguiled people, tricked and deceived, then took advantage of them. Could that be right? Or was it an exaggeration? Maybe Bishop had nothing to do with the murders. But she had used a stolen credit card. If she needed to steal to take the ministry team to dinner, wasn't it strange that she'd committed such a large lump sum to Saint Vladimir's for the roof? What was that all about?

Leo stopped in front of a gray bungalow with a columned porch extending across the front of the house. Past the porch rail, she saw a glider. Someone sat on it, rocking. She got out of the car wondering why anyone would sit outside in this muggy heat. At least the house faced east and the porch was shaded.

A middle-aged man in shorts and a bright orange t-shirt slumped on the glider. He held a half-eaten apple in one hand.

"Hello," she called out as she made her way up to the porch.

He rose, chewing the apple, frowned, and forced a swallow. "Hi. How can I help you?"

She introduced herself as she came up the stairs. He gestured to a wood Adirondack chair across from the glider, and she examined it skeptically. Once you got down into those things, they were comfortable, but they were never a lot of fun to get out of. She lowered herself to the edge and perched.

"I'm here to talk about Saint Vladimir's, the roof, and Victoria Bishop."

He gulped so hard she saw his Adam's apple bulge. "What do you want to know?"

"For starters, have you talked to Reverend Trent today?"

"No. My wife and I just returned from a fishing weekend about an hour ago. We missed today's service. Has something happened—to Victoria Bishop? Or the roof?"

Was that a glimpse of hope on his face? The expression flitted by so quickly Leo couldn't be sure. "There's definitely something odd going on regarding the roof. We—"

The front door opened and a round, pleasant face peeked out. "Jim? You need anything?" She glanced politely toward Leo, and her curiosity was clear.

"No, darling. Well, wait a minute. Could you bring us some lemonade?"

"Sure." The door smacked shut.

"I'm investigating Victoria Bishop, Mr. Lucas. I've talked to Jo Ellen Wiesniak, and she thought I ought to touch base with you."

He flushed a deep red and stuttered a moment before finally getting out a high-pitched, "Me? Why me?"

"Something's not quite right regarding Ms. Bishop, and I'm hoping you can help me."

"Oh, my..."

Leo bit her tongue and let the guy think. Suddenly Lucas was sweating profusely. He ran a hand over his bald head and shuddered.

The front door opened, and in a firm voice, Leo said, "Let us pray. Please, Pastor."

Jim Lucas immediately bent forward and intoned a rambling prayer asking for strength and courage during difficult times. Mrs. Lucas stood in the doorway, two glasses in hand, and respectfully inclined her head, too.

When he said, "And this we pray in Jesus' name," Leo joined him in a resounding "Amen."

Sarah Lucas bustled forward and offered her an ice-filled glass beading with drops of water. She was a short, round woman with graying brown hair and intelligent eyes. She wore a multicolored, calf-length skirt and a sleeveless blouse.

"I'll need just a few more minutes of Pastor Lucas's time," Leo said. "I apologize for interrupting your Sunday."

"Think nothing of it," she said. Turning to her husband, she said, "Let me know if you need anything else, hon."

He grasped her hand for a moment, a look of defeat on his face. With her head held high, Sarah Lucas marched into the house. Leo could tell the woman knew something was up, but she was too polite to embarrass her husband with questions.

The lemonade was tart and refreshing. Leo set the glass on the arm of the chair. "Back to Victoria Bishop, a woman who seems to be a sore topic today."

"What is it you want, Ms. Reese?"

"Apparently many in the congregation think the woman is a gift from God, but others tell different stories."

He leaned forward and put his elbows on bony knees. "It would be unseemly of me to tell tales out of school."

"Let me make some guesses, then. You can confirm or deny. Victoria Bishop came to the church, and she was a breath of fresh air, like no one you'd ever met before. She was pretty and helpful and oh-so-charming. You fell for her hook, line, and sinker. She sank that hook deep, reeled you in, and once you'd been somehow compromised, she changed completely."

Jim Lucas sat clutching his lemonade, his face horror-stricken. She felt sorry for him.

"I apologize for being so blunt, Pastor Lucas. I can tell by the look on your face that I'm not far off the mark."

"Not at all," he whispered. "She dropped her mask and became a devil."

"What did she want? And what did she threaten?"

"She said she'd go public. Tell the congregation, tell my wife." Haltingly he said, "Last year—in the spring, we chaperoned the church kids at the National Youth Gathering. We—I—" He closed his eyes and winced as if in pain.

"I understand, sir. She took advantage of you. Got you in a compromising situation. What happened then?"

"After—after that, she was—she held it over my head."

"What did she demand in return?"

"She wanted free rein on the finance committee. She wanted me to support her for a position on the church council. I hated to do it. She said she'd tell my wife, so I had to."

He was near tears.

"Look, Pastor, I don't care about what happened intimately between you and Victoria Bishop, and I'll keep this confidential if I'm able to. I'm not sure your experience with her will come up, but I want you to tell me one thing. What is your assessment of her? Try to put aside your feelings as a man and think about it solely from the angle of a church leader and minister."

He swallowed and stared out toward the street for a full minute before finally turning back to meet her gaze. "I never thought, as a man of God, that I'd say this, but she's one of the most intensely evil people I've ever encountered. Pure evil. If her goal was to get on the finance committee and be part of the church's guiding council, she could have asked me, and I'd have helped. Instead, she sought to humiliate me. Nothing I've said since last spring could convince her otherwise, and in fact, she twisted it all around like it was my fault. Suddenly, she was the victim, and I was some sort of oppressor, guilty of God only knows what. Please, Ms. Reese, please understand."

"I do. You're not the only person she's abused and betrayed."

"Oh, my Lord, I feel sorry for anyone else going through this kind of hell. I succumbed to her wiles once. Just one time. It was wrong, and I've prayed and asked God's forgiveness. I don't know how I'll ever forgive myself. But I don't deserve this terrible campaign she's carried out against me. Since the youth conference, she's made a point of seeking me out, smiling knowingly, as though we shared a naughty secret, as though she'd vanquished my ethics, my morals. Which, indeed, she has. And the worst of it is that by her unspoken actions, she managed to give enough hints for my wife to suspect what happened. That's why we went away for the weekend—so I could confess to my wife and ask forgiveness. I hope God will forgive me."

He set the lemonade glass on the floor and leaned forward, head in hands. The picture of Victoria Bishop had sharpened in focus, and Leo felt a wave of cold fury toward the woman. How many men had she done this to? How many lives had she destroyed? How many churches and employers had she defrauded? Leo suddenly felt the intense desire to get every bit of information she could about this woman and contact the FBI or the State Bureau of Criminal Apprehension. This extortionist, this murderer and rip-off artist wasn't new at this. The level of sophistication, the extorted silence, and the damage left behind was too calculated, too precise. She was a master. Bishop had no doubt done this before, and she'd probably do it again. She had to be stopped.

"Anything else you can tell me, Pastor Lucas?"

He sat up, took a deep breath, and suddenly looked resolute, as though he were ready to face things head-on. "Why, yes. There is one more thing. She said she'd tell my wife everything if I didn't give her an alibi for last Monday night."

"And you told the police she was with you."

"I did. I regretted it the moment it came out of my mouth, and I've been debating for days whether to retract it. While we were gone, I prayed about it and decided to return home and tell the truth, no matter what the consequences."

"So she wasn't with you?"

"No. I have friends in the ministry who will verify where I was, and she most certainly was not with me."

Leo said, "You've been so helpful. I'm sorry to put you through this, but with any luck at all, your ordeal will soon be over."

He sat back on the glider, looking subdued. "I don't know if it'll ever be over."

"Don't count on it. I think you'll see your whole world change dramatically once we get her out of your church."

"I'll pray for that."

Chapter Twenty-three

ELEANOR KNELT IN front of a dresser, rooting at the back of the bottom drawer to pull out the last of some clothing. Callie had cram-packed the dresser full, and Eleanor was boxing up the items and getting them ready for Goodwill. Despite her periodic weepiness, she felt considerable satisfaction. All day she'd been working in fifteen- and twenty-minute spurts, then sitting down to rest and recover from crying. She'd accomplished more than she'd expected.

The armoire was full of necklaces and earrings. Most of them she would save for Callie's daughter, Olivia. Eleanor had requested Callie's rings from the funeral director. Now she opened the armoire and put the sealed plastic ziplock inside, retaining just the one ring that she had bought for Callie all those years ago. She slipped it on the ring finger of her right hand and admired their two birthstones on either side of the diamond.

"Miss Eleanor?"

"Yes?"

Habibah Okello stood in the doorway. "Are you coming for dinner? Dottie is serving now."

Eleanor rose slowly to her feet, grasping the top of the dresser to pull herself erect. "I'm feeling all rickety tonight."

"Yes, ma'am. I can understand."

"I have a few more things to do here, Habibah, so I may be late. Don't have Dottie wait. If this takes me too long, I'll pop out to a restaurant later. I'm making such good progress though."

"You are! I cannot believe how much you have packed."

"Slow and steady wins the race."

In the distance, Eleanor heard the ring of a telephone. "Uh-oh, that's probably for me." She hastened across the hall and paused at the entrance to her suite. Was she finally strong enough to cross the threshold?

Habibah looked at her oddly as she headed toward the café, and that sealed it. Eleanor stepped into the room and grabbed the phone.

No one said anything for a moment, then she heard a woman's voice. "I almost hung up. I thought no one was home."

"I'm here."

"Is this Eleanor Sinclair?"

"Why yes, who's calling?"

"This is Bonnie Yarborough. I work at Saint Vladimir's Church. Some children playing in our churchyard found a credit card with your name on it." She read off a number. "Is that yours?"

"Yes, it is."

"Lucky I found you listed in the phone book then. The church is open until nine p.m. for Bible Study. Would you like to come by and get this tonight?"

"I most certainly would, Ms. Yarborough. I can be there in half an hour."

The woman gave Eleanor the address and general directions, and Eleanor hung up feeling triumphant. If it hadn't been handled too much, she wondered if the police could still get fingerprints off the card. Grabbing her purse and a sweater, she hurried to the parking lot.

AT THE CHURCH, Eleanor parked on the deserted street and went up the stairs to the side door Bonnie Yarborough had instructed her to enter. All the way over from Minneapolis, she wondered about her accounts and if she'd ever get her money back. Would it be possible for the police to crack the case? She was lucky her broker had only managed a portion of her funds, but still, the theft of nearly a quarter million dollars was such an egregious crime. Every time she thought about it, she felt a rush of rage.

She pushed the door open and entered a vestibule. Bonnie had told her to go through the doorway straight ahead and down the hall to the left, but she hesitated. The farther in she moved, the darker it was. She sure hoped that the Bible Study was lit better than this corner of the church.

The passageway to the left grew increasingly dim, but an Exit sign gleamed red at the end, and Eleanor oriented toward it. One hand on the wall, the other clutching her shoulder bag, she took slow, even steps. Under the Exit sign, she pushed open a door and found herself in the church's main entryway. She frowned, thinking she must have misunderstood the directions. Surely the secretary's office was nowhere near the narthex.

She took small steps across the carpet until she came to the entry to the sanctuary. Next to the open door, three sets of metal folding chairs leaned upright against the wall. Otherwise, all seemed in order. The only light was cast by three lancet windows up high, a candle under a red globe near the altar, and a spotlight on the larger-than-life body of Jesus on the cross. She thought the representation must be of Christ after death. His body was too scarred and bloody, and he slumped just like a real crucified dead body would. She shuddered. The whole altar looked downright spooky.

She decided to retrace her path. A noise squeaked behind her. She started to turn. "Hello? Anyone—"

Something struck the back of her head. She fell, out of control, and could do nothing to stop the headlong pitch forward. She hit the floor and let out a whimper. A bitter taste flooded her mouth, and she couldn't see. Gasping, she tried to draw enough breath to speak. She lay on her left side, clutching her bag under her arm, unable to move or respond.

"You miserable rotten bitch," someone said. "And now just watch—you'll weigh a ton, too."

Cool metal bumped against Eleanor's forehead. What in the world was happening? She wanted to call out, but waves of pain radiated through her head and made her sick to her stomach.

"I should've fucking killed you the first time around. And her, too," a soft, matter-of-fact voice said. "You ruined everything. Fucking bitch."

Hands grasped under Eleanor's arms, yanked her up, and dragged her roughly onto a cold metal surface. She lolled there, unable to fight back.

She blacked out for a moment. The next time she felt bodily sensations, there was a dampness under her that smelled like the bitter tang of urine. Had she wet herself? Her head hurt so much that she gave the indignity no further thought. Without warning, bad-tasting bile came up, and she vomited.

She forced her eyes open and squinted to make sense of what she was seeing. Her vision went from foggy to somewhat clear, but it took a moment before she finally identified that it was the ends of pews going by. She lay on her back, her head turned to the side, on some sort of cart. Someone was rolling her up the middle aisle of the church. The cart jerked to the left, traveled a distance, and stopped.

"What a fucked up mess," the woman said.

She stepped away, and Eleanor had a clear view of her face as she stabbed a finger at an elevator button. I know her, Eleanor thought. I can't remember her name, but I know her. What's her name?

"Jesus, hurry up. Damn church has the slowest goddamn elevator ever built."

The woman continued to mutter until the door opened, then she came back and moved the cart forward. A huge figure loomed over Eleanor. She was afraid the giant would hurt her, maybe hit her some more. She thought she might throw up again if anyone touched her. The figure swam into focus, and she realized it was church statuary. Eleanor winced with pain when the cart smacked into the elevator doorway. The pounding in her head increased, and she closed her eyes again and made herself relax.

"Oh, right. Now you go ahead and die. Couldn't die right the first time, but now you drop dead with just one crack to the back of your head. Great. That's no fun for me, you damn bitch."

The last thing Eleanor heard was another string of epithets made all the more dreadful by the fact that they were uttered at the feet of the statue of the Blessed Virgin Mary.

Chapter Twenty-four

MONDAY MORNING COULDN'T come fast enough. Leo was in the office before eight a.m. itching to find the elusive con woman and get the case resolved. Before she'd even gotten settled, Fred Baldur was in her doorway.

"Leona, I've been more than patient, but I must get the completed report on Rivers' Edge. I need you to move on, work on other cases."

"It's wrapping up, Fred."

"That's what you said last week!"

He sounded so whiny that Leo took a deep breath before answering. "Murders are obviously not going to be open-and-shut cases. I'm sorry that it's more involved than you'd planned for."

"I certainly hope you're getting all these witness transcripts squared away."

"Transcripts?"

"Yes. You do need to have the tapes readied in case they need written documentation for every single discussion and interview. Haven't you been labeling them and ensuring that they're ready for transcription?"

Leo bit her lip as she nodded. She'd been so good about taping talks early on, but she couldn't remember the last person she'd spoken to with the recorder running. Ooops. She wasn't about to admit that to Fred Baldur.

"How about we get this piece completed today, all right?"

We? Did he have a mouse in his pocket, or what? He'd done nothing but nag. "Wait a minute, Fred. Didn't you hear there was another murder at one of the Rivers' complexes?"

"What? That's not possible. I don't have a police referral."

"You're sure to get it soon."

"You must be mistaken."

"I was out at Rivers' Bloom yesterday."

"Nonsense. Yesterday was Sunday, and you weren't scheduled to work."

Was this guy the stupidest man in creation? Was he calling her a liar? Or did he have so little imagination that he couldn't possibly envision anything happening except by official channels?

"Fred, Detective Flanagan called me yesterday. Both Thom and I went out to Rivers' Bloom and talked to a few people. I followed up with some additional interviews in the afternoon."

"That's comp time, then. To get credit, you'll need to file a special form. Monique monitors that for Ralph. You're actually supposed to get comp time preapproved."

"I don't care about comp time. I care about finding out who killed Callie Trimble."

He stood blinking in the cubicle entryway, a puzzled expression on his waxen gray face. "This isn't working out. You were brought on to help us catch up. It's not working."

From down the hall, a voice called out, "What's not working, Baldur?"

The look of dismay on Fred's face was enough to make Leo laugh out loud, but she pushed down the desire. Fred stepped aside and Leo could see Thom's legs and part of his wheelchair in the hallway. He leaned forward and peeked around the edge of the cubicle. "Good morning, Leo." He sat back, and she couldn't see his face anymore, but she could hear him clearly.

"Now, Fred, what's your problem today?"

"I was just telling Leona the department is in a shambles. I'm doing all I can to knock down the paperwork, but we've got multiple visits to make and the reports are stacking up. You weren't brought down here from Duluth to devote all your time and attention to one single case. The complaints are pouring in faster than I can read them. I can't run this department all by myself."

"And we don't expect you to. Leo is probably hours away from finishing off this murder investigation. We're going to check a mail drop, get an address, and after we find the witness, I'll work on the other cases for most of the day. We'll make a dent this week, don't worry."

"Excuse me, boys." Monique Miller squeezed past to hand Leo a couple of sheets of paper. "This fax is marked RUSH, so I brought it over rather than stick it in your mailbox."

"Thanks," Leo said.

"What's with all of you crammed into this miserable little hallway? We do have a conference room if you need it."

Fred let out a huff and shouldered his way past Thom.

Monique said, "He's getting grumpier by the minute."

"I'll say," Thom said.

Leo glanced at the cover page, which identified the sender as Jo Ellen Wiesniak at Saint Vladimir's. She flipped back the cover page to find a photo of six people around a picnic table. One of the women was circled in thick black pen.

"Holy shit, Thom, we've got to go."

"To the mail drop?"

"Nope, we can skip that completely."

ON THE WAY out to Plymouth, Leo called Flanagan's work and cell phones, but couldn't reach him. She left a message relating what she'd learned the day before in her interviews with Jim Lucas and Jo Ellen Wiesniak.

"Good thinking," Thom said. "I should have been there, too."

"You deserved your weekend, especially since you had Twins tickets."

"Yeah, but they lost in the ninth. Total bummer." Thom wheeled into the Rivers administrative building lot.

"I hope you're getting reimbursed for gasoline," Leo said. She put her valise on the floor, but kept her cell phone.

"Yup. I'm keeping track." He hastened to get his wheelchair out.

She went around the back of the vehicle and watched him drop smoothly into the chair. "Your exit reminds me of those old Westerns where the cowboy jumps from the upper story of the saloon down onto his horse."

"That's me, all right. Giddy-up." He slammed the van door, and they rushed inside.

The office was quiet, and once more, the nap of the carpet lay in perfect, vacuumed lines that they disturbed as they approached the main counter.

Leo hit the bell on the counter, but no one answered. "Hello? Anyone here?"

Thom said, "Ring it again a couple of times."

From the distance, a voice called out, "Coming." A dark-haired woman emerged from the office. She was younger than Leo, perhaps in her mid-twenties. "Sorry. I was in the workroom. May I help you?"

Leo said, "Is Martin Rivers in?"

"Not today. He's out at the construction site."

"What about his assistant?"

"I'm his assistant. I'm Iris Fullerton, and chances are good that whatever you need help with I can handle."

"We really need to find Claire Ryerson. Do you expect her in today?"

"Oh, no, you just missed her. She's on vacation for two weeks."

Leo looked at Thom. He got out his ID, and she flashed her Saint Paul Police badge. She didn't know how much her badge would help since she wasn't in her jurisdiction, but she figured it couldn't hurt. "It's critically important that we speak to Ms. Ryerson."

"Sorry. I was gone on vacation last week, and now it's her turn. She's flying out today."

"Where to?"

"Gee, I don't know. She and I aren't close. Seems like she usually goes somewhere warm so she can keep up her tan." Her tone had changed, become stiffer, more hostile.

Leo took a chance. "Ms. Ryerson is in big trouble, Ms. Fullerton. We need your help."

"Really?" She brightened considerably.

"Yes, and this may be a matter of life or death."

"I don't know what I can do."

Leo asked, "Did she leave any paperwork at her desk?"

"No, she dropped by to tidy up and print something then left."

Thom said, "What did she print? Maybe an e-ticket?"

"I couldn't say. I wasn't paying attention."

Thom said, "Would you mind if we checked it out?"

Iris winced. "I don't know if I should."

"Please," he said, smiling, "I promise I won't disturb anything." Before she could respond, he rolled around the side of the counter and through the office door. "Ms. Fullerton, you've got a dandy printer over there."

"Yes, it's brand new."

"Do you work off a main server or are your desktops linked?"

"We both have access to the same records. I guess they're linked."

"Have you printed anything since she left?"

"No, I've been assembling packets in the storeroom."

"Your system can reprint recent documents. May I?" He gestured toward the computer, and she shrugged.

Leo waited in the doorway, watching, then thought to take the opportunity to redial Flanagan's cell phone. No answer. She tried again. Nothing.

Thom rolled his chair over and grabbed a page from the printer. "Sun Country to Dominican Republic. She flies out of Humphrey in less than an hour. Let's go."

"Iris," Leo said, "did she leave by taxi?"

"Yes, only a couple of minutes ago."

As they hustled toward the door, Leo called out, "We'll get back to you as soon as we can." When she glanced over her shoulder, the young woman was standing behind the counter with a pleased smirk on her face. Leo wished she had time to find out what Claire Ryerson had done to her.

In the van, Thom was grim. "We've got miles to travel in bad traffic. It's possible we might not catch her."

"We have to. Just drive like a bat out of hell. She's only got a few minutes on us."

"You think she's going on vacation? Or that she's not coming back?"

"I'd bet money she knows this gig is up. She'll fly down to the Dominican Republic, catch a charter somewhere else from there, and that'll be that. We'll never find her again."

Thom cut into the fast lane and expertly passed a slow-moving car. "You're probably right. I went to Puerto Plata with a bunch of guys on spring break my freshman year in college. We joked about ditching school and hopping a flight to Europe or South America. There were more airlines down there than we have in the Twin Cities. Of course, it was easier to travel before the 9/11 restrictions."

"That won't stop her. Victoria Bishop, or Claire Ryerson— whichever name is right—is shrewd. No doubt she set up the identity she needed long ago. If she's been flying back and forth periodically to keep up her tan, I'll bet she's got this exit all figured. We have to catch her before she boards that plane, or we'll never see her again in Minnesota."

"Does the Dominican Republic have criminal reciprocity? Will they extradite her?"

"Heck if I know," Leo said. "We can't take that chance."

"Call Flanagan again."

Leo tried once more with no success. "Damn him."

"Call the department. Call the airport police. Just call 9-1-1."

"I'll try Flanagan one more time."

The phone rang twice, and a sleepy voice answered.

"Flanagan, thank God. Leona Reese here. We've got a lead on the Callie Trimble killer."

"What? Huh?" He mumbled for a moment, then his voice was sharp. "What the hell? We've already got the murderer."

"You've got the wrong guy."

"Dream on, lady."

"Listen, Flanagan, at the very least Claire Ryerson is Trimble's partner in crime. She's the one who used the Sinclair credit card."

"Ryerson? From the Rivers main office?"

"Yes."

"I've been in bed for two whole hours, Ms. Reese. Can't this wait until my shift starts?"

"She's flying out of the country *now*. To the Dominican Republic. You need to take her into custody before she gets away forever. Listen to me. Get someone over to the Humphrey International Terminal or we'll never find her again."

Thom pulled into the ramp, took a ticket from the dispenser, and inched the van forward as the arm slowly rose. Once through, he raced around the ramp and came to a screeching halt near the elevators.

"Get out, Leo. I'll park and catch up with you."

She didn't argue. Phone to her ear, she took off running as she gave Flanagan the flight information. She hung up and poured on the speed.

The muscles in her legs protested. She felt stiff and sore all over, especially her quadriceps and across her shoulders. That'd teach her to let so much time pass between workouts.

The Humphrey Terminal was much more compact than the Twin Cities' main Lindbergh Terminal. While Lindbergh served nearly every major carrier that flew throughout the world, the Humphrey airport facility was a home to charter airlines and to the much smaller carriers such as AirTran, Icelandair, Midwest, and Sun Country. She'd never flown out of this terminal and hadn't picked anyone up from it in years, not since the new facility was built and expanded, so she didn't know her way around.

She assumed the skyway would lead from the ramp to the check-in area but was surprised when she emerged from the tunnel near the gate security and above the check-in concourse. The ticketing area below was bright, with enormous panels of glass illuminating the counters, X-ray machines, and passengers checking in. She started for the escalator but paused at the rail to make the best of her vantage point, quickly examining each traveler below.

She saw surprisingly few people compared to the usual heavy foot traffic at the main terminal. Everyone seemed to be moving at a leisurely pace. No long lines. No pushy jerks nipping at anyone's heels. Five people, business travelers by the looks of them, stood in line at the check-in area. A young couple dragged a cranky two-year-old onto the escalator as he protested loudly. An elderly man and woman hobbled toward the elevator.

Could the taxi have been that far ahead? Had Bishop already been checked in and gone through security?

Leo honed in on the area around the metal detectors. A bored Transportation Security worker stood waiting at the checkpoint, picking at the latex gloves he wore. Behind him, a wide hallway stretching to the left and right was lined with shops and eateries. Far off to the left, the waiting area for the gates bustled with activity. Was she in there? Leo had no way to enter and check without assistance and permission from the airport police. Though she carried her badge in one pocket and her cell phone in the other, she doubted whether either would get her in quickly enough. Where were Flanagan's forces? Why hadn't any cops made an appearance?

She turned back to survey the area below. Two taxis pulled up outside, and clumps of travelers emerged. She watched a woman lean into a cab's front window and pay the driver. Close, but she was far heavier than Bishop. Two men in summer suits, wallets open, stood by their wheeled suitcases and haggled. One laughed, plucked some money from his billfold, and tossed it to the cabbie.

Leo scanned the area below again, looking closely at every woman. She paused to squint at a tall, stately brunette ambling away from the check-in counter. She wore a waist purse strapped around her middle and pulled a carry-on case on wheels. Her linen pants were tan, her navy top a simple, short-sleeved button-up shirt, and her tennis shoes were so stark white that they had to be new.

Not Bishop, Leo thought. The stride wasn't graceful, and besides, her hair was wrong. The woman paused and opened a pocketbook, shuffled some papers, knelt down and zipped something into her suitcase.

Thom appeared to Leo's right and startled her. "Whoa. Wheels on carpet. Very sneaky, Thom."

"What have we got?"

Without taking her eyes off the woman, Leo said, "What do you think of that woman? The one to the right of the TSA guy? Hair's wrong, but is that her?"

"Could be."

"Nobody else fits. Wrong builds. Wrong height."

"Let's check that one out. You keep an eye out from here, and I'll take the elevator down to flank her."

Leo wished she had binoculars. If only she could get a better look. If the woman was Victoria Bishop, she'd likely recognize Leo right away, so it was better to stay out of her line of vision. Feeling exposed, she moved over toward the wall, angling away from the direct line of sight of anyone who took the stairs or elevator.

The woman zipped up the bag, adjusted the handle, straightened, and strode forward. As she drew closer, Leo examined the line of her jaw, the tilt of her head. The suitcase shortened the woman's stride slightly, changed her gait, but yes, it was the woman she knew as Claire Ryerson.

From the corner of her eye, Leo saw Thom's chair roll into view. He was on course to cut Bishop off before she reached the escalator.

Time to move. Leo hastened to the top of the staircase. She wasn't willing to get stuck on the escalator or to take the elevator down if it meant letting the woman out of her sight. If Bishop managed to come up the escalator or to reverse and escape out the front, at least Leo had options by using the staircase.

She halted halfway down the steps. Thom raised a hand to intercept the woman, as though he were merely asking the time. Bishop stopped politely, nodding. She glanced toward the windows. Her head swung gradually across the terminal until her gaze met Leo's, passed idly by, and jerked back.

Bishop let go of the suitcase handle. The luggage rolled back, and a man hurrying behind her tripped over it but managed not to fall. Bishop whirled. Thom grabbed her forearm. She tried to pull away, but he had a strong grip. As Leo scrambled down the stairs, she was amazed to see Bishop lean down, grab the footrest of Thom's chair, and flip him over.

The onlookers let out a collective gasp but were too surprised to do anything other than stand staring. Bishop wrenched her arm from Thom's grasp and took off for the front entrance.

"Thom!" Leo reached Thom, on his back like a marooned turtle.

"Go, Leo. Go! I'm fine."

She changed course and charged past him.

"Get her, just get her," he called out as she rushed away. "I'll find the airport police."

Victoria Bishop hit the front door, but was slowed by a knot of people trying to get in.

"Hey!" someone said. "Watch where you're going."

By the time Leo got to the glass door, the group had turned back to enter, but they quickly got out of her way when they saw her coming.

"What's with the chicks in flight?" some guy grumbled.

She blasted through the door, fumbling for the badge in her pocket. Bishop led by a few yards. A block ahead, a taxi pulled in behind a line of other cabs. Leo had to stop her before she got to that taxi stand. Overruling stiff muscles, she pumped with her arms and pushed herself harder.

She felt naked without her gun, but in street clothes, it was probably better that she didn't pull a gun anyway. Some overzealous airport cop might take a shot.

"Stop her!" she hollered. She didn't see anyone who could help, but it was best to identify herself. "Stop! Police!" She passed a knot of travelers, all pulling suitcases, and held up her badge. They gawked as she ran by.

Bishop slowed at the front taxi, but Leo hadn't played football with Kate and the neighborhood boys for nothing. Before she could get the door open, Leo hooked Bishop's waist with an arm and they both went crashing to the cement.

Bishop rolled, kicking and fighting like a wildcat. She caught Leo in the jaw with a fist. A fingernail scratched Leo's arm.

Shrieking, she twisted and squirmed to get away, but Leo was stronger. She forced flailing arms down and pinned them with her knees. "Don't make me sock you."

"Hey," a man's voice said softly. A cabdriver stood nearby, his eyes wide under a plum-colored turban. Other cabbies exited their cars, but they didn't seem to know what to do. One bent and picked up her badge.

"Saint Paul Police," Leo said, through gritted teeth. "That's my badge. Somebody please get the airport police."

Leo stared down into the blue eyes below. The face was pretty, but the eyes were ice-cold. She glared up with such fury that Leo shuddered. "Why? Why would you kill those poor old women?"

Victoria Bishop's expression was triumphant, like a cat that had just eaten a particularly lovely songbird. She hissed, "Because…"

"Why?"

"Because I can." She smiled sweetly then grimaced and kicked, but Leo had too firm a hold for her to squirm lose.

"You think you're so smart, such a clever savior," the woman said. "You'll see soon enough that you're not."

The words were unsettling. Victoria or Claire—or whatever her name was—glared at Leo with such venom that Leo was reminded of a predatory snake poised to sink its fangs into some unsuspecting victim.

Thom called out Leo's name. She saw the wheel of his chair in her peripheral vision, but she didn't dare turn her face away from Bishop.

"Cops are coming," Thom said. "You nailed her. Good job. But you're bleeding."

"I'm okay." She couldn't quite catch her breath, and her right shoulder and knee burned painfully.

"Hang on, kiddo. Just hang in there another minute."

An airport police officer came jogging up. Thom held his State ID high in the air. "Minnesota State Investigator. She's Saint Paul Police."

"What's going on?" the airport cop asked.

"We're arresting this suspect," Leo said. "Will you please cuff her and take her into custody?"

The moment Leo clambered to her feet, the other woman broke into tears. By the time Leo got to her feet, Bishop was clinging seductively to the brawny cop. "She assaulted me, Officer. Look, I'm bleeding."

The pitiful expression on Bishop's face was so patently false that Leo wanted to barf, but it seemed to be working on the cop.

"What's this all about?" he asked, looking from Leo to Thom

and back at the woman.

Thom said, "This woman is wanted in connection with two murders and multiple financial crimes."

"Ridiculous!" Bishop said. "I never hurt anyone." She sagged against the officer, managing to pat his chest and smear blood from her torn palm onto his shirt.

Leo dug her phone out of her pocket. Though it was cracked, she still got a signal.

"Flanagan? We've got her. Get over to the Humphrey Terminal now. And I mean now."

She hung up. "The Minneapolis Police will be here momentarily." She hunted for the cabbie who had her badge and found him standing by the door of his taxi. "May I have that, sir?" As she reached out to accept the badge, she realized she'd burned away a lot of the skin on her wrist, forearm, and elbow. A drop of blood fell to the pavement. "Ouch, I might need a Band-Aid."

Thom said, "I think you might need a paramedic."

Chapter Twenty-five

AFTER THE PARAMEDICS stanched the flow of blood from her arm, Leo got to ride with them over to Hennepin Medical Center. She didn't want to go to the hospital, but the medics advised it. Dirt and bits of gravel were ground into the deep scrapes in her arm and knee, and the medics insisted a doctor irrigate the wounds. Naturally, Victoria Bishop/Claire Ryerson only bruised her elbow and scratched her hand. Leo fumed about that. Wasn't the bad guy the one who was supposed to end up in the ambulance?

She was on the scene at the terminal long enough to see Flanagan arrive, soon followed by DeWitt. They wanted to talk to Leo but Thom said, "Let her go. I'll update you, and she can fill in the blanks later." He waved her on. "Go, Leo. I'll be over to get you as soon as I can."

The medic pulled the door shut and belted her into the padded side seat. Leo held a compress to her arm and examined her torn, blood-stained pants. They'd cost her sixty bucks, and she regretted going all Rambo in them.

Before the bus spirited her off, the last thing she saw through the narrow window in the back was Bishop being led to a police car. She stared toward the ambulance, caught Leo's eye, and smiled before she was unceremoniously stuffed into the back.

The smile had been gleeful, diabolic. Leo shivered. What had Pastor Jim Lucas called her? Pure evil? Why hadn't Leo seen it before? Why hadn't anyone else noticed? Clearly, Victoria Bishop/Claire Ryerson was a great actress.

Leo couldn't wait to hear what evidence Flanagan and DeWitt could turn up to make a case. What was in the traveling bag Bishop ditched? Cash? Gems? Documents? Leo hoped for damning evidence. She was pretty sure they could put Bishop away for the financial crimes, but the murders might be another story. The case wasn't going to be an easy one to prove.

Ten in the morning is a good time to frequent the ER. Leo was happy to see it was deserted, and the medics got her right in. She'd left her valise in Thom's van, so she had to do some fancy talking to postpone the insurance paperwork, but by the time she'd gotten out of her torn clothes and been treated and bandaged, Thom arrived, her valise on his lap.

"Hey, smart guy. Thanks for bringing that. Apparently the

insurance company won't honor my SPPD badge."

"I figured as much." He handed up the valise. "Amazing bandage on your knee there. You okay?"

"Absolutely as okay as I could be sitting here half-exposed in this silly show-my-whole-behind hospital gown."

"I hear you. When I broke my back, I lived in those damn things for months. I'll go hang out in the waiting room." He wheeled partway around then stopped. "You know, if you give me your insurance card, I can go out there and get the paperwork underway. Expedite it, you know."

"You don't have to bother with that."

"What else do I have to do? It's my specialty. I may not be able to run down a suspect, but I can surely do paperwork. Hand over the card."

She opened the valise and found her wallet. Out of the corner of her eye she sneaked a look at Thom. He hadn't frowned much in the brief time she'd known him. Now his expression was troubled. He reached for the card, but she pulled it back.

"What's the matter? Did the detectives give you a hard time?"

"Oh, no, not at all. They're sort of shell-shocked, but after I gave them the scoop, they perked right up."

"What's wrong then?"

He exhaled, shaking his head. "Nothing. Don't worry about it."

She tucked the valise behind her and smoothed the gown with one hand. "You're bullshitting me."

He looked up, surprised.

"Come on. What's up?"

"She dumped me over. That worthless bitch knocked me on my ass. I play murderball and don't get blown out of my chair as easily as that."

"She caught you unaware. She's a lovely, elegant-looking viper. Nobody expects her level of cunning. I had her on the ground, pinned, and she was spitting and kicking like a cornered animal."

"Still—"

"Thom, you're not listening. We got off lucky. You didn't see into her eyes." She paused and took a deep breath. "I looked into those evil eyes. There's nothing there. Nothing. She doesn't care about anyone. I asked her why she killed those innocent old women. You know what she said?"

"What?"

"She said, and I quote, 'Because I can.' As if it were a game. The way I see it, we're lucky as hell she wasn't carrying a gun or a knife. I think if we'd surprised her anywhere else but at the airport, she might have killed you."

"Oh, great. That doesn't make me feel any better. She didn't have a gun or knife, but she was easily able to tip me on my ass and run."

"I hear there's a sale on cow-catchers—you know, like they used to have on old-fashioned trains."

With a wry grin, he said, "I know what they are." His face went serious, and he pounded his fist on the chair arm. "You could have been seriously injured tackling her."

"Ah, so what you're really saying is you should have been the one tackling her, huh?"

"Yeah, in a perfect world."

"How very gallant of you. And sexist."

He sighed. "I don't mean it that way."

"Maybe I'll have to get some tips from you then. Every time I've tackled someone, which is only four or five times over the last decade, I've always gotten dinged up. It sure isn't as easy as they make it look in the movies."

"I definitely could teach you some tricks. There's a way to slow yourself at the last moment, grab on, and drag the person down."

"I thought that's what I did," she said dryly.

"Well, not exactly. You launched yourself like a torpedo, and—"

The doctor entered the room, clipboard in hand. "Excuse me, am I interrupting?"

"No," Thom said. "I'm on my way to update the billing clerk." He held out a hand, and Leo gave him her insurance card.

"Now then, Sergeant Reese," the doctor said, "I'm prescribing a five-day course of antibiotics. You had a lot of crud in those wounds." He ripped off two pages and handed them to her. "Contact with the pavement like that scraped away a couple layers of skin. It'll burn like a son of a gun for a while. If you find you need it, the second scrip is for a mild painkiller."

"So I can go?"

"You bet. Keep the wounds clean and call your regular doctor if you have any fever or excessive pain."

"My clothes?"

The doctor looked at her like she'd asked for a hot air balloon and a passport to Mars. "I don't deal with that. I'll get the nurse in to help you."

IT WAS AFTER one o'clock before Leo finally made it home to change into a clean, blood-free outfit. Thom stopped at the drive-through pharmacy on the way, then tried to tell her to take time off for the rest of the day. But what was she supposed to do? Sit around the house and wait for four hours to pass so she could take the next antibiotic pill?

"Wait for me," she said as she exited the van stiffly. "I want to go to the office and get Fred's damn report done. I've got to get my car anyway."

She was standing in a clean bra and underwear when the downstairs front door slammed. For a moment, she thought Thom had decided to come in to wait for her, then she realized there was no way he could have navigated the front stairs. For the first time it occurred to her that their house wasn't handicap accessible.

"Daria?" she called out. She heard a heavy tread on the stairs, and Daria stopped in the doorway, face grim and pale. "Why are you home so early? What's wrong?"

"The jury came in."

"Uh-oh. Not good."

"No, not good at all. In record time they convicted Dunleavey on all counts."

"I'm so sorry." Leo picked up a long-sleeved blouse from the bed and shrugged it over her bandaged arm.

Daria narrowed her eyes and for the first time actually studied her. "What the hell happened to you? Your knee? Your arm?"

"I took down a suspect and got scraped up."

"Judas Priest! You've been on the police force all these years, and you've never been bandaged like that. What the hell is this temp job doing to you?"

"This was an unusual incident. I was in street clothes and short sleeves. If I'd been in my heavy-duty uniform, it wouldn't have been so bad."

Daria crossed the room and helped her into the blouse.

"Ouch. Don't squeeze there."

"Sorry. How'd you manage such a nice bandaging job?"

"I had a great doctor at the hospital."

"What? You went to the hospital and you didn't call me?"

"Cripes, so I'm a little scraped up. It's minor."

"If it's so minor, why all the bandages?"

"Just a lot of scrapes, hon." She buttoned up her shirt and went to the closet for some pants. "Don't overreact. I'm fine."

Daria fell back to the bed, kicked off her shoes, and lay there, arms spread. "What a shit-ass day."

Leo stepped into her pants and zipped them up awkwardly. Her arm didn't want to bend, so she moved it gently. "What's going to happen with your job?"

"For all I know, the partners will fire me."

Leo stopped in the middle of tying her shoe. "You're kidding, right?"

"I don't know. They were furious. If they keep me, you can bet I won't be seeing first chair again for a long time, if ever."

"Are you taking the rest of the day off?"

"I think so. I decided I'd better make myself scarce until they all calmed down."

"Good plan." Leo leaned a hip on the edge of the bed and took her hand. "No matter what happens, we'll get through."

"This is the worst day of my life. I lose the case, you get injured, I might lose my job, and you could lose your eye."

"Thanks for reminding me and for using that joyous word lose, lose, lose. I'd actually forgotten about my eye for a few hours."

"I can't believe how our lives have gone to shit. What did we ever do wrong?"

"Nothing, Daria. Into every life a little rain does fall. It's our turn for the deluge."

"It's not funny."

"No, it's not."

"Then why are you taking it so lightly? This sucks."

"I know, but we just have to keep on track as best we can. And I've got to go now."

Daria sat up. "You're kidding, right? You should stay home and rest."

"Oh, please. I've got work to do. Besides, my car is still over at DHS."

"I'll drive you then." She slid off the bed and nabbed one of her shoes with a toe.

"You don't need to. My coworker Thom is out front waiting."

Daria slumped back on the bed. "Jesus, I need a drink."

"Go take a whirlpool instead. Please don't get drunk. I'll be home in a few hours, and we can go out to dinner and commiserate."

Daria put her forearm over her eyes and mumbled something noncommittal. All Leo could do was lean down and kiss her jaw.

"I'll come home once these case details are sorted out."

Chapter Twenty-six

LEO ARRIVED HOME shortly before five p.m., but Daria wasn't there. Once she lowered herself into the recliner, Leo fell into a deep sleep and wasn't awakened until much later when a booming crash of thunder shook the house. Lightning flashed so brightly that it stabbed through the cracks in the blinds and illuminated the room briefly. Even after the storm moved off into the distance, Leo continued to hear wind howling and rain crashing down against the side of the house.

She didn't move from the chair. Her arm throbbed in concert with a pulse beating behind her eye. A painkiller would help, but she was too tired to get up for it. She didn't feel at all rested, but a feeling of satisfaction kept her from grumbling about her cuts and scrapes.

After her hospital visit and as soon as she'd arrived at DHS, Ralph Sorensen summoned her and Thom to his office. He heard their story, congratulated them, and gave a five-minute speech about how their jobs weren't to solve crimes but to clear DHS cases. He was pleased they'd helped catch a murderer, but he encouraged them to quit being hotdogs and focus on the backlog.

She did have to chuckle at Fred Baldur's expense. He still hadn't gotten the report he kept demanding.

Sorensen sent them off to the Minneapolis Police Department, and they were there for hours answering questions and sharing their findings and paperwork. The time passed quickly with the exhilaration of closing the case keeping her going every bit as much as the coffee she kept downing.

But all that caffeine had worn off, and she was glad to be home. She hoped Ted Trimble had been cleared of the charges against him. She was certain he was innocent. She hadn't often come into contact with such a cold, heartless bitch as Victoria Bishop. She recalled a drug dealer who'd sold poisoned crack despite knowing it was bad. Three people died, but he didn't care. Over the years, she'd arrested a number of other felons who lacked consciences: thieves, rapists, wife beaters, and child abusers, but it was amazing how often lying con artists like Victoria Bishop could stay hidden. They put on a good show and simply didn't care about anybody else but themselves.

Because Bishop couldn't care about other people, Leo had a hard time believing Ted Trimble had anything to do with her.

Sociopaths like her didn't have the capacity to collaborate with others. They hatched and carried out their devious plots alone. If they had a sidekick, he was usually a real dummy — and real temporary as well.

She shifted in the chair and lowered the footrest. Already her cuts and abrasions had sealed up, and if she moved the wrong way, it felt like she was ripping open the scabs. Shuffling along like an old woman, she went to the kitchen to make a snack.

In the middle of eating toast and tea, her cell phone rang. The connection was scratchy, and she didn't understand the caller's accent at first. After twice asking the man to repeat himself, Leo realized it was Franklin Callaghan from Rivers' Edge.

"I am sorry to call so late, lass, but I am concerned about Eleanor. We heard that Miss Callie's killer is arrested, so has Eleanor been with the police today?"

"Not that I know of. What's wrong?"

"She's not been home all day. She whisked out of here last night like a bampot. Not even a word of goodbye to me."

"A — a what? Like a vampire?"

"Oh, no — like a bampot. As though she was slightly unhinged."

"When was this?"

"Around dinnertime last night. She jumped in her auto and roared off and didnae come back all through the night. Habibah listened for her. I meself was up until midnight, and she never returned."

"Has anyone called the police?"

"Mrs. Hoxley said she would if Eleanor didn't arrive by tomorrow morn, but I'm fair worried now. I know she's only been here a few months, but it's not like her to bolt with not a bit of explanation."

"I'll check on this. Thanks, Franklin."

"It's me pleasure to help, lass. I hope she turns up and the ruckus is all for nothing."

After they hung up, Leo sat for a moment contemplating. Did Eleanor have a cell phone? She didn't recall ever getting a number from her. Leo stood, bones aching and skin pinching, went to her valise, and pulled out her notebook. The only phone number she had listed for Eleanor was marked "LL" — landline.

She called Thom's cell and explained the issue.

"Have you talked to Flanagan or DeWitt?" he asked.

"Not yet."

"You ring Flanagan, I'll try DeWitt. Call me when you get off the phone."

When Leo reached the homicide cop, Flanagan was curt. "She's a big girl," he said. "She can go wherever she wants."

"But she's reliable. This doesn't sound like her."

"Contact me in 72 hours if she doesn't turn up." He terminated the connection.

Leo cursed under her breath. She knew he was tired and overworked, but she hated when cops weren't helpful. She called Thom back.

He said, "I couldn't reach DeWitt."

"I probably got through to his ass of a partner quicker, so he knew not to pick up." She told Thom what Flanagan had said.

"Guess it's up to us, Leo. Let's go looking."

"But where?"

"Let's start with the family. I'll come by and pick you up in the van."

Leo grabbed a shoulder bag and stuffed in her badge, notebook, and wallet. On second thought, she added her holstered off-duty weapon. She didn't think she'd need it, but it never hurt to have it. Cell phone in pocket, and she was ready to go.

VISITS TO THE houses of Ted Trimble and his father, Howard, turned up no news. Ted informed them he'd been trying to call Eleanor all day and requested that when they found her she should call him ASAP.

Back in the van, Leo suggested Thom drive by the library in Saint Paul. Eleanor's branch was open, but they didn't see her car in the parking lot, and Leo verified she wasn't at the weekly book group.

Back in the van, Thom asked, "She took her own car, right?"

"That's what Franklin Callaghan said."

"Where else do we look?"

Neither of them had an idea, so they cruised around Saint Paul, up on Rice Street behind the capital, down into Frogtown, and along Snelling Avenue toward Hamline University.

Leo sat delicately, wincing with every bump they hit. Her stomach felt like she'd swallowed lead. Strange thoughts bothered her. What had Victoria Bishop said? *You're not as smart as you think you are...* Something along those lines.

"Thom, did we ever discover where Victoria Bishop lived?"

"No, I didn't. Maybe the police did? Call 'em."

She was shocked that Flanagan picked up again, but he was surly. "What now?" he demanded.

"Did you ever find out where the Bishop woman lived?"

"Yes. In Saint Paul. Crime scene techs have been processing the apartment all day."

"What's the address?"

"Why the hell do you need to know that? You can't get in there now. It's a crime scene."

"I don't want to get in, Detective. I want to know if there's a basement or laundry room or storage locker or someplace on the premises that Victoria Bishop could have stashed an old lady."

"You still all het up about the Sinclair woman?"

"Yes. I've got a bad feeling something's wrong and that Bishop's responsible."

He let out a sigh. "All right. I'll tell you the address, but you promise me you won't step foot across the threshold."

"I promise." For a moment she thought of sending Thom in — he couldn't "step foot across" — but she wasn't going to press her luck.

"Ring the bell if you like and tell the techs I sent you to ask about a damn hidey-hole. They'll let you know you're worrying about nothing. I'm sure they've gone over the place with a fine-tooth comb."

The address he gave her was just off Lexington Avenue. Thom reversed course and headed that way.

"You going to claim this as overtime?" Thom asked.

"Didn't occur to me. You?"

"Nah, no need to. I didn't have anything else to do tonight anyway. Twins got rained out in Oakland, and my pals are crashing early. Or hey wait — maybe we should claim the OT and torture old Baldurdash. He gets his knickers in a knot anytime anyone gets comp time or OT."

"You torture the man way too much, Thom."

"He deserves it."

The rain had stopped, but the sky was overcast and the sun nowhere to be seen. "It's getting late," Leo said.

"Yup." Thom waited at a light and turned down a side street.

Up ahead, a couple of blocks down, Leo saw the spire of a church steeple. "Isn't that Saint Vladimir's?"

"You bet."

"No wonder Victoria, or whatever her name is, went to that church. It wasn't far from her house after all."

"Nope. Here's the address for Ms. Bishop, oh she of the Narcissistic Personality Disorder. Or maybe it's Anti-Social Personality Disorder. She's definitely disordered —"

"Thom," Leo interrupted, "I think we should swing by the church, then go to the apartment."

"Ohhh-kay. Why?"

"I don't know. I just have a hunch."

Leo pointed to a car parked on the street near Saint Vladimir's side entrance. "Wonder if that's Eleanor's car?"

"Long shot."

"I'm checking." Leo phoned the Saint Paul Police Department, identified herself, and asked to run a license plate on a green Saturn sedan. After a moment she flipped the phone shut. "Unbelievable. It's actually hers."

"Let's go," Thom said.

Leo was already exiting the van. She ran up the stairs and pulled on the handle for the side door. Locked. By the time Thom was in his wheelchair, she'd jogged to the front entrance and found it closed as well.

"Did you knock?" Thom asked.

"I bet no one's there." She hurried past him to the van, pulled out her bag, and dumped the contents on the seat.

Thom rolled the chair over and waited on the sidewalk. "Hey, you brought your gun."

"I did. I've felt naked these last few days without it."

Jokingly he said, "Are you going to use it to shoot the locks off the church door?"

"Nope." She scooped up her notebook and thumbed through it. "I'm calling Jo Ellen Wiesniak and hoping she's home."

Jo Ellen picked up on the second ring, and Leo quickly explained what she needed. She hung up and, still standing, leaned back against the van's seat. "She said she'll be here in a few minutes. She has a key."

Leo felt like a bird dog on the hunt. She could smell her quarry, and she was antsy to start tracking. She looked up at the darkening evening. As she gazed up at the unfinished church roof, she saw movement in the steeple, and a flock of birds rose into the dark gray sky. Squinting, she realized the creatures weren't birds — they were bats. The sight gave her the shivers.

A sleek red sports car motored down the avenue and came to a stop across the street. Jo Ellen hefted herself up out of the low-slung convertible and hurried across the street, keys in hand.

"I got here as fast as I could."

"Thank you." Leo slammed the van door and hastened down the sidewalk, introducing the woman to Thom as they headed to the front of the church.

It seemed to take forever for Jo Ellen to force the door open. "I never use this key," she said. "It's an ancient old thing."

Once inside, all was dark. Leo said, "Thom, why don't you check the back halls and the pastoral offices?"

Jo Ellen said, "I'll look in the balcony."

Leo went up the center aisle of the church, moving quickly toward the bloody Jesus dangling overhead. The body hanging above still gave her the willies and a deep sense of foreboding. Under the dimness of the sanctuary candle, she hunted around the altar area and in the sacristy and its walk-in closet. Nothing. She stood thinking behind the chancel rail. Where could a slender older woman be hidden? Obviously not here in the commonly used section of the church. She almost missed a door across from the choir area. When she opened it, she found the giant pipes from the organ, but no Eleanor Sinclair.

Jo Ellen came hustling down the center aisle and called out, "Nothing upstairs or in the Cry Room or the front restrooms."

Thom came through the side door and wheeled swiftly along the west transept to meet Leo and Jo Ellen at the sanctuary crossing. "I couldn't get into every office," he said, "but they all have windows in the upper half and I couldn't see anything out of order."

Jo Ellen said, "Let's go downstairs." She led them to the elevator around the side of the sanctuary. As soon as she pushed the call button, the door opened.

Leo's stomach was tight, and her head had gradually begun to pound. As the door opened to the lower level, she remembered the bats outside and shuddered.

The basement was dank and chilly, and the air smelled like nothing fresh had made its way down there for ages. A sharp pulse of pain ripped through her right temple. She didn't know why odors did that to her. She hoped they could make a quick search and find Eleanor so she could get the hell out.

The walls were a sinister green, and the dim passage didn't afford enough light for Leo to see very far ahead.

Thom said, "I feel like we should be saying, 'Lions, and tigers, and bears, oh my.'"

"Yeah," Jo Ellen said, "it's creepy down here. Even during the day. I'm not looking forward to searching these little rooms."

"They're like cells," Leo said. "Let's each take a room and look, then move on. I wish I'd thought to bring a flashlight. Is there a main light panel we can access?"

"No," Jo Ellen said, "just feel inside the door. Each room does have a light switch—they're just not all in the same place on the wall. You have to hunt."

Great, Leo thought. I'll just feel around while saying, "Spiders, and insects, and bugs, oh my," and hope nothing drops into my hair.

The first room she entered was full of janitorial supplies. She couldn't find any secret entrances or hidden alcoves, so she left the light on and moved down the hall to the next darkened room. She felt around for the switch and illuminated thirteen upright vacuum cleaners standing along the wall three rows deep, like skinny metal soldiers kept from the battle. Along the interior wall adjacent to the corridor sat six more canister vacuums that weren't viewable from the hallway. Leo opened a closet door and dust wafted out. She sneezed.

"Bless you," Thom hollered. He rolled by the doorway. "Nothing so far."

Jo Ellen said, "When I get to work tomorrow, I'm going to arrange to have all this crap carted off to the dump. I mean, really! Do any of those vacuums even work?" She flicked on the light for the council room and stepped inside.

Thom wheeled out of the last room. "I don't think she's down here, Leo."

"Her car's here. Where else could she be?"

"Bishop could have taken her from the car and never come in the church."

"Let's look one more time upstairs," Leo said.

"Maybe we should look more carefully in the offices. From chair level, maybe I missed something."

Jo Ellen snapped off the light to the council room. "I'll get the keys to the offices."

But back upstairs, nothing new was revealed. Leo's head kept on pounding, and her sense of doom intensified. "Maybe we should walk the grounds and check in the flower beds."

Jo Ellen took the lead from the altar toward the entry, and Leo followed Thom. With every step Leo took, her head pounded more. She put her fingertips to her temples and rubbed. At the doorway to the narthex, she paused and closed her eyes, breathing deeply as she tried to soothe the pain. When she opened her eyes, she nearly missed it. She'd even taken a step toward the front door when the realization hit her, and she turned back and squatted down. Her bandaged knee screamed with pain, but she ignored it.

"You guys, wait!" She reached down to the bright red carpet and touched a misshapen spot the size of the palm of her hand. "I think this is blood." The fibers in the short nap were stuck together by something dry and dark. If it had been fresh blood, she might never have noticed, but it had been there long enough to turn rust brown and contrast with the carpet.

She rose and inched down the aisle, followed by Jo Ellen and Thom. She didn't find any more stains down the east transept, but when she went to the west and around the corner to the elevator, she found several more spots they'd overlooked.

"Is there an exit from the basement?" she asked.

Jo Ellen shook her head. "No. There are only those fake windows in the council room, and you can't open them. If there's ever a fire we'll all roast."

"We must have missed something downstairs," Leo said. "Let's look again."

Back in the creepy passageway, they agreed to search different rooms than they had examined the first time. This time they knocked on walls and searched for any kind of cabinet or alcove. They found the same supplies and vacuums, boxes, and junk. Jo Ellen even moved the boxes out of the way in one cell to see if there was a secret door behind them. No luck.

Leo turned on the light to the council room. The bookcases looked suspicious. She tugged on shelves and knocked on the walls behind the books. Everything was solid. There were no secret passageways behind the faux windows or where the Stations of the Cross hung. The room was empty of all but the giant council table and chairs.

She exited to find Thom holding both hands in the air, palms up. "Dead end, Leo."

"Okay, let's look over the grounds, then call in the cops. I think I can get the Saint Paul police to open a missing persons case." She paused. "Did you hear something?"

"Like what?" Thom asked.

"A squeak? A whimper?"

They listened, but no sound came.

Jo Ellen made a face. "Probably a mouse. This whole place is shot through with them. And bats, too."

Leo reached back to turn off the light in the council room.

"Wait," Thom said. "What's that underneath there?"

He nearly rolled into Leo. She jumped back to get out of the way and bent to gaze under the table. A piece of gleaming silver metal resembling a roll bar lay on the floor. From an upright position, neither Leo nor Jo Ellen could see it.

Thom grabbed a chair and wrestled to pull it out. Leo and Jo Ellen moved other chairs aside. Leo looked under the table edge. A rolling cart without a handle sat beneath the center of the table. The piece of metal lying on the floor fit into holes at one end of the cart, but without removing it, the cart wouldn't have fit underneath the table.

She squinted at the bundle of rags piled on the cart's silver surface. "Oh, my God," she said. Paying no heed to her knee, she scrambled underneath. "Eleanor? Eleanor! Can you hear me? Jo Ellen," Leo called out, "can you help me?"

Jo Ellen was already crawling up beside Leo. They pulled the cart out as gently as they could and knelt there in silence. Thom rolled up next to Leo, and they all stared.

"Oh, crap," he said.

In the light, Leo saw a crumpled figure, her hair matted with blood and her face death-gray. She lay in a fetal position on her side, her arms encircling her purse and up against her torso. The smell of urine and vomit was so strong Leo wondered why they hadn't noticed it earlier.

"Eleanor, this shouldn't have happened," Leo whispered. How long had she lain there? Had she died in pain? This was what Victoria Bishop had referred to, her last brutal ha-ha. A surge of rage passed through Leo. She wanted that woman executed. She wanted to drop the cyanide or inject the lethal drugs herself. Not for the first time, she wished Minnesota were a death penalty state.

Tears flooded Leo's eyes, and she couldn't see clearly. Not even thinking, she followed on-duty protocol and reached for the older woman's wrist. The skin was cool, but not cold. She pressed fingers against Eleanor's pulse point. Did she feel something? She thought she must be wrong.

"I'm not getting cell service down here," Thom said. "I'll go upstairs and call the police."

A quiet wisp of sound. "Yesss..."

"Eleanor?" Leo said. She leaned over the body. "Mrs. Sinclair?" She touched her neck, and it felt slightly warm. Leo turned to Jo Ellen. "It's hard to believe, but I think she might be alive. Call for an ambulance, too, Thom."

He was already heading for the door.

Jo Ellen said, "I've got an afghan in my office. I'll go get it. Don't move her."

"Don't worry, I won't."

Eleanor's hand trembled. She managed to reach out a few inches, then her arm dropped.

Leo gently put one hand against Eleanor's back and the other on her upper arm. "Eleanor, it's Leona Reese. We'll have the medics here shortly. Just stay still and relax. You're going to be okay."

"Claire..."

The voice was so quiet, Leo could hardly hear it. "Don't try to talk. Save your strength."

"No, no...Claire Ry...she did this...to me."

"Shhh, it's okay. We know. We caught her."

"Good... That's...very...good." She relaxed under Leo's hands. For a moment, Leo worried she'd died, but when she pressed her palm against Eleanor's back, she could feel the faint beat of her heart, pounding in concert with the pain in Leo's head.

Chapter Twenty-seven

BY THE TIME Leo arrived at the Episcopal church in Saint Paul, the rain had stopped, but the sky was still overcast. She sat in the pew and eyed the casket in the front of the church as the funeral director closed and sealed it. The sorrow she felt about the woman's death was only eclipsed by the satisfaction she felt due to the rapid recovery Eleanor Sinclair had made from the severe concussion she'd suffered. She had a heavy bandage affixed to the back of her head, and it would take some time for her hair to grow back, but the wound was healing.

Callie Trimble's funeral had been delayed a few days, but as soon as Eleanor was released from the hospital, it was rescheduled. Leo observed Eleanor and the Trimble family. Ted sat in the front row with Eleanor and his sister, Olivia, between him and his cranky father. Franklin Callaghan, Sherry Colton, Habibah Okello, and the four Merry Widows were in attendance, along with a few dozen others Leo hadn't met, including three older women who stayed close to Eleanor and comforted her.

The service was somber, and afterwards, Leo intended to leave, but she was surprised to see Thom in the narthex. Today he was dressed in a pale-gray suit and a somber black tie.

"When did you get here?" she asked.

"A few minutes late. I didn't want to interrupt anything, so I hung out in the back." He wheeled his chair and kept pace as she walked to the exit. "Are you going over to the graveside service?"

"I hadn't planned on it. You?"

He said, "I'd like to offer my condolences to Eleanor Sinclair. Want to ride with me in the funeral procession?"

"Okay."

Leo felt a strange sense of déjà vu as they approached Oakland Cemetery. Callie Trimble was being laid to rest in the same place where Leo's mother was buried. She couldn't remember the last time she'd visited her mother's grave, and the thought troubled her.

Thom pulled his wheelchair to a halt on the cement a few feet away from the grass. He waved Leo on, and she walked toward the stark white tent that sheltered the casket. The ground, still wet from the previous night's rain, squished beneath Leo's feet as she moved to stand with the others around the grave site. The final service was brief, and when the priest said the final benediction, the family placed red roses on the casket.

Leo couldn't bear to watch anymore. She moved to leave, but someone touched her arm, and she stopped.

"Leona, thank you so much for coming," Eleanor said. She was remarkably composed for someone who had just buried her life partner while suffering the aftereffects of a concussion.

"You're welcome, of course."

"Thank you for your dedication to finding Callie's killer. You've probably saved the lives of a lot of vulnerable women like her, not to mention saving mine."

"I wish we'd figured it all out sooner and saved you the hell you went through."

"I can't tell you how grateful I am — that we all are, especially Ted. I still can't believe how that woman framed him."

"What I can't believe is that she tried to kill you."

Eleanor smiled. "She thought she had. Even in my wounded state, I knew enough to play dead. I tricked her, and I look forward to making a victim statement at her trial and rubbing that in."

"You go, Eleanor." Leo laughed. "You're the best witness against her. The attempted murder is a lot easier to prove than all the cases we have that contain only circumstantial evidence. The vengeful attack on you will help put her away for a long time."

Eleanor frowned. "She'll be put away for good, won't she?"

"Oh, yes, I think so. It's incredible what she's done, where she's been, and how much pain and anguish she's left in her wake."

"She seemed like such an attractive woman. What a trickster she turned out to be."

"She's a heartless sociopath. The police have already tracked crimes in six states over the last ten years, and I'm sure they'll find more embezzling and murder as they continue to investigate. It's lucky you kept that Post-it note she put on your mail and didn't smudge it up. Detective Flanagan ran it through fingerprinting, and bingo. Nailed her. She'd wiped down the entire Rivers office and the place where she'd been living. The thumbprint on your Post-it was a big help in identifying her and connecting her with other crimes. I don't think we'll even begin to find all the places she's been, but other jurisdictions will take a crack at her when we're done."

"I just don't understand how anyone could think they'd get away with this."

"Normal people would never imagine such a thing, but Eleanor, the woman is cracked in the head. It was all a game to her, outsmarting everyone. She's gotten away with it for a long while. She visited each complex monthly to get the lay of the land and waited until the managers were on vacation, then she could go in unnoticed, steal the mail, assess who to steal from, and run her scams. Notice how she chose women who had little or no family."

"But Callie had family."

"Yes, but you don't. She brought down her house of cards when she killed the wrong woman."

"The wrong woman? Oh, my. I guess Callie saved my life then. I think she would have wanted it that way." Eleanor let out a wistful sigh.

"It's a terrible shame you've had to go through this. I'm so sorry."

Eleanor leaned in and gave her a hug. As Leo patted the other woman gently, she felt her own tears stinging. "I'll keep you in my thoughts and prayers, Eleanor." Leo stepped back and wiped her eyes.

Eleanor said, "I'll soon be moving elsewhere. I'll make sure to send you my change of address in case there are follow-up issues." She walked with Leo back to where Thom waited. Eleanor patted Thom on the shoulder and thanked him for his help and hard work on the case. She invited them to return to the church for lunch, but Leo told her they had to get back to work. With a final farewell, she and Thom headed for the van.

"Pretty muddy," he said.

"Yes, you were smart not to try to roll over there. You'd have gotten mud all over your hands, your chair, probably your suit."

Thom scowled. "I've got to admit that I get damn tired of making accommodations for this stupid chair."

"You're amazingly mobile, if you ask me."

"Well, Leo, I think we should get some lunch, then swing by Saint Vladimir's."

Leo realized she must be looking at Thom blankly because he made a face at her and went on. "We ought to tell them in person now that we have proof Victoria Bishop gutted their Roof Fund."

"Good point," Leo said. "I think they'll get their funds back eventually, but it's probably going to take a long while."

"I still find it unbelievable that she bilked a church."

"No kidding."

"And twenty grand isn't even all that much money. Why did she bother?"

"She liked the game, I think," Leo said. "It was the challenge of the con that kept her amused. That's the only thing that makes sense."

"I suppose. I've read that sociopaths have problems with feeling real emotions."

"Yes. Seems like everything they do is extreme, just so they can feel something."

"I hope they lock her away forever."

"That's what Eleanor was just saying." She glanced toward the far corner of the cemetery. "Thom, you go on ahead, and I'll meet you at the van shortly. My mother's grave is a ways down, and I'd like to stop by."

With each step she took, the air grew warmer. The rain clouds were burning off swiftly, and she unbuttoned her raincoat. The walk was farther than she'd reckoned, and it took her longer to locate Elizabeth Reese's grave than she expected. She stood near it for a moment, scanning the area. The grass was neat, the weeds minimal. The words etched on the stone, *Beloved Mother,* had been suggested by Mom Wallace, and to this day, they remained appropriate.

She squatted next to the stone, pulled some wild clover weeds growing at the edge of the marble, and thought of all the decisions she had to make. She wasn't one of those people who went to the graveside to kneel and talk to their loved one, asking for guidance, and hearing heaven-sent advice. She'd never once considered doing that, and it felt strange to see such a contrivance on TV and in the movies.

Leo owned a box of memorabilia, a scrapbook, and a jewelry case that had been passed from great-grandmother, to grandma, to her mother. From these possessions, she could still feel her mother's spirit, but here, in section 5, row 6, plot 33, was the last place where any of her mother's actual physical presence remained. Leo would spend the rest of her days, however many she had, missing her.

She hadn't meant to cry, but without warning, tears tracked down her face. Her head throbbed. Soon she'd have to decide what to do about this cancer. She didn't like any of the three options she had to choose from: cut out the tumor by removing the eye, try the radioactive plaque therapy that the specialist said he didn't believe would work, or do nothing and see what happened.

Whichever course of action she chose would cost dearly, and none of them came without a huge dose of remorse.

The sun shone down, hot across Leo's shoulders. She touched the top of the glossy headstone, caressed it for a moment, and rose and walked away.

The End...

...until *A Very Public Eye: Book 2 in The Public Eye Series*

Greed? Hatred? Retaliation? Or a Cover-up?

Winter has not yet set in, but young Eddie Bolton will never see another snowfall in his hometown of Duluth, Minnesota. A diabolical killer has murdered him in what should have been a secure juvenile detox ward at the Benton Dowling Center. Leona Reese, a state licensing investigator, has been out of commission for three weeks due to surgery. On her first day back on the job, she's faced with the aftermath of the 17-year-old's death and is shocked by the brutality. Working with the local police, Leona discovers far too many people with motives for the killing...and precious little evidence. As she uncovers long-buried secrets, someone else is murdered and Leona realizes she, too, is in danger. In the midst of her own emotional turmoil, is Leona strong enough and smart enough to confront and catch a clever and ruthless murderer?

Other Quest Titles You Might Enjoy:

Veiled Conspiracy
by Michele Coffman

Throughout the time of man, history offers evidence that following the rise of Great Empires, comes their swift and total destruction.

Elaina Williams works hard as a mid-level reporter for Channel Seven news, from finding and writing the stories, to a part-time anchor fill-in for the stories nobody else wants. All this for her dream that one day she will find herself sitting behind the anchor desk, viewed as a respectable newscaster. Luck seems to turn her way when her ex-girlfriend Kim, a conspiracy-seeking journalist, requests a private meeting in which she tells Elaina "the story of a lifetime." It is this story that forces Elaina into a dangerous world of solitude and peril.

Samantha Kelly has worked her entire adult life at trying to forget the horrors of her past. After graduating from high school, she enlisted into the Army where she served eight years attached to a Military Police unit. She went on three different deployments into combat zones, and struggled through the bloody chaos of battle. The sudden death of her parents sends Sam back home to care for her younger sister Rachel who is still in high school. To accommodate her new responsibilities, Sam joins the Police Force and settles into a normal everyday life.

Unfortunately, normal life in the United States does not last long when unforeseen events rock the foundation of the country, and the American people are sent into a downward spiral full of pain and turmoil. Could this be the end of America as we know it? Is there enough patriotism left in the country to make a stand for what is right? Will there be enough of America left to stand and fight? For Sam and Elaina nothing is certain, except that they both find themselves in way over their heads.

ISBN 978-1-935053-38-5

Rescue At Inspiration Point
by Kate McLachlan

Rescue at Inspiration Point is the second book in the Rip Van Dyke time-travel series. Van is taken hostage at a local prison, and Patsy is stuck in the role of hostage negotiator. Jill sends Bennie back to 1974 to learn more about the hostage taker and his crime. "Do nothing," Jill warns. "Just observe and report back." But the instant Bennie lands, she breaks Jills # 1 rule. As Bennie pursues her own agenda in 1974, the hostage crisis in 1988 escalates. Can Bennie rescue Van from fourteen years away? Or will her actions only make things worse?

ISBN 978-1-61929-005-1

More Lori L. Lake titles

Gun Shy

While on patrol, Minnesota police officer Dez Reilly saves two women from a brutal attack. One of them, Jaylynn Savage, is immediately attracted to the taciturn cop—so much so that she joins the St. Paul Police Academy. As fate would have it, Dez is eventually assigned as Jaylynn's Field Training Officer. Having been burned in the past by getting romantically involved with another cop, Dez has a steadfast rule she has abided by for nine years: Cops are off limits. But as Jaylynn and Dez get to know one another, a strong friendship forms. Will Dez break her cardinal rule and take a chance on love with Jaylynn, or will she remain forever gun shy? *Gun Shy* is an exciting glimpse into the day-to-day work world of police officers as Jaylynn learns the ins and outs of the job and Dez learns the ins and outs of her own heart.

ISBN 978-1-932300-56-7

Under the Gun

Under the Gun is the sequel to the bestselling novel, *Gun Shy*, continuing the story of St. Paul Police Officers Dez Reilly and Jaylynn Savage. Picking up just a couple weeks after *Gun Shy* ended, the sequel finds the two officers adjusting to their relationship, but things start to go downhill when they get dispatched to a double homicide—Jaylynn's first murder scene. Dez is supportive and protective toward Jay, and things seem to be going all right until Dez's nemesis reports their personal relationship, and their commanding officer restricts them from riding together on patrol. This sets off a chain of events that result in Jaylynn getting wounded, Dez being suspended, and both of them having to face the possibility of life without the other. They face struggles—separately and together—that they must work through while truly feeling "under the gun."

ISBN 978-1-932300-57-4

Have Gun We'll Travel

Dez Reilly and Jaylynn Savage have settled into a comfortable working and living arrangement. Their house is in good shape, their relationship is wonderful, and their jobs — while busy — are fulfilling. But everyone needs a break once in a while, so when they take off on a camping trip to northern Minnesota with good friends Crystal and Shayna, they expect nothing more than long hikes, romantic wood fires, and plenty of down time. Instead, they find themselves caught in the whirlwind created when two escaped convicts, law enforcement, and desperate Russian mobsters clash north of the privately-run, medium-security Kendall Correctional Center. Set in the woodland area in Minnesota near Superior National Forest, this adventure/suspense novel features Jaylynn taken hostage by the escapees and needing to do all she can to protect herself while Dez figures out how to catch up with and disarm the convicts, short-circuit the Russians, and use the law enforcement resources in such a way that nothing happens to Jaylynn. It's a race to the finish as author Lori L. Lake uproots Dez and Jaylynn from the romance genre to bring them center stage in her first suspense thriller.

ISBN: 1-932300-33-3

Ricochet In Time

Hatred is ugly and does bad things to good people, even in the land of "Minnesota Nice" where no one wants to believe discrimination exists. Danielle "Dani" Corbett knows firsthand what hatred can cost. After a vicious and intentional attack, Dani's girlfriend, Meg O'Donnell, is dead. Dani is left emotionally scarred, and her injuries prevent her from fleeing on her motorcycle. But as one door has closed for her, another opens when she is befriended by Grace Beaumont, a young woman who works as a physical therapist at the hospital. With Grace's friendship and the help of Grace's aunts, Estelline and Ruth, Dani gets through the ordeal of bringing Meg's killer to justice.

Filled with memorable characters, *Ricochet In Time* is the story of one lonely woman's fight for justice — and her struggle to resolve the troubles of her past and find a place in a world where she belongs.

ISBN: 1-932300-17-1

Different Dress

Different Dress is the story of three women on a cross-country musical road tour. Jaime Esperanza works production and sound on the music tour. The headliner, Lacey Leigh Jaxon, is a fast-living prima donna with intimacy problems. She's had a brief relationship with Jaime, then dumped her for the new guy (who lasted all of about two weeks). Lacey still comes back to Jaime in between conquests, and Jaime hasn't yet gotten her entirely out of her heart.

After Lacey Leigh steamrolls yet another opening act, a folksinger from Minnesota named Kip Galvin, who wrote one of Lacey's biggest songs, is brought on board for the summer tour. Kip has true talent, she loves people and they respond, and she has a pleasant stage presence. A friendship springs up between Jaime and Kip—but what about Lacey Leigh?

It's a honky-tonk, bluesy, pop, country EXPLOSION of emotion as these three women duke it out. Who will win Jaime's heart and soul?

ISBN: 1-932300-08-2

Stepping Out: Short Stories

In these fourteen short stories, Lori L. Lake captures how change and loss influence the course of lives: a mother and daughter have an age-old fight; a frightened woman attempts to deal with an abusive lover; a father tries to understand his lesbian daughter's retreat from him; an athlete who misses her chance—or does she?

Lovingly crafted, the collection has been described as a series of mini-novels where themes of alienation and loss, particularly for characters who are gay or lesbian, are woven throughout. Lake is right on about the anguish and confusion of characters caught in the middle of circumstances, usually of someone else's making. Still, each character steps out with hope and determination.

In the words of Jean Stewart: "Beyond the mechanics of good storytelling, a sturdy vulnerability surfaces in every one of these short stories. Lori Lake must possess, simply as part of her inherent nature, a loving heart. It gleams out from these stories, even the sad ones, like a lamp in a lighthouse—maybe far away sometimes, maybe just a passing, slanting flash in the dark—but there to be seen all the same. It makes for a bittersweet journey."

ISBN: 1-932300-16-3

Shimmer & Other Stories

In these tales of hope and loss, lovers and found family, Lori L. Lake has once more given us an amazing slice of life. A frightened woman stumbles through her daily existence, unsure of her place in the world, until she comes into possession of a magic coat... Tee has a problem with her temper, and now that she's being tested again, will she fail to curb it again? Kaye Brock has recently been released from prison and doesn't have a single friend — until Mrs. Gildecott comes along...

These women and many others, unsettled and adrift and often disillusioned, can't quite understand how they arrived at their present situations. But whether rejected, afraid to commit, or just misunderstood, even the most hard-bitten are not without some hope in the power of love.

Lori L. Lake's talent shines like never before in this collection of glittering tales. Sharply rendered, the tone of these stories reflects their title: silver and gray, shimmery and wintery, yet also filled with the shiny hope of summer. These are stories that bear rereading.

ISBN: 978-1-932300-95-6

The Milk of Human Kindness: Lesbian Authors Write About Mothers and Daughters

Edited by Lori L. Lake, this anthology contains stories, essays, and memoirs by some of the brightest stars in the lesbian writing world:

Cameron Abbott + Georgia Beers + Meghan Brunner + Carrie Carr + Caro Clarke + Katherine V. Forrest + Jennifer Fulton + Gabrielle Goldsby + Ellen Hart + Lois Hart + Karin Kallmaker + Marcia Tyson Kolb + Lori L. Lake + SX Meagher + Radclyffe + J.M. Redmann + Jean Stewart + Cate Swannell + Therese Szymanski + Talaran + Julia Watts + Marie Sheppard Williams + Kelly Zarembski.

Don't miss this unforgettable collection!

ISBN: 1-932300-28-7

Snow Moon Rising

Mischka Gallo, a proud Roma woman, knows horses, dancing, and travel. Every day since her birth, she and her extended family have been on the road in their vardo wagons meandering mostly through Poland and Germany. She learned early to ignore the taunts and insults of all those who call her people "Gypsies" and do not understand their close-knit society and way of life.

Pauline "Pippi" Stanek has lived a settled life in a small German town along the eastern border of Poland and Germany. In her mid-teens, she meets Mischka and her family through her brother, Emil Stanek, a World War I soldier who went AWOL and was adopted by Mischka's troupe. Mischka and Pippi become fast friends, and they keep in touch over the years. But then, the Second World War heats up, and all of Europe is in turmoil. Men are conscripted into the Axis or the Allied armies, "undesirables" are turned over to slave labor camps, and with every day that passes, the danger for Mischka, Emil, and their families increases. The Nazi forces will not stop until they've rounded up and destroyed every Gypsy, Jew, dissident, and homosexual.

On the run and separated from her family, Mischka can hardly comprehend the obstacles that face her. When she is captured, she must use all her wits just to stay alive. Can Mischka survive through the hell of the war in Europe and find her family?

In a world beset by war, two women on either side of the conflagration breach the divide-and save one another. *Snow Moon Rising* is a stunning novel of two women's enduring love and friendship across family, clan, and cultural barriers. It's a novel of desperation and honor, hope and fear at a time when the world was split into a million pieces.

ISBN: 978-1-932300-50-5

Like Lovers Do

Kennie McClain is a security guard who, unbeknownst to her tenants, owns the Allen Arms where she works. In her off hours, she rehabs apartments and nurses a broken heart. She's still recovering from the loss of her partner three years earlier and has moved from upstate New York to Portland to escape bad memories.

Lily Gordon is a nationally-acclaimed painter who lives in the penthouse. She's beautiful, accomplished, and haunted after her lover ditches her.

Sparks fly in a big way when Kennie and Lily finally connect...but then in one shattering moment, Lily betrays her, and Kennie's world comes crashing down around her, leaving her untrusting and in deep emotional pain. Can Kennie rise above these losses and ever risk her heart again?

ISBN 978-1-935053-66-8

OTHER QUEST PUBLICATIONS

About the Author

Lori L. Lake is the author of two short story collections and ten novels, including four books in The Gun Series and this first book in The Public Eye Mystery Series. Her crime fiction stories have been featured in "Silence of the Loons," "Once Upon A Crime," "Women of the Mean Streets," and "Write of Spring." Lori lived in Minnesota for 26 years, but re-located to Portland, Oregon, in 2009. She is currently at work on the second book in The Public Eye Mystery Series. When she's not writing, she's at the gym, the local movie house, or curled up in a chair reading. For more information, see her website at www.LoriLLake.com.

VISIT US ONLINE AT
www.regalcrest.biz

At the Regal Crest Website You'll Find

- The latest news about forthcoming titles and new releases

- Our complete backlist of romance, mystery, thriller and adventure titles

- Information about your favorite authors

- Current bestsellers

- Media tearsheets to print and take with you when you shop

Regal Crest titles are available from all progressive booksellers including numerous sources online. Our distributors are Bella Distribution and Ingram.

CPSIA information can be obtained at www.ICGtesting.com
Printed in the USA
BVOW081135260812

298844BV00004B/77/P

9 781619 290013